Hailing from Sioux Falls, South Dakota, Megan DeVos is twenty-six years old and works as a Registered Nurse in the operating room. Her debut Anarchy series amassed over 30 million reads on Wattpad, winning the Watty Award in 2014.

THE ANARCHY SERIES

Anarchy

Loyalty

Revolution

Annihilation

Anarchy

MEGAN DEVOS

ORION

First published in Great Britain in 2018 by Orion Books,
an imprint of The Orion Publishing Group Ltd
Carmelite House, 50 Victoria Embankment
London EC4Y 0DZ

An Hachette UK Company

1 3 5 7 9 10 8 6 4 2

A CIP catalogue record for this book
is available from the British Library.

ISBN 978 1 4091 8384 6

Typeset by Input Data Services Ltd, Somerset

Printed and bound in Great Britain by Clays Ltd, Elcograf S.p.A.

MIX
Paper from
responsible sources
FSC
www.fsc.org FSC® C104740

www.orionbooks.co.uk

For my readers, who have been here from the start.
This book wouldn't be the same without you.

Chapter 1 – Raid
HAYDEN

My shoulders shifted, readjusting the thick strap of the assault rifle that dug into my muscles while I walked. The metal of the gun was hot as it seared through my thin shirt to my skin, heated from recent use. Nobody gave the weapon slung across my shoulder a second glance as I passed; they were used to the sight.

I could hear the heavy crunching of my boots on the ground as I walked down the dirt path toward the raid building. A light breeze tickled at my hair, which was tied back in a bandana to keep it off my face. It really had got too long but I couldn't find enough in me to bother with a haircut. Of all things I had to worry about, a haircut was not one of them.

Faces flashed by as I walked, my pace brisk and purposeful. It was nearing dusk, and I wanted to get the raid on the way before darkness completely enveloped us all. My eyes scanned the crowd for the faces I was searching for, but they didn't appear. The dirt road I walked down was bordered on either side by makeshift huts that were made of things rummaged from the city. Scraps of wood, metal, and glass were thrown together to produce surprisingly sturdy buildings that served as people's homes. Trees stood tall around us, masking our wooded encampment from any prying, unwelcome eyes.

1

While everyone ignored the weapon draped over my arm, people of all ages watched me with a sense of awe as I walked by. My relatively young age made my rise to the top all the more impressive. I was only twenty-one, but somehow I had found myself in charge of these people. All these people, ranging from just little kids to those so old they could hardly walk, and I was responsible for protecting them, providing for them; I was in charge of keeping them alive.

The weight of this responsibility didn't escape me, and I quickly found it taking over my thoughts as I ducked my head to enter the raid building. It was one of our sturdiest buildings, made entirely out of metal with actual locks on the doors as opposed to the simple sliding wood hatches we'd constructed in everyone's huts. There were, at all times, at least two people here to guard our supplies. As the keep for our weapons and ammunition, it was one of the most essential places in our entire settlement.

I nodded at the two in charge of guarding it now: a middle-aged man I recognised by face but not by name, and a boy of ten whom I knew very well. I sighed, wishing it were anyone but him on duty at the moment because I knew what would surely follow.

'Hi, Hayden!' he said cheerfully, jumping to his feet immediately and racing to my side. I glanced down at him before moving to one of the gun cases held in the building. Swinging the strap over my head, I removed the weapon to put it back to its rightful place. He looked just as haphazard as ever with a mop of hair falling in his eyes and clothes that were far too large for him. He was practically swimming in his T-shirt, and his jeans dragged along the floor whenever he took a step.

'Jett, you're supposed to be on duty,' I reminded him, raising an eyebrow. A look of concern flashed across his face before he erased the smile and put on a mock-serious expression.

'Yes sir, I know that—'

'Don't call me "sir",' I grumbled immediately. It was something a lot of people had started to do, especially the younger kids, and I hated it.

'Right, sorry si—, um, Hayden,' he said, almost repeating his mistake. I ignored him and pulled out a 9mm handgun. After slipping the clip out, I discovered it to be half empty.

'So, um, I was wondering—'

'No,' I said flatly, already knowing what he was going to ask. I pulled some bullets out of the case to load into the gun.

'But *why*?' he whined. 'I'm old enough! Let me come with you!'

'You're not old enough. One more year,' I said gently. As annoyingly over-eager as he was, I could admit he was determined, and I had to admire that. For years now, he'd been bothering me to come along on a raid only for me to deny him every single time.

'You said that last year,' he pointed out, his tone disgruntled.

He was right but I wasn't going to admit that. I'd thought a year ago that he would *maybe* be ready by now, but he was still far from it. He was just a kid, too young to realise the severe danger that went along with raids and too unskilled to defend himself. He would only put everyone, especially himself, in danger.

'Next year,' I repeated. I slammed the clip back into the gun before reaching behind me to shove it into the back of my jeans. The metal was cold against my skin where it touched my back, but it gave me an odd shot of adrenaline; it was almost time for the raid.

'All right, let's get this show on the road,' a voice said suddenly, booming through the relatively small building. My eyes were averted from Jett's disappointed face to see Dax and Kit coming through the door. Dax, as always, looked ecstatic to be going on a raid while Kit's expression was that of stony seriousness. Both men were around my age and absolute opposites of each other, but I wouldn't dream of going on a raid without both of them.

'Hayden.' Kit nodded at me in greeting before moving to a different crate across the room to gather his supplies. Dax loped over to join Jett and me at the case and grab a gun of his own.

'Jett, what's the deal, you coming with us finally or what?' he asked lightly, grinning down at the boy. I frowned, irritated that Dax insisted on encouraging him.

'Hayden won't let me. He says I'm too young still,' he grumbled, glaring at me out of the corner of his eye while I stuffed a switchblade into my pocket.

'Nope, I won't,' I assented, turning my back on the two to gather some more supplies. I grabbed a small backpack before shoving some first aid materials and a bottle of water into it.

'Aw, don't worry, your time will come, little man,' Dax said, clapping him on the shoulder a bit harder than he probably meant to. Jett's body jerked a few inches to the side from the force, proving yet again how unfit for a raid he actually was.

'But I want to go *now*,' he muttered, dropping his gaze to the ground and digging the toe of his shoe into the dirt that covered the wooden floor.

Dax reached out to ruffle his hair with a good-natured chortle before joining me to grab a supply bag of his own. Instead of a first aid kit, however, wires, batteries, and an

4

assortment of other electrical equipment were stuffed into the backpack before he slung it over his shoulders. Dax was the resident technology expert and was capable of getting nearly anything, no matter how decrepit and broken down, back into working condition. He was one third of the essential team of he, Kit and I.

Kit, on the other hand, handled the majority of the surveillance and, when necessary, weaponry. He was the one who more often than not ended up firing the guns we all carried or using the deceptively large knife he hid in his back pocket. When it came to raids, he was the last one anyone wanted to mess with if they wanted to make it out in one piece or even alive at all. Kit was the way he was for a reason, and he had more than a few kills under his belt to justify it.

My role in the trio seemed to change depending on what we were raiding for and where we were going. I covered all areas – tech, comms, fighting, surveillance, recon, everything. It was one of the reasons I'd risen so high, though I hadn't meant to at the time; all I'd been trying to do was stay alive, not run an entire camp. I'd never asked for this responsibility, but it was mine now and I embraced it with everything I had.

Jett watched closely as we all gathered around the central table that was lit by a single lamp dangling from overhead. There were only three buildings in our encampment that had electricity in the form of generators: the kitchen, the infirmary, and the raid building; the rest of the buildings were lit by lanterns and candles. The hanging lamp was the only light in the room, so our shadows were cast in sharp contrast against the walls. With our weapons and supplies ready, we only had one thing left to do.

'All right, so,' I started. My thumb rubbed across my lower lip as I thought of the best plan of action. 'We're going to Greystone, and we need kerosene for the lanterns. *That's it.'*

'What?' Dax protested immediately. 'We're going to bloody Greystone and all we're taking is kerosene? What's the point then?'

'The point is we need kerosene and we're not going to risk taking anything else when it isn't necessary,' I said firmly. I glared at him, annoyed at his insistence to think of raids as something fun instead of dangerous. It would get him hurt one day if he kept it up. 'Especially at Greystone.'

Dax frowned at me, disappointed our mission wasn't one of the larger ones but accepting my ruling. Not that he really had a choice – I was in charge, after all. Both he and Kit were my closest friends and allies, so it was difficult for me to give them orders without feeling like a power-hungry arsehole. I trusted them with my life, and they trusted me with theirs.

Trust was essential in times like ours. You could trust your group and no one else. Depending on what we were raiding for, we took different amounts of people. Since this was a relatively small raid, we only needed the three of us. It was how I liked it the most, because large raids with loads of people made me nervous for the group's sake. The more people you take, the greater the risk of getting caught and killed.

'Can we at least get some ammo while we're there? We're running out of shells,' Dax stated, giving his idea one last shot.

'We have plenty of shells,' Kit said from across the table. His face was, as always, serious as he listened to the plan. 'Now shut up and take your orders.'

'Yeah, yeah. Loosen up a bit, would ya?' he said, shaking his head in disappointment at our lack of enthusiasm. I ignored him.

'Now that we've cleared that up, everyone remember where it is?'

They both nodded.

'Left side of their camp with one guard going by every ten minutes,' Kit said. I nodded.

'That's it. Let's get going before it gets too dark to see without a light,' I said.

Jett, who had remained fairly quiet so far, let out an indignant huff that he was being left out.

'Stay put, little man,' Kit said, shooting him a rare grin. Jett had a special place in everyone's hearts, even the always-serious Kit.

'Little man,' Jett muttered, crossing his arms over his chest before letting out a quiet scoff. 'I hate when you guys call me that.'

Dax let out a hearty laugh, his spirits once again high after I'd briefly shot down his more extensive raid idea. He couldn't resist a raid, no matter how simple.

'Let's go,' I said, growing impatient. With our backpacks on and weapons secured, each of us grabbed a torch before saying goodbye to Jett and the man on guard.

It was already much darker outside now than it had been when I'd gone inside, and I wanted to get through the woods before it got completely dark. It was nearly pitch black beneath the thick canopy of trees, and using a torch to manoeuvre through the trunks was a sure-fire way to blow your cover.

Together, we trekked through the camp, nodding at people as we passed by but mostly focusing our heads to prepare for the raid. We were quiet as we neared the edge of the huts and grew quieter still once we disappeared into the trees. Our feet moved deftly over the branches and twigs that littered the ground, our years of practice making us nearly silent as we shifted among the shadows.

Greystone was the closest settlement to ours at about a mile away. While our camp was hidden among the woods, Greystone sat about one hundred yards off the tree line, completely exposed. While it might seem like a bad idea to have literally no cover over your camp, it was all purposeful and strategic: Greystone was probably the most dangerous to us of all the individual camps; with their abundant weaponry and a penchant for people who loved to fight, they were not the group you wanted to mess with, much less steal from in the dark of the night. The lack of trees around their camp made of stony buildings gave us virtually no cover and made it easy for their on-duty guards to spy incoming intruders.

Other encampments, such as Whetland and Crimson, were far less well-protected and much easier to raid, but were significantly farther away. For extensive raids, we would make the journey through the wasteland of a city and back, but for small raids like this, we preferred to sneak into Greystone. There were still other groups of people living together, all with their own loyalties to each other and no one else. Clusters of people, all living in makeshift villages in a ring around the city, had formed years and years ago. It had been like that nearly all of my life.

Aside from the organised camps, were those that dwelled within the city – the most dangerous, brutal type of people who killed for fun. They lived in the shattered shells of buildings, living off food stolen from unsuspecting passersby and using whatever they could fashion into weapons to carry out their threats. These were the people who seemed to have reverted a bit in evolution, relying on their most barbaric instincts and nothing more for survival. We called them Brutes, and they were another reason we preferred to sneak into Greystone rather than risk going through the city.

Everyone was divided and nobody trusted anyone but those in their own camp. That was how it worked – you fight for your own camp and that's it. If you needed something, you either stole it or risked going into the city to scavenge for it. You steal, you sneak, you lie, and you fight, all to survive. You do all this, or you die.

'I can see it,' Dax whispered, slowing his pace as he pointed ahead. My focus was ripped from my thoughts as I blinked into the darkness. Sure enough, past where Dax's finger was pointed I could see the dark outlines of stone houses. Their camp was set up in a circle, with the most important buildings and resources held in the middle. Guards, just like the ones we had, patrolled the area continuously to deter thieves such as ourselves. They were armed with guns, and they weren't afraid to use them. More than once, we had lost members of our camp to gunfire from those in Greystone.

We hovered on the edge of the tree line and squinted across the hundred-yard gap between us and the outer edges of their settlement. Silently, each of us pulled our guns from their various holding places to have them ready by our sides.

'There,' Kit breathed. His eyes were fixed on a shadow moving between the small buildings, the outline of a barrel of a gun visible in his silhouette. 'He'll be back in ten.'

'Shouldn't we wait to double check?' Dax asked. His eyes, too, followed the moving shadow.

'No, it's always ten. Every time,' Kit replied. I nodded silently, more to myself to them. Kit was right; every single raid I'd ever been on, their guard had passed by in ten minutes. No more, no less, and I had been on a lot of raids.

'Remember, left side,' I whispered. The shadow was nearly gone now and our window of opportunity had just opened. 'Go!'

Without a moment's hesitation, the three of us sprinted from the trees like silent shadows, our feet whispering across the patchy grass without a sound. My muscles revelled in the stretch, the exertion of running making them feel alive after walking for so long. I pulled in deep, even breaths while I ran to keep up the fast pace. I could hear Dax and Kit doing the same beside me, our bodies in excellent shape from the sustained physical exertion. My eyes constantly scanned the houses for another shadow, another guard, or maybe just a person out wandering from their home, but I saw none.

After a few moments, we reached the first building and threw our bodies silently against the wall, flattening ourselves shoulder to shoulder as much as we could to hide from view. Everyone's breath remained quiet and even despite having just sprinted a hundred yards. My ears pricked for any sound of someone approaching or calling warning to our arrival, but none came. I nodded at the two before cautiously poking my head around the corner. My heart pounded with the adrenaline that only a raid could deliver.

'Clear,' I whispered before slinking around the building. They followed silently behind me. Silence was second nature to us by now.

It was very dark in Greystone, as they seemed to have the same electrical problems we had, but candles flickered here and there to give enough light to illuminate our target. The building we aimed for was relatively unremarkable, and the only thing that distinguished it from the other bland, grey buildings was a small, intricate carving of a fire on the door – fire that can only burn with kerosene.

My eyes scanned the area once more and saw nothing.

In my mind, I could feel the minutes ticking by, each pause wasting more and more of our precious time to get in, get our supplies, and get out. I gave a tiny flick of my hand to signal them to follow me before sprinting across the path and landing by the door. I paused for only a second to press my ear against the door, listening on the off chance someone was inside. Silence greeted me.

I turned the knob to let myself in, quickly followed by Kit and Dax. Our prize lay all around the room, piles upon piles built up along the walls. The moment we entered, we each gathered up several gallons of kerosene, throwing one in our backpacks and carrying another to leave one hand to wield a weapon.

'Hayden,' Kit whispered. 'We're good, we'll go first then signal you.'

I nodded, waving them out the door to see them disappear into the darkness before turning back around to see if there was anything else useful. They were only gone a few seconds when I heard it. All of a sudden, a loud clang sounded from behind me followed by a hushed gasp.

I jolted around, searching for the guard and expecting to see a gun in my face. What I saw was worse. There, standing in the doorway next to a pile of toppled kerosene cans, stood Jett with a look of surprise on his face and a hand clamped over his mouth.

'Jett!' I hissed. 'What the hell are you doing here?'

'I wanted to help on the raid!' he replied, whisper-shouting more than whispering. He looked eager and enthusiastic and far too happy about our current situation, especially after making such a racket, and it was as if he didn't fully realise the seriousness of it. He had probably alerted their entire camp, half of who would be on their way toward us in a matter of moments.

'I'm sor—'

I shushed him to cut him off, my eyes wide in anger. What an idiot to follow us here; now he was going to get us all killed.

My eyes darted toward the door and I was relieved to see no sign of Dax or Kit. At least they had made it out. Jett stood with his chest puffed out as best he could, trying to appear brave and unafraid. His little fists were clenched by his side in determination.

'Jett, we have to go. Now,' I seethed, rushing forward and yanking him by the arm. He grumbled quietly, muttering something about 'just wanting to help'. My grip on him was tight as I hovered by the edge of the door, glancing around to look for guards. It was, miraculously, clear.

'Come on,' I whispered, tugging him forward. I stepped forward, pulling our bodies out of the cover of darkness into the dim lighting provided by the streets.

'Hold it,' a voice directly behind me said. My heart plummeted in my chest. I heard the distinct click of metal on metal – the sound of a gun loading into place. I closed my eyes in a grimace as I shoved Jett in front of me, shielding him from whoever was behind me. I heard the terrified gasp break through the false bravado he was trying so hard to maintain, giving way to the fear he should have been feeling all along were it not for his disillusioned sense of things.

'Turn around,' the voice commanded. A girl's voice, I was surprised to discover, though it certainly didn't lack any authority. I turned slowly on the spot, tucking my gun into my waistband discreetly on the way and managing to keep Jett shielded behind me. After dropping the jug of kerosene by my feet, I raised both of my hands in the air by my head, more concerned with getting the terrified Jett out of here than myself.

12

My eyes moved from the ground, up her body, and to the gun in her hand pointed straight at my chest before finally locking on her eyes. They were a deep green, and her face was framed by wisps of blonde hair that fell from her haphazard bun. She was, without a doubt, absolutely beautiful, and she was fully prepared to kill me.

Chapter 2 – Weak

GRACE

My hands were steady in front of me, arms extended to keep the gun aimed at his chest. His features were set in a solid expression, masking any fear he might have felt even though he didn't strike me as the type to easily be afraid. His hard gaze met mine and I was momentarily stunned by the depth of green in his eyes as they narrowed at me.

He hadn't seen me before he'd stepped out of the door, his hasty glance looking in every direction but to his exact left where I'd stood hidden by the shadows. I hadn't been surprised when a smaller shadow followed him out the door because of the racket they'd made in the building, but I hadn't got a good look at either of them until he'd turned around to face me. I almost wished he hadn't because even as I held a gun to his chest, there was no denying how attractive he was. He was about my age, twenty-one or so, and with his messy, dark hair pushed back in a bandana, it was easy to see the sharp line of his jaw, the piercing green of his eyes, and the stony look of determination written on his face.

A quiet whimper sounded from behind his back, shaking me from the spell I seemed to momentarily have fallen under. For the first time, a flicker of worry flashed in his eyes beneath his tightly knitted brows. I stepped closer, determined to uphold my composure just like I would with any other raider who was caught in the act.

'Who's behind you?' I demanded sharply, nodding over his shoulder.

'It's just a kid,' he answered. His voice was deep and gravelly as he tried to keep it down and avoid drawing any more attention to us. He must have noticed I hadn't alerted anyone to his presence yet, although I knew others were already on their way.

'Let me see him.'

'Put your gun down first,' he returned firmly. His hands were still raised by his sides but I could see the flexed muscles beneath his skin, his body tense and ready to react.

'Nice try.'

As I spoke, a small hand gripped the side of the shirt he was wearing before a head peeked around from behind his back. A set of wide brown eyes peered out at me, very obviously terrified. He let out a tiny squeak when he saw me looking at him before ducking behind the man's back again. My gaze travelled back up to his face, gun never leaving his chest.

'Where are you from?' I asked. He stared back at me defiantly, not answering my question as he set his jaw tightly. I hadn't really expected him to. That was one of the first rules of raiding: you get caught, you stay quiet, and most of the time, you die. There was a reason hardly anyone dared to raid Greystone, and it was the reason he wasn't giving me any information now. He knew he probably wouldn't make it out of here and didn't want to risk retaliation on the rest of his camp.

That wasn't always the case, however. Many times, the person caught would give up all sorts of information if there was even the slightest chance it meant they'd escape with their life. Whoever he was, he was loyal and brave.

15

'Why'd you bring a kid with you on a raid?' I questioned again. My tone held a hint of annoyance. I didn't like being put in this situation, because I knew I should shoot them both and I really didn't like the idea of having to shoot a kid. He was so small and terrified, it hardly seemed justifiable, even if he was on a raid.

'I didn't,' he said through gritted teeth. The skin was pulled taut on his neck as he watched me closely. His eyes darted to the side, leaving mine for the first time since his gaze had locked on mine at the sound of someone calling my name.

'Grace!' the voice called. His eyes snapped back to mine, an eyebrow rising as if questioning that it was me they were calling for.

'Look, at least let the kid go,' he said shortly. It was almost as if he were irritated that I hadn't shot him yet. I stared at him, gun still raised and ready.

'*Grace!*' the voice repeated, much closer this time. I recognised it now as my older brother's. Jonah, who was ruthless and had a quick temper, wouldn't hesitate before shooting the both of them. Another petrified whimper sounded from behind the man's back, breaking my will. Before I even fully decided, I was lowering my gun.

'Get out of here,' I grumbled. It irritated me to let them go but I couldn't bring myself to shoot an innocent kid. 'But if I catch you here again, you're dead. I don't care who you have with you.'

He nodded sharply before turning around. The muscles in his back flexed beneath the thin black shirt he wore as he hunched over to speak to the kid.

'Now we run, little man.'

He gripped the kid's arm while I watched in silence, confused by the gentle way he spoke to him after being so defiant with me. They looked around once before taking a few steps away. The kid took off at a sprint for the nearest house while the man surprised me by pausing and turning back around to look at me once more.

'Thank you,' he said, somewhat grudgingly. I blinked in surprise before I forced a scowl on my face, determined to remain hard even though I was shocked by his behaviour.

'Go!' was all I said, ignoring his thanks. He nodded once more before turning and breaking into a sprint. The back of his shirt that billowed out behind him as he ran had just disappeared around the corner when my brother came running from the opposite direction. I sucked in a breath as he skidded to halt next to me.

'What the hell was that?!' he bellowed, telling me he had indeed seen him before he'd disappeared. His chest heaved out in anger as he glared at me. I couldn't tear my gaze away from the shadow that had swallowed the stranger, even though I felt my brother staring at me.

'I let him go,' I answered as if it were obvious. I wasn't in the mood to deal with his temper after such a strange incident.

'You let him go,' he repeated flatly. '*Why?*'

'He had a kid with him,' I replied, finally turning to meet his angry gaze with one of my own. He may have had a short temper, but mine wasn't far behind, and nothing set it off quite like he did.

'So?' he spat.

'*So,*' I started. 'I didn't think it was necessary to kill a little kid.'

'I didn't see any kid.'

'Yeah well, that's because you were too slow to see him,' I muttered, turning away to walk back to the main part of camp. My body was jerked backward when his hand clamped over my arm, yanking me back to face him once more.

'Ow, get off!' I said angrily, shoving his chest hard enough for him to release me. I shot him a disgusted look and was half tempted to pull my gun on him just to get him to leave me alone.

'Where the hell do you think you're going?' he seethed while continuing to glare down at me.

'I'm going home, my rounds are over,' I said. My tone challenged his and it clearly annoyed him that I didn't back down. When I was younger, I let him boss me around and tell me what to do, but the past few years I'd grown much stronger, harder, and altogether much more resistant to authority.

'I don't think so. You have to report the raid to Celt. And tell him how you *let him go*,' he growled. I rolled my eyes at him.

'Fine.'

I turned abruptly to stalk away from him and was annoyed when he followed. His feet were loud as they slammed into the dirt with each step.

'I know where it is. You don't need to come with me.'

'I do if I want to make sure you tell him the truth,' he replied flatly. I ignored him as I stomped down the path between the makeshift houses. It was completely dark now, and the path we walked down was lit sparingly with lanterns here and there. We walked in stony silence, both of us annoyed with one another while we drew closer and closer to the command building where I knew Celt would be.

Jonah shot me another glare as I raised my hand to knock at the door, more of a formality than anything.

'What?' I grumbled quietly, beyond annoyed at his presence and insistence on being horrible. He didn't say anything and merely shook his head as someone answered from inside the door.

'Come in.'

I turned the handle and threw my shoulder into the door to push it open, the shape of the building making it tend to stick. The only light in the room came from a candle sitting on the desk that was scattered with papers. Celt sat at the desk, his face drawn tight in an expression of concern before his eyes flashed up to meet mine. The shadows threw the fine wrinkles in his skin into sharp relief and seemed to highlight the sparse grey hairs that had started to show, making him appear older than he actually was. A smile pulled at his lips when he saw me.

'Grace! Come on in, have a seat,' he said, gesturing to the chair across from his desk. I gave him a weak smile as I entered and sat down, followed closely by Jonah.

'Jonah, you too, of course,' he added. Jonah ignored the offer and stood next to me with his arms folded across his chest. Celt shot him a disapproving look before turning his gaze back to me.

'To what do I owe this pleasure?' Celt asked. He gathered some of the papers he had been looking at and stacked them neatly in front of him. Jonah scoffed indignantly next to me.

'Yeah, tell him, Grace,' he said tightly.

Celt watched me closely as his expression turned more serious.

'What happened?'

'Um, there was a raid in the kerosene building,' I said, leaving out the most important details.

'And . . .' Jonah said.

'*And* they got away.'

'And why did they get away?' he said. I turned to glare at him, furious he was trying to make me look like an idiot in front of Celt.

'Because I let them go,' I muttered grudgingly. My jaw was clenched when I spoke.

'Grace, why would you do that?' Celt asked. He rubbed his hand over his temples as if I'd caused him great stress. 'You know we can't let that happen.'

'He had a kid with him!' I said in my defence.

'Yeah and guess what? That kid was on a raid which means it's only a matter of time before he's pointing a gun at *you*,' Jonah growled from beside me.

'No way. That kid was terrified. I'd be surprised if he ever even left his camp again,' I said, shaking my head.

'Did you find out what camp they were from?' Celt asked. His tone held a hint of disappointment that made me feel like absolute shit.

'No,' I admitted.

'You're so useless,' Jonah spat. 'You're weak.'

'Will you shut up? Just because I'm not a heartless arsehole like you doesn't mean I'm weak,' I shot back. I had half a mind to get up and punch him in the jaw.

'Celt, will you do something about this? We can't have her running rounds if she's too afraid to kill anyone,' Jonah said exasperatedly. He threw his hands in my direction as if he couldn't possibly comprehend how I'd managed to let them go.

'You know that isn't the case,' I replied. I'd killed before and he was well aware of that so the fact that he even dared to hurl something like that in my face now infuriated me. I didn't like it, but I did what I had to do to survive.

'Just because it was some guy you wanted to screw—'

'*What!* No it wasn't—'

'—doesn't mean that's any reason to let him go. You're *weak*,' he repeated, digging at what he knew would irritate me the most. I hated being called weak just because I was a girl.

'You're such a dick—'

'Stop!' Celt roared suddenly, both of our heads snapping round to face him. I hadn't even been aware of it, but I'd risen to my feet and was now standing face to face with Jonah. I took a step back and blew out a solid breath before forcing myself to sit back down.

'You two need to stop this pointless bickering and get along. How are people supposed to trust you to keep them alive if you're constantly at each other's throats?'

Neither of us said anything as he reprimanded us. Humiliation tinged my cheeks red; I hated disappointing Celt.

'Sorry,' I muttered. Celt's eyes darted to Jonah expectantly.

'Sorry,' he mumbled unconvincingly.

'I thought you were raised better than that,' Celt said, adding insult to injury. He shook his head slowly before looking back at me. 'And Grace, I appreciate your character but you know the rules. You catch a raider, you kill them. That's it.'

'I know,' I muttered sheepishly.

'So what are you going to do next time you catch someone?' he prodded.

'Kill them,' I said through clenched teeth.

'That's it. I know it's gruesome but that's just how it is. We can't let it get around that we're allowing raiders go free or soon we'll have nothing left,' he said gently.

'Yes, Celt.'

'Come on now, you know I don't like it when you call me that,' he said, a hint of a smile pulling at his lips now. I sighed, rolling my head back before pulling it forward again to meet his gaze.

'Yes, Dad.'

Chapter 3 – Spontaneous

HAYDEN

Fury burned through my veins as I ran after Jett, my strong legs allowing me to draw even with him quickly while he fled. He shot me a terrified look out of the corner of his eye while we ran, and I slowed my pace to allow him to keep up. My jaw clenched in anger as I tried to hold back from cursing him for being so incredibly reckless.

'Stupid,' I couldn't help but mutter. He didn't reply, but I could hear the heavy puffing of his breaths as he ran, his body unaccustomed to the physical exertion required for a raid. The edge of the tree line was quickly approaching, and I knew Kit and Dax must have been hiding just beyond sight, waiting for us. I slowed enough as we approached to let Jett run through the gaps in the trunks before me.

As soon as we were covered, I reached forward to grab his arm and yank him back to face me.

'What the *hell*, Jett?!' I demanded, struggling to keep my voice quiet. Even though we were covered, we still weren't completely safe. I glared down at him, his pitiful expression doing nothing to soften the hard anger I felt.

'I said I was sorry!' he protested weakly. His wide brown eyes stared up at mine, remorse filling them completely.

'Jett, you idiot!' Kit interjected, appearing from behind a

tree. He looked absolutely livid. 'Are you *trying* to get your-self killed?'

'No,' he murmured sheepishly. He hardly even dared glance at Kit as he glowered down at him.

'You can't just follow us, little man. It's not safe,' Dax said, his tone the kindest of the three. It took a lot to piss Dax off, but it was still clear he disapproved of Jett's reck-lessness. I watched Jett as he chanced glances at the three of us. He looked intimidated, the glares from us older and bigger men breaking down his tiny bit of courage.

'I just wanted to be tough and brave like you guys,' he said quietly, dropping his gaze to stare at the ground. I let out a heavy sigh and crossed my arms over my chest.

'Being patient is being brave, Jett,' I told him. He lifted his soft gaze from the ground to look at me.

'You guys went on raids at my age,' he said quietly. That was true: Kit, Dax, and I had been going on raids since we were hardly ten years old, but we had always been better than those our own age. We were smarter, faster, stronger, and just as lethal as anyone else years older. Jett didn't understand that no matter how much he wanted to be, he wasn't like us.

'We'll know when you're ready,' Dax said, saving me from telling Jett the embarrassing truth: he just wasn't cut out for it yet.

'Okay,' Jett mumbled. 'I really am sorry. I didn't mean to put anyone in danger.'

'Keep that in mind next time,' Kit said harshly, hitching his bag over his back. 'Now let's get out of here before they come after us.'

'Good idea. We hardly got away as it is,' I said. I read-justed the gun beneath my waistband to make sure it was secured after running so quickly. Everyone nodded as we started our trek through the darkness of the trees, heading back to our own camp. We were silent until we'd moved a good distance away from Greystone.

'Wait, how did you get away?' Dax asked suddenly as if just realising what I'd said. 'Did they catch you or what?'

'A girl did,' I said. Her face flashed before my field of vision, the burning green eyes narrowed at me in determination. 'She had a gun but she let us go.'

'What?' Kit asked incredulously. He glanced at me sceptically, his face barely decipherable through the darkness.

'She let us go,' I repeated, shrugging.

'She was pretty,' Jett piped up from between Dax and me. 'But really scary.'

'Why the hell would she let you go? I've never heard of anyone getting caught at Greystone and making it out alive,' Kit questioned.

'I don't know,' I said honestly. Her actions were mysterious to me, but I remembered the annoyance her voice had held when she'd asked about Jett. 'I think it was because of Jett. She didn't want to shoot a kid.'

'She must be the only one over there,' Dax muttered. Greystone was notorious for being brutally heartless when it came to those they killed.

'So I saved you?' Jett said suddenly, his voice lifting excitedly.

'No. You were the reason we got caught in the first place,' I snapped, quickly shutting down his irrational thought.

'Oh.'

No one else spoke as we carried on, our journey nearly complete as the flickering lights from our camp blinked through the trees. The quiet sloshing of the kerosene in the few barrels we had managed to steal on the raid accompanied our soft breathing while we moved. It was much later now and completely dark, so I assumed most of the camp would have retired back to their individual huts for the night.

I saw that I was right as we re-entered the camp, the pathways relatively deserted, apart from those making their rounds while on guard duty. I nodded at the middle-aged woman and teenage boy that passed, glad to see they had their guns ready in case a threat appeared.

'Jett, go to Maisie. You better tell her what you did, otherwise she'll hear it from me,' I told him. He let out a quiet squeak, anxious to tell her. Jett's parents were both gone, victims of the world we now lived in. Maisie had taken him under her wing, acting as his adoptive mother as well as the mother of the entire camp. She kept us fed, working in the mess hall to keep the camp well nourished. In her forties, she was gentle and kind, but strong-willed and highly unlikely to put up with any nonsense. Everybody respected her, and while he loved her dearly, Jett was a little bit afraid of her; surely he wouldn't be too pleased to tell her what he'd done. She would be furious.

'Yes, sir,' he squeaked, nodding at me and scurrying away before I could reprimand him for calling me 'sir'.

'You're too soft on him,' Kit grumbled from beside me. I glanced at him and raised an eyebrow.

'He doesn't respond to people being mean,' I said. Jett was too fragile to be helped the way Kit wanted me to treat him.

'Hmmph,' he muttered, switching the jug of kerosene to his other hand. We walked in silence until we reached the storeroom. Dax threw the door open and greeted the guard loudly, making him jump at our sudden intrusion.

'Not sleeping, are you?' Dax teased, raising his eyebrows at the elderly man who was on duty.

25

'Never, Dax,' the man said with a smile. There wasn't anyone in the camp that didn't like Dax.

I waited patiently for Kit and Dax to deposit their items, taking the one jug I'd managed to steal out of my bag and placing it next to theirs. I nodded at the man before we left the building to return our guns and supplies to the raid building. After several more minutes of walking in silence, we reached the building and went inside. Our guns were placed back inside the cases and our backpacks were returned to their rightful places.

Kit said a stony hello to the guards, a different man and woman from before, as we made our way out into the night. We walked together, heading back to our own huts that were situated on the right side of our camp. We were nearly there when a man of about fifty appeared from his own hut as we were passing.

'Hayden,' he greeted. He extended his hand, which I shook firmly.

'Barrow,' I said in response, nodding at him.

'Back from the raid, I see?' he observed, nodding at Kit and Dax beside me.

'Yep.'

'And it went well?' he questioned.

'I wouldn't say well but we're back,' I said. Dax snorted next to me, already finding our dangerous situation funny.

'Well, glad to hear it,' Barrow said, smiling at us. 'I tried to find you before you took off but I must have just missed you – we need wiring.'

I sighed, running my fingers along my lip in frustration. 'Wiring? What for?'

'The generator in the kitchen and mess hall is going out,' Barrow said. 'It's all burning up and we'll be out of power soon if it blows.'

26

'We'll have to go into the city for that,' Kit said from beside me. I frowned.

'I know.'

Barrow frowned at me apologetically. 'Want me to put together a team? I can go.'

'No, that's all right,' I told him. I could see Dax grinning beside me. 'We'll go tomorrow.'

Raids into the city were best done during the day, even if it meant we were more easily spotted. The city at night was the most dangerous place you could go, because it was when the Brutes came out to play. It was their territory, and they knew how to defend it.

Barrow nodded at me. 'Okay. Get some sleep, boys, we'll want you all back safe.'

'You know it'll take more than a few Brutes to take us out,' Dax said lightly, grinning at Barrow as he nudged his shoulder. Barrow grinned, appreciating the enthusiasm. He still went on raids once and a while, but not nearly as many as he used to. After a trip to Crimson had gone horribly wrong, he'd wounded his left knee pretty badly and now found it difficult to keep up with the fast pace of a raid. He never said it, but I knew how much it devastated him to have to stay behind whenever we went on raids. He was the one who had trained us all.

'Yeah, yeah, the invincible trio,' Barrow said playfully. 'See you later, then.'

'Good to see you, Barrow,' Kit said evenly, grinning at him as much as he ever did. With that, Barrow went back into his hut to leave us to get to ours. We covered the remaining short distance before we found ourselves outside our homes, which all happened to be next to each other's.

'Shall we take off around nine tomorrow?' I asked them. Kit picked at his fingernail as he nodded.

'Yeah, sounds good.'

'Sweet dreams, boys! Glad your lucky arse is still here, Hayden,' Dax said lightly before turning to head inside. Kit chuckled deeply, the stress of the situation wearing off slightly now that we were home.

'Me, too,' I laughed, a grin breaking across my face for the first time in what felt like ages. With that, we each disappeared into our huts to get some sleep before the raid in the morning. Usually we didn't go on raids two days in a row, but the wiring for the generators was too important to put off. If we had no electricity in the kitchen, we didn't eat.

I reached my hand behind my head to grip the back of my shirt and haul it over my head, knocking my bandana off in the process. My hair fell forward into my eyes as I undid my boots and jeans before letting them drop to the floor. Within moments, I was falling into bed, my body crashing down onto the mattress. I was asleep the moment my head hit the pillow, the stress of the day knocking me out quickly.

It felt like only seconds later when I was abruptly awoken by someone pounding on my door.

'Hayden, mate, let's go!' Dax shouted.

'Yeah, get out of bed, you lazy pile,' Kit added. He sounded surprisingly happy for Kit. I let out a heavy sigh, pressing my face into my pillow before my arms flexed beside me to push myself up.

'All right, all right, give me a minute,' I called back. Without much thought, I pulled on the jeans that lay discarded on the floor before throwing a navy flannel over my chest. I grabbed the headband off the floor and pushed it onto my head, keeping my hair out of my face while I tied my boots. I moved to the makeshift sink in the little bathroom that had been added to my hut, to splash water on my face.

28

As the leader of my camp, I was one of the few who actually had their own bathroom. A bucket filled with water served as the sink and a hanging perforated bag that could be filled with water served as a shower. People like Dax had managed to rig a rudimentary plumbing system that allowed water to drain from the floor and run outside. I even had a latrine with a system that drained the waste away from camp while the rest had to use the communal latrines. I was lucky; I had it better than a lot of others.

Sunlight blazed through the doorframe when I whipped open the door, revealing a surprisingly excited-looking Kit and Dax standing outside.

'Morning, sunshine,' Dax said, shoving a gun and backpack into my hands. 'Got your stuff for you, let's get on with it!'

'Where's my—'

I was cut off by Dax flicking open my switchblade inches from my face, grinning as I jerked back at his sudden movement. I frowned disapprovingly at him as I took it, closing the blade back into the handle.

'Thanks.'

'Let's get going. I want to be back in time for lunch. Maisie's making that special chicken,' Dax said excitedly.

'All right, all right,' I muttered. I threw the backpack over my shoulders and pushed the gun under my waistband where I always kept it. My bag was considerably heavier than it had been last night, and I knew Kit and Dax had loaded it with more ammunition and supplies since we were going into the city. It was bright and sunny as we made our way out of the camp, our pace quick and purposeful.

Sometimes we chose to take one of the vehicles we had, but on days like today when our load would be light, we chose to walk and save precious gasoline. Before long, we were making our way through the trees that surrounded our camp, heading in a different direction than we had gone last night. The city wasn't much farther than Greystone, so the trip didn't take very long.

The ruins of the city rose before us, the decrepit grey buildings crumbling more and more with every visit we made. Weeds had started to grow through the cracks in the cement, making the once metropolitan area look even more desolate. We moved cautiously as we crept through the streets, our eyes constantly scanning the alleys and buildings for shifting shadows of those who could potentially harm us.

We hadn't moved far when we came across a broken down bus, a prime target for wiring. I nodded at Dax silently and saw his eyes light up at the prize. He was the technology expert, so it would be up to him to get the necessary wiring out of the bus. With our guns drawn and extended, we moved towards it, never letting our eyes linger in one space for too long.

The door to the bus was yanked open, and I moved stealthily as I entered it slowly. I scanned the inside of it carefully, gun pointing ahead of me in case I needed to fire, but it was deserted. I nodded behind me, indicating Dax come inside and do what he needed to do. Kit positioned himself at the door, his back to us so he could keep watch for any incoming enemies.

'Go, Dax,' I said quietly. He whipped off his backpack, crouching to the floor to dig out the necessary supplies and start taking apart the dashboard. I looked out of the windows carefully for any signs of movement. I jumped as Dax pried open the dash, the loud squeak it let out setting my nerves on edge. He worked quickly, pulling wires from sockets and cutting what he needed out of the dash.

A sudden bang echoed out to reveal a familiar sound: a gun going off not far from us.

'Shit,' Kit cursed, arms tightening as he turned toward the direction of the sound. Dax cursed from his position on the ground as he shoved the supplies into his backpack and slung it over his shoulder.

'I'm done, let's get out of here,' he said. 'Guarantee that was a Brute and they'll be here any minute.'

'Get down!' Kit hissed suddenly, climbing swiftly aboard the bus and ducking below the dash. I followed suit, sitting just high enough to see out of the windshield to figure out what Kit had seen.

'Ten o'clock,' Kit whispered. I averted my eyes and sure enough, a group of four was slinking through the ruins of the city, guns drawn as they peered around. One of them was limping slightly, and they all looked flustered.

'Bet they found some Brutes, yeah?' Dax said, appearing beside me to glance at the people. They hadn't seen us, too distracted by whatever they had just encountered. My eyes travelled down their line, taking in the two middle-aged men and a younger man of about twenty-five before landing on the final member of their party. A girl with blonde hair and striking green eyes who had held a gun to my chest only hours ago.

The girl from Greystone.

My jaw fell open slightly in shock as I watched her move, her body strong and well trained to avoid making any noise. Kit moved beside me, drawing my attention as he raised his gun. Dax did the same at my other side.

'I'll hit the first two if you can each take another,' Kit murmured, taking aim at one of the men.

'Got it,' Dax said. It was standard procedure to take out any enemies you encountered on a raid. The fewer raiders

31

the other camps had, the better. My heart pounded, uneasy with at the thought of someone killing the girl who had spared my life.

'Wait—'

A gun shot rang out, the sound of the bullet echoing off the walls around us as I saw the first man fall to the ground. My eyes jerked to the side to see a surprised look on the faces of Kit and Dax. They hadn't fired the shot, but someone had just shot one of the four, and it wasn't us.

My eyes jerked forward again as a second shot rang out, the bullet ricocheting off the cement next to the younger man as he tackled the girl to the ground and out of the line of fire. The remaining man darted off, disappearing between two buildings before the younger one jumped to his feet to go after him. My eyes widened in surprise when the girl followed suit, setting off at a sprint after the two men, leaving the first behind. The pool of blood around him was already too large; he was dead.

She sprinted quickly, arms pumping and blonde hair flying out behind her as she ran. We all watched as yet another shot rang out from the unknown source. Almost instantly, she fell to the ground, landing heavily against the cement as the bullet buried itself in her leg. Without even pausing, she tried to push herself to her feet. Her face contorted in a grimace as her leg gave out, the slightest pressure she tried to put on it causing too much pain to allow it to support her.

Yet another shot echoed around us, landing in the dirt only feet from her head as she tried to crawl behind a broken down car for cover. My heart pounded anxiously, waiting for someone from her camp to come back for her, but no one did. She was alone in the street, injured and completely vulnerable to the attack from someone that would surely arrive soon.

Before I knew what I was doing, I was on my feet and throwing myself out of the door of the bus. I could hear Kit and Dax shouting my name in surprise and outrage as I sprinted away from them, but I didn't stop. I raced towards her as fast as I could, determined to reach her before someone else could. I jumped over a pile of rubble, landing smoothly on the other side before closing the remaining distance to reach her.

'Hey!' I shouted, reaching my hand out to her. She looked up in utter shock, her eyes meeting mine while her jaw fell open.

'What—'

'Let's go,' I cut her off, reaching down to grab her arm and pull her up as another bullet whizzed past us. She didn't argue as she threw her arm around my waist, using my body to prop herself up and move the best she could. Pulling my gun out, I twisted around to fire a shot in the direction the gunfire was coming from, hoping it was enough to hold off any more shots from whoever was trying to kill her.

Or rather, kill us.

Chapter 4 – Responsibility

GRACE

Pain seared through my leg as I tried to put weight on it, the shredded muscle in my thigh too weak to support me on its own. If it weren't for the pain distracting me, I would have been thoroughly confused and apprehensive about the situation I found myself in. He had appeared out of nowhere, the man I'd held a gun to last night, offering his hand to me to lift me up instead of pulling a gun and finishing me off like he should have. His arm was slung around my shoulders, holding me up while I moved as quickly as I could away from the source of gunfire.

I gritted my teeth, angry with myself for getting hit. We'd run into a Brute and killed him, but he must have had at least one friend with him that we hadn't seen, because he'd shot down one of the men from my raiding party. I didn't even try to look back to see the body – I knew he was gone. Gone, just like my pathetic excuse for a brother who had left me without a glance over his shoulder. Jonah and the other man on the raid had left me to die in the decrepit streets of the city simply to spare their own lives. I was practically seething with anger.

My unsteady feet scrambled over the debris of the street, tripping occasionally only to be hauled back upright by the mysterious boy next to me. He was more of a man than a boy, with hard, muscled arms, a sharp jaw, and a certain confidence only someone of great importance could carry. I didn't dare glance at him for fear of tripping once more to send us both sprawling to the ground.

His breathing was steady and unlaboured as he practically carried me away, not saying a word while we fled. He fired another shot behind us, holding off whoever had shot at me in the first place. We were heading toward a bus, which would provide the first solid barrier between the gunfire and us. I was starting to feel a little lightheaded but was determined to remain strong; I didn't know what he would do as soon as we were out of the line of fire.

The bus was only feet away now, and I felt an immense sense of relief when he led me behind it. I leaned against the bus, releasing my arm from around him and shrugging his off my shoulders. Quiet pants escaped my lips while I tilted my head back against the metal of the vehicle, closing my eyes to try and get a grip on the pain. My relief was only momentary, however, as I opened my eyes and saw three men standing in front of me, two holding guns to my chest.

With only one fully functional leg, I couldn't bring myself to let go of the bus, but I managed to raise my hands in the air. I stared back at them and immediately noticed that the one who had saved me, the one I had spared last night, was the only one not holding a gun to me. Irritation flashed through me that he had saved me from one gun only to drag me in front of two others.

'What do you think you're playing at?' one of the gun holders said, directing his question at the man who'd saved me. All three of them eyed me with mistrust, though it was more pronounced in the two with the weapons. Why, I wasn't sure, because they were the ones with guns, while I proceeded to bleed out from the leg. There was very little I could do to them even if I wanted to.

'Put the guns down,' he said, glaring at the other two. His voice held an unmistakable authority, and they obeyed despite looking very disgruntled about it. I glared back, my harsh gaze focused on the one who had spoken first. He had light brown hair, dark brown eyes, and a very prominent scowl on his otherwise handsome face. A wave of blurriness swept across my eyes, the stinging pain and loss of blood starting to affect me.

The one I'd been glaring at held my gaze while the other turned to my rescuer, hissing words at him I could hardly hear.

'Okay, great, you saved her, now let's get out of here,' he said, glancing sideways at me over his shoulder. His face didn't hold the same blatant hatred as his friend's, but he definitely didn't look pleased. The one who was obviously in charge looked at me, my gaze switching to meet his green eyes as they narrowed slightly before darting to the wound on my leg.

'She'll bleed out if we leave her,' he said, looking at me. I knew he spoke the truth; the bullet hadn't hit my artery, but it had ripped a considerable amount of flesh that would be more than effective in killing me.

'Exactly,' the angry one growled. 'One less to worry about.'

'No,' he said. 'We're taking her with us.'

'*What?*' the other two hissed at the same time.

'Hayden, you're bloody insane,' said the gentler of the two, shaking his head vigorously. Hayden. The one who saved me was called Hayden.

'We should just shoot her and kill her before her leg does,' the angry one said, glaring at me once more.

'We're going to save her because she's the one who saved me at Greystone,' Hayden said firmly, shooting them a challenging look. They blinked, realisation dawning on their faces as they all turned to look at me.

'This is the girl? The one that caught you and let you go?'

Hayden nodded, his lips pulled into his mouth and brows tucked together over his studious gaze.

'You're helping her then, mate. She's not my responsibility,' one of them said.

'Shut up, Kit,' Hayden muttered reproachfully. His wide shoulders shifted as he readjusted his bag, tightening the straps by pulling down on them. His forearms flexed easily whenever he moved, and I noticed he was approaching me once more. He loped gracefully toward me before stopping a few feet in front of me.

'Who are you?' he asked. I stared at him, jaw set to try and hide the excruciating pain I was feeling. He let out a huff of frustration before speaking again.

'I'm not going to kill you.'

His hard gaze was set on mine, and despite years of training, I believed him. That didn't mean, however, that I wanted to answer him. Believing that he wouldn't kill me and trusting him were two completely different things. I didn't even know where he was from while he knew very well where I was from; I didn't want to give him any more information. I stared at him defiantly.

'You're Grace,' he said, a hint of annoyance laced into his voice. I couldn't stop the momentary look of shock that fell over my face before I managed to mask it again. How did he know that?

'How—'

'They were calling for you last night,' he explained flatly.

37

Oh. 'Now let's go before you die and I end up owing something I can't repay.'

That explained his motivation. He felt like he owed me for saving his life and wanted to repay the favour as quickly as possible. Before I could protest, he slung his arm around my shoulders again in the position we'd adopted earlier. He didn't wait for me to ready myself before hauling me away from the bus, legs nearly collapsing beneath me. He held me up so I could see, through slightly blurred vision, the other two begin to head out of the city.

Kit — that was what he had called the angry one. The angrier one, I suppose.

'You should let me go home,' I said through clenched teeth. My leg was throbbing now.

'You'll never make it home on your own,' he said flatly.

'I'll be fine,' I argued. He stopped walking suddenly and pulled his arm from around me, causing me to promptly fall into a heap on the dirt. I hissed as the impact stung my wound, fists clenching involuntarily against the ground. I pounded one against the dirt to try and relieve some of the frustration I was feeling while my eyes clamped shut to try and block out the pain.

'Yeah. You'll be fine,' he remarked. My eyes popped open in shock as he crouched down, grabbing my thighs and pulling them apart. I was about to punch him in the face before he pulled his bandana from his head and tied it around my leg in a type of tourniquet. He raised an eyebrow at me, judging me for my dark thoughts. Then he scooped me up again and dragged me back to my feet.

'They'll be looking for me,' I warned. Despite believing that he wouldn't kill me, I didn't trust his other friends as far as I could throw them. And who was to stop him from letting someone else kill me once we got to his camp? You don't go to other camps unless it's on a raid – not if you plan to make it out alive, at least. His camp was the last place I wanted to be.

'No, they won't,' he said simply.

'Yes—'

'They left you,' he said sharply, cutting me off. He didn't look at me, and his hard gaze faced forward as we followed his friends about twenty feet behind them. His words stung because I knew they were true. My raiding party, what was left of them, had left me, including my own brother.

'They'll come back,' I lied, forcing the resentment from my voice.

'No, they won't,' he repeated tensely. 'Now shut up.'

I would have argued, but the pain in my leg was making it extremely difficult to walk and think at the same time, much less talk. My mind raced through the haze that had settled over it, trying to come up with a way to escape. He held his gun in his hand away from me, but he surely had other weapons hidden on him somewhere. Did I dare risk the one chance I would surely get to steal one?

A nagging thought lingered in the back of my mind that I couldn't ignore.

You won't make it back alive if you do that.

I knew he was right about everything he'd said: I would never make it back on my own and no one was coming for me. Worse, if I stayed I'd end up stuck alone in the city, waiting to either bleed out, or for the inevitable night to come during which the inhabitants of the city would kill me however they pleased. I had no choice but to go with Hayden.

'Where are you from?' I asked. I was annoyed that my voice sounded weaker than before, the injury taking its toll on me. He ignored my question, forcing me to carry on forward with him. We were approaching the tree line and I was suddenly struck with a pang of trepidation. If we were going into the woods that could only mean one thing . . .

'Blackwing?' I whispered, my voice equal parts awe, apprehension, and, despicably, fear. Greystone, my own camp, was second only to Blackwing. Blackwing was, without a doubt, the most lethal of all the camps. I'd only been on a handful of raids there, all of which had been hideously unsuccessful. Every time, we'd lost someone to their guards.

I'd been raised to hate them, trained at every turn to never trust them, and without a doubt, kill any member of Blackwing I should ever come into contact with. They were dangerous, lethal, and not to be provoked unless you wanted to face dire consequences.

As determined as I was, I couldn't deny that I was more than a little nervous to be heading to the infamous Blackwing in less than prime condition.

I winced as a branch from a tree we passed by scraped against my wound, sending a shock of pain through my body. My eyelids fluttered involuntarily, the trees swooping before my eyes as the pain hit the highest level yet. It grew harder and harder to lift my feet over the uneven ground, and I could see the black creeping in around my vision as I tried to cling to consciousness. Despite my efforts, I'd lost too much blood and the pain was too high. The last thing I heard before I succumbed and blacked out was Hayden muttering next to me.

'Nearly there . . .'

Everything was black and my body felt like it weighed ten times its normal weight. I tried to lift my arms, but couldn't thanks to the straps that bound my wrists in place. A vague digging could be felt in my thigh, the site of my wound, and it took me a few minutes to remember how to open my eyes. When I did, I clamped them shut almost immediately to ward off the blindingly bright light overhead.

I sucked in a breath and forced my eyes into a squint to try and figure out what was happening. Once I adjusted to the brightness of the light, I was able to see a tall man hunched over my leg, his arms blocking my view of whatever he was doing. It didn't necessarily hurt, but there was an annoying pressure every time he moved.

Quiet murmurs reached my ears, their tones decidedly tense. I tried again to lift my arms, but they didn't budge. An attempt to move my legs proved impossible thanks to straps around my ankles, binding all of my limbs to the table I was lying on. I turned my head to the side, trying to see anything else in the room.

'Best stop moving, girl. I'm nearly done,' the man said, his voice impossibly deep and slow. He turned to glance at me, dark skin making the whites of his eyes stand out in sharp contrast. He looked to be about sixty-five years old.

'What are you doing?' I asked tightly. I tried to sit up, but all I managed to do was lift my head off the hard surface.

'Fixing your leg. Just missed your femoral artery and didn't hit any bone. You're a lucky one, you are,' he answered. His words were aimed at my leg as he refocused on his work.

'Why doesn't it hurt?'

I'd experienced wounds before that had required some medical attention, but every time the pain had been excruciating. This lack of pain scared me.

'I had a little anaesthetic left,' he explained.

'Shouldn't have wasted it on you,' another voice said from behind me. I turned my head sharply in an attempt to see who had spoken. My eyes landed on the three I'd encountered earlier: Hayden, Kit, and the other one. It had been Kit who had spoken, his dark eyes glaring at me once more. Hayden approached, leaving the others to linger against the wall.

'Docc says you nearly bled out,' Hayden said slowly, steady gaze falling on me. The news didn't shock me.

'That bloody bandana of his saved your life, girl,' the older man said. Docc, apparently. He put the finishing touches on his work before standing up to his alarmingly tall height. He towered over everyone, including Hayden who was fairly tall on his own. I jerked my arms up, silently indicating I wanted to be untied. Being completely helpless and surrounded by men I did not know with a wide variety of tools they could use against me made me extremely uneasy.

My eyes were on Docc, waiting for him to undo the binding when I felt a touch on my other hand. I turned my head sharply to see Hayden's fingers pressing into my wrist, steadying me as he undid the strap. As soon as my arm was free, I twisted to the other side to undo the second one. I managed to loosen it enough to free my other arm and sat up quickly, regretting it immediately. The room spun around me, my body very clearly still recovering from the loss of blood.

'Easy, girl,' Docc said, shaking his head while he undid the straps on my ankles. I blew out a heavy breath and swung my legs to the side, perching myself on the edge of the table while praying for the room to stop spinning. My eyes focused on my leg, where I was surprised to see a fine line of sutures running along the skin, sewing my flesh neatly back together.

'You're going to want to rest up for a few days,' Docc added, seeing I was clearly unfit to move.

'No, I need to get back,' I said, suddenly feeling frantic. How long had I been gone? I needed to get out of here before Hayden decided his debt was paid and he allowed someone else to kill me.

'No way. You nearly died, you need your rest,' Docc answered firmly. My gaping expression turned from Docc to Hayden.

'Let me go home,' I requested. My eyes locked on his as he watched silently.

'No,' he said. My heart sank. 'You won't make it on your own and I can't spare anyone to bring you back.'

'I don't need help,' I said defiantly.

'You won't make it thirty feet,' he said sceptically. 'Docc says you need to rest a few days and what Docc says goes. That's final.'

He turned his back to me and strolled to his friends, who still looked rather upset. They all made to head out of the room and were nearly to the door when Docc spoke.

'Hayden.'

He turned around and looked at Docc.

'What?'

'She can't stay here,' Docc said firmly but respectfully. Even this huge, older man respected Hayden. He must have been pretty high up in their ranks if such a man spoke to him so humbly.

'What? Why not?' he hissed, jaw clenched.

'I have work to do. The infirmary is no place for her to stay.'

'What am I supposed to do with her?' Hayden asked, speaking as if I wasn't even there.

'Told you we should have left her,' Kit muttered, shooting a look at his friend behind Hayden's back. The other one nodded slightly as he pinched his lips together in agreement.

43

'That's on you, Boss,' Docc said, shrugging. 'But she's your responsibility.'

Hayden let out a heavy sigh and ran his hand across his face, clearly irritated with the situation. He looked as if he was starting to regret bringing me here. He pinched his lower lip between his thumb and forefinger while he thought before looking up at me.

'We'll put her in an extra hut and put a guard outside. She doesn't leave until I say so. Can't risk her stealing anything,' he said firmly. He glared at me as if this were all my fault.

'No way,' his friend said in protest. 'We can't spare someone to guard her – they're all on a fixed schedule and it'll screw everything up. This is your responsibility to handle, Hayden.'

'Dammit Dax . . .' Hayden muttered, addressing him. Dax. That was the other one's name.

Hayden frowned again, face twisting in irritation as he thought. I waited with bated breath to hear whatever solution they would come up with, sure I would hate it no matter what it was. I felt like I was a prisoner.

'All right . . .' Hayden said. He sighed heavily and pushed his hand through his now bandana-free hair. I held my breath as I waited for him to finish his thought, my heart pounding with anxiety and stress.

'Okay. She'll stay with me.'

Chapter 5 – Important
GRACE

I stared wide-eyed at the various people in the room. Kit and Dax looked irritated and relieved all at once, glad the responsibility for taking care of me had fallen to someone other than themselves. Docc was studying Hayden closely, his expression curious as he watched him. Hayden looked even more irritated than Kit and Dax as he threw a glare in my direction. Like any of this was my fault. He was the one who had dragged me here in the first place.

'I've got tower duty,' Kit said, breaking the uncomfortable silence. 'Don't do anything stupid.'

I wasn't sure if he was talking to me or to Hayden, because everyone in the general vicinity seemed to be irritating him at the moment. With that, he and Dax left the room, leaving me alone with Docc and Hayden. I wished I could just stay there with Docc. At least he seemed less annoyed with my presence.

A heavy sigh blew through Hayden's lips as he shoved his hand through his hair.

'Let's go, then,' he grumbled, eyes locking on mine. I opened my mouth to protest but decided against it as I heaved myself off the table I was sitting on. My leg almost buckled under my weight but I managed to grip the table to hold myself up. Hayden made no move to support me like he had before. I took a deep breath and focused on moving my leg, which was still weirdly numb from whatever Docc had done to me. At least it didn't really hurt.

I walked shakily toward Hayden, teeth gritted tightly. He watched me with his brows pulled low over his eyes. I focused on keeping my breathing even as I got closer, watching as he turned around to walk out of the room, silently indicating I follow.

'Thank you,' I said suddenly, turning back to look at Docc. He nodded solemnly, giving me the closest thing to a smile I'd seen from anyone since arriving here.

'You're welcome, girl,' he said, his deep voice mellow. I gave him a small nod before turning back around to follow Hayden. I was surprised to see it was completely dark out now as he opened the door without turning around to see if I was following or not. I must have passed out for a few hours if it was already dark.

My eyes studied Hayden, the wide expanse of his back shifting while he walked, the stress of the day weighing on him. He was clearly athletic and fit, though not in a bulky way. Despite his wide shoulders, his body was lean, with sharply defined muscles hidden beneath his skin and clothing. I shook my head and looked away from him to observe the camp. I'd never actually been in Blackwing – only around the boundaries while other brave members of Greystone attempted to raid it. They were always unsuccessful.

We were in what appeared to be the main part of their camp, with several larger buildings built more sturdily than the numerous square huts that fanned out from the centre. There were few people out, but those who we passed along the dirt pathways shot me looks of confusion, mistrust, and most prevalently, hatred. They knew I wasn't part of their camp; I was an outsider, a stranger. I was someone not to be trusted.

As we moved through the camp, we left behind the larger buildings and circled around to an area made up completely of huts, the pathway lit here and there by candles and lanterns. I didn't say anything as I continued to take in my surroundings, still somewhat shocked that I was actually in Blackwing.

My eyes locked on those of an elderly man with wispy white hair, his eyes narrowed in disgust as he watched me following Hayden. I frowned at him in apprehension as he took a menacing stop towards me. I sped up a little, closing the distance between Hayden and me to put some space between myself and the man. He took a few more steps, quicker this time until he was only feet from me.

'I'd go back inside if I were you,' Hayden said suddenly, his voice forceful. My gaze jerked to him, surprised to find him glaring at the man rather than at me. His hand gripped my upper arm, shifting us so he was between the man and me. The man muttered something, more of a growl than anything, before turning around to head back into his hut.

'Thanks,' I muttered grudgingly. All it would have taken was one punch to the old man's throat to get him away from me, but surely attacking a member of Hayden's own camp right in front of him wouldn't have gone over well.

'Just keep up, will you?' he replied flatly.

After passing a few more huts, Hayden veered to the left, approaching a hut that was just slightly bigger than those around it. He pushed the door open to reveal a pitch-black expanse, the sparse lighting from outside failing to reach within. He held the door open and flicked his head, telling me to go inside as he pressed his back against the frame to let me pass.

I walked into the darkness, stopping a few feet into the hut so I wouldn't run into anything. I gasped quietly when he let the door slam shut, enveloping us completely in total darkness. My heart sped up a little, the vulnerability of being in the complete dark with this stranger, this enemy, making me extremely uncomfortable. I could hear him moving even though I couldn't see him. A sudden flare of light from a match came from the corner where he lit a candle before picking it up to light a few others in the small home.

The light made it possible to see the space around me, which was unsurprisingly relatively simple. The room consisted of a bed, a couch and table, a desk, and a dresser. There was little else to the room, nothing fancy or unnecessary. Everything in here had been scavenged from the city years ago. A door was closed on the other side of the room.

Hayden turned around and walked toward me, his face lit up eerily from the flickering candle he held. He put it down on the coffee table by my knees. Papers were scattered across it, as if he'd spent many hours sitting on the couch poring over them there. He bent to pick them up, shuffling them into a stack before carrying them to his desk and sliding them into a drawer.

'You can sleep on the couch,' he said gruffly. He moved to his bed and pulled a blanket off the end of it before tossing it to me. I caught the blanket and looked at the couch, which had definitely seen better days. It looked to be made of scratchy brown material and like it had long ago lost its firmness, but at least I didn't have to sleep on the ground.

He sat on the edge of his bed and started unlacing his boots while I stood and watched him. Everything about this was so surreal — stuck in the enemy camp with a fairly serious injury that had now been fixed while being forced to stay in this weird shack thing with someone I did not know in the slightest.

'Aren't you afraid I'll kill you in your sleep?' I asked, studying his movements. He didn't react much as I spoke before he sat up slowly to kick his boots off.

'No.'

'Why not?' I asked, sitting down on the couch. It sagged easily beneath my weight.

'Because if you do that you'll never make it out of here alive,' he said calmly, as if it were obvious. He had a point.

'Aren't you afraid I'll kill you?' he added, shooting me a curious look. He shocked me slightly when he stood and yanked his shirt over his head, gripping the collar to pull it off. I blinked and averted my eyes when I saw his hands moving to undo his jeans, but not before I'd got a good look at his long, tightly toned body I had started to notice outside. I blushed slightly as I stared at the floor.

'No,' I said, uncomfortable that he was undressing in front of me. I heard him pull a drawer out of his dresser followed by the whispers of fabric. When I looked at him again, he'd pulled on a pair of shorts but left his torso bare. His very attractive, firm torso. It was then that I noticed tattoos littering his left arm, accented by a few across his chest. How had he got those?

'Why not?' he pressed, shooting my own questions back at me. I could have been wrong, but I thought he sounded slightly amused at my obvious discomfort.

'Because then everything you've done so far would be for nothing,' I said. If there was one thing I understood about him after such a short time, it was that he didn't want to owe me anything. He wouldn't kill me because I hadn't killed him. He looked slightly impressed with my answer as he sat

49

back down on his bed. I was surprised he hadn't told me to shut up yet.

'Who are you?' I asked when he didn't speak.

'Hayden,' he said simply.

'You know what I mean,' I pressed. 'You're somebody important here.'

'What constitutes important?'

I rolled my eyes at his avoidance of my question. 'Those people out there . . . they all listen to you. Even the older ones.'

'And?' he asked, raising another sceptical eyebrow at me.

'Most people don't listen to twenty-something-year olds like that unless they're important,' I stated. Even though we were from different camps, it was something I suspected to be true universally.

'So what if I'm important then?' he asked. 'What does it matter?'

'It doesn't, I guess,' I muttered. I broke the steady gaze he had fixed on me to settle into the couch, which was already uncomfortable. I threw the blanket over me and tried to ignore the heat of his gaze. His unwillingness to answer my question pretty much confirmed what I'd begun to suspect – he was a leader here, if not *the* leader. It was so strange for him to be in charge at such a young age, especially when compared to my father, Celt, who was in charge of Greystone.

He was quiet again for some time before he pushed himself off his bed. He moved through the small space, blowing out the candle on his desk and the one by his bed, leaving only the one on the coffee table by the couch. My eyes focused on him as he walked toward me, his commanding presence stealing my breath. His green gaze found mine as he bent over slightly, the muscles in his stomach contracting tightly as he did so.

'Remember, Grace,' he said, his voice deadly quiet. 'You try anything, you die.'

I gasped slightly at his words before his full lips curled into a circle to blow out the remaining source of light, plunging the room into darkness. His feet padded lightly across the floor, and I heard the soft sound of blankets moving as he climbed into bed. My heart pounded a little faster in the complete darkness, my years of training setting warning bells off in my head. It was never good to lose one of your senses, especially in my current circumstances.

'Are you really going to let me go home?' I asked, my voice quiet. He didn't answer right away and I began to wonder if he was already asleep.

'Yes, Grace,' he finally answered. 'Then we're even.'

I prayed he was telling the truth, because I wanted nothing more than to get out of this hut, this camp, this entire situation. I wanted to go home where I knew everyone and could settle back into my routine. I also wanted to kick my brother's arse for leaving me, something I couldn't very well do in the confines of Blackwing.

A sudden loud banging on the door of Hayden's home interrupted my thoughts. I jumped, thankful for the darkness so Hayden didn't see. He swore quietly under his breath before I heard him push himself off his bed. I clutched my blanket tightly to try and calm my already frazzled nerves while I listened to him move toward the door. Soft light from the candles outside flitted into the room, illuminating the sharp cut of muscle in Hayden's stomach. I averted my eyes again, blinking furiously to try and keep my focus.

'What?' Hayden asked, addressing whoever was outside. All I could see was a silhouette.

'The tower saw raiders coming from the south,' the voice

51

said. It sounded familiar, and his face popped into my head before his name. Dax.

'Okay?' Hayden said sharply. 'So why are you here instead of taking them out?'

'It's a larger party. Barrow wanted you to come to the tower to verify,' he said, lowering his voice before leaning toward the frame to try and get a look at me.

'He and Kit can't handle a raid party?' he asked in irritation.

'Hey,' Dax said, raising his hands. 'Just delivering the message for Barrow. He wants you in the tower just in case.'

'So what am I supposed to do with her?' Hayden asked, throwing his hand in my direction. 'You going to watch her?'

'No way, man. You wanted her, you take her with you,' Dax said, shrugging. 'I'm not a babysitter.'

'Neither am I,' Hayden grumbled.

'Should have thought of that sooner, mate,' Dax said, not sounding the least bit apologetic. 'Better hurry. Barrow's getting antsy.'

'All right, all right,' Hayden said, shooing Dax away. Dax left, leaving Hayden to light the candle he had just extinguished not too long ago.

'Get up,' he said to me as he pulled a shirt over his body.

'What are we doing?' I asked, pushing the blanket off me to tie my boots. Hayden pulled on a pair of sneakers that he'd had under his bed.

'We're going to the tower,' he said flatly. I had to admit, hearing this excited me slightly. The tower was one of the reasons Blackwing was so formidable; it rose seven or eight storeys high and gave the people of Blackwing a 360-degree view of their camp, allowing them to see anyone coming from miles around. It must have been some type of lookout tower before the world fell apart, but now it served as the main defence for Blackwing. They knew raiders were on their way almost before the raiders did.

I stood and stretched my leg, the anaesthetic Docc had given me having worn off. I winced. Hayden saw me stretching it and shot me a look.

'Hope that leg of yours is up to it,' he said before heading out the door. 'Let's go.'

I followed, determined to keep up with him after his snide remark. We moved through the settlement, which was much more deserted now than it had been earlier. The tower rose over the camp and the top of it disappeared into the darkness even as we approached its base. Steep stairs made of steel allowed our ascent, and I looked at them with slight apprehension as we started to climb. Hayden made me go first.

The first few flights weren't bad, and almost helped ease some of the dull ache from my muscles. It almost felt good, and reassured me that my leg was still functional after suffering damage. Luckily, it seemed most of the wound had been in the fleshy part of my thigh, leaving my nerves and arteries uninjured. That was a good sign.

After the fifth flight, my leg began to throb again from the exertion, but I refused to slow down. I kept up the quick pace, determined to make it to the top without pausing or giving him any reason to think of me as weak. By the seventh flight, my lungs were burning with the effort to hold back the pain that seared through me, but still I kept going. A soft glow could be seen at the top, a lone candle illuminating the peak of the tower just enough to see that we'd reached it.

'Hey,' Hayden said, announcing our presence just as I climbed the final step. My nostrils flared with the effort of keeping my breathing even; Hayden didn't appear winded in the slightest. Damn. I placed my hands on my sides as I

53

glanced at the two men on top of the tower – Kit and a man I assumed to be Barrow, a fifty-something-year-old with speckled grey hair. He reminded me of Celt despite the disgruntled look he threw me before conferring his attention to Hayden.

'Three o'clock,' he told Hayden, pointing off in the distance. Sure enough, a small group could be seen thanks to their flickering lights. It was hard to tell how many there were because they were still so far away, but it was definitely more than a few. I glanced around in the other directions, but it was impossible to see anything besides darkness. Surely the view was amazing in the daylight. I would have no such luck in seeing it.

'You sure they're raiders?' Hayden asked.

'Damn sure. What else would a group that large be?' Kit said. It was then that I noticed the vast assortment of rifles set up at the top of the tower, all aiming outward in different directions and ready to be fired at a moment's notice. Kit and Barrow had additional guns slung over their shoulders.

Hayden was quiet for a moment as he stared out at the group that was slowly drawing closer.

'Take them out,' he said softly. Kit nodded instantly as he crouched down next to a rifle, eye aligning with the viewfinder to aim. Barrow copied him, and Hayden did the same. I stood back in mild shock as I watched them prepare to snipe a substantial amount of people.

'I count twelve,' Hayden murmured, eye pressed to the viewfinder.

'Me too,' Barrow agreed. Hayden continued to watch for a few seconds before speaking again.

'All right, take down a few and see if they turn back,' Hayden ordered. Neither of the other men responded, but it became clear that they'd heard when they both fired their rifles. They repositioned once and fired again, totalling four shots. Hayden, I noticed, hadn't fired his weapon yet.

'Four down,' Hayden stated. He watched a bit longer. 'They're still coming.'

'Firing again,' Kit muttered, squinting through his viewfinder. He waited a second to get his aim before shooting once more, Barrow doing the same next to him. They repeated their process, aiming and firing until they'd fired off twelve rounds.

'Okay,' Hayden muttered. 'That's it.'

He stood from his crouched position, a frown deeply set on his face. He looked surprised when he saw me standing behind him, as if he'd forgotten I was there. I suddenly felt like an intruder.

'Have a good watch,' Hayden said to the other two before starting toward me. He surprised me by grabbing my upper arm again to steer me back down the stairs.

'Hayden,' Barrow said, stopping him in his tracks. He turned around to face him.

'That girl,' he said, nodding at me. 'She's the one from Greystone?'

'Yes,' he said warily. I noticed people here had a habit of talking about me as if I wasn't even there.

'She's seen quite a lot, yeah?' Barrow continued, studying Hayden. Hayden seemed to catch on to where he was going, but he didn't answer, his glare daring him to continue instead.

'We've been talking, Hayden,' Kit said, drawing my attention. I didn't like the sound of that. Hayden remained silent as Kit continued.

'We've decided . . . she's seen too much. We can't let her go home.'

'Excuse me?' Hayden challenged.

'You know we're right, mate. She's seen too much of the camp, how we work. We can't let her go back and tell all of Greystone about it or we'll all be in danger. She either stays here as our captive or you kill her. Up to you,' Kit said, his tone gravely serious. I got the distinct impression that if it were up to him, he'd throw me off the side of the tower and be done with it. He'd just shot six people and hardly blinked an eye, killing me would be absolutely no problem for him.

I held my breath as I waited for Hayden's response and tried to decide which I was more afraid of: death, or staying in Blackwing as a prisoner for ever. At that exact moment, it was impossible to choose.

Chapter 6 – Ultimatum
GRACE

'You're giving me an ultimatum, Kit? *Me?*' Hayden asked, the anger barely masked in his voice. I couldn't help but notice the way his hands clenched into tight fists by his sides. Clearly, he did not like having his authority questioned.

'Not just me, mate. Dax, Barrow, everyone. You shouldn't have brought her here. You're putting everyone in danger,' Kit said firmly.

'No one's coming after her. They're not dangerous,' Hayden said firmly.

'Maybe not, but she is. She's from Greystone and she was on a raid. You bet your arse there's more to her than meets the eye,' Barrow said. I felt oddly comforted by his words despite the fact that it would probably work against me. I was more than capable of fending for myself and was pretty confident I could at least hold my own in a fight against any of them. They were stronger, but I was willing to bet I was faster.

'She's dangerous, Hayden,' Kit added.

'I'm standing right here,' I interrupted, unable to stop the words from falling from my mouth. I was sick of people talking about me as if I wasn't even present. Three pairs of heated eyes looked at me, my own glare burning back at them. Everyone was silent until Hayden spoke.

'I'm not killing her,' he said calmly, referencing Kit's ultimatum.

'Fine,' Barrow said, standing suddenly. 'Then I will.'

I took a step back as he rose, my back colliding with the meagre railing around the top of the tower as he swung his gun to point in my direction. I clenched my jaw tightly, determined not to give way to fear. The gun was cut from my vision, however, when Hayden stepped between Barrow and me. He lowered the gun immediately, shooting an irritated look at Hayden.

'I'm not killing her, and no one else is, either,' Hayden clarified firmly. I could hardly see Kit and Barrow over the wide expanse of Hayden's back.

'Looks like we've got ourselves a prisoner, then,' Kit said, his eyes dancing back and forth between Hayden and me. 'Should be fun.'

'Brilliant,' Hayden muttered sarcastically. 'Now get back to your watch.'

With that, he spun to face me, his chest nearly colliding with mine when he saw he was much closer than he had anticipated. He took a step back before grabbing my arm once again and tugging me toward the stairs. I jerked it out of his grip defiantly, sick of him treating me like a disobedient child. If I was going to try and escape, it wouldn't be now on top of a tower full of loaded guns with testy people behind the triggers.

He frowned, before pinching his lower lip between his thumb and forefinger, the way he did, in concentration. 'Come on.'

I didn't argue as I followed him down the stairs, glad to get off the top of the tower. Hayden didn't speak as we descended, his movements jerky and unnatural as if he were fighting a silent battle with himself. Once we reached the base, dirt practically flew out from beneath his feet as he stomped down the path back toward his home. The door to his hut was flung open wildly, the wood slamming against the various materials that made up the structure.

I returned to my place on the couch, sitting silently as I observed him some more. He kicked his shoes off hurriedly, a deep scowl set on his face. He looked infuriated.

'Hayden?' I ventured calmly.

'What?' he snapped, throwing me a surly look. I frowned.

'Why didn't you shoot anyone?' I asked.

He paused, hands freezing as he reached to rip his shirt over his head again. He recovered quickly, however, and proceeded to tug the fabric from his body. It had struck me as odd – this boy, who I was pretty sure was in charge of all of Blackwing, had neglected the opportunity for a few easy kills. Almost everyone I knew from Greystone would have jumped at the chance, their eyes lighting up with glee at the opportunity to take out a few enemies. Not Hayden.

'Kit and Barrow had it covered,' he said, his voice monotone. I caught a hint of something else beneath his words – a tiny note of deception. He was lying.

'Yeah, but you could have helped, right?' I prodded. He was silent as he threw himself into bed. He hadn't even bothered to light any candles this time, using only the sparse light that managed to creep through the cracks around the door and the one musty window. He was silent for so long I was starting to think he wouldn't answer at all.

'Goodnight, Grace,' he muttered, ignoring my question. The anger had drained from his voice now and he simply sounded tired. I sighed.

'Goodnight, Hayden.'

*

The first thing I registered when I woke up in the morning was that my back was extremely sore, followed shortly by a throbbing burn in my leg from where I'd been injured. The second thing I noticed was that there was the sound of running water coming from behind the only door besides the entrance into Hayden's hut. It must have been some kind of bathroom, and I was surprised to hear what sounded like running water.

I glanced at the door hiding the source of the sound and was surprised to see it cracked open an inch or so. Through the crack, a flash of skin from Hayden's wide back caught my eye, dripping wet as he stood beneath a makeshift shower. I jerked my head forward again, blushing even though he hadn't seen me accidentally spying on him.

What was it with this guy and being shirtless around me? It was distracting enough to have to watch him undress time and time again, much less catching a glimpse of him completely naked. Why couldn't he have just shut the door?

I jumped when the sound of the water ended, unsure of what to do with myself. In a moment of sheer panic, I threw myself back down on the couch and pretended to be asleep. My eyes closed quickly, but not before I saw Hayden stroll out of the bathroom with nothing but a towel around his waist.

Oh my god.

'You're shit at that,' Hayden said, his tone amused. My eyes opened against my will to catch him shooting a smirk at me. I frowned in confusion.

'At what?'

'Pretending to be asleep. Stiff as a board, you were,' he said. He made no effort to cover his body, which I couldn't help but notice was covered in tiny droplets of water, making his firm muscles stand out even more.

'Oh,' was all I said. At least he seemed to be in a better mood than last night. I tried not to stare as he pulled a red plaid shirt over his arms, not bothering to dry off his chest at all. When his hands moved to undo the towel around his waist, I forced my eyes away as a blush crept across my cheeks.

I was surprised he affected me so much because usually I took no notice of nakedness; boys, girls, men, women, none of it really seemed to matter. I saw nudity in a clinical way, a necessary step to help heal those who were wounded. Much of my time in Greystone had been spent helping heal those in need, so nakedness was not uncommon.

This, however, was a completely different circumstance and I was not prepared to deal with it. I was relieved when I heard the subtle zip of his jeans, indicating he was finally fully dressed, and much less distracting. His showering and redressing, however, reminded me that I hadn't had a shower or a change of clothes for a while now. I probably smelled like something dead.

My stomach rumbled loudly, interrupting the quiet of the hut. Hayden pulled on his boots before standing and shooting me a surprised look.

'Hungry?' he asked.

'Starving,' I replied honestly. I pulled on my boots quickly and was ready in a few seconds thanks to my lack of clothes to change into.

'Come on, I'll take you to the kitchen,' he said. His mood was lighter this morning and I found myself not hating him for once. He was much more pleasant when he was alone than when under the watchful eyes of those in his camp.

I was pleased to see the sun shining brightly outside. For some reason I had been expecting clouds, rain, wind, anything that pointed to the stormy welcome I had received so far. Hayden led me down the path we'd come by last night, weaving through huts that were positively crawling with people in the morning light.

'So,' Hayden said, drawing my attention away from a mother playing with her two young children on a patch of grass. That kind of thing didn't really happen in Greystone, and it was oddly pleasing to see.

'So,' I repeated calmly.

'So if you're going to stay here—'

'Imprisoned here,' I corrected, cutting him off. He clenched his jaw before continuing.

'If you're going to *stay* here, you need to know how it works,' he said, a hint of apprehension in his voice as if he was unsure if he should really divulge any more information to me.

'Okay,' I said, urging him on.

'Meals are in the kitchen and mess hall. It's the same building as you'll see in a minute. Latrines and showers are on the other side of the camp but you can use mine. You'll go nowhere near our raid building or ammunition holds unless you're with me. Anywhere else you need to go, I'll take you.'

I hadn't expected any access to anything potentially dangerous, so his words didn't shock me.

'All right,' I agreed.

'And, you're with me from now on. I can't trust you to run around here alone and I don't trust anyone else to watch you without one of you picking a fight,' he said. His face was hard to read.

'What makes you think I'd be stupid enough to pick a fight with someone in the middle of Blackwing?' I asked, somewhat insulted. There was probably no more idiotic move I could make.

'I didn't—'

'Hi, Hayden!' a voice chirped, interrupting whatever Hayden had been about to say. A boy appeared at his side, around ten or eleven, and I immediately recognised his wide, brown eyes. It was the kid from the raid. I leaned around Hayden to get a better look at him. He blushed fiercely and fell back behind Hayden as he walked with us.

'Morning, Jett,' Hayden returned lightly.

'Hayden, is it true?' he asked. He tried to keep his voice to a hushed tone but it didn't work, and I heard him easily.

'Is what true, little man?' he asked patiently. The use of the nickname sparked a memory of what he'd said to him the night I let them go.

Now we run, little man.

'That you're letting her stay here?' Jett whispered in awe. He peeked around Hayden's body to glance at me, only to squeak and retreat when he saw me staring back.

'I'm making her stay here,' Hayden corrected. 'She doesn't want to be here.'

'Then why don't you let her go home?' Jett questioned.

'Because,' Hayden said simply. 'It's not safe to let her go home.'

I grinned, pleased he was finally admitting I could be dangerous even if it was only to explain my presence to a kid.

'Oh,' Jett said flatly. His face screwed up in concentration as he tried to understand what Hayden had told him before remembering something. 'Oh yeah! Maisie said we need firewood for the stoves in the kitchen.'

'Is the storeroom out?' Hayden asked. Jett paused, causing Hayden and I to stop as well. He just shrugged, bringing his shoulders almost up to his ears as his lower lip pouted. He shot a somewhat fearful look at me before turning back to Hayden.

'It's just what Maisie said to tell you,' he replied.

'All right, tell her we'll get some,' Hayden said. Jett nodded and scampered off. Hayden turned sharply, veering off the path we were on to head between a few huts.

'I like him,' I said, unable to hold back a soft smile. He glanced at me in surprise.

'It's hard not to,' he admitted. We walked through the huts and entered the edge of the woods, presumably to retrieve some firewood.

'So I have to stay with you all the time?' I asked, frowning. That sounded awfully exhausting.

'Yes,' he said, bending to pick up a few pieces of wood from a stack near a large tree. We stood in a small clearing surrounded by trees just outside the ring of huts in camp.

'I don't need you to protect me,' I said, folding my arms over my chest. He sighed before setting down the logs he'd gathered to stand to his full towering height. He was well over six feet tall.

'Oh really?'

'Yeah,' I said firmly. We stared each other out.

'Prove it.'

'Prove what?' I asked, unsure of what he wanted me to do.

'Prove you don't need me to protect you.'

I blinked once. Was he asking me to fight him? He raised his eyebrows expectantly, confirming my thoughts. My hands rose from my sides as I shifted my stance, taking a small step towards him. He countered my move, deflecting to the side away from me. A fight, it seemed, was exactly what he wanted. A satisfied grin fell across my face. Finally.

I raised my fists in full guard of my face and body. He did the same, green eyes lit in a smirk. Every step I took, he matched, circling away from me but never out of my reach. Adrenaline pumped through my veins at the promise of a fight as I sucked in a deep breath and lurched forward, throwing my fist toward his jaw.

My blow was deflected easily with his forearm, causing me to miss my target. A second blow from my other fist followed quickly, but it only managed to graze his ribcage. Every move I made sent a slight stinging sensation through my leg, but I ignored it determinedly. I blew out a steady breath as I took another step forward, quicker than his retreat, as I managed to swing my knee up to his side to collide solidly. Again, my attempt at hitting his jaw was rebuffed as my fist swung through the air, his palm easily swatting it down.

He didn't attack, merely deflected and defended against my offence. His feet moved quickly and deftly, and my confidence that I was faster than him appeared to have been misplaced. Every step I took was matched with one of his own, and the only blows I managed to land were those he had softened first with his forearms or body. He was an excellent fighter, and it was frustrating me.

'Come on, Grace, you can do better than that,' he goaded, smirking at me once more. I could feel sweat starting to prickle at my forehead as I launched forward again, this time leading with a kick rather than a punch. My first solid hit landed with a thud on his side, and he blew out a heavy puff of breath. I pressed forward, feinting with my left hand before following through in a swing with my right. A heavy thud sounded as I finally connected with his jaw, snapping his head to the side.

I cheered silently, celebrating my small victory in my head. Before I had a chance to continue my assault, however, he recovered and grabbed both of my wrists easily, twisting me around and pushing me forward until he pressed the front of my body into a nearby tree trunk. I landed against it with a thud as a heavy puff of breath was forced from my lungs. My cheek pushed against the rough bark while his hands gripped my wrists against my lower back

'I have to say, I expected more from you,' he said, his voice an almost menacing whisper as he pressed his body into my back, pinning me to the tree. Excuses flashed through my mind: I hadn't eaten properly in days, I'd just got shot in the leg, he's much bigger than I am, but I didn't say any. I didn't want to give him the satisfaction of hearing an excuse.

'Then you won't be afraid to do this again some other time,' I said firmly, pushing back against his weight to try and get him off me. He didn't budge.

'Still think you don't need me to protect you?' he whispered. I shivered when his lips tickled against my ear when he spoke, and I hated myself for liking it. My breath was slightly shallower than I would have hoped, but I told myself it was because I was weaker than usual thanks to the circumstances.

Right.

'Hmm?' he hummed, his lips nudging against the shell of my ear again when I didn't answer him. Without hesitation, I threw my hands down, straightening them out as best I could though they were held behind me, to catch him off guard with a shot to the groin. He fell backward with an audible groan, surprised by my sudden attack. I swept a kick around his feet, knocking him to the ground.

I dropped down instantly, pinning his arms beneath my knees as I bent over to put my forearm over his throat. His jaw tightened as he tilted his head back to ease the pressure.

'You tell me,' I said, hovering over him. It was impossible to miss the glimmer in his eyes – he was impressed. He didn't respond but held my gaze for a few seconds; I was surprised to feel a stirring of something in the pit of my stomach. My breath hitched in my throat when his head lifted from the ground below to inch closer to mine. I slackened the pressure at his throat from my forearm. His eyes darted to my lips, lingering there for a second too long while my mind buzzed with confusion.

All of a sudden, my entire body was flipped over as Hayden threw me off him and into the dirt before he landed on top of me. The weight of his body was too much for me to throw off, his hips pinning mine down while his hands covered each of my wrists to push them into the ground. I sucked in a breath when he lowered his lips to my ear once more.

'Maybe you're not the one who needs protecting,' he said quietly. Once again, his lips nudged against my ear, causing another shudder to run through me. He pulled back enough to look me in the eye, his face inches from my own as he hovered over me. 'Maybe I'm protecting them from you.'

Chapter 7 – Tension

HAYDEN

My breath snagged as my gaze caught Grace's, her stunning green eyes only inches from mine. I could feel the heat of her body pressed against mine as I hovered over her, my hips pinning hers down while my hands enclosed her wrists, with her back in the dirt. Her lips were parted as she blew out heavy breaths, the physical exertion she'd expended winding her slightly.

For a moment, I forgot how we had even ended up in this position. It seemed strange that she'd given up on fighting me, her face looking slightly bewildered by what I'd said to her. I hadn't meant for my lips to press into the shell of her ear, but I hadn't exactly tried to avoid it either because, despite my better judgement, I liked the feel of it.

Maybe I'm protecting them from you.

That was what I'd said to her, and it was the absolute truth. She had already proven that she didn't need anyone to protect her; the fight she'd put up against me was more impressive than from any other girl I'd ever seen, even if I'd won in the end. She'd been shot only a day ago but had made no complaints or excuses, trudging along after me without a word of protest. There was a strength in her, a bravery, that I couldn't help but admire.

I could feel the tension between us as neither of us spoke,

our eyes regarding each other from only inches away. Finally, she opened her mouth to speak, drawing in a breath, but she was interrupted before she could start.

'Oi! What the hell are you two doing?' a voice demanded, shattering the spell we seemed to have fallen under. I tore my gaze from hers, practically jumping to my feet to see Dax standing a few feet away with an incredulous look on his face. Grace soon leaped to stand next to me, hastily brushing the debris off her clothes. Was I seeing things, or did I see a slight blush on her cheeks?

'Nothing,' I said flatly, strangely irritated at him for interrupting. We hadn't been doing anything, so why did I feel annoyed that the moment was over?

'Didn't look like nothing,' Dax muttered, his gaze switching between Grace and I. The blush I'd thought I'd seen was gone now, replaced by a scowl on her face as she folded her arms over her chest. Hmm.

'I don't care what it looked like,' I said dismissively. 'What are you doing here?'

'We need firewood,' he said matter of factly. *Oh, right.* We were in the middle of the area where we stored the wood – it was the reason we were here in the first place. I seemed to have forgotten. Grace, I noticed, turned around abruptly and started walking away from me. For a moment, I thought she was trying to make a run for it, before she stopped in front of a pile of logs and stooped to gather some. My chest relaxed a bit even though I hadn't noticed it tighten in the first place.

Dax and I followed suit, gathering our arms full of as much firewood as we could carry. After we were sufficiently loaded down, the three of us moved back toward camp and allowed Dax to lead us to the kitchen. Grace didn't say anything as she walked beside me, although she scowled every time Dax turned around to cast a curious glance at us.

The mess hall portion of the kitchen was booming with the sound of numerous people talking, the sunny day making people extra energetic as they ate their breakfast. Several said 'hi' to me only to frown in confusion at Grace. Surely most people had heard of her presence here by now, although there were probably more than a few that hadn't believed it until they'd seen her. Word travelled fast here, and people usually didn't react well to change.

Grace ignored the spectacle as she followed me, her face set to give away no emotions. Dax pushed through the door to the kitchen and we were immediately met with the sound of Maisie's voice shouting instructions to those helping her.

'Ah, boys!' she greeted us fondly, a wide smile forming when she saw us. 'Thank you. You're life savers.'

'Any time, Maisie,' I responded. We dumped our wood into the large hearth we'd built, the fire beneath it blazing back to life as soon as the fuel source was renewed. The large griddle we'd fashioned over the fire sizzled as it cooked the meat Maisie was preparing for breakfast. From what I could see, it looked like the deer we'd hunted earlier in the week.

'And who's this?' she asked, somewhat breathless as she wiped her hands on her apron and regarded Grace. For the first time, someone didn't appear disgusted by her presence.

'Maisie, Grace. Grace, Maisie,' I introduced, waving between them.

'Captive from Greystone,' Dax piped up. I frowned at the word 'captive' even though it was technically what she was.

'Ahh, the girl Jett has been blabbering about,' Maisie said, nodding her head in recognition. 'He was right – you are a pretty thing, aren't you?'

'Um . . .' Grace said, glancing at me as if unsure of what

to say. Her eyes shifted back to Maisie. She seemed embarrassed. 'Thank you.'

'You'll be staying here with us, then?' Maisie asked.

'That's what they tell me,' Grace responded dryly. Maisie nodded pensively.

'Well, no use in treating you like an alien. Eventually you'll have to start pulling your weight around here so enjoy the honeymoon while it lasts,' Maisie said. I was glad that at least *someone* from my camp wasn't treating her like a dog.

My gaze fell on Grace regarding Maisie, and I was surprised to see a soft smile pull at her lips.

'Yes, Maisie,' she said evenly, her hint of a smile expanding. I noticed the way her eyes lit up a bit when she did that. I shook my head, feeling myself staring at her. *Stop it, Hayden.*

'Excellent. Now you three, get yourself some breakfast before it's gone. Busy day today, Hayden,' Maisie said, nodding at us in dismissal. I shot her an appreciative look before I walked to gather three completely non-matching plates, prizes from scavenging through the city ages ago. After handing one each to Grace and Dax, we filled our plates, carried them out to the mess hall, and sat down at an empty table.

I dug in right away, the mixture of meat and eggs delicious as it landed on my tongue. Maisie raised chickens, and people in Blackwing took turns hunting to provide meat. Occasionally we got fish from the river, though it was quite a long way so it wasn't really practical. Living in the woods made hunting a much more reliable option for food. We also had stores of cans gathered up over years of raids and we grew a few crops, though we hadn't been very successful in growing much.

71

'So,' Dax said through a mouthful of food. 'Busy day, huh?'

I swallowed and nodded. 'Yeah, got to meet with Barrow to do an inventory on our ammunition and then with Docc to assess the medical stuff. And Malin mentioned something about some of the huts having unstable structures so I should probably look into that.'

'You do all of that?' Grace asked suddenly, drawing both my attention and Dax's.

'Someone has to,' I said.

'Yeah, lucky you, meeting up with the big man here,' Dax said, clapping my shoulder. I rolled my eyes while he grinned.

'I'd rather have a big man than a little one,' Grace shot back, a hint of a grin on her face. I almost choked on my food at Dax's shocked expression. He recovered quickly however, and let out a chuckle of appreciation.

'You're not too bad, for the enemy,' he said lightly, giving her a tiny nod of approval. It appeared as though now that it had been made clear she would not be returning to Greystone, he'd lightened up considerably, not that he was ever very serious to begin with.

'The enemy,' she repeated quietly, more to herself than us as she frowned in disdain. Her lips pursed together in thought. 'Right.'

We finished our food soon after that, and our conversation grew a little lighter in the wake of the sudden cheeky exchange between Dax and Grace. Kit made a stony appearance at the end of the meal but didn't say a whole lot beyond the confused and questioning looks he kept shooting at everyone. The light tone of our conversation clearly surprised him.

Kit and Dax left to go take care of their various duties

for the day, leaving Grace and I to venture out on our own. Again, people shot glares and whispered behind their hands as she passed, and again, she ignored them. Her inner strength showed through once again as we made our way outside.

The day was relatively uneventful, though I couldn't tell if Grace as getting bored or not. First we visited the raid building with Barrow, who despite his unwelcoming greeting last night largely ignored Grace's presence altogether as she jotted down some notes. I kept Grace within a few feet of me at all times, still not fully trusting her near our ammunition and weapons.

After determining what we would need on the next raid for weapons and ammunition, we travelled to the infirmary to visit Docc. He greeted her warmly and was pleased to have the chance to look at her leg, which he deemed to be healing nicely. He scolded me lightly for making her run around on it so much, but Grace insisted that she was fine and denied the pain medication Docc offered her.

I didn't know much about medical supplies, so I took the list Docc handed me without much questioning. He knew what we needed and left it up to me to collect the items for him on raids. Grace, however, appeared to be fairly knowledgeable about the medical supplies Docc had listed for us and even offered a location she knew of that would have some of them.

The last errand of the day went uncompleted, as it turned out Malin, one of the architectural experts in Blackwing, was busy working on something and couldn't meet with me. The other errands, after a late lunch in the mess hall, had taken most of the day. It was still early evening, but the beautiful day was coming to an end as dark clouds started to gather, rolling closer and closer in a turbulent cluster.

'It's going to storm,' Grace noted, her eyes fixed on the sky.

'Yeah,' I said, nodding in agreement. 'Soon, too.'

The clouds were nearly here now, and from the way they streaked downward it was clear they carried rain. Flashes of lightning could be seen lighting up sections of the ominous clouds, followed quickly by a distant booming of thunder. The wind picked up around us, blowing strands of my hair in front of my eyes and causing my shirt to billow out from my back. Grace struggled beside me to control her haphazard mess of blonde hair before giving up and letting it tangle around her like a beautiful blonde halo.

Thankfully, we were almost back to my hut when the first droplets of rain fell. My shirt speckled a bit darker where the drops splashed down, the liquid cool on my skin. Grace kept pace with me, following me inside before I closed the door to stifle the howling of the wind outside. She blew out a heavy breath and pushed her hair off her face before moving to sit on the couch.

'How well does this thing keep the rain out?' she asked, glancing at the roof sceptically. It was made of tin and had almost no leaks.

'Really well, actually,' I said proudly. 'It's loud as hell, but at least it doesn't leak.'

Sure enough, the droplets started to fall faster and faster, their descent on my roof causing a loud plonk to echo throughout the hut with every drop. The tin did little to stifle the sound, so I almost had to shout to be heard. The rain was pelting down on the roof relentlessly, drowning out her words as she opened her mouth.

'What?' I shouted, the small distance between us making it feel odd to shout. I was surprised when her face split into a smile, and I was momentarily stunned by how beautiful she looked. I shook my head once more, clearing away the thought.

'I said, what do we do now?' she shouted back, a grin on her face as if she found the situation funny. I thought and shrugged, stumped. Usually, I didn't have to keep someone entertained all of the time. I worried about myself and the good of the camp, that was it.

She rose to her feet once more, folding her arms loosely across her chest as she walked slowly around my home, looking for something to do. She paused at my desk and a flare of panic rose inside me as her hand passed briefly over the leather-bound journal sitting there. Before I could stop them, my feet carried me over to grab the journal and stuff it behind my back.

'What are you doing?' I demanded. She shot me a surprised look, taken aback by my sudden action.

'Nothing,' she said innocently.

'Don't touch my stuff,' I said sternly. She didn't appear fazed by my words.

'All right.'

The rain continued to pound down on the roof, our close proximity making it much easier to hear now. Her eyes narrowed benignly as if trying to determine something. I opened my mouth to speak just as a loud pounding sounded at my door. I groaned, my hand coming to run down my face before falling exasperatedly at my side.

I stalked toward the door, tired of the constant interruptions. It was nothing new; people came to me all the time with problems. It was part of being in charge, but I had never had someone with me at all times to witness it. I hated myself for resenting those that came now simply because I didn't want to be interrupted.

I flung the door open to reveal a completely soaked Kit, his light brown hair plastered to his skin.

'Hey, sorry, but the well is caving in again,' he said

75

quickly, not bothering with any small talk. I swore under my breath before starting to leave the hut without hesitation. I was nearly off my porch, following Kit, when he turned around abruptly.

'The girl?' he asked, nodding back inside.

'Shit,' I muttered, momentarily forgetting I had to keep her with me at all times. 'Grace!'

She appeared immediately in the doorway, as if expecting me.

'Come on, you're helping,' I said. She frowned slightly but followed anyway, closing the door behind her as she followed Kit and me into the torrential downpour. My hair was almost immediately soaked, the long strands sticking to my face despite my efforts to push them off. The thin fabric of my shirt clung to my body as the rain soaked it thoroughly, a problem I noticed Kit was experiencing as well.

I glanced at Grace and immediately looked away. The fabric of her shirt was plastered to her body, outlining the curves easily as she made no efforts to cover herself. I stared determinedly forward as we advanced toward the well, refusing to glance at her body again and notice the way her bra was nearly completely visible through her shirt or the way the tones of her skin were highlighted through the fabric.

No, I would not look and notice those details.

I blew out a deep breath as we closed the remaining distance to the well, which already had four people gathered around it, their hands busy at work to keep it from caving in. Whenever we got a heavy rain, we had this same problem. The mud around the well started to shift, causing the heavy bricks to lose their rigid form. If the well caved in, we would have no source of fresh water for two miles, in which case we'd be forced to make daily trips to the lake.

Dax was already there, working with two older men

to keep the bricks from falling down the hole. He was absolutely covered in mud, as were Kit and the other two working. My feet sunk into the mud as I approached, and I knew it wouldn't be long until I resembled the rest of the crew.

Grace surprised me by moving straight to Dax's side, helping him grab a large section of the well to pull it back upright. For the first time, no one seemed to notice she was there; she was just an extra set of hands that were much needed for a task like this. Her hair stuck to her face, which was set in a grimace as she exerted as much strength as possible to help Dax until they had their section completely righted.

I moved to help Kit steady the base of the well, sinking down into the mud to get better leverage. Together, we worked until we had corrected the section that had started to buckle. More than once, each of us slipped in the mess of mud and dirt.

'I think we're good,' Dax called from the other side. I stood up, which was more difficult than it should have been thanks to my feet sinking several inches into the mud. My back and chest were completely covered, and the mud had managed to seep beneath my shirt to cake my skin. My eyes scanned our work and I was satisfied that it wouldn't cave in this time.

'Yeah, we are,' I agreed, shouting over the sound of the rain. 'Good work, guys.'

Nods and waves were exchanged as people parted ways, yanking their feet forcefully from the grip of the mud to make their way back home. I turned to see Grace approaching me, nearly losing her balance before she righted herself enough to get out of the deepest part of the mud. Her clothes, skin, and face were splattered with brown smudges.

'Well, that was fun,' she said flatly, a hint of sarcasm to her voice. A deep chuckle rumbled from my chest as I took in her messy state, still unable to ignore her stunning green eyes.

'Come on,' I said, tilting my head back towards the way we came. 'Let's get cleaned up.'

We moved as quickly as possible back to my home, some of the mud washing away thanks to the heavy downpour, although most of it managed to cling to our clothes and bodies. The small awning in front of my door did little to stop the rain as we spilled into the hut, stopping only a few feet in so as not to track mud through the entire place.

'Shoes off,' I muttered, kicking off my own and placing them next to the door.

I wasted no time in stripping off my shirt, the fabric heavy with water and mud. My hands moved to undo my belt, nimble fingers easily releasing the buckle and fastenings of my jeans to shove them off along with my socks. It wasn't until I was left in my briefs that I felt the heat of her stare and turned to look back at her.

She jerked her head away quickly, embarrassed to be caught staring. I couldn't help but smirk. She stood awkwardly next to me, now staring firmly at the ground instead of at my mud-covered, almost naked body.

'Well?' I said. Her eyes locked on mine in confusion.

'Well, what?' she asked.

'You think I'm going to let you get my home all dirty? Strip down, you need a shower.'

Her jaw dropped and she stared at me blankly. 'With you?'

'Unless you want to stand out in the rain, yeah. I only have so much water in here,' I explained.

The 'shower' only held fifteen or so gallons on a good

78

day, not enough for two separate showers when we were so completely covered. I expected her to protest, but she surprised me when she set her jaw in determination before gripping the hem of her shirt. The fabric was lifted over her head, streaking mud across her smooth skin on the way, then she moved to undo the fastenings of her jeans. She held my gaze, brows knitted together in a type of scowl as if she resented me for making her take a shower.

I regarded her steadily, determined not to let my eyes travel down her body. When her jeans hit the floor, she straightened up.

'Happy?'

'Yes,' I said evenly.

I bit my lip into my mouth as she cocked a challenging eyebrow at me. If her point was that she looked fantastic in a bra and underwear, then I was more than convinced of it. I allowed myself one more quick glance at her body before shaking my head and moving to the bathroom. I could feel her following me, just as I could feel her gaze burning into my back.

Once I reached the shower, I turned around to face her. It seemed odd to shower in our underwear, but I wasn't about to force her to get fully naked in front of me. She came to stop a few feet away, not nearly close enough for the spray of the shower to reach her. My gaze held hers as she stared back unwaveringly.

'You need to come closer,' I told her gently. She swallowed but maintained the look of determination as she stepped a foot closer. Her green eyes were locked on mine.

'Closer,' I said, my voice dropping in volume.

Tentatively, I reached forward to put my hand on her hip, curling my fingers around her soft skin to tug her nearer to me. She sucked in a breath, moving to stand only inches from me now. She broke our steady gaze as her eyes dropped to my chest, eyes focusing on the mud streaked there. I felt my lips tug to the side in a small lopsided smirk as I reached up to grab the handle that would start the shower. I tugged on it, releasing the stream of cold water that cascaded over us.

She gasped at the temperature, jumping forward slightly to collide with my chest involuntarily. Her eyes, wide with surprise, flitted up from my chest to meet mine once more. The contact seemed to increase the energy in the small space, adding to the odd tension I'd been starting to feel all day around her.

'Sorry,' she muttered, backing up an inch or so. My heart pounded, thanks to the thick electricity I felt between us.

'It's all right,' I said slowly. Something about having her so close seemed to be messing with my mind. My thoughts felt skewed, as if her proximity was clouding my judgement, but I couldn't stop myself from thinking how nice it felt to have her so close.

The water poured over my head, dripping down the sides of my face before splashing down to my chest. Her skin was covered in droplets of water too, mixing with the mud to create dark trails that streaked over her curves. Her eyes flicked down to my lips when I spoke, and I felt myself moving towards her to close the gap once again. I tried to ignore the temptation that sizzled through my veins, but it was impossible.

She sucked in another breath as the inches between us evaporated, our bodies pressing together under the cold stream of water. It was as if my body acted of its own accord, blocking my mind from thinking rationally about anything at the moment. I couldn't help the way my head ducked down to let my lips hover inches from hers. I lingered, waiting for her to stop me in some way, hit me even, but she didn't. She was shaking slightly against me, and I could feel the way my heart pounded in my ribs. Even my pulse could be heard echoing in my ears. Her lips were less than an inch from mine now, getting closer every second, but still she didn't stop me.

When my eyes flitted up to hers one last time, I was pleased to see hers fixed on my lips. Without stopping to think what I was doing or why it was a terrible idea, I leaned forward, closing the tiny remaining distance between us to press my lips into hers. She didn't respond for a half a second as if stunned by my action, though she didn't pull away from the pressure. My lips lingered on hers for a few anxious moments before she recovered enough to return the pressure, her hands finding their way to my chest. My stomach flipped over, and I felt an undeniable flash of heat from the contact.

I had just kissed my prisoner, my enemy.

What the hell was wrong with me?

Chapter 8 – Paradox

GRACE

My heart beat erratically as Hayden's lips pressed to mine. Though the water was ice cold on my skin, an undeniable heat spread from wherever he touched me. The tension between us had been building from the moment I first made eye contact with him, and despite my efforts to ignore it, it had finally taken over.

His lips melted against mine, encasing my lower lip as he kissed me. My arms had somehow shifted from his chest to wind around his neck after recovering from their momentary shock, hugging him to me. His skin was hot against mine, and I couldn't stop my fingers from tangling into his dark, shaggy hair. A haze settled over my mind while butterflies danced in my stomach.

My back arched into him as he deepened the kiss, interpreting my return as consent. His tongue pushed into my mouth and his hands came up to hold either side of my face, the kiss growing more desperate as he pushed lightly until my back collided with the wall. The wall was cold, contrasting with the heat of his body. I found it difficult to draw a full breath.

I felt myself starting to spiral out of control. He was everywhere – his hands on my face, his lips on mine, his tongue in my mouth, his body pressed tightly against mine, skin on skin with only minimal clothing serving as a barrier . . .

Suddenly, my hands unwrapped themselves from his neck to press my palms on his chest and shove him away. He moved back a few inches, disconnecting his lips from mine with a small gasp. His eyes looked slightly bewildered when he looked at me, brows knitted together as a frown formed on his face. Muscular arms dangled by his sides as he released his grip on me, his body separated from mine now by a little bit of space.

'What?' he asked somewhat breathlessly. He seemed a bit annoyed I had stopped him. His chest heaved as he stood beneath the falling water, which slid over his skin in thin rivulets, curving around his firm muscles. I ripped my eyes from his torso to meet his gaze, which practically burned a hole through me.

'We can't do this,' I said, silently cursing myself for how breathless I sounded. He stared at me, nostrils flaring slightly as he blew out a deep breath. His expression changed from annoyance to one of thoughtfulness.

'You're right,' he agreed, stepping back from me to widen the distance between us to more than a foot now. I ignored the pang of disappointment in my stomach even though I was the one who had stopped it. 'That was stupid, I don't know what I was thinking.'

Despite his distance, my heart was still pounding against my ribs, much to my annoyance. His words did little to calm me.

'It's all right,' I said flatly, struggling to maintain a look of indifference.

'I wasn't apologising,' Hayden said, his voice deep in the confined space. I blinked, unsure of how to respond.

'Oh.'

He flicked me a glance before stepping under the full force of the water, letting it run through his hair as he pushed his hands through the strands. His eyes closed under the stream while I stood there stupidly and watched him, unsure of what to do. The way the water slid down his body, glistening as it trailed over his skin, was distracting. He tilted his head back down after rinsing his hair and opened his eyes, which immediately locked on mine.

'Finish your shower, then,' he said, the annoyed tone back in his voice as he stepped out from under the stream. Mud was still streaked down his skin.

'Wait,' I said, stopping him. He turned around to look at me without a word.

'There's still mud on your back,' I told him. He twisted slightly to look over his shoulder but was unable to see anything.

'Come here,' I said, exasperatedly. I tentatively raised my hands to place them on his shoulders, turning him around so his back was to me. I expected him to flinch from my touch, but he didn't. My hands moved down his back, washing the mud from his skin.

This was the first time I'd been near enough to him, and not distracted by him kissing me, to notice his skin had flaws. As the mud cleared away, it became evident that his body had suffered years of damage only to attempt to heal itself. More scars than I could count littered his skin, some a faint white in colour from years of healing while others were a darker pink, indicating they were more recent. Some were long and thin, some round and smooth, while still others were jagged and uneven, as if they hadn't really been treated properly before healing.

Hayden was silent as my fingers feathered over his skin, the pads of my fingertips tracing each scar as I cleared the mud. His head turned to the side, watching me cautiously out of his peripheral vision while my hands explored the wide expanse of his back. My fingers traced a particularly jagged scar, the raised edges of it rough beneath my fingertips. It was as if the story of his years of combat was written in his skin.

'What are these from?' I asked quietly, unable to tear my gaze from the marred flesh.

'Raids and things,' he said vaguely, his voice soft. My mind whirred as it tried to figure out how many he'd been on to sustain such damage. It had to be hundreds, and he'd survived every single one. I was silent as this impressive realisation settled over me.

'Why? Why put yourself through all that?' I asked. Surely he'd paid his dues by now, if his back was evidence of anything.

'I have to protect them . . . All of them.' As if it were the most obvious concept in the world.

'That's a lot of pressure,' I said, stunned by his devotion. The more I learned about him, the more I realised what a selfless leader he was. He truly cared about these people and sacrificed a lot of himself for them. It was a rare thing, these days, when so many were only selfishly concerned with their own wellbeing.

'It has to be done,' he said finally after a few moments of silence.

My hands cleared away the last of the mud while we remained silent. He was a walking paradox, with his physically intimidating nature, his natural fortitude for leadership, and the harsh way he dealt with reality, compared to this selfless dedication to keeping those around him safe. His selfless side and determination to protect everyone else contrasted sharply with the way of the world. He was a combination of things I had never experienced before in anyone, much less a leader.

My hands stopped brushing against his skin, stilling to move only my thumb across a long scar over his ribcage. Water streamed over his back, clear now that the mud had washed away. He must have sensed my slowed movements, because he turned cautiously to face me, causing my hands to graze across his ribs as he spun. His features pulled into a curious uncertainty as he observed me observing him.

Again, my heart beat a little faster in my chest and my breath hitched in my throat. His muscles flexed beneath my palms on his ribs as he inched forward for a second, his body arching toward mine. I thought he might kiss me again, but his actions were halted as he drew back suddenly when the water abruptly stopped flowing. He blinked as if breaking out from some sort of haze.

'Shower's over,' he muttered, dropping his gaze to my lips once before stepping away from me. My hands fell to my sides while my body lurched forward slightly as if pulled by his movement backward. He turned to grab two towels, tossing one to me before running his own through his hair.

I stood dumbly in the shower, which felt much colder now that he was gone. He ran the towel over his body briefly, tugging down the hem of his briefs dangerously low before straightening back up and leaving the bathroom. I sucked in a deep breath, and it felt like it was the first full breath I'd taken in years.

After quickly drying off my body the best I could, I wrapped the towel around my now soaked undergarments and followed him into the main room of his hut. He had already pulled on a fresh set of briefs and shorts and was in the process of tugging a shirt over his head when I entered.

'Um, Hayden?'

'Yeah?'

'I don't have anything to wear,' I said. He turned to observe me standing there in a towel before his eyes darted to the soiled pile of clothes by his door.

'Oh, right, umm . . .' He looked around as if something would suddenly appear. He frowned at his dresser before moving to pull some clothes out of it. He tossed me a large grey sweater and a pair of shorts before running his hand somewhat awkwardly through his hair.

'You can wear these until we get you some clothes tomorrow,' he said.

'Thanks.' The sweater was far too large for me as I pulled it over my still wet bra, the hem falling to my mid-thigh. The shorts were also far too big, but luckily there was a drawstring to keep them up.

'Yeah. We should get some sleep. We have to go into the city tomorrow for Docc to get that medical stuff,' he said, avoiding looking at me.

'Okay,' I said, nodding as I sat down on my couch. I was physically exhausted; the long day I'd had of following Hayden around, fixing the well, and the fact that my wound was still healing wearing me out. My mind, however, was buzzing as it tried to comprehend what had happened and how I felt about it.

I hadn't been expecting Hayden to kiss me, almost certain the tension I felt between us was only me imagining things. There was no denying the jolt that had shot through me as soon as his lips touched mine and the automatic way I responded, but it worried me. He was holding me here against my will, and I definitely shouldn't have wanted him to kiss me. Worse, I shouldn't have enjoyed it.

I shook my head, attempting to clear away the thoughts before I lay down on the couch. My eyes darted to Hayden, surely witnessing my inner turmoil. I blinked, pursing my lips together as I averted my eyes and pulled my blanket up around me, embarrassed at having been caught thinking about it as if he could tell.

'Goodnight, Hayden,' I muttered, my voice stifled by the blanket. He was quiet as he settled into his bed.

'Yeah. Goodnight.'

My thoughts as I fell asleep were a mixed jumble of surprised euphoria, deep confusion, and certain anxiety that sat like a rock in the pit of my stomach. This was a complication I hadn't seen coming, and I desperately wanted to go back to a few hours ago when none of it had happened. Back to when I was simply a prisoner, with no lingering questions about kissing her captor.

'Grace . . .'

A quiet groan came from my throat as I squeezed my eyes shut even tighter, fighting off whoever was trying to wake me. I tugged my blanket up over my face only for someone to pull it back down.

'Grace, come on, wake up,' the voice said, a hint of impatience lacing the tone. I opened one eye just enough to peek out when I felt a hand on my shoulder. Hayden hovered over me, his face blank as he watched me.

'I'm up, I'm up,' I said, my voice tight as I stretched my back.

The couch was not treating me well. Hayden removed his hand from my shoulder and moved away from me to pull his boots on. He was dressed in his usual jeans with yet another plaid shirt and a grey strip of fabric tied around his head to hold his hair back. When his hair was free, the wavy, dark brown strands dangled just below his ears and had a tendency to fall into his face. I rose stiffly from the couch, cringing when my back popped loudly. I glanced down at my outfit – Hayden's much too large clothes – and decided to remind him today of his promise to get me some clothes of my own.

'Hurry up, they're waiting,' Hayden said impatiently. I shot him a glare as I crossed to put on my mud-caked boots, completing my mismatched outfit.

'All right, let's go then.'

He huffed before pushing past me to head outside, his mood stony once again. I followed him to see that it had stopped raining, something I had completely forgotten about last night. The grass was squishy as we walked quickly toward the centre of the camp.

'Who's coming with us?' I asked, hurrying to keep pace with him.

'Kit and Dax,' he said gruffly. I frowned at his unhappy tone. If he had any feelings about what had happened last night, he hid them well now with his grumpy attitude.

'Hayden—'

'No,' he said, cutting me off.

'No, what?' I shot back, growing irritated.

'No, I don't want to talk about it,' he snapped angrily. I glared at him.

'That wasn't what I was going to say,' I said, suddenly very annoyed at him for being so ill-tempered.

'Right.'

'It wasn't!'

'What were you going to say, then?' he asked back dubiously. He continued to walk quickly, as if trying to distance himself from me.

'I was *going* to say I could show you the place I was telling Docc about yesterday. Where they'd have the stuff he wants.'

'Oh.'

'Yeah, you jackass,' I muttered, increasing my pace even more to pull ahead of him. He appeared slightly stunned before hurrying to catch up with me.

'Watch it, Grace,' he threatened.

I scoffed. 'Right. Got it.'

He seethed next to me, even more irritated now. Had I really *wanted* him to kiss me last night? We turned the corner to come face to face with Kit and Dax, both of whom were leaning casually against a truck, waiting for us. Kit watched us approach while Dax took in our leaden expressions.

'Jesus, who pissed in your coffee this morning?' Dax joked, raising his eyebrows. I glanced at Hayden and saw his surly expression.

'Shut up,' Hayden muttered, stalking past everyone to jump in the driver's seat. Dax shot me a bemused look, clearly not offended by Hayden's surly mood. Kit surprised me by nodding curtly at me before jumping into the passenger seat, leaving the backseats to Dax and I. I was surprised to see a breakfast biscuit of sorts sitting on a napkin in my seat. I paused, trying to determine if it was for me or not.

'Eat up,' Dax said, nodding at it as he strapped himself in. 'Big day!'

I obeyed and picked up the food before climbing in, silently pleased he'd thought to bring me something; my stomach was already grumbling.

'Thanks. Why are we taking a truck?' I asked Dax. He was the only one who didn't appear to hate it when I spoke to him this morning.

'When we get medical supplies, we take as much as we can and it's hard to transport a lot without breaking it when we run. The truck is more obvious but it's better for getting what we need,' Dax explained, gripping the handrail as

90

Hayden started the truck and began driving.

The road was rough, filled with divots and potholes as we drove, and trees bordered us narrowly on each side, but it was much faster than trekking through the woods on foot. Kit and Hayden talked in the front seat, largely ignoring Dax and I. Dax didn't seem to mind as he looked out of the window, taking in the scenery as it flew by. Before long, we were approaching the edge of the city.

'You need to turn left at that big supermarket,' I said, leaning forward between Hayden and Kit's seat. Hayden glanced at me, and his forearm flexed as he gripped the wheel. Reluctantly, he turned left just as I had instructed.

'Right through the alley,' I continued, giving instructions to the hidden pharmacy I usually raided. No one else seemed to know about it because of the odd location. Again he listened.

'How do we know you're not leading us right into an ambush?' Kit asked suspiciously, turning to look at me.

'I'm not,' I said flatly. I'd done nothing to make them distrust me and I was quickly growing tired of their suspicion. True, I wanted to go back home, but I wasn't stupid enough to think I'd have any way of escaping. I would have to earn their trust enough for them to voluntarily let me leave. I didn't have a lot of hope that day would ever come, but it was worth a shot.

'Relax, dude. She'd have no way to organise that even if she wanted to,' Dax said, defending me. I felt a rush of gratitude for him.

'Exactly. It's on the right,' I said, redirecting my words at Hayden. He pulled the truck to a stop and leaned forward over the steering wheel to peer out through the windshield. He must have deemed it worthy, because he turned off the engine and stepped out of the car. I noticed the flash of metal as he did so as his shirt rose over his back to reveal the gun stored in his waistband. Kit and Dax also got out of the car, so I followed.

All three of them pulled weapons from various locations, arming themselves against the unknown. I felt extremely vulnerable without a weapon, no way to defend myself other than my hands.

'Do I get a weapon?' I dared ask, fully expecting to be denied.

'No way,' Kit and Hayden said at the same time. I huffed in frustration before following them towards the door. We moved in a stealthy line, all three of them with their guns raised in case of enemies. Hayden paused at the door, leaning against it to press his ear to the metal. Apparently he heard nothing, because he reached to turn the handle and let himself in. He moved cautiously through the frame, eyes sweeping the pharmacy for any signs of movement, but there were none.

We followed him inside the dimly lit building silently, the three of them automatically splitting up to search for what Docc had requested. Kit and Dax pulled their backpacks off to reveal yet another duffle bag and immediately started filling them with supplies. I stood near the door, feeling useless and unsure of what to do since I had no bag or weapon. I moved toward Hayden.

'Let me help,' I requested firmly, coming to stand next to him.

'Keep watch, that's how you can help,' he replied shortly, stuffing a bag full of medicines he pulled off the shelves.

'There's only one way in and it's the door we came through,' I said. 'Tell me what to look for and we can get out of here even faster.'

Hayden huffed out a short breath of irritation and I

resisted the urge to call him a jackass again. 'Fine. Docc needs bandages, go find some.'

I nodded before moving away from him, heading toward the back where I knew they would be. Sure enough, the shelf was nearly full of them. I filled my arms with as many as I could carry before heading back to Hayden. He looked up from where he was examining some vials of liquid, a moderately impressed expression crossing his face.

'Bag?'

'Here,' he said, pulling one out of his belt loop. I stuffed my materials in it and waited while he filled the rest of his two bags with supplies. Kit and Dax reappeared by my shoulders, laden down with medical materials. Clearly, this raid had been lucrative. I hoped that my contribution would make them a little more inclined to like me, seeing as I was the one who told them about this place.

'All right, let's get out of here,' Hayden said, swinging his bags over his arm while still gripping his gun. He led the way, heading back to the door and peering out in all directions.

'Clear,' he whispered, streaking out toward the car. I followed with Dax and Kit right behind me. The boot was thrown open quickly for us to set our bags inside. Hayden slammed it shut and moved to jump in the car before we all copied him. We were almost in the car when a sudden bang echoed through the alley – a gunshot going off at close distance.

Everyone ducked to the ground, my legs dropping instinctively before I even registered what happened. Hayden descended beside me and threw his arm over my shoulders protectively to haul me into his side. Kit and Dax were on the other side of the car, but I could hear muttering coming from their direction.

'Shit, shit, shit,' Dax said, his voice frantic. *'God dammit!'*

Hayden ducked down beside me, looking under the car to see what was going on. His face slackened at whatever he saw before jumping up to sprint around to the other side of the car.

'Hayden!' I shouted, waiting for another gunshot to sound and rip through him; nothing came. I jumped to my feet, sprinting after him to round the car. I rounded the hood and came to a halt, feet skidding in the dirt when my eyes settled on the sight before me.

Hayden and Dax were huddled over Kit, his body flat on the ground and convulsing unnaturally, with blood pouring from a gaping wound in his neck.

Chapter 9 – Focus
GRACE

My eyes focused on the thick, red fluid gushing from Kit's neck. Hayden's hands hovered uselessly over his throat, unsure of what to do while Dax crouched next to him, pale with shock. My body reacted before my mind did, jerking my feet forward to carry me to them. I moved across from Hayden and promptly shoved Dax out of the way, shouldering him roughly to take his place next to Kit, who was growing paler by the second.

'No!' Dax shouted, snapping out of his shock when I shoved him. He threw his shoulder into mine to knock me back away from Kit. 'You set us up! You'll kill him!'

Another shot fired through the alley, missing us narrowly as the bullet collided with the dumpster behind us. Hayden's head whipped around toward the source of the sound, eyes scanning frantically back and forth looking for the enemy.

'No, I didn't!' I shouted, shoving my shoulder into him again. Kit coughed below us, deep red blood sputtering from his lips. 'Now move!'

'This is your fault,' Dax said, his voice losing conviction as he watched a shockingly large amount of blood begin to pool around Kit. My hands went to his neck, feeling the jagged flesh there to assess where the source of the bleeding was. It was hard to see through the vast amount of fluid pumping from his neck.

'Brute!' Hayden said suddenly as yet another shot echoed through the alley, missing yet again. Dax seemed to react automatically, despite the state of shock he appeared to be fighting off. He sat up and raised his weapon to aim where Hayden indicated before firing a single shot. I didn't need to look to know he'd hit the target; a guttural shout ripped out before a loud thud sounded, the body of whoever had been shooting at us falling from where it had perched above the alley. A sickening series of cracks told me whoever had fallen hadn't survived.

'Holy shit . . .' Dax muttered, slumping next to me after shooting down the enemy – just a random Brute, a dweller of the city, not someone I had summoned from my own camp to take them out, as he had suspected moments ago.

All of that registered in less than a second, however, as my hands continued to work at Kit's neck. Hot, thick blood quickly tinged my skin a dark, sinister red. Kit's eyelids fluttered, telling me he was still alive while he continued to bleed out. My fingers sifted through the marred flesh, searching for the opening. I cringed when I felt a bit of jagged muscle, torn from where it should be. Finally, my fingers sunk into the deepest hole, the source of the bleeding and the deepest part of the wound.

'Shit,' I muttered, leaning even closer.

'What? What is it?' Hayden demanded, his voice tight. Dax appeared stunned next to me as he watched me prod at his best friend's neck.

'It hit one of his arteries,' I muttered, my eyes focused intently on Kit's neck. I sunk my fingers into the wound as deep as I could, plugging the flow of blood to the best of my ability. The artery was warm and sticky with blood, the flesh around it spongy and resistant to my touch. My other hand frantically swiped away what had already spilled over, trying to clear it so I could see.

The world started to fall away around me as my mind and body focused only on saving Kit's life. All the training I'd had at Greystone kicked in as my reactions took over. This had been part of my job on raids – helping those who were injured. There wasn't really anything I could do to heal him right now, but I could at least stop the bleeding enough to get him back to Docc, who was surely better equipped to deal with such a major injury.

'Is he dead?' Dax asked, recovering enough to lean forward and watch what I was doing more closely. He quickly realised I was trying to save Kit's life, not finish the bullet's job.

'No, you idiot,' I snapped. My fingers pressed harder into the wound, causing blood to squeeze out around them, but it was blood that had already escaped. I was managing to staunch the gushing, but as soon as my fingers were removed I knew it would start all over again. I could feel the gentle pulse – it was faint and slow, but it was there.

'Get us back to camp,' I instructed firmly. 'You need to lift him and I need to keep my fingers in his artery or he'll bleed before we get him in the truck.'

'Okay,' Hayden agreed instantly. They both jumped to their feet and I was relieved they didn't question me. Hayden positioned himself at Kit's shoulders while Dax moved toward his feet. 'When you're ready, Grace.'

'Now,' I said, standing to my feet while they lifted, making sure to keep my fingers firm at his throat. We moved as quickly as we could without causing further injury, and luckily the door to the truck was still open. Hayden backed himself in, hauling Kit's limp but still living body after him.

I managed to squeeze in beside him, keeping my fingers in place until we had him laid across the back seat. I sat on the floor, pressed in uncomfortably but hardly noticing as I focused on keeping the bleeding at bay.

Hayden and Dax both made sure we were situated before rushing to their respective seats. Hayden wasted no time in starting the car and speeding out of the alley, twisting backward to see out of the rear window as he drove. The vehicle whipped around as he backed completely out before throwing it into drive and jerking forward. I struggled to keep my fingers as steady as possible, my entire body tight with concentration.

'Could you try not driving like a maniac?' I hissed, nerves completely frazzled. He slowed down a fraction but didn't respond. Dax turned around in his seat to cast an anxious glance at me that I could hardly see. My stomach lurched as Hayden took a violent corner. I ignored the wave of nausea and focused on my hands at Kit's neck.

His skin was even paler than before, the loss of blood and his waning consciousness draining all the colour from his face. His chest rose and fell slowly, the movement so subtle it was difficult to see at all. Hayden was driving straight now, his speed gathering as we left the city behind.

'Almost there,' Hayden said from the front seat. 'How is he?'

'Just hurry,' I said through gritted teeth. My muscles were straining from the effort of holding still. He sped up a little more at my words. Trees flashed by the windows now, telling me we were almost back to the camp. Not a moment too soon, either, because Kit's pulse was even fainter now than it had been before.

After a few more turns through the bumpy woods, Hayden began to slow enough to manoeuvre through the camp. Dax rolled his window down to shout at someone nearby.

'Kit got hit, go tell Docc!' he yelled.

Hayden continued to drive until we reached the infirmary, stopping the car as smoothly as possible before jumping out. We repeated the process of carrying Kit, not stopping as people gathered around to see what was happening. Someone managed to open the door for us to let us into the building.

Docc was there, hastily preparing his limited supplies of whatever was necessary to save Kit. Hayden and Dax laid him on the table Docc had cleared, my fingers never leaving his artery.

'Hayden, get the bags,' I instructed firmly. He nodded and sprinted back to the car to get the medical supplies we had just gathered. I didn't know exactly what Docc would need but the more supplies, the better.

'What is it?' Docc asked quickly, his voice deep and calm. Years of practice clearly had made him collected under strenuous situations.

'He got hit in an artery,' I said. 'I don't know if the bullet went through or if it's still in there, though.'

Docc nodded, pulling on a pair of gloves and bringing a table of tools next to Kit's table. Hayden returned quickly with the bags of medical supplies in his hands. He brought them over to us, setting them on the floor at Docc's feet. Docc glanced down at the bags as Hayden unzipped them quickly, assessing the materials inside. He nodded to himself before looking at me.

'All right, Grace. I'll need your help with this,' he said quickly yet calmly. I nodded, my body still on autopilot. 'Count of three, you remove your fingers.'

'Okay,' I said firmly.

'One, two, three.'

HAYDEN

My feet carried me back and forth, tracking a path in the dirt. Dax sat against the wall on the ground, his head bowed down over his forearms that rested on his knees. He'd started out pacing just as I had before adopting that position while we waited for news on Kit.

Docc had kicked us out moments after instructing Grace to help him, saying we were a distraction and a potential infection risk. We'd obeyed his wishes only because we knew he knew what was best, but it was beyond difficult to leave Kit without knowing if he'd make it. Kit was like my brother, and the constant state of not knowing what was going on was driving me nuts.

It had been nearly two hours now and we still had no word on what was happening as the only people allowed in the infirmary were Docc and Grace, both of whom were understandably busy. My nerves were twisted into knots throughout my body, every step I took jolting them even tighter. I'd seen neck wounds like that before, but I'd never seen anyone survive one.

'I can't believe this, mate,' Dax muttered into his knees. He'd been saying things like that for the last hour, repeating his disbelief over and over again.

'I know,' I agreed lamely, my voice deep with tension. I tilted my head to the side to try and stretch out the tight muscles in my neck but to no avail. My feet continued to pace back and forth over the dirt.

'And Grace, she . . . Jesus,' he mumbled. He wasn't really making sense, thanks to his state of shock.

'This wasn't her fault,' I snapped, surprising myself at

how quick I was to defend her. 'That was a Brute, not some-one from Greystone.'

'I know,' Dax agreed solemnly.

'She didn't set us up,' I added, glaring at the ground. My pace increased frantically.

'I *know*,' Dax agreed, lifting his head from his knees.

'Because if you say it's her fault—'

'Bloody hell, will you shut up? I'm agreeing with you!'

I didn't respond, too disgruntled to really get into an argument with Dax. He agreed with me now, but he'd been awfully quick to accuse Grace before. That bothered me a lot more than it should have. My brooding was interrupted, however, when the front door of the infirmary opened, revealing a thoroughly blood-soaked Docc.

Dax jumped to his feet before both of us rushed towards Docc, whose expression was hard to read.

'Well?' I demanded instantly.

'He's alive,' Docc said, sending a flood of relief through me. Dax and I both physically sagged at his words, released from the tension. 'He lost a lot of blood, but thank-fully we were able to use some from the store you guys started.'

I nodded numbly as the words sunk in: Kit was alive. A few months ago, raiders started getting their blood drawn for Docc to keep in stores just in case a situation just like this arose. One of three generators in Blackwing powered the refrigerator used to keep the blood stores cool. It had been, ironically, Kit's idea after he'd suffered a fairly deep cut to the calf on a raid.

'Grace saved his life,' Docc continued. 'Smart little thing, she is. Plugging his artery like that. He would have died in minutes if she hadn't thought to do that.'

Dax blew out a shaky breath next to me while I nodded,

trying to absorb what Docc was saying. My best friend was alive because of Grace.

'Can we see him?' Dax asked. Docc frowned before speaking.

'He's still unconscious but he's stable so you can see him.'

That was all the permission we needed, pushing past Docc to head into the building. Somehow, Grace and Docc had managed to move a now blood-free Kit to a different bed. Bandages looped around his neck, secured under his arm to hold them in place. Thick pads of gauze were held beneath the bandages to absorb any bleeding that might escape Docc's careful stitches. Colour was starting to return to his face, which had been scarily pale before.

'He should wake up in a few hours,' Docc said from behind us where he had silently followed.

'Hang in there, mate,' I said quietly, unsure of what to say exactly or if he would even hear me. Dax leaned forward to inspect the bandages before straightening up again.

'Good work, Docc,' he said, impressed.

'I had a bit of help,' Docc said. As if on cue, the back door to the infirmary opened, revealing Grace. She was still wearing my shorts, which were completely soaked with blood, but had lost my sweater at some point. She must have shed it after saving Kit's life with Docc. Now she was left in a plain black tank top she must have got from Docc, which was relatively free of blood.

She glanced at Dax and me nervously, as if afraid we still blamed her for what had happened. Before I realised, my feet were carrying me towards her. She seemed slightly stunned when I reached her and pulled her into my chest, wrapping my arms around her shoulders to hug her tightly. She responded after a slight pause, winding her arms around my torso to return the hug.

'Thank you,' I mumbled, my words stifled by her hair. She seemed stunned but didn't pull away.

'You're welcome,' she replied into my chest. A sudden clearing of his throat announced Dax's presence next to us. Grace pulled away from me, shooting me a tentative glance before focusing on Dax.

'Grace, I'm so sorry,' he said sincerely. 'I shouldn't have blamed you so quickly. Then for you to go and save him . . . just, thank you.'

A soft smile pulled at Grace's lips. 'Happy to do it.'

Dax nodded before he seemed to realise he had interrupted something. His eyes darted back and forth between us before a guilty expression settled on his face.

'Oh, right, um, sorry,' he muttered before turning and going to join Docc once more. 'Thanks again, Grace.'

Her soft smile widened a bit more before turning to look at me. I couldn't help but notice the streaks of blood running across her skin, decorating her collarbones, visible without my gigantic sweater. I suddenly found myself unsure of what to say to her.

'Do you want a minute with them?' she asked, nodding toward my friends and Docc. I shook my head.

'He won't be up for a few hours, right?'

'That's what Docc says,' she said, shrugging.

'I don't know what we would have done without you today,' I said honestly. Actually, I did know, but I didn't want to consider how things would have gone if she hadn't been there. Kit would be dead, without a doubt. This girl, this beautiful enemy, had saved my best friend's life and I had no way to repay her.

Her lips tightened as the same dark thoughts passed through her head that had gone through mine. 'Let's just consider ourselves lucky that I was there.'

'Fair enough.'

My hands rose to my head, then my palms slid down my face with a heavy sigh. I was exhausted and it was only the afternoon. My stomach grumbled loudly, reminding me that even though I didn't feel like eating, my body still required food.

'Are you hungry?' I asked. She nodded.

'Yeah.'

'Let's go and eat then come back to check on Kit,' I said. She nodded again. I reached forward to put my hand on her back and steer her toward the door before I realised what I was doing and retracted my touch. She didn't seem to notice, however, which was a relief.

'We're going to go and eat. Want us to bring you some food?' I called to Docc and Dax.

'Nah, I'll get something soon,' Dax replied. Docc nodded in agreement.

I turned to lead Grace outside, my chest considerably lighter now that I knew Kit was going to be all right. The reality of the situation hadn't really sunk in yet, but I found myself feeling light-headed when I thought of what could have happened. I shook my head, clearing the thoughts that I no longer needed to consider.

Grace was quiet as she walked next to me. I glanced down at her and instantly was reminded of her behaviour earlier. She had been so calm and in control, absolutely confident of her abilities and never doubting herself even when accused of causing the problem in the first place. Dax and I had watched, helplessly stunned, while she did what we could not.

'Hey, Grace?'

'Yeah?'

'There's something I want to show you tonight,' I said, surprised by the nervous tension I felt in my stomach.

'What is it?' she asked, glancing at me with her eyebrows together.

'Will you come with me?' I asked, ignoring her question. She frowned slightly as if confused by my questions. I was worried she'd say no, especially after the way I'd treated her this morning. Technically she had to, but that wasn't why I asked; I asked because I wanted her to *want* to go, not go because she had to. My heart thumped nervously as I waited for her response. She took a deep breath, her lips parting as she did so.

'Yes.'

Chapter 10 – Gratitude

HAYDEN

Yes.

My heart leaped when Grace responded, agreeing to go with me later that day. We walked together through the camp, heading towards the mess hall to get some food. I noticed a few of the stares that had been harsh and reproachful before were now focused on her with a gentle curiosity; it appeared word of her rescue had travelled fast. Even as we gathered our food and sat at a table, I noticed a middle-aged woman named Helena shoot her a soft smile, at which Grace seemed taken aback then altogether pleased.

We didn't talk as we ate, my mind too consumed with the thoughts raging through my skull. After what she'd done for my best friend, I felt the need to thank her somehow. While I knew I lacked the ability to verbalise even the most basic of emotions, I hoped that what I had planned would express my gratitude after I'd been a complete jackass to her earlier this morning.

I hadn't meant to be, but it had sort of just happened. In a moment of weakness, I'd given into temptation. After I'd kissed her, I felt an odd sense of betrayal, like I was letting down my entire camp by associating myself with a member of an enemy camp even though she didn't *feel* like an enemy. I hated the guilt that had flashed through me almost instantly, but even more so, I hated that I had enjoyed it. Quite a lot, actually, because I'd been more than a little annoyed when she'd practically shoved me off her, as if she, too, were feeling the same conflicting emotions.

I shook my head as I scooped up the last bit of my meal, clearing the thoughts. I couldn't dwell on what had happened because it couldn't happen again. We needed to remain separate, unlinked, if I wanted to retain the respect I'd worked so hard to earn. Even now, watching her glance cautiously around the mess hall, I felt a strange pull that I knew would make it difficult. However, I was determined to keep things between us strictly platonic, which almost seemed like too friendly a word for us.

She was still a prisoner, a stranger; she was still the enemy.

I just had to remind myself of that over and over again and I would be fine.

Tonight wasn't about pursuing her or trying anything; it was about thanking her for what she'd done for Kit and that was it. I hated owing her for things. How was I ever supposed to be even and remain even with her if she insisted on acting in such a way? After tonight, we would be even, and I could move on with my life how it had always been.

'Hayden?' Grace said, drawing my attention from my thoughts. I blinked before allowing my eyes to refocus on her.

'Yeah?'

'Are you done?' she asked, nodding at my plate. I looked down to see it was empty.

'Oh. Yeah, let's go.'

She stood, grabbing her plate to bring it to the discard area to be washed while I followed. I noticed she was still very much covered in blood and was surprised she hadn't wanted to wash up before eating. I supposed it didn't really bother her much anymore. The sight of her in the black tank top she'd procured from Docc reminded me of my promise to get her some clothes of her own.

'We can stop by the storage on the way back and you can shower if you like,' I offered, slightly surprised by my kind tone. She appeared surprised too, but grateful.

'That would be great,' she replied, following me as I led her out the door of the mess hall.

The storage building was right next to it, so we didn't have far to go. We didn't keep a guard here, but whoever was on patrol was responsible for checking on it every time they went past. In this building, we kept clothing and comfort supplies, like towels, bedding, and other things one would need in a home. Everything in here had been obtained on raids over the years and saved. We never threw anything out. I led Grace to a shelf that held clothes about her size.

'Pick whatever, just don't take too much,' I said, nodding at the shelving.

'Where do you get all this from?' she asked somewhat in awe as she reached forward to examine the clothes. They were nothing special – simple T-shirts or tank tops with standard jeans, shorts, or pants, basics for underwear, but they did the job.

'Raids and . . . people who have passed,' I said, wishing she hadn't asked. I didn't want her to think about running around in the clothes of someone who had died. 'But mostly raids.'

She didn't respond right away, fingers sifting through the fabrics to pull out a few of each item until she had enough to keep her clothed.

'I see,' was all she said. 'I think I'm all set.'

I nodded and turned, glad she made no further comment

about the clothes, not that I really expected her to. It didn't seem like there was much left in the world that could shock her, a fact that made me both impressed and a bit sad. What kind of world did we live in where vast amounts of killing and gore no longer had an effect on a person?

I hated it. All of it.

Grace followed me as I led her back to my home, and I noticed the sun starting to slip away in the sky. It would be dark soon, and I wanted to at least be on the way before night completely overtook us. We arrived quickly at my hut, entering it before Grace proceeded to stand somewhat awkwardly with her arms full of clothes. I sighed before pulling out a drawer in my dresser.

'You can put your things in here,' I said.

'Thanks,' she said quietly. She seemed tired and I suddenly found myself afraid she'd change her mind about coming with me tonight.

'Do you still want to go tonight?' I asked, the tone of my voice hiding my uncertainty.

'Yes,' she said quickly, straightening up from where she'd hunched over to put her things away. Her green eyes focused on mine as she nodded earnestly. 'Just let me take a shower and then I'll be fine.'

'All right,' I said, nodding. 'I'll just . . . be here.'

Her lips pulled into a flat line as she nodded, ducking once more to pull the necessary articles of clothing from the drawer before turning to head into the bathroom. Just as she was about to shut the door, her head appeared through the crack, her eyes finding mine.

'No peeking,' she smirked, before slamming the door shut. Of course I wouldn't 'peek'. I wasn't a fourteen-year-old boy. I had control of my hormones and wasn't about to let the presence of a girl mess with that. A beautiful girl, stripping down right now in my shower, about to have water sliding down her body . . .

'Nope, nope, nope,' I muttered to myself, shaking my head as my mind started to turn down a dark train of thought. I ran my palm over my face, drawing my lips down with it before dropping my hand back at my side. 'Don't even think about it.'

I heard the shower start and water colliding with the floor, making it even more difficult to think of anything but Grace in the shower. I flopped over on my bed, staring at the strange thatch work ceiling, focusing on counting the wooden beams across it. It didn't work well, because all that I could see was the way the water had run over her skin from the shower we'd shared and the way her lips had parted at the cold temperature.

I blew out a frustrated sigh, annoyed at myself for being unable to fend off such thoughts. I could block just about anything out – fear, pain, regret – but I couldn't block this. My hands gripped the covers of my bed by my side when I heard the water end, a sigh of relief blowing through my lips. After a few more agonising minutes, the door to the bathroom opened to reveal a now blood-free Grace, fully clothed in a plain white T-shirt and a pair of cut-off jean shorts that fit her surprisingly well. Her hair was still wet and slightly tangled as she ruffled it carelessly with a towel which she then hung on the hook on the door.

'Ready,' she said, bouncing slightly on her toes and breaking me from the slight stupor I seemed to have fallen under.

'Right, let's go,' I said, clearing my throat. I waited while she pulled her boots back on before leaving the hut.

'What are we doing?' she asked, glancing up at me while we walked toward the back of the camp.

'You'll see,' I said vaguely. I wanted it to be a surprise.

She huffed weakly next to me as she ran her hand through her hair, throwing it over her shoulder. There weren't many people out now as darkness started to suffocate the light of the sun, and we moved through the camp quickly. After passing through a small clearing of trees, we reached the large garage that housed our vehicles at the back of the camp; it was another building that had been constructed before our arrival, and we used it to our advantage like the tower. I stooped to grip the edge of the door before throwing it open, revealing the dark contents of the building.

Inside sat three vehicles, one of which we had taken earlier today, a few bicycles, and what we'd come for – my motorcycle. It was old, even for before when the world had gone to shit, but it ran and it was mine. The base and seat were black and the pipes were a muted silver. I glanced at Grace to see if she'd caught on to find her staring at it with wide eyes.

'Are we riding that?' she asked, in quiet surprise.

'Yep,' I responded. I looked for a hint of fear or apprehension, but of course none came. I was yet to find something she was afraid of, so it shouldn't have surprised me that this didn't scare her either. Her lips pulled into a slow smile while her eyes raked over the machine.

'Awesome,' she whispered, more to herself than to me. I couldn't help but grin at her enthusiasm. Moving farther into the garage, I grabbed the keys from the drawer that held them before taking two helmets off a shelf. I handed her one, which she accepted with a wide grin.

'Let's go, then,' I said, finally managing to tear her gaze away from the bike and lock it on mine. I tapped her helmet in her hands. 'And you'll want this on.'

She obliged, sliding it over her still wet hair before pushing the shield down over her face. I pulled my own helmet over my head before moving to mount the motorcycle. My long leg swung easily over the seat, the familiarity of it settling into my body. It felt good to be on it again; I hardly ever got to ride because petrol was so hard to find and the bike didn't do well on raids because it was so loud. Riding the motorcycle was a special occasion, but I figured Grace deserved it after what she'd done.

'You coming or what?' I asked when I noticed her standing and gaping at me. She jumped slightly before striding to me, gingerly setting her hands on my shoulders as she climbed on behind me. I could feel the heat of her body pressing into my back but tried to ignore it as her hands floated around my sides uncertainly.

'You're going to want to hang on,' I said. 'Tight.'

I turned the key and started the engine, the sound immediately filling the small garage. Her hands wound around my torso, locking tight over my stomach. I turned the throttle to lurch us forward out of the garage.

Air whipped past us as we flew down a path leading away from the camp, and her grip tightened on me even more as I increased the speed. Trees flashed by in a blur and the dirt kicked up behind us, but I easily kept control of the motorcycle as I manoeuvred through the familiar path that led us away from Blackwing, away from the city, away from everything.

A small squeak escaped her as I turned a sharp corner, sending us flying around a bend in the trees while our path started up an incline. An undeniable feeling of freedom settled over me as I pushed on, relishing the feel of the wind on my skin and the certain wild irresponsibility that came with riding the motorcycle. For once, I felt like I didn't have to worry about keeping hundreds of people alive as I left my worries and doubts behind.

I was surprised when I heard a laugh from behind me. Grace's grip was still tight around my waist, but I could feel her lean back slightly as if enjoying the way the wind whipped around her as we flew through the woods. Her quiet giggle turned into a loud, blissful laugh as she gave in to the carefree recklessness that I always felt on the motorcycle. She surprised me by releasing one of her arms from around me to let it drift carelessly out by her side, her hand moving through the air while her fingers wiggled slowly. A wide grin spread to my face, thrilled she was enjoying it just as much as I did.

We had almost reached our destination as the motorcycle continued to climb the incline. The trees were thicker than ever up here, and it was nearly impossible to see anything beyond the steep path we were on. Grace's carefree laugh was the only thing I could hear besides the rushing of the wind past my ears, and it filled me with a strange lightness I wasn't used to.

Finally, we reached the place I'd been countless times before, but always alone. I slowed the bike, causing Grace to crash lightly into my back as our speed reduced, and her hands found their way back around my torso. We reached a small clearing where I stopped the bike and killed the engine, setting the brake before reaching up to pull my helmet off. I held it steady as I waited for Grace to get off, her actions not quite as fluid as mine due to lack of practice. She stood next to the bike and pulled her helmet off while I dismounted and set my helmet on the seat.

'What'd you think?' I asked, fighting to keep the grin off my face.

'That was amazing,' she said honestly. She looked exhilarated; her green eyes were glowing brightly and a light flush settled on her cheeks, making her look more radiant than I had seen her yet.

'Isn't it? Best feeling in the world,' I said, accidentally divulging a bit of myself. She nodded quickly in agreement. 'That's only part one of the thank you, though.'

'The thank you?' she questioned, confusion darkening her glowing features slightly.

'Yeah, for what you did for Kit,' I explained. Something flashed across her eyes, dimming her excitement before she hid it.

'Oh, right,' she said, forcing her tone to be as bright as before but not quite managing. 'What's part two?'

'Come on,' I said, reaching forward to grab her hand and tug her along after me before I released it after a few feet, feeling strange at the contact. Captors don't hold their prisoner's hands, no matter how nice it had felt.

She followed me silently as I led her through the thick foliage away from the motorcycle. We battled the trees and bushes silently until we got to a clearing, revealing a steep cliff that dropped off drastically about twenty feet from the edge of the tree line. I smiled softly as I heard the predictable gasp leave Grace's lips as she took in the view.

We were very high above everything, the deceptively steep hill leading to an utterly breathtaking view. Below us, the forest we had just come through cascaded down, spilling out at the bottom enough to hide where I knew Blackwing to be. Aside from the tower, all that gave away our camp were the few sparse lights that managed to flicker through the thick trees, only visible after intense scrutiny of the woods themselves. Farther out, to the east, the lights of Greystone could be seen more easily, its lack of trees making it much less camouflaged than Blackwing.

'Wow,' she breathed next to me, approaching the edge of the cliff. I followed her, hovering a few feet back. Her eyes were wide with awe as she took in her surroundings, her gaze drifting over everything.

I saw her search for Blackwing and saw the tiny hint of recognition when she identified it. I saw her eyes travel over the shattered remains of the city and nearby suburbs, most of which had been blown to bits in the end of civilisation. I saw her squint off in the distance as she searched for signs of where she knew the other camps to be – Crimson and Whetland and others still. And finally, I saw the pang of sadness flit through her features when her gaze settled on Greystone, her home for probably most of her life.

For the first time, I wondered who she'd been forced to leave behind there. Did she have a family? Friends? A boyfriend, maybe? What had she lost after being taken captive here? A twinge of guilt twisted my stomach as her features slid into a soft frown, her gaze never leaving the Greystone settlement. I moved to stand next to her, gently taking her hand in mine to lead her to a large rock that I often sat on to observe this world I'd fallen into.

She sat next to me, features difficult to read but decidedly sad. I felt suddenly disappointed, as if my attempts to thank her had backfired horribly and only upset her. I was about to say something, anything, really, to interrupt the silence when she spoke first.

'Do you remember it? Before?'

She didn't look at me as her gaze stayed focused on Greystone. I observed the serious expression on her face and the way the wind soft breeze blew strands of her hair across her features.

'Yes,' I answered honestly. When she didn't respond, I spoke again. 'Do you?'

Her lips pinched together, pulling into her mouth as she shook her head slowly. Finally, her gaze left Greystone to settle on the wreckage of the city. From here, even in the dark, it was impossible to miss the craters fifty feet wide, the crumbled shells of buildings, and the shattered pieces of society that littered the grounds. Evidence of the end of life as it once had been lay before us, most of it destroyed before we'd even reached the age of five.

'That's not a bad thing,' I told her. More often than not, I wished I couldn't remember. Images of exploding fire, panicked people fleeing their homes, and the sound of screaming, so much *screaming*, filled my mind before I shook my head to get them off.

'I wish I could remember it,' she admitted. 'I want to know what it was like before the world tore itself apart.'

'Maybe it's better if you don't. That way you don't know what you're missing.'

She was quiet for a while as she considered my words before speaking again.

'What do you remember?' she pressed, finally tearing her gaze from the view to look at me. I hadn't really looked away from her face since arriving here. She looked a bit surprised to catch me studying her. I stalled as I tried to decide what to tell her. Before I could stop myself, my hand reached up to brush the hairs lightly behind her ears. She blinked in surprise but didn't flinch away from my touch.

I decided on the happier side of what I kept locked away in my brain, but that didn't stop the darkness from creeping up, the nightmares of memories threatening to take over.

Run, Hayden, run now!

I clenched my fist by my side, digging my nails into my palm to bring me back from the edge of dark thoughts I constantly hovered over, determined to keep from falling into them.

'I remember . . . riding these little plastic cars around my neighbourhood. Eating ice cream in the summer while my parents tried to teach me how to play sports. I remember going to the zoo to see all the animals I'd only seen in books. Stupid stuff like that,' I said, suddenly feeling embarrassed at the sharing of these memories. I blinked, clearing away the haze that had settled over me as I thought back to my few memories that didn't include people being slaughtered all around me.

'That all seems so . . .' she paused, searching for the right word. 'Weird.'

A sad smile pulled at my lips. How wretched it was that things we should have grown up doing now seemed so foreign to us. In a way, I envied Grace for her lack of memory; she didn't know what she'd missed and therefore felt no nostalgia for it.

'It didn't always seem weird.'

'I wish I could remember stuff like that,' she said, repeating the same sentiment from before. Now, more than ever, I was certain she was wrong; she was the lucky one to remember nothing. I was silent for a bit as I studied the huge crater in the middle of a suburb, lit only by the moon above but enough to see the gaping hole in the earth. The gaping hole exactly where my house had been so many years before.

Panic flooded through the streets as people ran desperately for their lives, clinging to each other with nothing in their hands but their loved ones. Bullets whizzed through the air, interrupted only by the all-too-frequent explosions that rattled the earth and shook us down to our bones. Both of my small hands were claimed by one from each of my parents, who ran on either side of me, no faster than I could manage on my short, stubby legs.

'Run, Hayden, run now!' my mother called down to me, her voice strong despite the overwhelming fear she must have

felt. I ran as fast as I could, keeping my eyes on the ground to avoid tripping over the bits of people's lives that were scattered across the street. A photo album thrown from a house. A chair ripped from someone's deck by an explosion. Most terrifyingly, a bloody stump of an arm that had long since lost the natural hue of human flesh . . .

'Hayden?' Grace said gently. I got the feeling she'd repeated my name more than once before catching my attention.

'Sorry, what?'

'What are you thinking about?' she prodded gently. Our roles were reversed now as I could feel her gaze on my face while I stared out at the shell of my former life.

'Nothing, Grace. Nothing at all.'

Chapter 11 – Exhume
GRACE

My breath seemed to get swept away with the wind as I sat next to Hayden on the rock overlooking the world as I knew it, the only way I knew it. Hayden's face was tight with his brows pulled low in concentration as whatever was going on in his head pulled him away from me. I had a strong suspicion he was reliving memories, or rather, nightmares, but he refused to share. I felt a twinge of guilt for bringing down his infectious, carefree mood from earlier by asking about his past.

We were both quiet for a while as we let ourselves get lost in the view and the thoughts that came with it. No matter what I tried, my gaze kept drifting back toward Greystone, my home for as long as I could remember. I knew that I, like Hayden, had spent the first years of my life in a relatively normal world, even if that world had been slowly crumbling around us before finally completely disintegrating. The only difference was that I remembered absolutely nothing before life in Greystone.

I didn't know much about why the world fell apart, but I knew the basics. The governments couldn't get along as we slowly but surely ran out of all resources essential to life. Wars started around the globe until every country stood alone, blasting each other to bits while the internal workings of our own country fell apart. Not only was the world at war with itself, but individual countries were ripped to shreds by people's desperation to survive within it.

It happened in our city, just as it had all over the world, as people started banding together, stealing and fighting other groups, their own friends and neighbours, within the network of the city. The day the bombs hit — weapons from several countries unknown to us — all hell broke loose. It didn't matter who had dropped the bombs, because everyone was an enemy. People fled, clinging to their loved ones and trying frantically to find the few others they trusted. That was how the camps were formed; those few who survived the bombs and managed to make it out far enough to avoid the carnage stayed with the few they'd already begun fighting with.

What started out as people living between rocks and under trees, nibbling on roots to survive, had somehow evolved into fully functioning societies, separate from all others and relying only on themselves to survive. Everything we had now had been taken painstakingly moved from the city to the camps, each and every item.

The world had fallen to ashes, ripping apart countries and cities alike, leaving only a few to survive and fight to carry on.

These were the things my father had told me. Other bits I'd learned from people who had survived and experienced the fall first hand. Hayden was the youngest person I'd met who actually remembered it, as if most people our age had somehow managed to block out the memory they'd held at a very young age. It made me wonder exactly how that came into play with him now; I suspected it had a lot to do with why he was the way he was — serious, protective, and despite his attempts to hide it, good.

Thinking of my father sent a wave of sadness through me as I realised how much I missed him. His face, my best friend's, and even my rotten brother's floated through my mind. It felt so strange to be here, in this enemy camp with people I didn't know, when I could see my home easily from where I sat now. I was a prisoner, but I didn't feel like one. Hayden wasn't exactly nice to me, but he was far from cruel. He was, surprisingly, decent. Despite all that, however, I still wanted to go home where I belonged.

My eyes flitted to his face, illuminated only by the light of the moon. The sharp line of his jaw cast a dark shadow down his neck, set strongly as he thought about whatever went through his mind. My eyes moved involuntarily to his lips, which were pursed together in thought. Looking at them now brought back the feeling of them on my own, his hands on my skin, and the butterflies that fluttered in my stomach when he'd kissed me.

I suddenly hoped he would do it again.

'Do you miss it?' he asked suddenly, jerking my eyes from his lips up to meet his gaze.

'Yes,' I answered honestly. 'I miss home.'

He nodded solemnly and turned back to look at Greystone.

'I'm sorry I have to keep you here,' he said quietly. I observed his profile and was somewhat surprised to see he actually looked like he meant it. 'Do you have . . . people you left behind?'

'Yeah,' I said simply. It hurt to talk about them because I didn't know if I'd ever see them again. He didn't respond as his eyes raked over my home. I noticed he had a habit of not responding unless it was really necessary.

'Are you really going to make me stay here for ever?' I asked quietly. A tiny, tiny part of me wanted to remain here solely because I was so intrigued by him, but for the most part I just wanted to go home.

'Yes.'

My heart sank at his words. I'd been hoping since I'd worked so hard to prove myself that maybe he would have a change of heart, but it didn't seem to be the case. As bad as he said he felt, it wasn't bad enough to allow me to return home. He turned to look at me suddenly, hand twitching in his lap. I thought he might reach out to brush my hair back again, but he didn't.

'I am sorry,' he started quietly. 'But I hope that you can learn to like it here. They're all good people who are just stuck in a shitty world.'

I nodded but didn't answer, his steady gaze stalling any words I might have said. A soft breeze blew around us, causing wisps of his chocolate hair to brush along his skin.

'We're all stuck in the shitty world,' I muttered. He was much closer than I remembered him being.

His hand reached up to grip the very end of my hair, twisting it around his finger once before releasing it.

'We should get back,' he murmured. Air whooshed out of my lungs in disappointment as he leaned back and stood up, offering his hand to me to help me up. I tried not to look disappointed as I accepted it and let him pull me to my feet, the contact dropping as soon as I was up. His eyes searched mine briefly before he turned and walked back in the direction we'd come.

I sighed quietly and followed. I felt extremely conflicted, because I knew I shouldn't want him to kiss me but I couldn't deny that I wanted him to. Really wanted him to, apparently, because the disappointment was sitting in my stomach like a rock as my feet carried me after him. We reached the motorcycle and put our helmets back on. His lanky leg swung easily over the seat, accustomed to the process. Again, I had to blink and force myself to focus on copying him rather than gaping.

I wasn't sure if he knew just how attractive he was, or if his behaviour was designed to show off, but my guess was that he was too humble to really notice. But that did not stop *me* from noticing.

I climbed on the back of the bike, placing my hands around his torso as I had before. I felt sort of deflated as he started the engine and took off. The ride was just as exhilarating as the way up had been, but I couldn't enjoy it quite as much. My arms stayed locked firmly around his waist, where I could feel his back expanding against my chest whenever he took a breath.

Before long, we'd made our way back down the hill, the path through the pitch black woods seeming all the more mysterious now that it was almost impossible to see anything beyond the beam of his headlight. The garage we'd taken the bike from remained open and waiting for us as he pulled in and killed the engine. Just as before, I climbed off and removed my helmet to put it back on the shelf.

My eyes stayed locked on him as he dismounted and carried his helmet and keys to the shelf.

'So that was all just to thank me?' I asked, unable to stop myself. I'd hoped, deep down, he'd done it because he actually had wanted to show me. Or at least, a small part of him had. I would take a small part. His eyes flitted to mine in the darkness where I stood just inside the door.

'Yeah,' he said quietly, turning to lean against the counter of a workbench. He studied me curiously. 'Why?'

I shook my head, pursing my lips together stubbornly in an attempt to appear nonchalant. 'Just wondering.'

My gaze stayed fixed on his as he approached, his height

towering over mine the closer he got. He paused about a foot away from me.

'I'm intrigued by you,' he admitted, his voice low and quiet but still managing to send my heart into a sudden flurry.

'Intrigued,' I repeated, testing the word. I decided it was a good word – far better than other options he could have used. He nodded slowly, his gaze fixed on mine.

'Despite my better judgement, yes.'

'Maybe you should trust your judgement,' I said quietly. He moved a bit closer, setting my stomach in knots.

'I should,' he murmured, nodding. His eyes flicked to my lips once as he moved even closer, his face inches from mine now. I stood breathlessly as I waited. 'But I don't really want to.'

My chest rose and fell rapidly as my breath shortened due to his proximity. A relentless thudding of my heart could be felt against my ribs as I silently urged him to come closer.

'Then don't,' I breathed.

The words had hardly left my mouth when his lips pushed into mine. A spark turned to a full-fledged fire as it spread through my body, the feel of his lips on mine waking every single cell. I felt his hands land on my hips, tugging me forward so my body collided with his. He increased the pressure of the kiss as my arms rose to wind around his neck, my back arching into him.

My fingers raked through his hair once before tangling between the strands to tug on them lightly, hands acting of their own accord. I allowed his tongue to glide lightly across my own as his hunger intensified. I returned the pressure, eagerly kissing him as the tension that had been building between us for days now spilled over into our actions, finally winning our silent battle against temptation.

I felt his hands slide over my hips and I gasped when he hitched them under my thighs, lifting me easily from the ground to pull my legs around his hips. He carried me backward until he pushed me onto the counter top he'd been leaning on, perching me right on the edge so his hips remained between my thighs. I locked my legs around him, drawing him as closely as I could while he continued to kiss me deeply.

His hands pushed up my thighs, his fingers and thumbs expanding over the expanse to grip me tightly, his touch very close to my centre. I gasped again when he ripped his lips from mine to trail them down my neck, peppering hot, wet kisses along my skin. He reached the base of my throat and nipped lightly, earning a quiet moan from me as I tipped my head back to allow him more room.

'Hayden!' a voice echoed around us suddenly, yanking us from the bubble we'd encased ourselves in. Hayden's lips pulled from my neck as he dropped his forehead to my shoulder in exasperation. I felt the warmth of his breath wash over my skin.

'You've got to be kidding me,' he muttered in irritation. He straightened up and I noticed his chest was heaving slightly from the shallow breaths that he, too, had been taking. Both of us appeared slightly wild and breathless, and his eyes were practically glowing in the darkness as he caught my gaze.

'I'm sorry,' he whispered, squeezing my thigh lightly before starting to move away from me to answer whoever was looking for him.

'Wait,' I muttered, grabbing his hand and yanking him back to where I sat perched on the counter. He allowed me to tug him back, coming to land in front of me. My hands rose to his face quickly, cradling his sharp jaw as I pulled him forward enough to press my lips to his one last time.

He reacted, moulding his lips against my own as if momentarily forgetting that someone was just outside looking for him. The kiss settled into my bones, heating me from the inside out before I pulled away. His eyes looked slightly wild, and I caught a hint of a smirk before he moved to the entrance of the garage.

'Hayden!' the voice repeated.

'What?' Hayden called, squinting out of the garage into the darkness. I took a deep breath to collect myself before jumping off the counter, certain my lips were swollen with the evidence of what had just happened. I moved through the dark garage to join Hayden at the opening, where I could see a figure appearing out of the night.

'There you are,' the voice said. This time I recognised it as the figure drew closer. Barrow appeared before us, shooting me a cautious look before glancing at Hayden. 'Been looking for you everywhere.'

'Sorry,' was all Hayden said, offering no explanation. 'What do you need?'

'Kit's awake,' he said. Hayden took a step forward automatically.

'Really?'

'Yeah. Has been for about an hour now,' Barrow explained.

Hayden nodded before starting to head back to camp at a brisk pace. I shot Barrow an awkward smile before following, not liking the idea of hanging out alone in the dark with the older man. I had to break into a jog to catch up with Hayden. I vaguely heard the garage slamming shut as Barrow closed it behind us.

I tried to think of something to say but couldn't, my body still buzzing from the kiss we'd shared. Hayden, however, appeared to be experiencing no such thing as he rushed

126

toward the infirmary. We arrived shortly, pushing our way through the doors with Barrow not far behind us. Kit sat up in bed, the large bandage still in place over his neck while a girl with dark hair tried to feed him soup.

'Hayden, Grace,' he greeted with a weak smile when he saw us enter. The girl, around my age, paused her coaxing to glance at us. I was struck by the beauty of her features; she had light blue-green eyes and long, dark brown hair that fell down to her waist.

'Hey, mate, how are you feeling?' Hayden asked, coming to stand by his bedside. I hovered back, not wanting to intrude.

'Alive,' he joked lightly. Hayden smiled gently down at him.

'He needs to eat,' the girl said, frowning at him.

'Not hungry,' he said, shrugging before wincing, as if the action had caused a lot of pain.

'You heard, I see,' Hayden said, addressing the girl. She nodded at him.

'Of course,' she replied. Kit glanced around Hayden, searching for something behind him.

'Hey, Grace,' he called.

Oh.

He was searching for me.

I stepped forward to stand next to Hayden, pleased to see the colour had returned to Kit's face after seeing him so starkly pale.

'You're looking much better,' I commented.

'I wouldn't be if it weren't for you. Docc told me what you did and I can't thank you enough,' he said sincerely. It was the most I'd ever heard him talk and by far the nicest he'd ever sounded.

'You're welcome,' I said simply, smiling gently at him.

127

'And I'm sorry. For being such a dick to you. I just have a hard time trusting the enemy, you know?'

'I understand,' I said, nodding. I fully understood the idea because it was how I'd been raised.

'Still don't trust you,' he added, chuckling lightly. 'But at least I know you're probably not gonna kill us now.'

I laughed calmly. I thought he was kidding, but I couldn't be completely sure. 'I'll take that.'

'So you're Grace, huh? The one who saved him?' the girl said, addressing me for the first time. She looked at me curiously, as if she didn't fully trust me.

'Yes,' I answered. It was strange how so many people knew who I was before they even met me.

'I'm Malin,' she answered, turning back toward Kit to try and feed him some more. I wondered if they were together from the close proximity she sat next to him. He'd never mentioned having a girlfriend of sorts, but then again he hardly ever spoke, much less to me, much less about personal things. I made a mental note to ask Hayden later.

Hayden, who I could feel watching me at that very moment. I turned to glance at him and was surprised when his gaze met mine, not bothering to look away or hide the fact that he'd been watching me. His lips were slightly darker than usual, evidence of our kiss that was just subtle enough that probably only I noticed. My stomach fluttered at the memory.

'You stay with Hayden?' Malin asked, breaking the moment between Hayden and me. I blinked and turned back to look at her.

'Yes,' I answered, unsure whether I should smile or not so I ended up just staring at her blankly. She nodded, glancing at me once again. Kit watched us interact in stoic silence.

'You come see me later tonight,' she said, smiling gently at me. I'd been having a hard time deciding if I liked her or not, but decided I did. 'I'll show you some things to make your life easier here.'

'That'd be great,' I said sincerely. There were certain topics I knew I'd have to face eventually that I didn't feel comfortable talking about with Hayden, so I was glad to have met a female around my age, hopefully to confide in.

'She's supposed to stay with Hayden at all times,' Kit interrupted, glancing around at everyone. Even now, after I'd saved his life, he still didn't like the idea of me walking around unattended.

'It's fine,' Hayden said, surprising me. 'As long as she's not completely alone. And not for very long.'

I couldn't help but grin at his decision, pleased I would finally have a few moments away from him, hopefully to be able to think straight. It was difficult to sort out what was happening when he was constantly overwhelming my senses and clouding my thoughts.

'Great,' Malin said with a grin. 'Now, hate to kick you out, but he needs to eat.'

'It's fine,' Hayden said, nodding. 'I'll see you later, mate, all right?'

'Yeah, all right,' Kit muttered. 'Leave me with the slave driver, here.'

'Oh shut it,' Malin answered lightly, grinning softly at him. My suspicions grew even more as I watched them interact.

'Feel better,' I said, waving at him as Hayden led me out of the infirmary into the dark camp.

'So you're really going to let me out of your sight, huh?' I asked, unable to suppress the grin at the tiny taste of freedom.

'Don't get any ideas,' he warned. 'Malin will kill you faster than anyone else around here.'

I blinked in surprise, not expecting that. 'I wasn't going to try anything.'

'Good,' he said, glancing at me with the tiniest ghost of a smile on his face. He was leading us toward his hut once again. 'And Grace?'

'Yeah?'

'Let's keep what just happened between you and me.'

Chapter 12 – Relief

HAYDEN

I frowned at Grace as she sat fidgeting on my couch. She was waiting for Malin to come and get her for whatever she planned to do, but the longer we waited, the more second thoughts I began to have. Half of my theory for keeping Grace with me at all times was to protect my people, but the other half was to protect her. I was fairly certain Grace wouldn't try anything, but the more I thought about it, the less I trusted her to be with Malin.

'You don't have to go tonight,' I offered, hoping she'd change her mind. 'It's getting late and you could just do it tomorrow.'

'Tonight's fine,' Grace said, her eyes flitting to me before she looked away.

She'd been strangely quiet since we'd returned, something I suspected had to do with my request to keep our secret between us. It had nothing to do with her and it wasn't because I regretted what had happened; it was because I didn't want the people that looked to me to keep them alive to see me as compromised or weak. If they knew what I'd done with Grace and what I wanted to do, it could completely change their opinion of me. Keeping my people's trust was more important than giving in to my selfish desires.

'I'm not going to say anything,' she said suddenly, as

if reading my mind, a pensive look on her face. I frowned and resisted the urge to let my eyes drop to her lips at the memory.

'I know,' I replied slowly. 'You know why you can't, don't you?'

'Because I'm the enemy,' she muttered, a hint of bitterness laced into her voice.

'Because they have to trust me with their lives. If they think I'm messing around with you . . . they might not anymore,' I tried to explain. It all made sense in my head why I couldn't get involved with her but seeing her sitting there on my couch, her face set in determination to show no emotion, was making it difficult. What had happened in the garage had felt like something a long time coming and as soon as I'd let it start, it had been nearly impossible to stop. It felt inevitable, like I was resisting the sun rising.

'It's fine,' she said coldly. I sighed heavily, a stone settling into my stomach. I didn't like it but it was how it had to be. I knew I was sending her mixed signals, but this had to stop. Nothing could go from here, and it was best for both of us.

I was saved from answering by a knock at my door. Grace practically sprang up from her perch to open it, revealing Malin behind it. Again, my stomach twisted at the sight of her as I began to rethink this more and more.

'Ready?' Malin asked her, ignoring me completely.

'Yeah,' Grace said. She shot me one last look over her shoulder that was difficult to read before she moved through the frame. 'See you in a bit, Hayden.'

'Don't kill each other,' I muttered, only half joking. Neither responded as they went out, closing the door behind them.

I sighed as I pushed my hand through my hair roughly to try and relieve some of the tension I felt. With my position in the camp, I was very used to stress and had got pretty good at blocking it out, but this was different. This wasn't stress, this was frustration.

It had been a long time since I'd even kissed a girl, much less slept with one. The phase I'd gone through very briefly a few years ago was stamped out forcefully when I came to be in charge of Blackwing, though I had started to grow out of it before then. Every now and then I saw a girl around camp that I'd slept with, only to look away and pretend nothing had ever happened. Only one of them had I seen on a regular basis, and she was currently with the object of my torment.

As soon as I thought of Malin, it became abundantly clear that the current situation was the true source of my anxiety; I was afraid Malin would tell Grace we'd slept together years ago. She'd never been more than that, however. No deep feelings had ever evolved, and we'd used each other as a distraction from the dark world we lived in. It wasn't something I was particularly proud of, especially now that she was with Kit, but there was no denying it had happened. Whatever it had been had been short-lived, running its course on its own even before I really grew out of that stage.

Yes, I definitely was not proud of that part of my life, but I'd learned to control any urges I might have had. Until now.

I huffed a sigh as I pushed myself off my bed. My hands pulled at my shirt, ripping it over my head in one swift motion before discarding it carelessly on the ground. My hands moved to my belt, easily undoing the clasp as I walked into the bathroom. I needed to take a shower and cool off. As soon as I managed to kick my jeans and briefs off, I shifted beneath the shower and started it, letting the cool water run over my skin.

I closed my eyes and tilted my head back to let the water wash over my face and soak my hair, matting some of the strands to my neck. My hands reached forward to press against the wall, body hunching over slightly as I hung my head forward to let my hair fall in my eyes. The water pelted down my back and I was reminded of Grace's fingers tracing my scars. She'd been so careful, as if afraid the pain of the wound remained in the remnants of marred flesh.

I imagined her touch, tickling gently across my skin on my back to trace around my ribs. I imagined her standing in front of me now, the water soaking through the thin clothes she had been wearing earlier to allow them to cling to her skin. I could almost feel her there with me – her hands trailing across my stomach to make the skin over my hips tingle, her lips parting slightly as she inched closer to me. It was like my body reacted to her even though she was nowhere in sight.

I sighed and let the water pour over me, attempting to block out the thoughts that were consuming me. The cool water did little to help distract me, and I noticed my hands clenched by my side. A huff of frustration forced itself from my lips as I shoved my hands through my hair, desperate to think of anything but her. It seemed as though it would be incredibly tough to keep myself from her, and it looked like I was in for a difficult ride.

GRACE

I followed Malin apprehensively, Hayden's warning that she'd be quick to kill me echoing clearly in my head. She hadn't said a whole lot as we approached one of the storage buildings but had shot me a small smile along the way.

'So,' she started as she pushed her way through the door.

134

'I'm assuming Mr Manly Abraham hasn't acknowledged your female needs.'

I choked slightly, turning my surprised sputter into a cough. This was what I figured she'd meant but to hear her say it so bluntly surprised me a bit. It also surprised me to hear something I hadn't known until now: Hayden's last name. Abraham.

'It hasn't come up,' I admitted. She nodded, pursing her lips together as she led me to a shelf way in the back. She studied it for a moment before reaching forward to grab some items.

'Here,' she said, stuffing a box of tampons in my hands. I accepted them gratefully before it occurred to me I had nothing to carry them in. She didn't seem to notice as she grabbed several other items – deodorant, toothbrush and toothpaste, what appeared to be face wash of some kind, a hairbrush, and most surprisingly, a razor.

'Treasure that,' she joked, pointing at the razor she'd shoved in my hands, which were now full of stuff. 'When it gets dull you can sharpen it so it lasts longer.'

'Thank you,' I said, very pleased at the luxury.

While it wasn't necessary to survive, it helped me feel more normal. Human. She nodded as she walked away, leaving me to follow her. She pulled a small backpack off another shelf before unzipping it and holding it out to me. I smiled gratefully and dumped my supplies in.

'You got all this on raids?' I asked, impressed. Greystone had a fairly substantial stash of their own, but I was surprised to see Blackwing's own collection.

'Yeah. We ration them out to make them last as long as we can before we try to get more,' she explained. I nodded but didn't reply; that was pretty much how it had worked at Greystone as well.

135

'See anything else you need?' she asked, gesturing around the room. I squinted around, the sparse candlelight making it difficult to see, but didn't spy anything essential.

'No, I think I'm all set,' I said. She clapped her hands together happily.

'Great! If you think of anything else, you can always come back. We can head out then,' she said, leading me back to the front door. I put the backpack on and followed her into the night.

'How's Kit doing?' I asked, hoping to hear good news.

'Stubborn as usual,' she said, rolling her eyes with a hint of amusement.

'Did he eat at all?'

'No but he sure didn't refuse the whisky Dax brought him when he came to visit,' she grumbled. I blinked.

'You guys have whisky?' Alcohol of any kind was a huge luxury around Greystone, and I had expected it to be the same in Blackwing. It was surprising to hear Dax had brought some to Kit so soon after his injury.

'Not much. It's usually for special occasions but I guess nearly dying is a special occasion around here.'

'I guess,' I said, nodding.

'Boys will be boys,' Malin joked lightly, glancing conspiratorially at me.

'Yeah . . .' I trailed off, unsure of what to say. I wanted to ask her about Kit but didn't want to seem intrusive. I decided to ask anyway. 'Hey . . . Are you with Kit?'

'Define "with",' she replied after a short pause. She didn't look at me as we walked and I wasn't sure exactly where in the camp we were.

'Are you guys dating?' I asked. I wasn't really sure what 'with' meant either.

136

'No,' she said, chuckling. 'I'd say we have more of a . . . physical relationship.'

'Oh,' I frowned. It had seemed to me that there was a bit more to them, but they probably had their reasons.

'Why? Are you interested in Kit?' she asked sharply, glancing down at me with an arched eyebrow.

'No,' I replied honestly. The last thing I wanted was for her to think of me as some sort of competition and decide she wanted to get rid of me after all.

'Because if you are, maybe I could help you,' she continued, sounding very much like she would despise fulfilling her offer.

'I'm not interested in Kit,' I reassured her.

'Okay,' she said, sounding slightly relieved. 'What about Hayden?'

'What *about* Hayden?'

'You're not sleeping with him, are you?' she said suddenly, her voice casual. This time I really did choke a bit, my breath catching in my throat before I recovered.

'What? No,' I said, praying my voice was convincing. Technically, I wasn't.

'Okay,' she said calmly. 'Because if you were we'd need to stop by Docc.'

'Why?' I asked, confused.

'He's got a pretty good stock of that birth control shot. You'll notice a bit of a lack of children around here and that's partially why. Not everyone wants kids now,' she explained. 'It hurts like hell but it's worth it.'

'You've got it?' I asked. I hoped I wasn't digging too much but I was curious.

'Yeah, you have to get it every three months. One shot, no babies. That's it,' she grinned.

'Huh,' I said thoughtfully. I hadn't really thought about

it, but there was a significant lack of younger children here. Come to think of it, Jett was one of the youngest I'd seen. It wasn't all that shocking; even in my own camp, people refrained from having children. No one wanted to bring a child into this desolate world.

'Keep it in mind if you find yourself settled in here,' she said, winking at me. I blushed already at the thought of going to Docc and asking him for a birth control shot. However, Hayden had just made it blatantly clear that it would never be necessary, so I waved the thought out of my mind.

Malin and I continued to walk through the camp, which was completely deserted. It had to be getting late, close to midnight if I had to guess, but she didn't seem to notice as we carried on. I was about to ask her a bit more about herself when I heard a snap of a twig to my right where the woods bordered the path we were on. My training kicked in as I carried on forward nonchalantly, as if I hadn't noticed.

'Malin,' I muttered quietly, careful not to look in the direction of the woods as I heard another branch snap.

'I know,' she murmured in reply, copying my casual attitude. We kept walking, but I could practically feel the eyes of whoever was hidden behind the tree trunks watching me.

'We have to find Hayden,' I whispered, my hands itching to grasp a weapon I did not have.

Malin nodded next to me as we quickened our pace discreetly. I could feel the adrenaline start to creep up in me that always came with raids, but it was different this time. Now, I wasn't protecting my own people. Now, all I really had to think about was myself, but my mind refused to stop flashing to Hayden. Our silence was interrupted by a sudden bang ringing out as a gun went off somewhere in Blackwing.

'Shit!' I cursed, breaking into a sprint just as Malin did beside me, both of us racing toward the sound. The first gunshot was followed quickly by several others of varying volume, as if several different calibre guns were going off. My arms pumped by my sides as my feet carried me closer to the source, my breath increasing with my pace. We had just rounded the corner when we saw dark shadows flitting between the houses, coming from the direction of the woods we'd just passed. Flashes of light were going off followed immediately by another booming bang from a gun as people fired at each other.

'Raid,' Malin muttered as we sprinted, her voice tight.

She pulled a gun from her waistband and charged forward while I raced along next to her, no weapon to defend myself. As yet another gun fired, I saw a shadow fall, joining several others already on the ground. My legs had almost carried me into the fray when I was suddenly jerked backwards, yanking the backpack from my shoulders to dangle off one of my wrists. My body slammed into another while a hand clamped over my mouth. A strong arm wound around my waist, hauling my back into a solid chest and pinning me there.

After dropping my bag to the ground, my arms struggled as they clutched at the hand over my mouth, but it was useless. Whoever had a grip on me was much stronger than I was, and I could do nothing to stop them from dragging me behind the wall of a hut, cutting my line of vision off from the chaos ensuing only a few yards away. Jets of air shot out my nose as I struggled to breathe thanks to the hand cutting off my mouth.

My body bucked wildly, trying to throw the stranger off me. I was about to drive my elbow into their groin when I felt a pair of lips at my ear, pressing into the shell tightly.

'Stop,' he muttered, his breath warm on my skin. I stopped thrashing but didn't stop trying to pull his hand from my mouth. My eyes darted down to the forearm holding me and saw a familiar smattering of tattoos inked the skin.

Hayden.

I tried to speak to tell him to let me go, but my words were too muffled by his strong hand to be decipherable. He held me tightly against him, his entire body hard from years of training and building his muscles. The bangs continued to echo around us as he leaned against the wall, keeping us out of view.

'Grace, knock it off,' he hissed when I continued to pull at his hand. I huffed angrily before dropping my hands, ceasing my efforts to escape. He leaned forward to peek around the corner, bringing my body with him as he did so. A final bang went off but neither of us flinched, more than used to the sound.

'I think that's all of them!' someone shouted from down the path. I could hear people muttering as they moved around and revealed themselves from behind their hiding spots, but still Hayden didn't let me go. Someone let out an angry curse while another seemed to kick something as a metallic clash rang out around us.

All of a sudden, another bang echoed around the huts, followed immediately by a thump of someone falling to the ground. Others shouted, their guns going off once more as they shot at whoever had appeared. I could hear frantic footsteps coming toward us, panting audible over the distant shouting as whoever it was approached, the gun shots missing their fleeing target.

Hayden held me tighter once again, his hand still planted firmly over my mouth while he flattened us against the wall. Whoever was running was even nearer now, and I knew it would only be a few seconds before they came into view. Sure enough, the sound caught up with my line of vision as a large, dark shadow blew past us. His clothes whipped out behind him as he ran, and his chest heaved while he gasped for air.

It wasn't until he turned his head to the side to glance back over his shoulder at those pursuing him that the light caught his face, illuminating his features. Had my mouth not been covered, I would have let out a loud gasp at the sight.

There, sprinting hastily through the darkness in Blackwing, was none other than my brother, Jonah. He hadn't seen me, and I had no way of calling out to him to get his attention. I struggled against Hayden as I watched Jonah's dark figure shrink while he sprinted away from us, growing smaller and smaller until he was finally swallowed by the darkness cast by the trees in the forest, leaving me behind once again.

Chapter 13 – Twofold

GRACE

My heart sank into the pit of my stomach as my eyes remained glued on the now empty space where my brother had disappeared. Hayden's hand remained clamped over my mouth while his chest pressed tightly to my back, holding me firmly against him. A crushing disappointment I hadn't been expecting swept through me, physically weighing down my body as the opportunity I hadn't realised I'd been hoping for disappeared before I could even consider the potential.

My chest was rising and falling far more rapidly than my lack of movement warranted, but the searing anger flooding through me was more than enough cause. I considered biting the palm of Hayden's hand to get him off me, frustrated with his restraint. Finally, after minutes without another appearance from Greystone and with much shouting from behind us, he removed his hand from my mouth. His other arm, however, slid smooth from my waist only to catch a tight hold of my forearm.

'Get off me,' I spat through clenched teeth. 'That was my brother!'

Whatever his reason was for restraining me, I was far from grateful for it. He'd stopped me from seeing my brother, and I was livid. Even though he was a selfish arsehole, he was still my brother.

'Are you going to run?' Hayden asked firmly, eyes locked tightly on mine as he looked down at me. He seemed completely unfazed by the revelation of my brother. I blew out an angry breath as I glared up at him.

'And go where? Ten feet that way for one of them to shoot me?' I grumbled sarcastically, throwing my one free hand aggressively toward the members of Blackwing who continued to mill around, inspecting the darkened shadows heaped on the ground. He frowned deeply at me, my anger surprising him.

After a few seconds of consideration, however, he released his grip on my arm, letting his hands fall to his sides. I glared at him and grabbed my bag out of the dirt before hitching it over my shoulder as best I could.

'Does anyone know you're here?' he asked suddenly, breaking our tense silence as he studied me closely. I would have been perfectly content to continue to glare at him in silence for the rest of the night.

'No,' I admitted reluctantly. As much as I would have loved to tell him someone knew I was here and that someone was coming for me, it would have been a lie. I looked past Hayden to the darkened lumps on the ground, the bodies of people from Greystone I most likely knew. Whoever had seen me in the woods had to have been one of them, but any chance they'd had of telling someone had gone with them to the grave.

The other possibility was that it had been Jonah in the woods when I'd walked by, but I knew that wasn't the case. If it had been him, he would have jumped out right away, killed Malin without a second thought, and taken me back. He was a fierce fighter, but he wasn't the best critical thinker. He would have reacted instinctively, revealing himself quickly to me rather than waiting in the woods for

143

a more opportune moment as the others must have done. He hadn't seen me when I'd walked by, and he hadn't seen me when he'd flown past Hayden and me behind the hut.

No, no one knew I was here. I was completely alone.

'Are you sure?' Hayden pressed, his eyebrows rising expectantly.

'I said no!' I spat, frustration getting the better of me. I sighed heavily before dropping my tone. 'They all think I'm dead, no thanks to you.'

'Well, what the hell, Grace,' Hayden seethed, losing his cool for the first time. 'What do you expect? You think I'm just going to let you have a nice little visit with your brother while he *raids* and *kills* people in my own camp? You think it's going to benefit me in any way if he knows you're alive?'

'No, I just thought—'

'Thought what? That if you played nice I'd let you go home?' he said, his voice on the edge of yelling. He looked livid now, his eyes narrowed tightly as he glared down at me. A muscle twitched in his jaw as he clamped it shut.

The sad thing was, that was exactly what I had thought. I maintained my sullen silence while my chest continued to rise and fall drastically in pace with my laboured breathing.

'This doesn't change anything, Grace. Just because you saw him here doesn't change the fact that you're never going home,' he said, his voice the coldest I'd ever heard. I felt like stamping my foot in irritation, punching my fists into his chest, crying ridiculous tears, anything to relieve the frustration taking over my body at that moment – but I didn't. All I did was glare back at him in stony silence, standing my ground until he shook his head angrily, a reluctant scoff leaving his lips.

'To think . . .' he muttered, his gaze dropping to my lips before returning to my eyes. He paused a second before pursing his lips, cutting himself off with another shake of his head. He blew out a deep sigh while trying to grab my arm again but I yanked it away. He shot me an irritated look and spoke. 'Come on.'

He turned his back on me, walking toward the chaos that was still unfolding down the path. I followed reluctantly and could feel the eyes of many a member of Blackwing on me, watching for an escape attempt I would not make.

I glared daggers at Hayden's back as I followed but was distracted by the solemn looks on people's faces as we approached. About ten people were gathered around, most of them holding weapons of some kind. From what I could tell as we approached, four separate shadows lay across the ground, none of them moving. My blood ran a bit colder as I realised what that meant; the warmth of life had slipped away from them, leaving only cold, empty bodies behind.

I noticed Hayden visibly tense as he neared, his features set in a stony expression. He was still angry from our fight, but the expression held a hint of something else that he tried to mask without complete success. Written across the features of his face was pain. I kept my eyes trained on his face as we got close enough to identify the people, too afraid to see someone I cared about lying dead on the ground.

Hayden came to a halt next to Dax, who I hadn't seen until now as I'd been too busy studying Hayden. I was surprised when a wave of relief swept through me when I saw he was not one of the unidentified deceased. My eyes squeezed closed tightly as I prepared myself to look.

'How many were there?' Hayden asked Dax solemnly.

'Four. One got away,' Dax muttered. The world was dark around me as I tried to summon the strength to look, the anger and frustration from my fight with Hayden giving way to fear.

'Do you know who that was?' Hayden questioned, leading up to the reveal.

I blew out a breath and opened my eyes, seeing a pair of feet that had struck at an awkward angle. Details of his ripped jeans and dirty, blood-stained shirt passed my eyes before I saw his face, a sigh of relief blowing past my lips when, remarkably, I did not recognise him.

Two more.

'Greystone,' Dax guessed correctly.

My feet carried me a few yards beyond Hayden and Dax, who continued to converse while I tried to keep myself calm. The body had landed on their front, the face turned away from me. Slowly, I moved around it before the face came into sight.

'That was her brother. The one that made it out,' Hayden informed him.

Dax sucked in a quiet gasp as I caught sight of the face. This one I did recognise, but didn't know his name. He was about thirty-five, and I seemed to recall seeing him with a woman about his age – a woman who would never see him again.

One more.

'Did he see her?' Dax asked after recovering slightly.

I began to feel the anger from before returning as I realised what had happened and exactly where I was. I seemed to have forgotten over the past few days who these people were and what they were capable of, but the evidence was here, right before my eyes. I moved towards the last body, the farthest away, that was being inspected by a member of Blackwing. Anger surged through me when I saw someone take a knife from the pocket of the deceased.

'Hey!' I shouted, rushing forward. I ripped it out of the man's hand, gripping it tightly in mine as about seven or eight guns pointed right at my chest. Before I even realised they were aiming at me, I threw the knife on the ground. I glared at the man before me, my hands shaking by my sides. 'You shouldn't steal from the dead.'

'That's the way the world works now, girl,' he growled, glaring back at me but not bending to pick up the knife. 'You should know that better than anybody.'

'What is that supposed to mean?' I spat, taking a tiny step forward even though I was now unarmed.

'You came from this filthy lot. You're no better,' he said, leering at me menacingly. Fury raged inside me as I clenched my fists by my sides, more than ready to knock his rotten teeth in when someone interrupted.

'That's enough,' Hayden's voice boomed from behind me. He didn't come to my side or move, but his words were commanding enough for the man to take a few steps back and lower his weapon. The man, instead, turned to glower at Hayden.

'Do they know she's here? Is that why they came?' he demanded. He still looked upset, but he was clearly intimidated by Hayden.

'No one knows she's here,' Hayden responded coolly. 'This had nothing to do with her. It was just a raid.'

I stopped listening as Hayden calmed the crowd, my eyes searching over the final body now that I'd interrupted the man from Blackwing. I took in the greying hair and the firmly muscled yet aged arms and a brief moment of panic set in as I imagined my father lying on the ground.

When I stepped closer, however, I saw that it wasn't him. This man didn't have the same piercing green eyes of my father, but dull, lifeless brown ones that had glazed over in his death. This man was not my father, but I recognised him, too. He was Winston, one of my father's closest friends, and

147

he was dead. I stared at his face numbly for a second, a thin red trickle of blood escaping his lips, before I managed to tear my gaze away.

I turned on the spot, closing my eyes as I faced the group again. Several pairs of eyes were fixed on me, mistrust evident in their gazes despite the fact that I made no more moves to escape or threaten anyone.

'Hayden,' a voice called from a little farther away. I turned instantly to see Malin standing solemnly on the outer edge of the ring. My gaze immediately shifted back to Hayden just in time to see the colour drain from his face, his jaw slackening before quickly retightening.

'What?' he asked, somehow managing to keep his voice strong. Malin opened her mouth to speak but only managed to draw a shaky breath before jerking her head back, beckoning him forward. His steps were jolted and unnatural as he stepped over a body to move towards Malin and the final remaining shadow on the ground. Without really realising, my feet carried me forward as well, following Hayden to see the final victim of the raid – someone from Blackwing. Someone my brother had definitely killed.

Hayden got there before I did, stooping down in the darkness to press his fingers along the wrist, his head hanging low when he clearly felt nothing there. I saw his shoulders sag as he sighed deeply, his hand pushing roughly through his hair in pain. When he stood, my view was clear enough to see the face of someone I did not know, but recognised.

She seemed too old to be here, in the middle of the chaos and slaughter, but there she was on the ground, blood spilling from a tiny hole in her chest that looked too minuscule to be so lethal. She was the kind woman who had smiled at me during our last meal – one of the few since I'd arrived to be openly nice. We hadn't spoken and I didn't know her name, but she'd been kind to me.

This small loss felt almost the same as losing the members of Greystone. Aside from Winston, I didn't know any of them. But they were all people who'd lost their lives fighting not just for themselves, but for those they were trying to provide for. They were just people trying to survive the only way they knew how. Sometimes I got so used to this malevolent world we lived in that I forgot what a true tragedy it really was.

Hayden's hands moved to his face, palms clasping either side of his temple while his fingers wove together over his forehead. He tilted his head back and closed his eyes as he blew out a slow breath. My heart ached for him despite my anger. It was already clear to me that he was a better person than most probably realised, but it was even clearer now as the weight of these deaths seemed to settle on to his shoulders.

'All right,' he said, dropping his hands and opening his eyes. 'Let's do this, then.'

Hayden shot me a tense look, the anger gone but replaced by stress. Whatever fury he'd held in the fight with me seemed to have ebbed away as things of more importance came up – these deaths. I watched him give people orders that were immediately followed. Dax, it appeared, was the only one not prescribed a job. I moved to stand next to him.

'Who was she?' I asked quietly, careful not to let Hayden hear me.

'Helena,' Dax answered bluntly. I nodded, storing the information. His eyes were narrowed in concern as he watched people gently lift the bodies to carry them away, the two people carrying the woman I now knew as Helena moving in a different direction.

'What will they do with them?' I asked, somewhat afraid to find out. I'd heard horror stories about things enemy camps did to those they killed. Even if they were only rumours, nothing seemed too vile for this world anymore.

'They'll bury Helena. Have a funeral, if they can. For those three . . .' he trailed off, glancing at me as if deciding whether to tell me or not. I pushed my lips into a flat line, preparing for the worst.

'They'll burn them,' he replied.

'Oh,' I responded blankly. All things considered, cremation was an honourable way to be sent off from the earth. Nightmares of leaving bodies to rot in fields and feeding them to dogs danced through my mind, remnants of things my brother had told me as a child to try and scare me. 'That's not so bad.'

'It was Hayden's idea, that,' he said. I hadn't realised, but I'd been watching Hayden as I spoke to Dax. He helped carry Winston's body away, following another pair as they disappeared into the trees. He didn't look at me.

'It was?'

Dax nodded. 'Yeah. About six years ago before he was even in charge. They used to just leave them outside the camp. In theory their camps could come and get them for a burial but no one ever did so they just ended up rotting. Smelled horrible . . .' he trailed off, seeming to get lost in his head as his nose crinkled up subconsciously.

'Hayden thought it was more respectful to cremate them as best we could,' he finished, snapping out of his head. I had to admit I agreed with Hayden. I watched in heavy silence as the last body was carried away, leaving only spattered pools of blood that were already starting to seep into the dirt as evidence of what had happened.

Hayden returned from between the trees, his head ducked

down and eyes fixed on the ground as he moved forward.

'He's better than the rest of us, you know?' Dax said quietly enough for only me to hear. My eyes stayed fixed on him as he moved toward us and took in the obvious weight that had settled on him after tonight.

'I know.'

We both watched him close the remaining distance between us in stoic silence. He came to rest a few feet away, finally glancing up from the ground to lock eyes with me. I was surprised to see how calm he looked now, as if he'd managed to push away whatever he'd felt initially.

'Malin's gone to tell Helena's family,' he said, his voice a deep monotone as he turned to Dax, who nodded silently. I felt like I was intruding on a private family affair, watching loved ones mourn someone I'd never even known.

'You should get some sleep,' Dax said gently, taking in the dark circles that had started to form under Hayden's eyes. They were similar, I noticed, to those forming under Dax's eyes and most likely mine as well. We'd all had an extremely difficult day that had seemed to drag on for years.

'You too,' Hayden muttered, nodding curtly at Dax before turning back to me. His hand lifted as if about to grab my arm again but thought better of it as it dropped back to his side. He stalked past me, barely giving me time to mutter a goodbye to Dax before rushing after him.

His pace slowed once I caught up, but he didn't look at me. Absolutely nothing came to mind to say. What could I possibly say to him after that? Our fight had been followed immediately by the grim reality of death, including one of his own camp. Words seemed to do no justice to the events of the day.

Though I hadn't recognised where we were, it turned out we were relatively close to Hayden's hut because before I knew it Hayden was throwing his shoulder into the door to push his way inside. His actions carried an odd strength, as if his mind was suffering but his body refused to let him sink. My own body often experienced something similar: when training took over, urging your body onward when your mind was too berated to try anymore. It was mental defeat coupled with physical resistance.

Hayden kicked off his boots quickly before heading straight toward his bed, falling over promptly without even taking off his clothes or settling under the covers. I followed suit, grateful I'd showered earlier as I kicked off my boots and set my bag of supplies down next to the couch. I lay down but instantly knew sleep would evade me despite being physically and mentally exhausted.

The reality of my situation started to set in. It was as if before, I hadn't really acknowledged the fact that this was permanent. I'd fooled myself into thinking that if I cooperated and behaved, maybe even helped out, they'd let me go. It was quickly becoming more and more clear, however, that that would never be the case. Hayden's harsh words earlier had drilled that into my head, making me feel stupid for thinking any other potential outcome was even possible.

I would stay here for the rest of my life, and I would never see my family again.

Unless, of course, they decided to raid Blackwing again like tonight and I caught a fleeting glance of them while they either escaped by a hair or, more horrifically, didn't make it at all. Seeing my brother tonight had made me realise just how much I really missed them and my home, the strange allure of Hayden had distracted me from this fact. I'd got too comfortable too easily, finding solace in the last place I probably should have. It had backfired on me magnificently.

A flash of heat went through my body as the moments

secluded in the dark with Hayden swam through my mind. The way his body pressed into mine and the way his lips smoothed over my own had felt undeniably amazing, although I doubted it would ever happen again after tonight. The raid carried out by my own camp would surely remind him who I was, what I was, and why we couldn't get into another garage-like situation again.

My despair brought on another memory – the memory of Hayden's hands holding me against him, restraining me from a fight I'd rushed toward despite being unarmed and uninformed. Confusion swept through me as I remembered the way his lips had pressed at my ear and the effort he'd put forth in keeping us hidden.

'Hayden?' I called out quietly, unsure if he was awake or not. He was silent for so long I had just decided he wasn't when he replied.

'What?'

'Why'd you do it?' My lips pinched together as I waited quietly, my eyes fixed on the ceiling of his hut.

'Do what?' he questioned. He sounded as distant as I'd ever heard him.

'Why'd you come and find me and stop me from fighting?' A burning need to know the answer to this question simmered in the pit of my stomach as I waited anxiously for him to reply. I fidgeted on the couch when he didn't answer, my patience wearing thin. After nearly a whole minute passed, it became clear he wasn't going to respond.

'Well?' I demanded, desperation leaking in my voice in my desire to know.

'What do you mean?' he asked evasively.

'Did you stop me so no one from Greystone would see me and know I was alive or did you do it to protect me because I was unarmed?' I asked, unsure which would be less painful to hear. He didn't answer again, but I could hear the soft sounds of his breath drifting through the darkness.

'Hayden!' I all but shouted, frustrated that he refused to answer me.

'What do you want me to say, Grace?' he asked, exasperation evident in his tone.

'The truth.'

'I did it so your camp wouldn't know you're here,' he said, his tone forced. My heart plummeted, disappointed.

'But . . .' he continued, surprising me. My stomach lurched hopefully despite everything we'd gone through tonight and how angry I'd been with him earlier.

'But . . .?' I prompted. My pulse quickened in my veins and I tried my best to lie still.

'But I'd be lying if I said it wasn't to keep you safe, first.'

Chapter 14 – Control
HAYDEN

I sighed deeply as I rolled over in bed for what felt like the thousandth time. No matter what I tried, sleep continued to elude me. I was physically and mentally exhausted, but my mind refused to quiet down and let me drift into the blissful oblivion of sleep. How I longed to get a few hours of respite from the trials of the day, but I had no such luck.

My body felt jittery as I lay on my back and stared into the darkness, like my limbs were vibrating despite my best efforts to calm them down. With another sigh, I gave up trying to sleep and sat up in bed, swinging my legs to let my feet settle on the floor. My elbows rested on my knees as I let my head fall into my hands, arching my back before I managed to push myself off the bed.

I moved deftly though the room, the only source of light a meagre amount that flickered through the grimy windows. I didn't need light; I knew my way around just fine. My feet carried me around the obstacles I knew were on the floor to bring me to my desk, where I lit a small candle on the surface and sat down on the chair. I cast a weary glance at Grace but was relieved to see she was sound asleep, her chest rising and falling slowly.

I cringed when the wood of the desk creaked as I opened the bottom drawer to pull out the old leatherbound journal.

Another quick glance at Grace told me she remained asleep. I opened the book to the last page I'd written on and let my fingers trace over the ink scrawled across the worn pages. It had been a while since I'd written in it, something I was none too happy to change.

More pages had been written on than were left blank, each one of them taking another little bit of me with it as I filled them with words. I wrote things I needed to remember, things I would forget if I didn't write them down. If no one kept a history, how would others know what had happened? How would people know who was here and who we were when we were gone and ground to dust?

I reached for the pen in the bottom of the drawer and started to write, the movement feeling foreign after so much time without using it. There wasn't much use for writing, these days, and doing something so simple felt odd. It took me a bit to loosen up, the words I scrawled disjointed and sloppy before I got used to it and wrote more freely. I ignored the sting of pain that poked at my heart as I recorded the words, blocking out the emotions in order to be as accurate as possible.

I'd been writing for a while when I noticed a subtle change in the atmosphere, a shift in the once steady breathing of the only other person in the room. I stopped work and glanced over at the couch, jumping slightly when I was met with a pair of beautiful green eyes watching me. She tugged her lip into her mouth at being caught and I suddenly felt like she'd intruded on something private.

'Hey,' she said, her voice soft and quiet. I cleared my throat and set down my pen.

'Hey.'

'What are you doing?' she asked, sitting up fully.

'Couldn't sleep,' I said, not offering anything further. She surprised me by standing up and walking toward me with a sad look on her face. Her eyes darted to the journal as she got closer, which I closed quickly to block her out.

'Writing?' she observed, returning her gaze to my face. I couldn't really deny it.

'Yeah.'

'What do you write in there?'

'It's private,' I said defensively. My voice mostly sounded tired. She frowned slightly as she leaned against my desk and looked down at me. I didn't like her being taller than me even though I was sitting. It made me feel vulnerable.

'You know it won't kill you to open up a bit,' she said gently.

'You're one to talk,' I challenged, raising an eyebrow at her. Both of us sounded worn out. 'Besides. It might.'

She rolled her eyes lazily, shaking her head as if she didn't have the energy to argue right now.

'Okay,' she said, trying again. 'Why couldn't you sleep?'

'Tough day,' I replied flatly. This day had felt never-ending with massive highs and immense lows.

'You have a point,' she agreed softly. Her gaze dropped from mine to glance at my journal again, which I pulled into my lap protectively as if she could see through the cover. Still I felt it was too vulnerable, so I returned it to the drawer and slammed it shut.

'Why are you up?' I questioned, turning it around on her.

'Couldn't sleep much either, I guess,' she said, shrugging. I felt a sudden flash of guilt as I realised what she must have been feeling. I'd lost someone today, but she'd lost three. And, on top of that, she'd been forced to listen to me tell her she'd never leave this place, never go home, and most likely, never see her family again. I'd had a tough day, but hers had arguably been even worse. I hadn't exactly been nice to her.

157

'I'm . . . sorry about yelling at you,' I mumbled. The words tasted foreign on my lips; I didn't apologise for things. 'Earlier.'

Her lips tugged up sardonically in the corner, as if she couldn't really help it. 'Are you really sorry?'

'Yeah,' I said, catching her gaze once more. 'I mean . . . what I said is still true – you can never leave here, but I'm sorry for how I said it.'

She nodded, sucking her lips into her mouth to wet them before releasing. Her gaze was fixed on the floor, her arms crossed loosely over her chest. I wasn't sure if that was an acceptance of my apology or not.

'It's just . . .' she paused, frowning. 'It hadn't really sunk in until today. That I won't be seeing them again. Or my home.'

A second wave of guilt flashed through me. My attempt to even things out and save her life had backfired so much she'd probably be better off if I'd just left her that day I found her. Now, instead of risking the chance to get back to her own camp or even get the relief of blissful death, she was stuck here for ever. Maybe she would have been better off without me.

'I'm sorry,' I muttered, unsure of what else to say. Her brows pinched together tighter at my empty apology, as if she wasn't fully convinced by it.

'Do you know what that's like? To know you'll never see your family again?' she said, an edge to her voice now. 'You don't.'

I tried not to feel bitter at her assumption.

'Yes, I do, actually,' I replied, finally managing to draw her gaze back to mine.

'Run, Hayden, run!'

I was back on the streets as terror reigned around me. The haunting remains of houses and people flashed by as I fought to keep up with my parents. Screams were so frequent now that it was impossible to distinguish the end of one and the start of another. Bombs echoed around us while gunshots blazed through the air, completing the soundtrack to our fight to flee. My tiny feet slipped on a shockingly large pool of blood, my parents' tight grip on my hands the only thing keeping me from falling to the ground.

'You've got it, Hayden, keep going!' my father shouted encouragingly, his eyes finding mine while we ran.

His strong face was set in determination to get us out of there, and I believed with every bit of my heart that he would. He was so tough and so strong that I didn't doubt for a second that we would be safe. A reassuring nod was aimed down at me as he tugged me along, but that was the last thing I saw before something changed. I watched in horror as the look of strength and resolve disappeared from his face suddenly, the bullet whizzing through his chest wiping his features blank.

'Dad!' I shouted. My feet halted instantly as his body fell to the ground, his firm grip on my hand yanking me backward. A chain reaction jerked my mother back, hauling her to her knees as I collapsed onto my father's chest.

'Dad, get up!' I pleaded, my little hands flopping uselessly over his chest as thick, hot liquid poured from the wound. 'We have to run, Dad!'

My voice had grown weak, cracking with tears that spilled from my eyes uncontrollably. His green eyes, so similar to my own, stared out blankly at the sky above us while terror continued to rain down from the skies. I felt my mother kneel beside me but I was unable to tear myself away from my father's now lifeless body.

'Dad,' I choked, leaning over him as if to protect him from further damage, even though I was barely five years old.

'Hayden, sweetheart, we have to leave him,' my mother said, her arms wrapping around me while her lips whispered in my ear. 'He's gone, love.'

'No, he's not,' I argued weakly. I knew she was right, though. His face didn't hold the same strength it had moments ago. No matter how much I pleaded, he wouldn't come back to me. I felt my body shaking as my mother turned me in her grasp, gripping either side of my head gently.

'He would want us to run, Hayden,' she said, tears pooling in her own eyes while she remained strong. I nodded weakly, sniffling and choking down the sobs threatening to take over.

'That's my boy. My strong, brave boy,' she said, hauling me forward quickly to kiss my forehead before standing up, her hand tightly gripping mine. 'Come now, love.'

With a final look over my shoulder at my father, we turned to run. My eyes focused on a large bridge a few blocks ahead that people had gathered under in a last-ditch effort to avoid the carnage around them. We just had to get to that bridge, I told myself, and we would be safe.

My little legs quickly tired as we sprinted forward, but we were getting closer. I could make out faces now among the crowd – people I'd recognised from when my parents would meet up with them to discuss things I did not yet understand. Still more faces appeared, some strange and unfamiliar. We were fifty yards away before I managed to let the hope I'd been fighting rise. We were so close, so close, to safety.

'Almost there, Hayden,' my mother called encouragingly.

'We're going to make it, Mum,' I called, sprinting as fast as I possibly could. We were less than twenty yards now and I could see the people there waving their arms, urging us forward. I was almost certain we were going to make it when I felt my arm tug backward sickeningly for the second time. My head turned to look, praying I wouldn't see what I knew I was about to.

With my grip still held tightly in hers, my mother had fallen to the ground, a gaping hole in her chest similar to my father's, spilling her blood out on the broken pavement. Too much had already bled from the wound, and there was no slowing it down as she took her last breath. The final sound that came from her was the soft whispering of my name, barely audible amongst the petrifying sounds of terror ripping through the air.

'Hayden.'

Within a matter of moments, both of my parents had fallen, leaving me helpless, afraid, and completely alone.

I shook my head with a jerk, wiping the painful memory from my mind as Grace's face came back into focus in front of me. She seemed to be able to tell I'd just experienced a painful memory because she didn't speak, letting me recover from what I'd just seen in my head.

'You're not the only one to know what it's like,' I muttered, suddenly resenting her a bit. At least her family was still alive. She studied me silently for a few moments.

'Did you lose your family?' she guessed correctly. I sighed deeply. I wanted to talk about literally anything else. Anything other than this.

'My parents,' I responded. 'They were all I had.'

'When?' she asked gently. She looked somewhat surprised I'd answered her.

'During the Fall,' I answered.

'And you remember it?' She sucked in a quiet breath as she spoke as if she felt sorry for me. I hated people feeling sorry for me.

'Yes.'

'I'm sorry, Hayden,' she said quietly. She sounded like she really meant it, which made me feel even weaker.

'It was a long time ago,' I said dismissively.

'But they were your parents,' she countered.

'It was a long time ago,' I repeated flatly. I didn't want to talk about this anymore.

'So you've been on your own since you were what? Five?' she asked, doing the maths in her head.

'Not alone,' I said, shaking my head slowly. 'Docc found me after they were killed and took me under his wing. And I had Kit and Dax. Barrow, Maisie . . . I wasn't alone . . . just wasn't raised in the traditional sense, I guess.'

'Nothing's traditional anymore,' she pointed out. I pushed my hand through my hair, sick of the heavy topic.

'Yeah,' I agreed.

'So who raised you? Docc?'

'Everyone, kind of. That's why these people . . . they're more than just people. They're like family and it's on me to keep them alive. I owe them my life.'

She didn't respond. I felt uncomfortable under her careful scrutiny but remained silent until she decided what to say.

'I've never met anyone like you,' she replied, surprising me. She surprised me again by reaching forward to grasp my hand on the desk, running her thumb over my knuckles slowly. A shock jumped through my skin, travelling up my arm and into the pit of my stomach as she did so.

I'd never felt that with anyone else. Malin and I had tried, thinking that our basis as friends could potentially lead to something more, but it never happened. Our time together had been a result of loneliness, but despite our best efforts, we hadn't been able to fall for each other. Simple things like that feeling I'd just got when Grace touched me had been markedly missing.

What a cruel twist of fate that the only person to ever make me feel anything was the one person I couldn't have.

I didn't know what to say back to her statement, my un-willingness to talk about myself shutting down my thought process. Truth be told, *I'd* never met anyone like *her*.

She seemed to sense my loss for words because she spoke again, withdrawing her hand from mine and sending a small wave of disappointment through me.

'Growing up with Kit and Dax must have been . . . interesting,' she said, shooting me a soft grin and starting on a less loaded topic. I chuckled softly, relieved to get off issues that made me feel vulnerable.

'Very,' I agreed. 'Dax has always been how he is now. He might have even got worse, actually, but Kit kind of hardened up a bit as we got older.'

'Do they remember things from before?' she asked out of curiosity, as if trying to figure them out a bit more.

'Bits and pieces. Not much, just flashes,' I replied. I knew Kit remembered more than Dax, but neither of them had much knowledge aside from what we'd learned growing up. It seemed I was the only one to have retained my full memory.

'I bet you three got into trouble,' she said with an indulgent grin, as if amused by the idea of younger versions of the three of us running around causing chaos in Blackwing.

'A bit,' I admitted, a soft grin pulling at my lips as a memory struck. 'We used to go and explore the woods all the time and always got in trouble for going out without an adult or whatever even after we were trained. Then when we were about ten we found this little pond thing that we could swim in when it was hot and we never really listened to authority after that. Hard to give up freedom once you've tasted it, I guess.'

'You guys sound like little shitheads,' Grace said with a grin. I chuckled again and glanced up at her.

'More than a little.'

'That place sounds great,' she said wistfully, looking away

from me, 'we didn't have anything like that in Greystone.'

'I haven't been there for a few years,' I admitted sadly. It had been my absolute favourite place to go when I was younger.

'Why not?' she questioned.

'I haven't had time. The last few years have been all about running this place and keeping things in order. Can't exactly go off to a little swimming hole just for fun.'

'Sure you can,' she argued lightly with a shrug.

'No, I can't.'

'You're in charge, aren't you? You can do whatever you want.'

'What I want is to keep these people alive,' I countered evenly. 'Besides, what I want and what needs to be done are not always the same thing.'

'I'm just saying,' she said with another shrug. 'The world won't end if you take a little time to yourself. You're so serious all the time. Unwind a bit.'

'The world already has ended,' I pointed out with a smirk. She laughed, filling the small room with the beautiful sound of it.

'All the more reason, then,' she said, smiling fully at me for the first time tonight. I liked it when she smiled.

'You really think I should go back?' I asked slowly, holding her gaze. My hand was dangerously close to hers and I could practically feel the heat from it pulling me toward her. I resisted.

'I really do.' She nodded sincerely.

'Would you like to see it?' I asked, nerves suddenly pinching at my stomach. I forced them down, determined to remain casual. She looked surprised but I didn't miss the hint of a smile that pulled at her lips before she reined it in.

'I'd love to.'

'Tomorrow?'

'You don't have anything you have to do?' she asked with a hint of surprise.

'Not until the day after tomorrow,' I said, shaking my head. I suddenly wondered if she had second thoughts so I continued. 'But if you don't want to, just say so. Don't beat around the bush.'

She frowned at my suddenly surly tone, as I'd gone from nearly happy to grouchy within a minute of time.

'I didn't say I don't want to go,' she said. 'I just don't want you to feel like you have to because I'm making you.'

'Like I'd ever let you make me do something,' I scoffed. She sighed and shook her head while shooting a weak smile at me.

'You're stubborn,' she told me.

'So are you,' I rebuffed. Even now, she stood with her arms crossed over her chest again, closing herself off from me despite the varying depths of our conversation.

She shrugged, not bothering to deny my claim. 'So does your offer still stand, or not? Because I really do want to see it.'

'It stands.'

'Okay, good. Tomorrow it is, then.'

'Fine,' I replied, feeling strangely defiant yet pleased all at once. It was like I was constantly waging an inner battle with myself when it came to her.

'Fine,' she repeated, rolling her eyes at me with an amused grin. 'Don't sound so happy about it.'

I could tell she enjoyed teasing me, but I wasn't sure how I felt about it. On the one hand, I liked seeing her smile. On the other, I didn't like not having control of the conversation. I was much more comfortable being in charge, but she made me feel like I was fighting a constant war for control – a war I was not always winning.

My nerves jumped again as she reached forward once again to place her palm over the back of my own hand, squeezing lightly once before she spoke. 'Go to bed, Hayden.'

My heart thumped at her touch, pleased and annoyed all at once that she made me feel things like that. I rose from my seat, standing to my full height to tower over her, just how I liked it. I held her gaze as I turned my hand over slowly, twisting it so my palm came to meet hers. Our hands were coming from opposite directions, so my fingers grazed slowly down her palm, curling upward as they did so before reaching the tips of her own.

'Goodnight, Grace,' I whispered, my lips much closer to her face. She sucked in a breath at my proximity, before I turned to move back toward my bed, leaving her standing there alone. I felt a gentle buzz run through me from the interaction, pleased I'd got the effect I'd desired.

Who has the control now, Grace?

Chapter 15 – Fear
HAYDEN

The sun was already high in the sky when I woke up, telling me it was late morning. A strangled groan rumbled from my throat as my back arched against my mattress, stretching the stiff muscles. I hadn't meant to sleep so late, but I hadn't exactly got the best night's sleep, either. After peeling my eyes open, I sat up in bed, shoving the covers off far enough to allow my legs to swing free.

My gaze landed on the couch as I heaved myself out of bed to see Grace still soundly asleep. She, too, had had an exhausting day, so it didn't surprise me that she was still out. After heading to the bathroom to get myself ready, I was slightly startled when I came out to find her standing over the couch. She had her back to me, and her hands were pressed low over either side of her spine as she twisted to the right and to the left, as if she were sore from the sleeping conditions.

'Hey,' I said, causing her to jump and turn around quickly. Her hand landed on her chest as if I'd frightened her.

'Hey,' she returned slightly breathlessly. I moved to my dresser to pull on a pair of shorts over my boxer briefs, different from my usual jeans. I could feel Grace's eyes on me as I pulled a plain white shirt over my head and I wondered if she realised I could tell. For some reason it didn't really bother me that she saw me walking around in my underwear all the time.

'Sleep well?' I asked, turning to face her. She averted her eyes quickly, confirming my suspicions that she'd been watching me.

'Not particularly,' she grumbled, bending to fold her blankets. I believed it. That couch was a nightmare.

'Hmm,' I murmured, choosing not to comment on it further. 'Well, get ready. We're leaving here in five minutes.'

She huffed out a breath, blowing the wisps of blonde hair off her face before nodding. She then turned and made her way into the bathroom. I took the opportunity to reach beneath my bed and retrieve the 9mm pistol I kept there, sliding it into the waistband of my shorts before tugging my shirt over it to cover the cool metal. I never went anywhere without a weapon, just in case.

I took a deep breath and let my neck roll to each side as I tried to relax the quiet nerves that had crept up. It occurred to me that she would be the first person other than Kit, Dax, or me to see this place and I wasn't entirely sure how I felt about it. Last night, it had seemed perfectly fine to offer to take her there, but now I began to wonder if the late hour and the comforting darkness had made my thinking a little hazy. Either way, it was too late. We were going because I refused to back out.

After a few more minutes, Grace emerged from the bathroom and pulled on her boots, the only pair of shoes she had, and we headed out the front door of my hut. Blackwing was busy in the morning hours; people criss-crossing the pathways, some heading places, others on patrol, and still others just enjoying the sunshine. The few children there were in Blackwing would be in school. Or rather, our version of school, which was really just a makeshift building where someone taught them the basics that were necessary to survive.

'We'll stop and get some food before we go,' I told her. 'It's a bit of a hike from here.'

'All right,' she said, nodding casually as she observed the people moving around us. If I didn't know any better, I'd say she actually looked a little excited at the prospects of the day.

The mess hall was crowded as we moved in, those who ate lunch earlier in the day filling the space. Maisie was at her usual post behind the counter, serving what appeared to be sandwiches of some kind to those in line. I cut to the front, stepping in front of a disgruntled looking Barrow before leaning over to speak to Maisie.

'Maisie, could you get us something to take with us?' I asked, shooting an apologetic look at Barrow. Maisie nodded at me. The meals she gave us to go usually consisted of some type of jerky, a bottle of water, and whatever other side she had at the moment. Today it appeared to be the slightly overly ripe apples we'd managed to grow, which she hastily stuffed into a plastic bag.

'There ya go, now move on, I've got people to serve,' she said with a gentle smile. I was thankful she didn't ask where we were going, because it would have been difficult to explain. I nodded at her before stepping out of the line and rejoining Grace by the door.

'Let's go,' I said, tilting my head so she'd follow me back outside. She didn't respond but followed me as I led her through the remaining paths out of the camp until we were under the cover of the woods. Once again, I was grateful we didn't run into anyone else who might have asked where we were going. I didn't want people knowing I was sneaking off into the woods with Grace.

Wait. Not sneaking. Simply exploring. Right.

It took me a moment to remember the correct way to get to the pond, but as soon as my feet started in the right direction they seemed to remember. Years ago, Kit, Dax, and I had made this journey nearly every day. It had been our way to escape the pressure of camp and the rigorous schedule we were subjected to in order to become the skilled fighters we were now. A sudden thought occurred to me that might make this entire trip pointless and I wondered if we should just stop right there and turn around.

'Do you know how to swim?' I asked, glancing down at Grace as she hiked along beside me. Sweat had started to form across her brow from the effort of hiking in the heat of the day.

'Yeah,' she answered, surprising me. Most people didn't know how to swim due to lack of experience or necessity. 'There's this little creek that runs by Greystone,' she explained, brushing her hair out of her eyes. 'It's only there for a month or two when it rains a lot but my brother taught me when I was little.'

'The brother who left you,' I clarified. I didn't miss the glare she threw in my direction.

'Yes,' she answered bitterly.

'Why'd he leave?' It was something I'd been wondering ever since discovering his identity. His face flashed through my mind from the day I first saw her in the city. He'd left her without a second glance after she'd been shot. My blood boiled angrily at the mere thought; he seemed like a rather despicable person, in my opinion.

'I don't know,' she answered, her voice on edge. I could tell she didn't want to talk about it but I didn't understand her desire to go back with him if he was such a selfish person. Families are supposed to look out for their own, not leave them behind.

'He shouldn't have left you,' I told her. She didn't answer me as we carried on through the trees. It appeared as if she was deep in thought and I suddenly wished I hadn't brought it up. I wanted her to enjoy today, even if I was feeling apprehensive about the whole thing.

We travelled almost a mile in silence before she spoke, breaking the somewhat awkward quiet that had settled over us.

'Why are you taking me here?' she asked. I wondered how long she'd been thinking about asking. In all honesty, I didn't know why.

'I thought you'd like it,' I answered simply.

'Okay,' she replied.

'We're almost there. It's just through those trees,' I said, pointing ahead of us. A thick line of trees cut off our path, but it was possible to negotiate them to get to the pond's location. I paused, holding one to the side to allow Grace to brush past me. The moment ended when she continued to push through the branches until she was finally free of their ensnaring reach. I felt a smile pull at my lips when she sucked in a quiet breath as she took in the scene before us.

The pond wasn't huge, but there was no denying it was beautiful. High rocks from the base of the cliff stood on one side, a thin wall of water running off it to form a waterfall there. Trees bordered all the edges that weren't contained by the cliff, secluding it from the rest of the world. It wasn't particularly deep, but enough to be dangerous if one didn't know how to swim. Dax had figured out years ago that there was a natural drain in the bottom, carrying the water away to the river a few miles off and keeping it fresh.

'Wow,' she said quietly, observing the clear water as it

swirled gently in the pond. 'This is not what I was expecting.'

'What were you expecting?' I asked with an amused grin, taking in the way her eyes lit up and a smile pulled at her lips. Her eyes widened slightly as if she hadn't been expecting me to be watching her.

'I don't know. A mildew covered little sink hole, maybe?' she said with a quiet laugh.

'Ah, sorry to disappoint you,' I said. It felt strange to have such lighthearted conversation. Strange, but nice.

She laughed, which made my stomach flip. 'Well, let's go!'

Her hands gripped the hem of her shirt, hauling it easily over her head to reveal the simple black bra she wore. It didn't seem to occur to her what she was doing until she'd stripped off her boots and shorts, leaving her in just her undergarments while I stood next to her fully clothed.

'Um,' she muttered, glancing down at her body once before letting her hands drift over her flat stomach, as if embarrassed. Before I realised, I reached forward to grab her wrists, stopping her self-conscious movement to cover herself. Her body was beautiful and it would have been a shame to conceal it.

'Don't,' I said quietly.

She sucked in a breath quietly at the contact, eyes finding mine before her lip tugged into her mouth. I focused on her face as I released her to pull my shirt over my head and kick off my shoes. I pulled the gun from my waistband before setting it carefully on top of my shirt. She watched me slightly breathlessly as I pushed my hand through my hair, righting the strands after sending them sprawling across my forehead.

'You can swim, right?' I challenged, a ghost of a smirk on my face.

'Yeah, wh—'

She was cut off, however, by my hands landing on either side of her waist just long enough to throw her into the water. Her head was submerged completely while a laugh ripped from my lungs. She burst from the surface, hair slicked back while she sucked in a breath. I was relieved when a wide smile spread across her face before she began splashing as much water at me as she could. It was cold on my skin but felt amazing in contrast with the beating heat of the sun.

'You ass!' she called, treading water while she shook her head at me. I continued to laugh, the sound of it echoing off the cliffs on the other side of the pond.

'Sorry,' I said, sounding as unapologetic as possible. She splashed me again, causing my hands to rise in defence.

'Did you come here to swim or just to push me in?' she accused. I returned her stare before raising my arms over my head, bringing my hands together briefly before diving into the cool water. The force of the water pushed my hair back off my face and soothed my heated skin, bringing memories from years ago flooding back. Why had I waited so long to return?

I drew in a smooth breath when I broke through the surface, my body relishing the familiar feel. A certain happiness settled over me and I felt the apprehension slipping away. Grace's gaze was fixed on me when I opened my eyes but she quickly averted them to a tiny cliff that jutted out next to the waterfall.

'Do you want to jump off it?' I asked.

'Can you?' she asked. Her eyes searched the side of the cliff for a way to the perch.

'Yeah. There are little rocks and things you can use to climb up there. We used to do it all the time,' I told her. It wasn't really that high, only about ten metres, but it was high enough to be dangerous to jump off. She frowned at the side as if contemplating my offer. 'Unless you're afraid.'

'I'm not afraid,' she said instantly, snapping her gaze to me. She glared at me as if insulted I thought she'd be fearful. 'You do it, if you're so brave.'

I shrugged, sloshing the water around my chest. 'I've done it. When I was much younger, mind you.'

She frowned, her brows knitting together in defiance. 'Fine, just show me where to climb.'

'All right,' I said, grinning at her. I liked the way she seemed to be fearless, even though I knew it wasn't completely true. Whatever it was she was afraid of, I was yet to see it.

She swam past me, her shoulder almost brushing mine as she did so. I followed her easily, swimming along behind her as the clear water slid over her skin. It looked so smooth. I wondered what it'd be like to touch it. I dunked my head under the water, plastering my hair to my face as I tried to chase off the thoughts.

We reached the edge of the cliff and I swam to the easiest place to start. A tiny ledge stood a few feet out of the water that served as the basis for the climb.

'There,' I said, pointing. 'Once you're up there, you'll be able to see.'

She frowned up at it, reaching her arms up but falling short. She was treading water, so she had no leverage to boost herself higher. She sank down, huffing in frustration as she glared up at the ledge as if it were its fault. I watched in amusement as she tried and failed to hoist herself up. I glided toward her silently, moving to rest behind her back.

She let out a quiet gasp as my hands landed on her hips once more, this time letting my touch linger longer than required to throw her into the pond. It took everything in me not to spin her in my grasp and push her against the rock, but I resisted. Her skin was warm beneath my palms as my fingers dug into her soft skin, lifting her easily out of the water enough for her to grab the ledge. Reluctantly, I released her hips to allow her to pull herself up.

She looked down at me, her body dripping with glistening trails of water as she stood against the edge of the cliff.

'I had it,' she said stubbornly. I pushed back from the wall a bit and let out a quiet chuckle.

'Sure you did.'

Now that she'd made it onto the ledge, she scaled the rest of the wall quickly, reaching the final perch in a matter of seconds. She stood on the edge, her toes curling around the end of the rock as she stood for a few seconds, her gaze fixed on the water below.

'You're sure it's deep enough?' she called, an almost undetectable hint of nervousness in her voice. I rolled my eyes and grinned.

'I'm sure,' I called back. Her brows were furrowed together once more as she stared down and I suddenly felt bad for goading her into it. 'Grace!'

'What?' she said, still not looking at me as if afraid to move.

'You don't have to do it,' I said gently. I didn't want her to be afraid. She took a deep breath, her chest rising and falling drastically as she did so.

'I can do it,' she said, convincing herself just as much as me. She shut her eyes for a moment before she launched herself off the cliff, her arms crossed over her chest while squeezing her legs together tightly as she plummeted through the air. A loud cheer left my lips, proud of her for jumping as she hit the water with a relatively small splash.

I swam over to where she'd gone under, ready to congratulate her when she resurfaced. It was difficult to see under the water because of the ripples from the waterfall nearby, but I made it to the general vicinity of where she'd disappeared.

The wide grin on my face started to fade, however, with every passing second that went by without a reappearance. More than the adequate amount of time ticked by than it should have taken. Fear flooded through me, causing my heart rate to increase dramatically.

'Grace?' I yelled, spinning frantically in the water as I tried to see below the surface. I could see nothing but the water splashing around me. I ducked under, diving down below the surface as my hands reached out blindly but felt only the cool water. Even with my eyes open, I could see nothing.

I resurfaced, taking a gasp of air before shouting her name again. 'Grace!'

I dove under once more, swimming to a different area to search for her. My pulse pounded in my veins as panic rose. I was suddenly very afraid for her. What if she'd got hurt? What if she'd hit a rock I hadn't known about or hit the water wrong?

Air was sucked frantically into my lungs as I surfaced again, my eyes scanning the surface without success. If she got hurt because I'd teased her into jumping off the cliff . . .

Or worse . . .

I shook my head, shaking off the dark thought before I even allowed it to be completed. I'd find her.

'Grace!' I called again, my voice straining with fear now as I searched below the surface.

I was running out of ideas, giving in to the fear that she was lost to me when a pair of arms roped around my neck from behind, hauling me under the water once before releasing me. I emerged at the surface, running my hand angrily through my hair to see a hysterically laughing and very much alive Grace bobbing in front of me.

'What the hell was that?!' I demanded, suddenly furious at her. She continued to laugh, but I couldn't even enjoy the beautiful sound of it as it echoed around me because I was so livid.

'Oh, relax,' she said, finally managing to stop laughing enough to get a few words out. 'You should have seen your face!'

'That wasn't funny,' I said. I was surprised the water wasn't boiling around me.

'It was a little funny,' she goaded, splashing me gently. I continued to glare at her. 'Oh come on. Lighten up! It was a joke.'

'An awful joke,' I spat, swimming away from her. I wasn't surprised when she followed but was surprised when she caught me quickly and placed her hand on my shoulder to stop me. I felt a flash of annoyance when a spark of heat ran through me at her touch.

'Hayden,' she said, stilling my attempts to swim away from her. She still looked amused, but not as drastically so as before. 'I'm sorry, I thought it'd be funny.'

'I didn't find it very funny,' I muttered. It was hard to hear my voice over the splashing of the waterfall a few feet away from us. I saw the amusement slowly leach from her features.

'I didn't mean to scare you,' she said gently.

'I wasn't scared,' I lied, glowering. She frowned softly, her body floating only a few feet away from mine. Although furious with her, I had to push down the desire to reach out and touch her.

'Oh, okay,' she said quietly.

Her gaze dropped from mine and she floated farther away

177

from me. I felt a flare of frustration. Why had she pulled that stupid prank and put a weight on a potentially enjoyable afternoon? Not only had I actually just felt terrified that something had happened to her, but now I was feeling guilty for making her feel bad.

My hand drifted out beneath the water towards her, but not far enough for her to see as she moved even further from me. She disappeared behind the curtain of the waterfall. I groaned quietly, dunking my head once to try and relax. I exhaled beneath the surface, watching as the bubbles floated up around me.

Quit lying, Hayden.

I emerged and drew in a breath, replenishing the oxygen in my lungs. I couldn't see her past the curtain of water falling down, but I knew she was back there, between the waterfall and the cliff face. The water pelted down on my shoulders as I moved under the spray, holding my breath until I emerged on the other side. There she was, just as I had expected. She looked almost sad, which only made me feel even guiltier.

I held her gaze as I moved even closer, not stopping until my chest was only a foot from hers. She didn't speak as I approached, but I didn't miss the tiny catch in her breath when I invaded her space.

'I was afraid,' I whispered, the roar of the water nearly drowning me out. She didn't reply but didn't drop my gaze. Tentatively, my hand rose out of the water to brush my thumb along her cheek, her skin soft beneath my touch. 'I was afraid something had happened to you.'

I finally admitted my fear out loud, and it was a surprising relief.

'I'm sorry I scared you,' she said quietly. She looked like she might have been holding her breath. I sucked in a deep breath of my own, fighting every instinct to shut up and move away from her.

'You do scare me . . . in more ways than one.'

Her lips parted in surprise as she took in my words, and my body drifted involuntarily closer to hers so that only a few inches separated us now. My hand didn't leave her face as my fingers wove into her hair behind her ear.

'You scare me, too,' she admitted breathlessly. My heart flipped over at her confession.

'Are you scared now?' My eyes searched hers for signs that she wanted me to stop but all I saw was a quiet vulnerability in her beautiful green eyes.

'No,' she answered, not quite sounding convinced. A rattled breath drew from her chest as she watched me.

'I don't want you to ever be afraid with me,' I told her honestly. After the paralysing fear I'd just experienced, the last thing I ever wanted was for her to get hurt or be afraid.

'I'm not afraid,' she whispered. Her chest pressed against mine as the little space between us disappeared. My lips were so close to hers that I thought I might explode. When I felt the light pressure of her hand on my hip, I took it as permission. I closed the distance between us, pressing my lips into hers and felt the instant fireworks going off in the pit of my stomach as I surrendered to what seemed like an inevitable kiss.

Chapter 16 – Succumb

GRACE

The moment Hayden's lips landed on mine, I felt a shock travel from my lips through my entire body. The tension of the afternoon, filled with a vast range of emotions, had built up so much between us that I'd felt like I was going to physically combust if he didn't kiss me. Finally, he had, and I could not have been happier.

I could feel his body pressed tightly against mine, pushing me into the rock behind the waterfall while our feet managed to find purchase on some rocks beneath us. His hips were firm beneath my palms as I gripped his sides, unable to stop myself from pulling him closer. His hand on my cheek seemed to be burning through my skin, but that was nothing to the heat I felt from his lips on mine. It was like we'd been fully engulfed in flames, the connection between us stoking the fires until we were completely incinerated.

He caught my lower lip between his, pulling it back lightly before he dove in once more. I gasped when he pushed his tongue into my mouth slowly so that mine could meet it. I was acutely aware of his other hand on my ribs, the large palm covering much of my skin beneath the water. As much as I tried to ignore it, I couldn't stop the overwhelming desire for him to drop it lower on my body.

Without meaning to, my hips pushed forward off the

wall, pressing into him enough to send another jolt through my body. He reacted immediately, his lips moulded against mine roughly now, the thick desperation growing more and more by the second. My arms rose from the water, hands leaving his hips to tangle into his unruly mop of hair. The strands were tugged between my fingers as my fists closed around them, giving me more leverage to kiss him even harder.

A quiet groan fell from my lips when his hand slid down my side, snaking over my skin slowly until he reached low on my hip. He squeezed and pushed his hips against mine to put pressure on my centre, which nearly caused me to fall further into the water. My entire body was already tingling at the contact, but I wanted more.

God, how I ached for him to touch me.

A ragged breath left my lips when he tore his mouth from mine, dropping his lips to my neck to suck on the skin below my ear. My back arched off the rock into him, setting me on fire little by little with every gently sponged kiss to my throat. When I felt his thumb drag slowly below the band of my pants, I felt my heart pound even harder.

'Grace . . .' he breathed against my neck. The sound of him saying my name sent a shiver through my body, making me want him even more than I already did. I couldn't even catch enough breath to reply.

His thumb repeated the movement, a little lower than he had the first time. When I didn't stop him, he brought his hand between my legs, cupping me over the thin material around my centre. A loud gasp from my lips caused him to bring his head up from my neck. His eyes found mine while his fingers readjusted their pressure between my legs. I bit my lower lip into my mouth to cut off the guttural groan that tried to escape at his touch.

He watched my reaction, searching for signs to stop. My entire body felt like it was melting under his gaze as his hand stayed on me, and he hadn't even touched me yet, not really. When I couldn't take his gentle teasing any longer, I pushed forward, reconnecting our lips and giving him permission to do what he was so close to doing. He recognised my silent statement instantly, returning the kiss hungrily as his fingers pulled away from me.

The momentary disappointment at the loss of his touch was filled quickly, however, when he slipped his hand beneath the thin material. I gasped into our kiss when I felt his fingers curl over my centre, dragging slowly until he reached the sensitive bunch of nerves. My arms wound tightly around his neck, hauling his chest as tightly into mine as I could manage with his hand between us.

A low whine escaped my throat when his thumb circled around my clit, putting the exact amount of pressure on it to drive my nerves into a frenzy. I let my tongue push against his in rhythm with the movements of his fingers. After a few moments of testing my nerves, I felt a finger trace around my entrance, teasing me lightly before pushing in all the way to fill me.

'Oh god,' I mumbled, my words stifled by our kiss. This seemed to encourage him, because his fingers slid in and out a few times, then stretched me deliciously, curling up inside me to hit the pressure points he knew were there.

In my haze, my back arched off the wall and my breathing was ragged as I ripped one of my hands from his hair. My palm travelled quickly down his chest, the firm muscles beneath it contracting and expanding quickly as his uneven breathing matched mine. My hand had just made it to the waistband of his shorts when he broke our kiss.

'Don't,' he breathed, hardly pausing before diving back in to kiss me again. His tongue pushed against mine roughly while his fingers continued to pump in and out of me, his thumb flicking over my clit torturously.

'Why?' I breathed, unable to understand why he wouldn't let me.

'Not yet,' he answered against my mouth. His tugged back my lip once more before breaking the kiss and looking at me. 'I just want to feel you.'

I sucked in a harsh breath at his words, beyond enthralled by them and the way his hand was working magic on me. I tried to hold his gaze as my breathing grew more and more desperate, but I knew I was almost at the edge and wouldn't be able to hold on much longer. He watched me closely as his fingers moved inside me, calculating exactly what every action he made did to me.

He seemed to sense I was ever so close to finishing. His lips crashed back into mine, my hands returning to tangle into his hair as his forearm flexed tightly between us to push his fingers into me again and again. With one more circle of his thumb over my bundle of nerves, I was pushed over the edge as my release flooded through me.

'Hayden—' my words were cut off, however, by the feelings ripping through my body.

My entire body shook between his and the rock, our kiss difficult to maintain as I gasped for air. My arms felt like noodles as they struggled to remain around his neck. His fingers worked me until he pulled his lips from mine, drawing back enough to watch my face as I came down from my high. My eyes closed lazily and my head tilted back against the rock as I felt the flush creeping up my skin.

'Holy shit,' I breathed. I jumped slightly when I felt his lips press at the base of my throat once, sending a wave of heat through my sensitive body. I finally managed to open my eyes enough to meet his heated gaze.

'You good?' he dared.

'I'm great,' I said honestly. I was still feeling the effects and I felt like I was about to float away, right out from behind the waterfall.

'Were you . . . okay with that?' he asked, his eyes blazing into mine.

'If I wasn't okay with it I would have stopped you,' I said, my voice still breathless as I tried to recover. He studied me a bit further, pausing before he spoke again.

'Good,' he said simply, his voice slightly deeper than usual. Our gaze stayed connected for a few quiet moments, a soft, half-smile on his face, before he spoke again.

'We should get back.'

I blinked, somewhat surprised but nodded in agreement. 'Yeah, okay.'

He nodded. His hand rose from the water, hesitating in the air between us before he brought it to my face to drag his thumb across my lip. My breath hitched in my throat as his eyes focused on my lips, a slight smirk on his features once more.

'Let's go.'

He withdrew his hand, turning around to disappear through the spray of the waterfall. I took a moment to suck in a deep breath and try to clear the haze that had settled over me, but it did little to help. I still felt like I was floating as I followed him through the water, swimming after him as he made his way back across the small pond.

I watched the muscles in his shoulders tighten and relax as he pulled himself through the water. Now that we were out in the open once more, it seemed like the intimacy we'd shared had vanished.

I reached the edge soon after he did and realised that we'd brought no towels. I frowned as I picked up my clothes, not exactly thrilled that they would get wet but too self-conscious to walk back to the camp in my underwear. I even felt self-conscious standing in front of Hayden now, until the moment before we'd got in the lake flashed through my mind: he'd stopped me from covering myself. He'd looked at me like I was beautiful.

'We can eat while we walk back,' Hayden said, breaking the silence.

'Okay,' I replied as I pulled my clothes back on. Hayden caught my gaze but averted it when he saw me pulling my shirt back over my head, refocusing his attention on getting dressed once more. After a few more minutes, we were both fully dressed again and Hayden had slipped his gun back into the waistband of his shorts. He handed me one of the lunches and we took off, heading back to Blackwing.

I felt like I should say something as we walked, but nothing came to mind. It was so strange how one minute Hayden could be kissing me and touching me then the next seem like he was in a totally different world. He didn't speak as we moved through the trees, focusing on letting his eyes scan for potential threats and eating the sandwich Maisie had packed for him. I ate, too, realising just how hungry I had been as I devoured the food.

After nearly an hour of walking with no more than five words spoken between us, I began to feel the overwhelming urge to say anything to break the silence.

'What do we have to do today?' I asked, grimacing at my own lame attempt at conversation.

'Nothing, really,' he answered, shrugging. 'I just don't like to be away from camp for too long in case something goes wrong.'

'Has something gone wrong before while you've been gone?' I asked, wondering what had put this belief in place.

'Yes,' he answered simply, not offering any further details. He glanced at me and seemed to realise I was just trying to make conversation. 'Sorry.'

'Sorry for what?' I asked, frowning in confusion.

'Sorry I'm not good at this.'

'At what?'

'Talking.'

'You're fine at talking when you don't mean to,' I laughed. It was when I caught him off guard that he revealed the most to me, as if he wasn't really aware he was sharing anything until it was too late.

'When I don't mean to,' he repeated, pondering my words.

'Mmhmm,' I confirmed, nodding.

'Well you're not great at it either,' he said. I glanced at him to see a ghost of a smile on his face, telling me he was teasing.

'You're not wrong,' I laughed. I was very aware of how terrible I was at sharing bits of myself. Just about the only personal thing I'd revealed to him was the identity of my brother. Everything else he'd learned about me had been through observation or through the very limited conversations we usually had. He shot me a slow smile, which I returned, glad to have finally broken the silence between us.

Huts started to come into view as we broke through the tree line, returning finally to Blackwing. I was relieved when things seemed calm, Hayden's comment about things going wrong before setting me slightly on edge. We passed a few huts before we made it back to the main part of the camp, where people continued to go about their lives. We were

186

just passing the hospital when someone shouted Hayden's name.

'Hayden!'

We both turned toward the direction of the sound to see Docc emerging from the infirmary.

'Docc, what's going on?' Hayden asked, concern flashing across his features.

'It's Kit,' he said, his face solemn. Fear flooded through me suddenly at his words. Hayden stiffened beside me tensely. 'He's got an infection and I don't have the right meds to treat it.'

'How bad is it?' Hayden asked seriously.

'I can cure it if I get the meds but I'll need them as soon as possible,' Docc said, rubbing his hands together anxiously.

'What do you need? I'll go on a run right now,' Hayden said quickly.

'I need antibiotics,' Docc said, handing Hayden a piece of paper. 'But there's bad news.'

'More bad news?' Hayden asked in frustration, pushing his hand through his hair, which had nearly dried now.

'I know for a fact Whetland cleaned out the city. They've got nearly all of it in their bunker.'

'Whetland?' Hayden repeated angrily. 'It takes hours to get there!'

'I know,' Docc said gravely.

'Can he make it that long?' Hayden asked, fear pinching his voice.

'I certainly hope so. We can't waste any more time. I've already got Dax preparing to go. You three should leave as soon as he's ready.'

'Okay,' Hayden said, nodding quickly. 'We'll hurry.'

'Good luck. Stay safe,' Docc said, nodding briefly at me before retreating in to the infirmary.

'Son of a bitch,' Hayden muttered, running his hand down his face in exasperation. 'Come on, let's go.'

He turned to head towards the raid building at the end of the path and I quickly followed.

'Hayden,' I started.

'What?' he snapped, his body tense as he stalked down the path. I ignored his rude tone, sure it wasn't personal.

'Let me see the list,' I requested. 'I might know where to find some of it closer than Whetland.'

Whetland was another camp just like Blackwing and Greystone. It was much farther away, however, and by far the fastest way to get to it was to go through the city, even if it was more dangerous. If we could avoid it, I would do anything I could. Hayden didn't speak as he handed me the list. My eyes scanned over the antibiotics Docc had requested, recognising all of them. Disappointment flashed through me, however, as I realised what Docc had said was true; the only place I knew of with these medications was Whetland.

'Shit,' I muttered, handing it back to Hayden. He looked at me tensely as we pushed through the door to the raid building, where we were greeted with a small stack of supplies Dax had gathered.

'Hey,' Dax said, casting a look over his shoulder from where he stood gathering supplies at a gun case. He turned, bringing two 9mm pistols with him. He was about to hand one to Hayden when his hand flashed behind his back, gripping the gun he already carried and waving it slightly so Dax could see.

'Never mind,' Dax muttered, starting to turn back.

'Wait,' Hayden said, stilling him. 'Give it to Grace.'

Was he finally going to trust me with a weapon?

'What?' Dax said through gritted teeth.

'We're down Kit and she's useless without a weapon,' Hayden explained. I ignored the slight sting of his insult when he called me useless but knew he was essentially right. It was hard to fight bullets with a fist.

Dax looked at us sceptically before handing the gun to me. The weight of it felt wonderfully familiar in my hand, and for the first time since I'd arrived at Blackwing, I didn't feel so utterly vulnerable. Finally, I had a real way to protect myself and those around me. I blinked suddenly as I realised that meant Hayden and Dax, and that I very much wanted to protect them.

'If you shoot me, I'm going to kill you,' Dax muttered, a half smile on his face lightening the dark words. 'I'll get the truck while you guys get whatever else you need.'

'Sounds good,' Hayden said, nodding. Dax left, leaving us alone in the raid room. Hayden looked at me apprehensively, as if questioning his decision to give me a weapon. I put the safety on and stuck it behind my back, tucking it into my waistband as Hayden often did. The cool metal felt reassuring against my back.

'I'm not going to shoot you guys,' I told him, rolling my eyes.

'I know,' Hayden said, letting his gaze linger on me for a few more seconds before moving to retrieve whatever else he needed. He moved through the room, throwing supplies into two separate backpacks before handing one to me. I looked inside to see more ammunition, two bottles of water, some food, a flashlight, and a small first aid kit. Light supplies for a long run, but enough to get us through it.

I heard the roar of the truck outside, telling me Dax had arrived. I was about to head toward the door when Hayden stopped me, his hand falling on my forearm lightly as his gaze reconnected with mine.

'Be careful,' he said quietly, his brows lowered as he watched me. My breath caught in my throat at his expression of concern.

'You too,' I replied, holding his gaze. He pinched his lips together once and nodded before dropping his hand from my arm to gather the supplies Dax had left on the floor. I held the door for him as he carried them outside and threw them in the truck, taking his place behind the wheel while Dax switched to the passenger seat. I jumped in the backseat and was immediately greeted with the harsh scent of bleach, reminding me of the blood that had been spilt and apparently cleaned up in the backseat the last time we'd been in this vehicle.

Hayden shifted the truck into drive, peeling away from the buildings as people cleared the way for us. No one spoke as we drove, everyone too tense for words. I tried not to think about how our last trip into the city had gone, but it was impossible as we grew closer and closer. I desperately wished that there was another way to get to Whetland other than going through the city, but there was no other option. To go around would take at least twice as long, which was time we did not have.

Sooner than I realised, we were surrounded by the shattered shells of buildings as we entered the edges of the city. Hayden swerved easily around piles of rubble that littered the streets, avoiding the chunks of cement and metal that were in the way.

'Watch out for Brutes,' Hayden muttered to Dax and I. I nodded even though he wouldn't see and reached behind me to pull the gun I'd been awarded to have it ready. We were entering the heart of the city now, where the most dangerous of the Brutes lurked. They were relatively inactive during the day, preferring to do their dirty work at night, but they wouldn't hesitate if they got the opportunity to take us out no matter what time of day it was.

The light of the day was quickly slipping away as evening approached, making me even more anxious than I already was. Hayden continued to fly through the city, and my adrenaline pumped even harder. I wasn't afraid to go into the city, but I'd be lying if I said it didn't put me on edge. As we blew past an alley, I caught a glimpse of three or four people huddled against the wall.

'In that alley,' I said, turning around to see if they'd emerged. 'They're not following, though.'

'Okay,' was all Hayden said. I noticed his jaw was clenched tightly and his knuckles were white on the steering wheel.

A loud bang sounded suddenly, different from that of a gunshot. The car sputtered as steam started to leak from beneath the hood, the engine stalling enough to stop the force of the wheels. Hayden swore loudly as he urged the car to continue, but to no avail. We were quickly losing speed, slowing down until we rolled to a complete stop in the middle of the street. The engine clunked loudly before shutting down altogether.

'No, no, no!' Hayden shouted, pounding his fist against the steering wheel. 'You've gotta be kidding me!'

'Shit,' Dax muttered, leaning forward to look at the hood through the windshield. I glanced around, certain we were going to be accosted by Brutes at any second.

'We have to get out of the street,' I said, very aware of the quickly slipping daylight. The last thing we wanted to do was get caught in the middle of the street in the city at night.

'No, we can fix it and keep going,' Hayden said determinedly. He tried to turn the key over but no sound came from the engine. He slapped his hand against the wheel again in frustration.

'Hayden, I don't know if I can fix it before dark,' Dax said tightly. 'I don't even know what's wrong and the sun's almost down. We can't risk it.'

'God dammit,' Hayden muttered, knowing we were right. 'Okay, get the stuff and we'll head into that building.'

He pointed at one across the street that had several floors. Dax and I nodded, jumping into action to gather the supplies as quickly as possible.

As much as we didn't like it, it looked like we were about to spend a night in the middle of the city. Perfect.

Chapter 17 – Never
GRACE

The three of us sprinted across the street as quickly and quietly as we could, our eyes constantly scanning for incoming threats. Luckily, there seemed to be no one around to witness our mishap or notice that we were here. The building Hayden had chosen was far enough away from where the truck had broken down so it wouldn't be obvious seeing as there were several other options closer.

Hayden paused at the door, backpack slung over his broad shoulders and gun drawn as he peered cautiously into the doorframe that was cracked open. It appeared to be some type of abandoned office building, three storeys high and not very wide. It wouldn't take long to sweep, which was another reason why I suspected he chose it.

He kept his gun raised as he pushed the door open slowly, not making any noise as he entered the building. I followed with Dax bringing up the rear, aiming our guns in different directions as we moved single file through the door. Hayden flicked his head to the side, indicating that before moving upward we should move through the entire ground floor in case someone was lurking there. I felt the thrill of actually doing something; I hadn't realised how much I'd missed the excitement and danger of a raid after being in Blackwing for so long. Despite breaking down, this was the first raid I'd gone on with Hayden where I actually felt like I had some control. The gun was probably helping significantly with that.

My eyes scanned the quickly darkening building while my gun swept around me, searching for targets or lurking danger. The bag on my back was lighter than I would have liked; lighter meant we didn't have many supplies, and we hadn't planned on staying overnight anywhere. I knew Hayden had hoped to make the trip there and back without stopping, making things like blankets and warmer clothing unnecessary, but he also hadn't planned on the truck breaking down in the middle of the city.

After moving through the heavily ransacked ground floor, it quickly became clear that there was nobody there. We kept our guns raised, however, as Hayden made his way back to the front door. We watched silently as he examined the door for a way to lock it, frowning when he saw the deadbolt hanging off the door after being broken. The muscles in his arms strained as he pushed it closed, the door banging against its warped frame. I cringed at the noise, as did Dax beside me.

'Nice,' Dax muttered, earning a glare from Hayden. My eyes scanned the ground for something to use to keep it shut before landing on a large filing cabinet tipped over on the ground.

'Help me,' I said, nodding at the heavy piece of equipment. I shoved my gun into my waistband. Hayden did the same, then grabbed the side of the metal box and helped me drag it in front of the door, blocking it from being opened from the outside.

'Good idea,' he whispered, nodding. 'Let's check the rest.'

I nodded, following him to a set of stairs that led to the first and second floors. The first floor consisted of more offices, similar to the ground floor, also showing no signs of being occupied. We continued on to the top floor which was separated into three different rooms: a bathroom, a large meeting room, and an office much larger than those on the floor below. It was slightly cleaner up here, as if raiders hadn't bothered to climb to the second floor to check for supplies before abandoning the building.

Hayden shifted the door to the bathroom open with his foot, aiming his gun into the dark room but finding no one. It quickly became apparent that the meeting room and the office were also empty, at which everyone breathed a quiet sigh of relief.

'This is as good as we could have hoped for,' Dax said, shrugging. He plopped down in the large chair that sat behind a handsome wooden desk as we let our weapons down for the first time since ascending the stairs. 'Suits me, doesn't it?'

He shot a satisfied grin at Hayden and me, to which I couldn't help but chuckle. Even in the most stressful of circumstances, Dax still managed to be light-hearted. He folded his arms behind his head and leaned back in the chair, stretching, while Hayden moved to the window to observe the street below.

'How long do you think you'll need to fix the truck?' he asked, searching for Brutes or other enemies but apparently he saw none because he raised no alarm.

'Depends what's wrong with it,' Dax said, shrugging.

The large desk sat in the middle, with two other chairs across from it. A trophy case of relatively useless junk stood with several large filing cabinets on the other side. I frowned as I realised there was nothing here that would really benefit us in any way besides the shelter of the building itself. There wasn't even a couch to sleep on.

I jumped as Hayden yanked the curtains closed, blocking

out what little remained of the sun's light. I moved to sit on the chair across from Dax, bumping into the desk in the darkness on my way.

'Ow,' I muttered, earning a laugh from Dax.

'Shut it,' I muttered with a hint of a grin nonetheless. I pulled off my backpack and set it between my feet to search for the flashlight I knew Hayden had packed. Dax found his before me because a small beam of light quickly illuminated the room, showing Hayden moving deftly to sit next to me on the remaining chair. It creaked when he sat down, causing his features to frown in distaste.

'So what happens now? We just wait until the sun comes up again?' I asked. I'd never actually got stuck in the city overnight but I knew the last thing you wanted to do was be outside when it got dark.

'Yeah, I suppose so,' Hayden said. He sounded reluctant, but it was simply too dangerous to try and fix the truck in the dark. Dax ignored us as he began rummaging through the desk, pulling out the drawers to search them.

'You can eat if you're hungry,' Hayden told me, nodding at my backpack.

'I'm all right,' I answered. He glanced at me and took a deep breath as if considering saying something before he thought better of it.

'Jackpot!' Dax exclaimed suddenly, emerging from where he'd been bent over to dig through a drawer. He grinned wildly as he raised his fist, clutching a brown bottle filled nearly completely with liquid. Whisky.

'This raid just got a lot more fun,' he said, setting it down on the table and running his hands down the sides reverently. 'I haven't had a drink in ages.'

'No way,' Hayden said, shaking his head sternly. 'Besides, you drank with Kit when he was in the infirmary.'

'No, I didn't. Kit drank it all, the lush,' he said, ignoring Hayden's stern look as he started to twist the top off. He gritted his teeth as he fought the years that had tightened the lid. With a triumphant cheer, he finally managed to unscrew with a quiet pop.

'No, Dax, we need to stay sharp,' Hayden said disapprovingly. 'We're in the middle of the city and you want to get drunk? That's a terrible idea.'

'Not drunk, just a drink,' Dax argued, drawing the bottle closer to him as if afraid Hayden would take it away. 'If you don't want any, fine. Grace and I can drink on our own, right, Grace?'

He surprised me by turning his gaze to me and grinning conspiratorially.

'Um . . .' I said, unsure of what to do. On the one hand, a drink sounded exactly like what I needed after such an emotionally draining day, but on the other, I didn't want to piss Hayden off. We were relatively safe in this building. One drink couldn't hurt . . .

Hayden glared at me as if he could see my inner thought process, which cemented my decision. I may have been his prisoner, technically, but after today I had to think that term was more loosely defined now. Hayden wasn't in control of my every move.

'Sure, let's have a drink, Dax,' I said, grinning at him. Hayden sighed heavily at my decision as he dug through his backpack, dropping his gaze from me. He rummaged around until he pulled out a candle and a book of matches, setting it down on the desk and lighting it so Dax could turn out his flashlight. Soft light flickered around the room, illuminating the desk and a few feet around us but leaving the rest of the room in relative darkness.

'Come on, Hayden, loosen up,' Dax said, grinning at him

as he raised the bottle to his lips and tilted it back. Liquid flowed into his mouth before he lowered it, and he grimaced as the bitter spirits slid past his tongue. He swallowed and blew out a heavy breath, whistling quietly as he raised his eyebrows.

'Hope you can handle your liquor, Grace,' he said, wiping his lips on the back of his hand. 'Strong stuff, that is.'

He passed it to me and I raised it to my nose to take a whiff. I immediately regretted it as the fiery stench entered my nostrils, surely burning off the top layer of cells there. I could feel Hayden watching me and was determined to drink the stuff without looking like a little girl, so I raised the bottle to my lips and tilted it back. It tasted like pure acid, making my stomach churn, but I managed to keep a straight face somehow as I swallowed my share.

'Hell yeah,' Dax said happily, clearly impressed as I lowered the bottle and passed it to Hayden. I was surprised when he accepted it and was pleased to see a look of slight shock on his face. 'Come on, Hayden. Don't make us drink alone. Just have one. Or two,' said Dax.

'Yeah, come on, Hayden,' I teased, grinning at him softly. I saw the tiniest spark of amusement flicker in his eyes before he shook his head and let out a low chuckle.

'Fine. You two are bad influences,' he muttered. He took a sip, handling it much better than Dax and I had. The only reaction Hayden gave was the tiniest of grimaces after he passed the bottle back to Dax, the residual burn of the liquor finally getting to him.

Dax let out a quiet whoop of victory as he accepted the bottle, pausing once it was in his hands.

'I need a moment,' he said, grinning sheepishly. He blew out a deep breath as if forcing his stomach to settle from the first sip he'd had.

'Knew you wouldn't stop at one,' Hayden muttered, leaning back in his chair.

'One sip hardly counts as a drink. No glasses means I get at least a few swigs,' he argued lightly. 'We've got some time to kill, wanna make this more fun?'

'No,' Hayden replied flatly. 'This is a raid. It's not supposed to be fun.'

'What'd you have in mind?' I asked. Having some motivation to drink more of the whisky might be helpful because I didn't know if I could choke down any more on my own. Hayden glared at me again, which I ignored as I glanced at Dax across the soft lighting.

'Never have I ever,' Dax said. 'Have you played before?'

'No,' I said. 'I've never played anything before.'

'That's the idea. You just say something you've never done and if we've done it, we have to drink,' he explained.

'Doesn't sound like much of a game,' Hayden muttered. He seemed very determined to have a bad time, which I guess was understandable considering the nature of our stay in the building.

'Let's try it,' I appealed. Hayden sighed and rolled his eyes before leaning forward as if he was indulging me.

'Fine. You first then, fratboy,' he said to Dax. It was such a strange reference for Hayden to use given the world we lived in now. I vaguely remembered my father saying something about that. Such things were lost long ago and not everyone would even understand what he meant these days.

'All right,' Dax said, rubbing the tips of his fingers together as he glanced back and forth between Hayden and me with a conspiratorial look.

'I've never lived in Greystone,' he said finally, looking pointedly at me. I rolled my eyes.

'Really?'

'Really. Drink up, mate,' he said smugly as he slid the bottle across the table at me. I could feel Hayden's eyes on me as I lifted the bottle and took a swig, the second time burning just as much as the first. My composure slipped more this time as I grimaced while I swallowed before putting the bottle back on the table.

'My turn?' I asked. Dax nodded. I racked my brain for something I could get them both with. 'I've never . . . slept with a girl.'

Dax snorted before taking the bottle enthusiastically to take a swig before pushing it toward Hayden. I felt my stomach twist uneasily as Hayden then took a drink, confirming what I'd suspected but didn't want to ask outright. So he *had* slept with someone before. It wasn't surprising given what he'd done to me earlier today; I had been with others before as well. My mind instantly wandered to the girls in Blackwing to try and figure out who it could have been. A terrible thought struck me that the person might no longer be there, so I shook my head and forced my train of thought elsewhere.

'Hayden, you go,' I said, nodding at him.

'All right. I've never crashed a perfectly good vehicle into a tree because I thought there was a spider on my face,' Hayden said, smirking across the table at Dax.

'That was *one time* and there *was* a spider on my face, thank you very much,' Dax retorted immediately, pointing a finger at Hayden before grinning and taking the bottle reluctantly. 'I'd like to see you keep your cool with that thing crawling on you.'

Hayden let out the first real laugh since we'd arrived, face splitting into a grin as he watched Dax take another swig. Dimples dotted into his cheeks and I was momentarily mesmerised by how beautiful he looked. I wished he'd smile more.

As if he could feel my gaze, Hayden's eyes darted to meet mine. I blinked and sucked in a quiet breath at getting caught but didn't divert my attention. His smile softened from one of amusement to one of contentment.

'My turn. I've never secretly wanted the person I'm supposed to be holding captive,' Dax said. I sucked in another breath as I jerked my gaze to Dax, just as Hayden did beside me. He watched us both with a smug grin on his face, clearly pleased at our reaction. Was Dax just trying to make us uncomfortable or did he really think that Hayden wanted me just from observing us? Did Hayden want me at all or were our moments together simply instances of weakness when he caved in to something he didn't want to?

We were both silent as Dax grinned at us. Hayden opened his mouth to reply, but was cut off by a sudden loud clang echoing from the street.

'Shit,' he muttered, blowing out the candle instantly and rising from his chair to move toward the window. Dax and I followed, kneeling so our faces were at the bottom of the window. Hayden picked up the curtain just enough to glance out at the street and I could see light reflecting off his eyes. Dax and I copied him.

Down on the street below, we could see our truck parked about halfway to the next junction. The light that was reflecting in Hayden's eyes came from lanterns being carried by four burly, rough-looking men. One was poking around our truck, trying to force his way inside while the other three stood and watched.

'Brutes,' I muttered.

Hayden nodded beside me. The Brute closest to the truck had a coat hanger and was attempting to shove it down the window to unlock the door, but appeared to be struggling. One of the others shouted something, his words muffled. They all appeared impatient and agitated as they looked on, alternating between keeping watch and observing the man struggle with the lock.

'If they get in, they'll strip it then we'll be screwed for sure,' Hayden whispered. It probably wasn't necessary to whisper, but the vicinity of the Brutes had put everyone on edge.

'Does the window open?' I asked. 'We can shoot them from here.'

Dax nodded silently, agreeing with me as Hayden looked up to inspect the window.

'I think it'll open,' he said, biting his lip as he reached upward to fidget with the lock. He flicked it open and flinched as it snapped loudly. The Brutes didn't appear to notice as they continued to bicker on the street below. Hayden then dug his fingers under the ledge and began to push it upward slowly, silently.

'We'll all have to shoot at once,' Dax said. 'And someone will have to take two.'

I nodded, agreeing. If we shot one at a time, the odds of one of them getting away and finding our location was much higher. We moved silently, aligning ourselves by the window as we all aimed our guns out the window.

'I got the far left, Grace you take the next one, Dax you get the two on the right,' Hayden instructed in a hushed tone, aiming his pistol while closing an eye and chewing on his lip.

'Got it,' I whispered as Dax nodded.

'On three,' Hayden lulled. 'One, two . . . three.'

Three bangs echoed around the street as three targets fell, all of us hitting who we'd aimed at. The final Brute, who'd been picking at the lock, bolted upright and spun around, searching for signs of enemies. His eyes had just landed on our window when Dax fired again, hitting him square in the chest. He dropped to the ground.

Hayden sighed heavily beside me, waiting for them to move. They didn't. He sighed again as he pulled the window shut, locking it. He searched the street for signs of any more Brutes, but none came. It was rare for them to travel in groups larger than two or three, much less four or more. It wasn't surprising that no one came to investigate the shots.

Hayden righted the curtain and moved back to his chair. He sat down and pushed his hand through his hair.

'That's enough for tonight,' he said heavily, nodding at the bottle. Dax didn't argue as he screwed the lid back on.

'All right,' he said.

An invisible weight seemed to settle on Hayden's shoulders. It wasn't the first time I'd noticed this when someone lost their life. No matter who it was, no matter what the circumstance, I knew it bothered Hayden. I hadn't had a second thought about killing the Brutes and even now, after shooting one, felt no remorse for them. Hayden, however, was troubled by it. Despite his high position in the camp and the vast number of raids he'd been on, killing still ate away at him.

I suddenly felt guilty for putting that responsibility on him. I could have volunteered to take the first two and spared Hayden the gore of doing it himself, but I knew he wouldn't have liked it. It was like what we'd just done had drained the light out of him, even if it had been necessary for our survival. Four people had just died without a second thought from Dax and I while Hayden was clearly subdued by it. Dax's words from a few days ago came back to me and

I knew he was right: Hayden really was better than the rest of us.

'Hayden . . .' I wanted to console him in some way but didn't know how. His face was set in a serious expression as he settled back into his chair, spinning it so he was facing the door.

'You two get some sleep. I'll take the first watch,' he said slowly, ignoring me. I didn't know what to say to him without embarrassing him in front of Dax, who apparently already suspected there was something going on.

Was there?

'Goodnight, Grace,' Hayden said when I didn't move, clearly dismissing me. He didn't look at me but I knew he could feel me watching him. I sighed.

'Goodnight, Hayden.'

I moved to join Dax where he'd settled between the desk and the wall with the window, the opposite side to where Hayden sat facing the door on the other side of the desk. Dax shot me a look as if he was very familiar with this mood of Hayden's. I pinched my lips together and shrugged lightly, returning his silent sentiment even though Hayden couldn't see us.

'Wake me in two hours, mate,' he called to Hayden as he settled on the floor, stretching his arms over his head before settling them over his flat stomach. Just like that, he closed his eyes and presumably fell asleep. No second thoughts, no ghosts to haunt him and keep him awake, nothing. Dax was out within seconds.

I lay a few feet away from him and attempted to get settled on the floor, but it was difficult. The floor was made of a pathetic excuse for carpet and the temperature was dropping quickly, making for very uncomfortable sleeping conditions. Despite the discomfort, however, the exhaustion of my body quickly took over, sending me plummeting into the darkness of sleep just like Dax a few feet away from me. My last thought before I succumbed to sleep was of Hayden and how I wished there was something I could do to lighten the load on his shoulders.

I felt like either minutes or days had passed when I was jostled lightly from my sleep. My eyes remained closed as I became aware of my own arms wrapped tightly around myself as I subconsciously tried to fend off the cold that had settled over the room. I lay stiffly on my side, unaware of what exactly had awoken me until I heard muffled voices.

'Hayden, mate, come on. You've got to get some sleep,' Dax whispered. He sounded farther away and I realised that his getting up must have been what had awoken me. I didn't move, desperate for a few more hours of sleep though I was doubtful I'd get any thanks to the cold that had settled into my bones.

'I'm fine,' Hayden replied, his voice hushed and deep.

'Nah, look, you did your turn now let me. I feel weird sleeping next to your girl, anyway,' Dax said.

'She's not my girl,' Hayden replied, a little too quickly. My heart jumped and I tried to ignore the disappointment in my gut at Hayden's denial.

'Whatever, either way, it's my turn. Now go sleep,' Dax said. I heard some rustling and the image of Dax physically trying to shove Hayden out of the chair floated through my brain, almost making me chuckle. A dull thud sounded followed by a quiet 'ow' from Dax as Hayden must have hit him softly. The chair squeaked, however, and I heard Hayden whisper once more.

'Fine. But wake me as soon as it starts getting light,' Hayden said.

'All right,' Dax replied, settling into the chair.

I heard Hayden's feet carry him closer as they padded softly on the carpet. I could feel him as he approached, pausing as he stood next to me while I pretended to be asleep. My body tensed slightly as he lowered himself next to me, close enough for me to feel his heat but not close enough to actually be touching me. I tried to keep my breathing low and even to make it look like I was asleep as I heard him let out a low sigh.

I jumped when I felt him roll sideways, his chest colliding lightly with my back. His arm snaked over my waist, pulling me into him and warming me instantly both inside and out. It was all I could do not to gasp when I felt his lips tickle gently at my ear.

'You're shit at that,' he whispered lowly, the phrase jogging a memory of when he'd said that to me before. 'Pretending to be asleep.'

I didn't reply but allowed the soft smile to pull at my lips, a grin stretching across my face in gentle amusement. My hand shifted to cover his, fingers tangling with his as my palm rested on the back of his hand. I squeezed it lightly in reply, relaxing a bit more into him as I let his warmth seep into me and lull me back to sleep. The last thing I felt before sleep pulled me back under was the gentle touch of his lips to the back of my neck. Just once, just for a second, but enough to feel and burn into my skin forever.

Chapter 18 – Care
HAYDEN

Warm.

That was the first thing I felt when I was slowly pulled from sleep; I was warm. The second thing I noticed was the soft tickle of breath washing over my neck, the pattern slow and even thanks to her current state. Grace was curled into me, chest pressed to mine and face buried in my neck. We both lay on our sides, facing each other, and I suddenly became aware of my arms cradled around her, as if protecting her from the terrors of the night.

Her head rested on my bicep while my arm curled upward, falling over her neck to cradle her to me while my other was slung easily around her waist, connecting us. Her arms were tucked between us, twisted in the fabric of my shirt as if she'd attempted to draw herself closer without realising while she slept.

I could feel the dull thumping of her heart and the heat of her body against mine; for a moment, I allowed myself to think we could stay like this all day – warm, lazy, with no responsibilities, but I quickly remembered our reason for being in that position in the first place. We were here to save Kit.

I heard a soft disturbance from the other side of the desk, telling me Dax was awake. My instinct told me to separate myself from Grace and hide it from him, but a weaker part of me very much wanted to not care at all what Dax thought. The weaker side of me won out, because my arms stayed curled around Grace's body.

Light began peeking through the small cracks in the curtains and I knew we'd have to get up soon, especially if Dax was already up. I was saved from waking Grace when I noticed a slight shift in her breathing, the momentary tensing of her muscles telling me she was awake before she remembered where she was and who was holding her. She relaxed once more. A breath I hadn't been aware I was holding blew out softly between my lips.

Without a word, my arms tightened, hugging her to me with more pressure than we'd had simply lying there. I didn't want Dax to know we were awake yet and I wasn't quite ready to part with the comforting warmth Grace provided. My heart seemed to skip a beat when I felt her nestle her face into my neck, returning the simple gesture and warming me even more.

It was so strange how the smallest of things seemed to have an effect on me, but I couldn't deny she held a certain power over me. I was drawn to her despite my resistance and reluctance, and I was growing tired of fighting it. What was the point? If it felt good to hold her, why couldn't I just let myself hold her without having an inner battle about it?

Because it makes you weak. Caring for people makes you weak.

I squeezed my eyes shut, fighting off the words that tormented my brain.

The more people you care about, the weaker you are.

My efforts to shut down my years of training were failing as every thought I'd grown up with cemented in my brain seemed to fight for attention. It's dangerous to care for people in this world, because sooner or later, everyone dies. The more you cut yourself off from caring, the less it hurts when you lose them.

And you can't save everyone.

My harsh thoughts were cut off by a tiny point of heat on my neck as Grace's lips pressed momentarily into my skin at my throat. I managed not to gasp at the surprise, but it didn't stop the tingling buzz I felt from flooding through my body. My arms loosened enough to allow her to pull back. For the first time that morning, my eyes connected with her green ones, sending a shock through my body.

She had a smudge of dirt running along her cheek, and her blonde hair had started to fall out of the ponytail she'd thrown it into, but there was no denying that she looked absolutely beautiful in the soft glow of the morning light. I opened my mouth to speak but was interrupted before I could manage any words.

'Oh, good, you're up,' Dax said casually, bending over the desk to look down at us. 'Sun's up, guns up, right?'

With that, he winked once and disappeared rather quickly over the edge of the desk where he'd appeared. I was surprised he'd said nothing about the way my arms were wrapped around Grace or the way we were mere inches apart after what he'd said last night.

Your girl.

She wasn't my girl, and I didn't want her to be. That would make me weak. She couldn't be mine, even if I was flat out lying to myself by saying I didn't want that.

I looked back to Grace and felt her sigh before connecting her gaze back with mine. She raised an eyebrow and shrugged softly before pulling herself from my arms and heaving herself off the ground. I silently cursed Dax for interrupting and copied her, standing to my full height. My

209

back ached dully from spending the night on the ground and my muscles in my shoulders were tight, but I ignored it.

'Sleep well?' Dax asked. It sounded like an innocent question but I was almost certain I could hear an amused undertone lurking beneath his words.

'Fine,' I muttered, my voice deeper than usual thanks to my sleep. Grace stood beside me, linking her hands behind her back and pushing them out to stretch. 'Let's get going, then,' I said, clearing my throat to rid it of the gravel that seemed to have settled there. 'We can eat while you fix the truck, Dax.'

'I already ate,' he said proudly. He appeared wide awake, which was surprising considering he'd only got a half a night's sleep.

'Good for you,' I muttered, gathering up my bags and stuffing what little I'd taken out back inside. Grace did the same, throwing her backpack over her shoulders once more. We were ready to go in less than thirty seconds.

'Let's do this,' Dax cheered, leading the way out of the office we'd called home for a few hours. He looked left and right, surveying the floor to make sure no one had intruded without our notice before proceeding toward the stairs.

'Hey, Grace,' I said, suddenly, spinning to face her. Her eyes widened in surprise at my sudden movement, but she recovered quickly. 'Be—'

'Careful,' she finished, grinning at me softly. 'I know. You too, yeah?'

My head jerked upward in a nod. 'I will.'

She shot me another soft grin before jerking her head up toward the door, silently shooing me to continue on. The corner of my lips pulled up into a satisfied smile as I turned and followed Dax down the stairs, gun raised and ready just as his and Grace's were.

After several cautious minutes, we ended up at the door on the bottom floor that was secured with a filing cabinet, undisturbed after hours of darkness. I stashed my gun quickly beneath my waistband to help Dax move the filing cabinet out of the way. The heavy object landed with a louder thud than I would have liked, making me cringe, but no more disturbances came from the street.

I pushed on the door and had to shove my shoulder to force it open, allowing sunlight to stream into the dark, musty room. I squinted through the crack between the door and the frame, but saw nothing.

'Come on, let's make this quick,' I muttered, moving through the frame and exposing myself to the outside world. Grace followed with Dax behind her as we sprinted toward the truck. The air outside was cool in the early morning. My lungs expanded gloriously to allow me to breathe and my muscles stretched as I ran, making me feel wide awake.

We arrived at the truck and were greeted with the sight of the four men we'd shot down last night. Their bodies lay undisturbed on the cracked pavement, the pools of blood that had leaked out around them long since coagulated in the dirt. I tried not to look at the faces, but it was impossible. Blank stares met my gaze, pale skin and lifeless features inking their faces into my memory forever, just like every other cold body I saw.

'Hayden,' Grace said softly, snapping me out of my thoughts. She was studying me with a soft frown on her face, as if she could tell the effect killing had on me.

'Help me move them,' I requested.

She nodded solemnly, walking over to join me at the body closest to the truck, where Dax had wasted no time in popping open the hood and beginning to work. I bent to wrap my hands around the wrists of the first man, his skin cold and mottled beneath my touch while Grace did the same at the ankles. Slowly, methodically, we managed to move all four of the bodies away from where we were working. They were placed in a neat row, their limbs tucked in as cleanly as their stiffening bodies would allow to at least give them a little bit of respect that every human being deserved.

They were Brutes – ruthless, selfish, and barbaric – but they were still human beings. Grace moved to stand next to me as we walked back toward Dax. I jumped slightly when I felt her hand land on my back, running up and down it once in a soothing motion before dropping down to hang by her side. Her simple touch had been comforting after a morning of such gore.

'One of you get behind the wheel, I need you to try something,' Dax requested.

Grace nodded and pulled the door open, perching herself behind the wheel. She took her backpack off and retrieved her sandwich, eating it casually as she relaxed back into the seat. She appeared so at ease that I couldn't help but admire her strength and bravery. Not many girls went on raids, much less thrived on them like Grace did. Time after time, she'd displayed herself as a more than capable contributor, stepping up when she was needed and waiting back when support was more important.

'Okay, try turning it on,' Dax called from beneath the hood. Grace leaned forward to turn the key. The engine sputtered weakly before going out again, causing Dax to curse quietly to himself. 'Hmm . . . maybe if I try this . . .'

He continued to mutter to himself while he tinkered beneath the hood. My eyes scanned the buildings and streets around us, searching for signs of movement, but it appeared completely deserted. The only benefit of having to stay the night here was that we got a much earlier start than anyone who dwelled in the city or those who braved its caving walls.

'Okay, try again!' Dax said. Grace obliged, turning the key again. This time, the engine sputtered for a few seconds before roaring back to life. A wide grin split across Grace's face as Dax let out a soft 'whoop' of joy. He emerged from under the hood and slammed it shut, patting the top of it proudly.

'She lives!' he exclaimed with a wide grin. 'Let's get this show on the road.'

'Good work, mate,' I said, feeling my spirits lift. That hadn't taken nearly as long as I'd thought, which meant we'd just saved precious time towards saving Kit.

Grace jumped down from the driver's seat, flashing me a stunning grin before climbing into her seat in the back. Our supplies were loaded in and soon we were peeling away from the carnage we'd inflicted in that part of the city.

'So what's the plan?' Grace asked after about twenty minutes of driving. We were nearly out of the city now and so far, we'd been undisturbed.

'They'll have the antibiotics stored near their infirmary, I'm guessing,' I said. 'Luckily it's on the edge of their camp so it shouldn't be too hard to sneak into. Hopefully since it's so early there won't be many people up.'

'I don't remember the last time I was at Whetland,' Dax mused aloud. 'Over a year, I think.'

'I was just there two months ago,' Grace said. 'Part of their camp flooded so things were sort of going to shit then.'

'It flooded?' I repeated, glancing at her briefly in the rear-view mirror.

'Yeah, the river overflowed after we had all those storms, I think,' she said. 'That's their own fault for putting their camp so close to the damn river.'

I chuckled, finding her low tolerance for stupidity amusing. She had a good point: it was stupid to put a camp so close to a river in a low land area.

We were nearly at the place we would have to park our truck and continue on foot now, and I felt the buzz of adrenaline begin to pump through me. Dax's knee jittered up and down in the passenger seat, telling me he was feeling it, too. It made me a little uneasy going to places we didn't go very often because of the unfamiliarity, but it was necessary to save Kit, and I would do anything to save one of my best friends.

We reached an old shed, bordered on one side by the river we'd just been talking about with sparse trees scattered around it. The trees would carry on and provide minimal cover until we reached Whetland, but not enough that we didn't have to be careful. They were different to the trees by Blackwing, which were thick and close together, providing much more coverage. I parked the truck and extracted the keys, hooking them onto my backpack as I jumped out.

'Remember, stick to the tree line but try to stay out of sight. They usually have someone on guard, if I remember right, but only one. Once we get to the camp, we'll head to the south side by the infirmary to get the antibiotics. Everyone stay together and don't shoot anyone unless you're shot at, so we don't alert anyone that we're there, got it?' I instructed, keeping my voice low.

'Got it,' Grace repeated quietly while Dax nodded, checking his gun to make sure it was fully loaded.

'Let's go,' I said, nodding at each of them before setting off at a jog through the trees. Light filtered through the sparse leaves to speckle the ground with bright patches, and the dirt was quiet beneath my feet as I padded softly. Grace and Dax jogged on either side of me, their feet just as quiet as mine while we approached the camp.

The huts were coming into view, constructed of mostly wood and a thatch work of reeds from the river for roofs. Most of the camp appeared to be asleep, but a sudden movement caught my attention, jerking my feet to a halt as I pressed my back into a tree trunk. My hands reached out automatically to grab Grace, hauling her into my chest to hide her from sight of the guard I'd spotted.

A short spark ran through me at the contact. Her chest collided with mine in a soft huff and her eyes locked on mine, her pupils blown wide as the adrenaline flooded through her. Her eyes darted away from mine to peer cautiously around the tree, taking in the scene before us. I watched her face for any negative reactions, but didn't see any.

'He's gone,' she whispered. 'Let's go. I can see the infirmary.'

I nodded silently and released her, ducking around the tree to see for myself. Sure enough, the coast was clear. The three of us moved again, darting now from trees to huts as we emerged from the tree line to infiltrate their camp. We were nearly to the infirmary when I heard a commanding voice echo through the air. Our bodies flattened against the hut we were pressed against as the voice drew nearer.

'. . . we've got the people from the flooded side of camp relocated but I still don't know what to do about the land. It's soaked now and completely useless . . .'

The voice trailed off as they continued past, oblivious to our presence. I let out the breath I'd been holding. The man speaking was tall and muscled, a few years older than me. He spoke to a woman who looked to be about forty and had a very commanding presence about her, just as he did. I recognised him instantly.

He was Renley, the leader of Whetland just as I was the leader of Blackwing. I made it a point to know who the leader of every camp was. The more I knew about the enemy, the better.

Renley had a reputation for being absolutely brilliant. His camp had been the first to figure out how to actually grow things in the rocky soil that surrounded our city, and they'd been the first to figure out a way to use the river as a source of power. He hadn't been in control of Whetland long, but it was already clear that he'd made them stronger. They didn't have a particularly big reputation as good fighters or effective raiders, but they were the most self-sufficient of all the camps, which eventually, I could only guess, would lead to improvements in other areas where they'd been previously weaker.

They might not seem like it now, but I knew in time, Whetland would be a force to be reckoned with.

Renley's voice drifted away completely now, leaving us in silence once more. My eyes were locked on the infirmary, and I was growing more and more anxious with every minute we spent in their camp. I glanced at Grace and Dax and nodded, signalling to them silently before I sprinted out from our hiding place toward the infirmary. My eyes constantly scanned the area, but no other guards or members of Whetland appeared.

My back pressed tightly to the door of the infirmary, listening closely as Grace and Dax waited beside me, guns drawn as they watched for enemies. I heard no noises from inside, so I turned the knob slowly and pushed. The infirmary was small, dark, and completely silent. I opened the door further and let myself inside, my eyes narrowed against the darkness as I peered around. Grace and Dax slipped in after me, closing the door softly.

Without waiting for permission, Grace darted across the room, heading straight toward a large cabinet on the back wall.

'Grace!' I hissed before following her immediately. She should know better than to rush through a room without fully securing it first. She had almost reached the cabinet when I caught up to her.

'What are you doing?!' I whispered angrily.

'Getting the meds,' she shot back, not looking at me as she pulled the cabinet open and began sifting through the bottles and IV drips located there.

'You're going to get yourself killed, don't do that again!' I demanded quietly.

'We're running out of time,' she replied as if it were obvious. Still, she didn't look at me as she focused on the medicines in front of her. 'Yes!'

She appeared to have located what we needed, because she grinned happily and began stuffing items into her backpack. As upset as I was with her for acting so rashly, I was pleased she'd found the right meds.

'Um, guys,' Dax whispered quietly.

'We got the meds, Dax,' I replied, helping Grace stuff as many as she could fit into her bag.

'Guys,' Dax repeated, a little more urgently this time.

'What?' I asked, noting his tense tone, and turning. As I turned, I froze. My eyes landed on a man lying on a bed in the corner of the room that I hadn't noticed before. He was asleep, but I noticed the gentle rise and fall of his chest, telling me he was very much alive and very capable of waking up at any moment to identify us.

'Shit,' I breathed, glancing nervously at Grace, who had also frozen in her tracks. A strange expression crossed her face as she took in the man's appearance. He was thin, very thin, and his skin hung off his bones as if his muscles had wasted away. His face was pale and slightly shiny with sweat, and his dark hair was plastered to his face. He looked like he might have been thirty, but the way his body seemed to be shutting down made him appear much older as he slept.

'I need your bag, Hayden,' she whispered, hardly daring to move. 'Mine's full and we need more.'

'Here,' I said, keeping my eyes locked on the man as I slid my bag off my shoulders and handed it to her. She traded me, handing me the full one to put on my back. I cringed when the bottles she'd collected clanked together loudly, fully expecting the man to wake up and raise the alarm. Thankfully, he remained asleep.

Grace continued to collect the medicine we needed while Dax and I stood helplessly, watching the man and praying he stayed asleep. Finally, after what felt like an hour of tense time, Grace slung the bag over her shoulders and closed the cabinet as silently as possible.

'Okay, we're good,' she whispered, glancing cautiously at the man.

'Let's get out of here,' I replied. Dax had moved to the door to keep watch. He signalled that the coast was clear, and the three of us bolted from the door. I didn't allow relief to hit just yet as we sprinted toward the trees. The last several outings I'd made had gone horribly, and I found myself very reluctant to hope for anything better. The bottles clinked in my backpack as I ran, as did the ones in Grace's, but we carried on.

After about a minute of sprinting, we reached the trees. I was surprised when no shots were fired, no warnings were called, and no one took any notice of our presence. We continued to sprint through the trees, constantly searching for guards or people who could see us, but none appeared.

When we reached the truck, I was certain it was too good to be true.

A moment of panic flooded through me when I couldn't find the key, only for Grace to hand it to me coolly as I remembered we'd traded backpacks. We piled into the truck and secured our bags so nothing would break. I was certain the vehicle wasn't going to start, that something would go wrong, but miraculously when I turned the key, the truck roared to life just as it had after Dax had fixed it.

I drove quickly, closing the distance between Whetland and the city in about half the time it usually took. The city remained as undisturbed as it had been that morning, and we made it through without a single sighting of anyone.

I didn't dare feel relieved until we were driving back toward Blackwing, meds safely in hand and no injuries to account for. A wide grin split across my face and I let out a sudden 'whoop' of joy, making both Grace and Dax jump. Dax laughed and let out a cheer of his own, the tension finally lifting as we left the city unscathed.

Grace let out a delicate giggle that set off butterflies in my stomach and I felt a sudden rush of appreciation for her. She'd risked her own safety, stupidly, admittedly, but she'd done so to speed up the process and get the meds faster. I'd have to reprimand her for that later, but now, it just felt good to have finally accomplished a successful raid.

Blackwing came into sight finally, and we were greeted with familiar faces as we drove through camp. I drove as fast as I could without being too dangerous as I rushed toward the infirmary, desperate to get the meds to Docc and Kit. I'd managed to block out the fear that he hadn't made it until that very moment, focusing solely on getting in and out of Whetland with what we needed. If Kit hadn't survived the night . . .

219

The truck pulled to a stop in front of the infirmary, all three of us jumping out immediately with our bags. We rushed forward and I tried to ignore the pounding of my pulse as I pushed through the door, bracing myself to see a lifeless Kit on the bed. I could feel Grace beside me and resisted the urge to take her hand.

Docc appeared suddenly, emerging from the darker part of the infirmary to greet us.

'Is he alive?' I asked immediately, terrified to hear the answer. Anxiety flooded through me and my stomach twisted into knots. I shoved the backpack full of meds into his hands, as did Grace with hers.

'Yes,' Docc answered. 'You're just in time.'

With that, he spun, taking the bags with him to administer the medications to Kit and leaving Grace, Dax, and me alone in the front area.

I felt like I was melting as a sigh so big left my body that I physically sagged. A half laugh, half gasp escaped my throat as I felt relief take over. Without even thinking, I spun to face Grace, taking her face in my hands and lowering my lips to hers in a sudden kiss. She appeared surprised but recovered enough to let her lips melt into my own. It felt so good to kiss her that I hardly noticed Dax standing feet away.

Watching us, with his jaw on the floor.

Shit.

Chapter 19 – Denial
GRACE

My heart hammered against my ribs, both from the delightful surprise of Hayden's kiss and the sudden realisation that a pair of eyes were fixed on us. Hayden dropped his hands abruptly from my face, taking a step away from me as he opened his mouth to speak. He failed to say anything, however, and snapped his jaw shut again, watching Dax as if he were a bomb about to go off. Dax's eyes were wide and his mouth was hanging open in shock. It appeared that, despite his many comments hinting at something between Hayden and me, he hadn't actually fully believed his own words and suspicions to be true until right in that moment.

'What the hell?' he finally sputtered, his eyes jerking back and forth between Hayden and I, both of us with guilty expressions on our faces.

'Dax,' Hayden said calmly, as if talking down someone about to do something drastic. 'It's not what it looks like.'

I felt a sting of pain jolt through my heart at his denial, although to be fair, I didn't actually know what was going on between us either. It *looked* like we were together, but that was very much not the case. It seemed every time we so much as touched each other, it happened on a whim. There had been virtually zero discussion of what was going on, leaving me completely in the dark as to what Hayden was feeling.

'Really? Because it looks like you just kissed her,' Dax said. He still sounded shocked and dumbfounded. My jaw stayed clenched tightly shut, not about to interject at all when I really couldn't explain. Hayden had been the one sending me so many mixed signals so he could handle this. He was so hot and cold that it was practically giving me whiplash, though I could feel that, despite his wishes, he held a small semblance of affection for me.

At least I hoped he did.

'Look, can we talk about this somewhere else?' Hayden said, glancing nervously over his shoulder. He didn't want anyone to overhear us and realise what had just happened. Dax gaped at him.

'Sure, Hayden, where would you like to go to discuss your *secret relationship?*' he said sarcastically. It was difficult to tell if he was mad or not through the surprise still written across his features.

'It's not like that, I just told you,' Hayden said in frustration. He shoved his hand through his hair and huffed. 'Let's go to mine and I'll explain.'

'Fine. Lead the way,' Dax said, throwing his arm toward the door of the infirmary. Without a glance in my direction, Hayden stalked out the door, leaving us to follow him. I couldn't deny that I was also looking forward to his explanation.

All I knew was that I liked it when Hayden kissed me and that I was feeling things for him that I definitely shouldn't have been. Every day we spent together, I learned more and more about him. I had learned he wasn't as tough as he wanted everyone to think, that he cared for people far more than he let on, and that he was far better than the rest

222

of us. Whenever he so much as looked at me, butterflies would erupt in my stomach and my skin would tingle with goosebumps.

I hadn't wanted it, but I couldn't deny it any longer: I had developed feelings for Hayden.

We arrived at Hayden's hut. I was already nervous to hear what Hayden would say, and I couldn't suppress the awful feeling that his words would hurt. Once inside, I moved immediately to the couch and sat down. My knees bounced nervously in front of me before I forced them to stop, irritated with myself for showing too much emotion. Dax sat next to me while Hayden remained standing, apparently too pent up to sit down.

'Well?' Dax said evenly, staring at Hayden expectantly.

'Well what?' Hayden asked, his voice already laced with irritation. I could practically see him silently berating himself in his head for being so slack with his emotions earlier by allowing himself to kiss me in front of Dax.

'What exactly is going on between you two?' Dax clarified shortly. It was still impossible to tell if he was mad or not.

'Nothing,' Hayden replied immediately, sending a sharp pang through my heart. His eyes darted to me for a half a second before refocusing on Dax. I tried to keep my face void of emotion but didn't know how successful I was.

'Nothing,' Dax repeated sceptically. He cocked an eyebrow at Hayden before glancing at me. I avoided his gaze and stared at the ground. Everyone was tensely silent for a few moments before Dax spoke again. 'I don't believe you.'

'Look, I was just really happy things went well and was feeling . . . grateful that Grace had been such a help. I don't know what came over me,' Hayden explained dismissively. My stomach twisted again painfully, unable to tell if that was the truth or if he was simply lying to Dax. I pathetically hoped for the latter.

'You were feeling grateful,' Dax repeated in the same tone as before.

'Will you stop repeating everything I say?' Hayden snapped, glaring at Dax as he paced back and forth across the floor. If he was trying to act like he didn't care about anything, he was doing a very unconvincing job of it. 'But yes. Grateful.'

'So you kissed her?' Dax asked. He frowned at me as if what Hayden had said didn't fully add up. 'Was that the first time?'

'Honestly, I don't see how this is your business,' Hayden said, sounding irritated.

'I feel like I have a right to know if you're fooling around with your *prisoner*,' he said, emphasizing the last word for effect.

'We're not fooling around, I just told you,' Hayden denied. Technically that wasn't true, but I wasn't about to contradict him. They were, once again, speaking as if I wasn't even there.

'So you don't like her?' Dax said, asking the question I'd been wondering myself. I waited nervously for Hayden to answer.

He stopped pacing and turned to face us, his face set in a deep frown as he glanced at Dax before fixing his gaze on me. He took in my anxious expression that I'd failed to hide as a flash of sadness crossed his face. I suddenly felt faint.

'No.'

There it was. Hearing him deny any feelings for me had hurt far more than I had imagined it would. My jaw clenched tightly as I forced myself not to react to his words.

'You're sure?' Dax pressed, his tone still unreadable even now.

'I'm sure,' Hayden said stiffly. His jaw was clenched tightly as well, and the muscle in his cheek twitched slightly before he resumed his pacing. I could feel Dax's gaze settle on me as I tried to appear nonchalant, like what Hayden had just said wasn't shredding me inside. I turned my head to meet Dax's stare, shrugging casually and raising my brows as if what Hayden had just said didn't affect me either way.

His light brown eyes didn't look angry when I finally looked at him, which surprised me. He looked . . . concerned. Sad, almost. He was studying me closely to observe my reaction. He took a deep breath before raising his eyebrows once.

'Shame,' he finally said. 'I thought you guys had something going on but I guess I was wrong.'

'Yeah,' Hayden said lowly, turning away from us to settle onto his bed. 'You were.'

'I'd be all right with it, you know,' Dax continued, turning his gaze from me finally to look at Hayden. I blinked, surprised to hear him say that. I'd been expecting him to be relieved to find out there was apparently nothing going on, but all he seemed to be was disappointed.

'There's nothing to be all right with,' Hayden said coldly, digging further into the ache in my gut. I felt anger starting to stir in the pit of my stomach, joining the disappointment and hurt there. It was one thing for Hayden to deny anything between us, but he was being colder than necessary, and it was frankly embarrassing for me because I was pretty sure he knew I'd started to develop feelings for him. He was throwing them back in my face now right in front of Dax.

'All right, mate, whatever you say,' Dax said, raising his hands in surrender, dropping the subject. He stood off the couch, tugging on his loose grey shirt to straighten it over

225

his shoulders before rubbing his hands together. 'You guys hungry?'

'No,' Hayden said flatly. I shook my head; I'd lost my appetite a while ago.

'Okay . . .' Dax said, frowning at Hayden's stiff tone. 'Hey, I've been thinking . . . that guy we saw in Whetland . . . you don't think he was contagious, do you?'

'I don't know,' Hayden said, sounding as if he couldn't possibly care. The way Hayden was acting right now was so far from the Hayden I'd come to know, and I had to admit I didn't like him very much.

'I wonder what was wrong with him,' Dax mused aloud, shifting toward the door as if eager to escape the thick tension that had settled over the room.

'He had cancer,' I said, speaking for the first time since Dax had discovered Hayden and I sharing a kiss. A kiss that had apparently meant absolutely nothing. My voice was flat and hollow as I spoke, and my eyes were fixed on the ground.

My statement was met with silence and I was suddenly aware that it was an odd thing to say with no further explanation.

'Cancer?' Dax repeated slowly, clearly confused. 'But he still had all his hair?'

'You lose your hair from the chemo or radiation, not the cancer itself,' I explained. My eyes rose from the ground finally to see them both staring at me curiously. I could tell they were both itching to ask how I knew that, but no one did.

Memories of her gaunt face floated before me, the padding from her bones stolen by her illness as she wasted away. I remember how weak she'd got in the end – so weak that she couldn't even hold my hand unless I scooped up her frail

226

fingers into my palm. There had been nothing we could do, as was the case with the man we'd seen, as the advanced medicines necessary were no longer an option in this world we lived in. Antibiotics were one thing, but chemotherapy treatments were another thing entirely. I blinked back the sting of tears I felt beginning to form as I shook my head, clearing away the unpleasant memories before I gave away more than I wanted to.

'You won't catch it,' I said flatly, glancing at Dax and giving him a weak smile. He nodded and shot me a sad smile before moving the rest of the way toward the door.

'Well . . . I'm going to eat. You guys can come if you change your mind,' he said somewhat awkwardly. He waved once before letting himself outside, leaving me alone with Hayden and the feelings rolling through me. A mixture of hurt, disappointment, disbelief, and anger seemed to fight for attention as I tried to look anywhere but at Hayden. I failed.

My gaze settled on him and I felt my eyes narrow into a glare, but I was determined not to say anything. If he wanted to deny everything that had happened between us, I wasn't going to give him the satisfaction of calling him out on it. He wanted to claim he had no feelings, so I could do the same.

'Grace,' Hayden said. He sighed as if he could feel my un-intentional glare before turning to look at me. I looked away from him and leaned back as casually as I could manage, picking at my fingernails rather than looking at him.

'What?'

I sounded angrier than I would have liked to let on but it was too difficult to peel the emotion from my voice.

'What I said to Dax—'

'You don't have to explain anything to me, Hayden,' I

said sharply, cutting him off. My anger seemed to grow more and more as I felt his stare linger on me. 'You've made it very clear where we stand.'

He was silent for a while and I couldn't stop my gaze from flicking toward him. He was watching me closely with a frown on his face.

'You're angry,' he observed. His voice sounded less tense than it had while Dax had been present.

'No, I'm not,' I lied tightly. I didn't sound very convincing as I felt the sting of anger drift through me.

'Grace . . .' he sighed.

'Stop saying my name like that,' I snapped. He sounded like he was constantly on the verge of telling me bad news and it was grating on me. I suddenly felt extremely stupid for thinking he could have feelings for me like I had for him. Of course he didn't. All he saw in me was an enemy. The reason all our moments together had been so random were because he hadn't wanted them and had only acted on them because he'd been caught up in the moment.

All but last night, when he'd held me while we slept.

I shook my head, clearing the thought. Obviously he didn't care about me or he wouldn't be sending me so many mixed signals and denying everything to his best friend, who had flat out said he'd be all right with it. Even then, Hayden had denied it when there would have been virtually no repercussions.

'What do you want me to say then, Grace?' Hayden said, irritation leaking back into his voice.

'Nothing.'

He glared at me across the room, his annoyance rising to match my own.

'Then why are you all pissed off? Stop acting like you're not because I can tell,' he said angrily.

228

'I'm not,' I repeated tightly. I stopped feigning inspection of my nails when my fingers curled into fists by my sides.

'Stop lying to me,' he growled, rising off the bed to come and stand in front of me. He crossed his arms over his chest and glared down at me, making me feel small. I rose to my feet to diminish some of the height advantage he held, but he still towered over me as I stood a few feet away.

'So I can't lie but you can?' I spat, finally cracking.

'When did I lie?' he dared to ask, staring incredulously down at me. My heart panged painfully once again at the confirmation that he hadn't been lying when he'd told Dax he didn't care for me.

'Never, apparently,' I muttered, walking away to put some distance between us. I didn't get far before his hand wrapped around my upper arm to spin me back to face him. I jerked my arm away angrily and glared at him.

'When did I lie?' he repeated, watching me closely.

'Is that how you really feel? What you said to Dax?' I asked, ignoring his question. His jaw fell open slightly before he clamped it shut again, his eyes narrowed as he focused on me.

'It's complicated,' he finally said, his tone tight once more.

'No, it isn't,' I spat, taking a step back from him. He was too close and it was clouding my mind.

'Yes, it is,' he said tensely. I was so frustrated I felt like screaming.

'How? Because I'm your enemy? I've gone on raids with you and saved your best friend's life. What else do I have to do to prove that I'm not going to hurt anyone?' I fumed. I was positively livid now. His excuses were running low and I was sick of them.

'That's not why,' Hayden said through clenched teeth.

'Then why, Hayden? What's so complicated?' I demanded.

229

'It just is,' he said stubbornly. Fury flashed through me, beyond frustrated with him.

'If what you said to Dax is how you really feel then you should just leave me alone, Hayden. I can't deal with you kissing me one second and then completely ignoring me the next,' I said, hating myself for the way my voice cracked when I spoke. My fists clenched by my side as I resolved to be stronger. Something sparked in his eyes as he watched me and took a step forward, which was met with my own retreat to maintain the distance between us. I couldn't let him close to me and risk my thoughts getting hazy.

'It's complicated because I *can't* care for you, Grace,' he finally admitted. 'Caring for people makes you weak and I can't be weak. Too many people are counting on me to be strong for them.'

'You're so full of shit,' I said incredulously, shaking my head at him.

'Excuse me?' he asked sharply. His voice was dangerously calm as he waited for me to continue.

'You want everyone to believe you don't care about anyone but you're not as tough as you think you are,' I said, poking him suddenly in the chest. His gaze dropped down to where my finger pushed into his muscle before raising it back to my face. He looked insulted.

'Oh really?' he challenged sarcastically.

'Really,' I spat. My hands shoved at his chest, trying to put more distance between us as we seemed to be getting closer still. 'You walk around like some hard case who doesn't care about anyone but it's so obvious that you care for every single person here. You risk your life on a daily basis for *them* and you're trying to tell me caring for people makes you weak. If you really believed that you wouldn't even be here in the first place.'

I hadn't realised it but my breathing had picked up considerably, causing my chest to heave with every breath. I was practically shaking for how mad I was, and somehow the space between Hayden and I had shrunk as I repeatedly shoved my hands into his chest. He was watching me closely, his own breathing speeding up as he listened to my rant. His nostrils flared as he breathed, and his jaw clenched tightly shut.

'That's fine if you don't care about me, but don't you dare try to tell me you don't care about *them*,' I continued, my voice strained with anger and emotion. 'Caring about people doesn't make you weak. It makes you human.'

'You're wrong,' he said slowly.

I rolled my eyes, fed up with arguing with him. 'Okay, Hayden.'

'You're wrong about a lot, actually,' he added. Anger bubbled inside me as I seethed on the spot. I was so angry that I was shaking.

'Of course I am. Tell me how I'm wrong,' I seethed. He glared down at me, none too impressed with my tone.

'Caring about you would make me weak because I'd want to protect you before myself,' he said, sounding as if every word pained him to say. He had somehow closed in on me again, standing only inches away as he glared down at me intimidatingly. I met his gaze determinedly.

'It's a good thing you don't care about me, then,' I said, my voice deadly quiet and loaded with bitterness.

The words had hardly left my mouth, however, when the distance between us disappeared as Hayden's lips collided with my own. His hands landed on either side of my face, holding me to him as my hands shoved at his chest, trying weakly to push him off. There was little conviction behind my actions, however, as I felt his lips melt into mine. The tension that had been building around us seemed to fall, cocooning us in our own world as I finally gave up trying to fight him off.

He held his lips firmly against mine, holding me tightly as I stopped resisting him. I finally relaxed and felt my hands settle on his chest, after straining fruitlessly against him. The heat of his lips and his hands burned away the anger I'd been feeling. My heart fought to escape from behind my ribs as he broke the kiss, breathing heavily as his forehead dropped to mine.

'Of course I care about you, Grace,' he whispered low. His eyes were closed as he spoke, but they flicked open moments after to observe my reaction.

My thoughts raced around distractedly in my head, making it difficult to sort out a reply. I didn't want to think him caring about me made him weak, but it seemed that he'd been drilling the thought into his head for years, making it difficult to erase.

'You don't have to protect me, Hayden,' I replied. I hoped to start breaking down his belief that he needed to weaken himself by protecting me first.

'I know,' he said quietly, running his thumbs slowly across my cheeks while he kept his forehead pinned against mine. 'But that doesn't mean I'm not going to try.'

Chapter 20 – Want

HAYDEN

I'd never felt more vulnerable and unprepared in my entire life than I did at that moment. There were too many different thoughts raging through my head. Despite my firm belief that it was dangerous to admit I cared for her, and my wish to remain unconcerned, I couldn't take back what I'd said or deny the truth behind it.

I cared about Grace and I wanted to protect her, even if it meant putting myself in danger.

This was very, very bad.

She drew a shaky breath between her parted lips, and her eyes appeared to be glowing in the dim light of my hut as she absorbed the last thing I'd said – my statement that I'd try to protect her even though I didn't have to.

'Why did you lie to Dax?' she finally asked, her voice quiet. Her hands fell from my chest, catching the hem of my shirt and twisting it between her fingers distractedly.

'I don't know,' I admitted truthfully. My first instinct had been to deny anything between us, the ingrained belief that caring for people made you weak ruining me.

She sagged slightly at my words, disappointed as she took a small step back. I followed immediately, to close distance between us, but let my hands drop from her face.

'Hayden—' she started, a strained tone to her voice.

'Look, don't start again,' I pleaded softly. 'I just . . . I'm not good at this.'

'At what?' she asked, her brows knitting together in concentration.

'This,' I said, shrugging, as I waved my hand back and forth between us. 'I don't even know what to call this. It's not a normal situation, Grace.'

'I know that,' she said, sounding slightly insulted before continuing. 'I don't know what this is either but . . . I need to know what you want.'

I frowned at her, unsure of how to answer that. What did I want? The answer to that was relatively simple, but I had absolutely no idea on how to go about getting it. I wanted a normal life, with no stress or pressure to keep countless people safe. I wanted things to go back to how they were before the world fell apart. I wanted to be able to go to sleep at night without worrying what unwelcomed enemies would try and infiltrate the place I worked so hard to keep safe. I wanted to be able to trust someone with everything I had, to lean on them when I wasn't good enough by myself, to learn what it felt like to love someone.

I wanted Grace.

But these were things I couldn't have. They weren't possible, feasible, or responsible, which meant they were things I would most likely miss out on in life, something I'd accepted a long time ago. The hardest part of realising I actually cared for Grace was the realisation that some of the things I'd wanted more than ever but never dreamed I could have seemed more possible than ever before, making it all the more painful to accept that I couldn't have them.

'For now, I just want to keep you safe,' I replied. 'What do you want?'

'Part of me wants to go home,' she admitted honestly, flashing her green eyes up to meet mine guiltily. 'To see my family again and let them know I'm okay. But another part of me . . . another part of me wants to stay here and see what happens.'

I nodded slowly. Part of me was ecstatic that she wanted to stay here at all, but I was also disappointed that she felt such a desire to go home even after all we'd been through. It shouldn't have surprised me, however. Of course she wanted to go home to her family more than she wanted to stay here. With me.

My stomach rumbled loudly, offering a distraction.

'Are you hungry?' I asked. She sucked in a deep breath, in acceptance at the end of the conversation.

'Yeah, let's go and eat,' she answered. I nodded slowly, letting my gaze linger on hers for another second before stepping back and moving toward the front door once more.

She followed me without a word, the weight of our conversation weighing down on both of us. There was no simple way to deal with what we were both feeling, and I couldn't stop my mind from continuously trying to resist the things I wanted to do.

We walked quietly through the evening light towards the mess hall, where the scent of grilling meat drifted through the camp, making my stomach rumble again. I seemed to forget simple necessities like eating when I was around Grace, something that my body was not thanking me for.

The mess hall was relatively full of people eating dinner and chatting pleasantly, unburdened by the things that tainted my daily life.

'Hayden!' someone called excitedly. I recognised the voice instantly and turned to see Jett waving at me enthusiastically from where he sat at a table alone. I waved back as

Grace and I moved up to the area where Maisie was handing out portions of food. Tonight, it looked to be venison someone had shot on a hunt.

'Glad to see you're back, Hayden,' she smiled at me before handing me a plate of food. 'And you, Grace.'

Grace appeared somewhat surprised by Maisie's kind statement but allowed a small smile to pull at her lips. 'Thank you.'

She accepted her plate and glanced at the ground, unable to hide the gentle smile that remained. I nodded appreciatively at Maisie, thankful she'd managed to make Grace smile after such a draining day. I could see Jett practically bouncing in his seat, waiting anxiously for me to join him at the table. I wove through the crowd and accepted the greetings people aimed in my direction as I passed them.

'Hayden, you're back!' Jett exclaimed excitedly when I sat down across from him. Grace sat next to me but kept a few feet of space between us.

'Yep,' I said casually before starting to dig into my food. I noticed Jett cast an apprehensive look in Grace's direction before continuing to speak.

'Hi, Grace,' he said, sounding as though he wanted to sound brave and casual but coming off as slightly terrified. He was clearly still very afraid of her even though she'd done nothing to him after the first incident when she'd had a gun to my chest in Greystone.

'Hi, Jett,' she said, smiling softly at him. She appeared pleased he'd spoken to her directly. 'How are you?'

'Good,' he replied automatically, casting a wide-eyed glance in my direction as if I should be impressed he was talking to her. I suppose all he really knew her as was the enemy who was being forced to stay here, so it was understandable for him to be uneasy around her.

'Have you seen Kit, Jett?' I asked before shoving another forkful of food into my mouth.

'Yeah,' Jett said excitedly. 'Last night and this morning! He was sleepy, though.'

'He's sick,' I clarified. I wasn't sure how much Docc had told him but I felt he needed to know the truth.

'Is he going to get better?' Jett asked with wide eyes.

'Hopefully. Grace, Dax and I got him some medicine earlier today so we'll see if Docc can fix him up.'

'You helped?' he asked, turning to stare at Grace in disbelief.

'Yeah,' she responded humbly.

'She saved him, didn't you know? He got shot in the neck and she stopped it bleeding long enough to get him back to Docc,' I explained. Grace fidgeted beside me as if she was uncomfortable with me bragging about her.

'It's not that big a deal,' she muttered quietly.

'You did all that?' Jett asked in awe. His eyes were still wide and he was looking at Grace now in admiration rather than fear.

'I had help,' she said modestly. She'd saved Kit's life and wouldn't even admit it to an impressionable kid.

'Whoa,' Jett breathed. I chuckled as I finished off my plate, feeling much lighter now that we'd escaped the tight confines of my hut where the emotions seemed to have got trapped.

'Hey, Jett,' I said suddenly as an idea struck me. 'Plans tonight?'

'No! Why?' he asked excitedly, his features lighting up.

'Want to practise your shot?'

'Really?! Yes, yes!' he said, practically jumping off his seat. Grace laughed at his enthusiasm before finishing her own plate of food.

'All right, finish up,' I said, nodding at his plate. 'Can't shoot on an empty stomach.'

'Okay!' he exclaimed, abruptly shoveling the rest of his food into his mouth.

'You can practise, too,' I told Grace, turning to shoot her a grin. Her jaw fell open before a smirk split her face.

'Excuse me, my shot is just fine,' she threw back. Her eyes crinkled slightly in the corner thanks to her grin.

'If you say so,' I said, cocking an eyebrow at her before standing to bring my plate to the clean-up area. Jett jumped out of his seat, his mouth still stuffed with food that he was barely managing to chew as he followed me. Grace copied us, following us outside after disposing of our dishes.

'Lead the way, Jett,' I said, nodding at him.

'Yes!' he said excitedly, pumping his small fist in the air as he started walking briskly towards the raid building where we kept our guns. Grace and I followed behind, letting him create a bit of a lead in his haste.

'You're teaching him to shoot?' she asked, her eyes fixed on him in amusement as he stumbled over a rock in the ground, righting himself at the last moment so he didn't go sprawling into the dirt.

'I'm fine!' he called back to us, a wide grin on his face.

'Yeah, someone has to. I've been trying for about two years now but he just can't seem to get the hang of it,' I told her. Jett pushed his way into the raid building, speaking excitedly to whoever was currently on guard duty.

'Maybe the problem is with the teacher, not the student,' she joked lightly, nudging her shoulder into my arm.

'That's definitely not it,' I laughed. 'I'm an excellent teacher.'

'I'm sure you are,' she said, the hint of sarcasm in her

voice nearly undetectable. I shook my head in amused disbelief. 'You're not intimidating at all.'

'Hmmph. Getting brave, you are,' I muttered lightly as I pushed my way through the door to the building, brushing off her comments. Jett was inside, loading a small duffle bag with several rounds of ammunition, some hand-painted targets Maisie had helped him make, and some empty cans that were already riddled with holes from me trying to show Jett how to aim. He'd only hit a target once, and I was pretty sure it hadn't been the one he'd been aiming at.

'Got it all, little man?' I asked, inspecting his supplies.

'All but the gun,' answered the man who was on duty.

'He wouldn't give me it until you got here. It's not even a real gun!' Jett pouted, glaring at the middle-aged man who sat in the corner. He shrugged casually, not denying Jett's statement.

'As he should have,' I agreed, nodding. I moved to the case and pulled out a single .22 pistol, selecting a less powerful weapon for practice. My usual gun was a 9mm and much more lethal than this one, but a gun was a gun, meaning it was always dangerous when handling them with unpractised hands. I checked to see that the safety was on before stowing it beneath the waistband of my jeans for safe keeping.

'Let's get moving, we're running out of daylight,' I told Jett. He grinned happily and scooped up the bag with his precious supplies before darting out the front door.

A few minutes later, we arrived at the place I usually practised with Jett. It was a small clearing just outside the camp, with enough of a cleared space to aim at without having to shoot in the direction of Blackwing. Jett wasted no time in setting out his targets and cans, determined to finally make his own holes in them.

'He really wants to learn, doesn't he?' Grace observed, watching Jett bounce around the clearing.

'He thinks if he learns he'll get to go on raids,' I answered. My stomach twisted a bit at the thought of this hopelessly clueless boy on an actual raid. No way would I allow that until I was absolutely certain he could handle himself, which at this rate would be several years.

'He's been on one,' she reminded me, clearly thinking back to the first night we'd run into each other.

'He wasn't supposed to be,' I muttered. I was still bitter about that.

'You won't let him, will you?' she guessed. 'You're protective of him.'

I didn't reply, absorbing her words as Jett finished his preparations and returned to us. I could feel Grace's gaze on me but I ignored it, pulling the gun from where it had settled against my skin.

'Okay, Jett,' I said, stepping up to stand next to him. 'What's the first rule?'

'Never point the gun at anyone,' he recalled dutifully.

'That's right. And rule two?'

'Always make sure the safety is on unless I'm shooting,' he said, nodding his head to punctuate every other word.

'Very good,' I said proudly. 'Now show me the *wrong* way to hold it.'

Jett raised his hands, folding them together while extending his index finger as if holding an invisible gun. He twisted his hands so they were parallel to the ground, his palms facing toward the ground and the sky.

'This is bad,' he said, squinting past his finger at the targets.

'Correct. What's the right way?'

'Like this,' he said, straightening out his hands so his thumbs were pointing upward.

'Good. You ready to try and shoot a few rounds?' I asked, hoping this session went better than our last few and that he'd actually manage to hit something he aimed at.

'Yeah!' he cheered, bouncing on the balls of his feet. I kept the gun aimed at the dirt as I handed it cautiously to him. He gripped it gingerly, as if afraid it would explode at the slightest touch. I saw him swallow harshly, as his eyes widened at the sight of the gun in his small hands. He focused intently as he raised it in front of him, holding it upright as he'd just demonstrated for me.

'Like this?' he asked, not looking away from the end of the barrel.

'Yes,' I reassured him, nodding. 'Remember to aim. Use the guides.'

He squinted one eye closed, his little tongue poking out between his lips in concentration while he aimed. His finger shifted slightly to undo the safety. He took a deep breath, his tiny chest expanding farther than usual as he tried to settle his nerves. He was too small for his age, thanks to the scarcity of food.

'One,' I started, hoping a countdown would relax him a bit. 'Two . . . three!'

He pulled the trigger, setting off a bang as the bullet shot out of the barrel. His weak arms did little to stop the light kickback, sending the barrel of the gun jolting upward a few inches and causing the bullet to completely miss its target, lodging in the dirt behind them.

'Damn,' he muttered, his shoulders sagging with disappointment.

'Hey, it's just the first one,' I reassured him. 'Try again.'

I turned to look at Grace, almost having forgotten that

241

she was there. She was watching us with a contemplative expression, and it was hard to decipher what she was thinking. A second shot jerked my attention back to see Jett miss again.

'Keep trying,' I said. 'Go until you run out of bullets and we'll reload.'

Several more shots rang out through the clearing, every single one missing their targets. A final empty click sounded, indicating Jett was out of ammo before he switched the safety back on and trudged to where I stood, his shoulders slumping dejectedly.

'I can't do it,' he said sadly. 'I'll never hit a target.'

'Sure you will, you just have to practise more,' I told him. I wanted to believe that he would get the hang of it, but it had only taken me a few weeks to become a relatively decent shot, and I'd been at this with Jett for nearly two years now; not to mention I'd been much younger when I'd learned. It wasn't a promising start and we both knew it.

'Jett, do you shoot with one eye open or two?' Grace asked curiously, stepping forward to join us while I took his gun to reload it for him.

'Hayden says one,' he said, glancing at me as if suddenly not trusting my decision.

'That's because you're supposed to use one,' I told him flatly.

'Have you ever tried two?' Grace asked him, ignoring me.

'No . . .' Jett answered slowly, as if the thought had never occurred to him.

'Try two,' she said, tilting her head back knowingly.

'Okay!' Jett said, a renewed excitement clear in his voice after being so discouraged only moments ago. I frowned as I handed him the gun back, freshly reloaded. He bounded back to where he'd been standing and raised the gun,

242

keeping both eyes open this time as he unlocked the safety.

He squeezed the trigger, sending another bang echoing out around us as the bullet whizzed through the air. A tiny hole appeared on the very bottom edge of the target Jett had been aiming at.

'Yes! Did you see that, Hayden?! I did it!' he shouted happily, spinning around to face us.

'Whoa!' I said, throwing my hands up in front of me automatically as he spun the gun wildly with him. My body jerked to the side without permission as I subconsciously threw myself in front of Grace. 'Jett! What's the first rule?'

'Oh, no!' he said, his eyes widening suddenly as he realised his mistake, aiming the gun at the ground once more. 'Don't aim the gun at anyone.'

'You've got to remember that no matter what,' I scolded. 'But good job. See if you can do it again. And really try to keep your arms strong so you don't have as much of a kickback.'

He nodded eagerly before returning to his stance and aiming once more, firing another shot that nicked the edge of the target. He let out a whoop of joy and prepared to shoot some more. I glanced at Grace with a hint of embarrassment at my sudden instinct to put myself between her and the gun. It was difficult to tell if she'd noticed or not as she met my gaze with a curious look. I refocused on Jett in front of us.

'Still think one is better?' Grace muttered smugly next to me, coming to stand at my shoulder. I peeked down at her, annoyed her way had appeared to work better for Jett than mine.

'I learned with one. I shoot just fine,' I told her stubbornly.

'One's better for things that aren't moving,' she said. 'But how often do we really shoot at things that aren't moving?'

I sighed in defeat; she had a point. 'True.'

Jett shot again, this time managing to land a shot within the outer edge of the rings painted on the cardboard that served as a target.

'Hayden!' he called excitedly, catching my attention.

'I see it, good work,' I called encouragingly. I dropped my voice slightly before speaking to Grace once more. 'I fear we've just created a monster.'

She let out a light laugh, her eyes focused on Jett as he fired the last shot, striking closest to the centre of the bull's-eye as he had yet.

'Soon he'll be hitting moving targets and you'll have no choice but to let him go on a raid,' she said lightly.

'No way. It takes more than hitting a few targets to go on a raid,' I said, suddenly stern.

'Well, obviously,' she said. I could practically hear her rolling her eyes. 'I was joking.'

'Hmm,' I hummed. Jett turned and moved back to us, his gun empty once more.

'You had enough for tonight?' I asked. The sun was quickly setting and soon it would be too dark to see the targets.

'One more round?' he begged. 'Please?'

'One more,' I agreed. 'But you have to load it yourself.'

He cheered and started to dig through the duffle bag, extracting the bullets to set them aside. He struggled to remove the magazine from the gun, but finally managed to free it and load the bullets into the slot before shoving it back inside with a soft 'click'. He looked pleased with himself as he moved back to where he'd stood, aiming once more before starting to shoot.

This time, all of his shots hit the target within the rings, holes appearing faster than they ever had before in the cardboard. Grace let out a low laugh.

'I'm not going to say I told you so but . . .' she trailed off smugly.

'Yeah, yeah,' I muttered. 'You were right. Don't get used to it.'

Jett rejoined us once more, handing the gun back to me before darting off once more to gather the targets.

'Thanks, Grace, you were right!' he called as he pulled the stakes attached to his target from the ground and hauled it over to us. He held it up proudly to display the new holes in the material. 'Look! I did that!'

'You did!' she agreed happily. 'Happy to help.'

'I've never hit a target before! Except once on accident,' he said, blushing slightly.

'Well, get used to it. You've got the hang of it now so you'll only get better,' Grace told him sweetly. I smiled softly as she observed him with a certain endearment.

'Yes, best night ever!' he shouted, throwing his fist into the air again as he set the target down and retreated to retrieve the rest. I chuckled as I crouched down to stuff the target into the duffle bag.

'Thank you,' I said quietly to Grace. 'For helping him.'

'It's no problem, really. Told you it was just the teacher,' she teased. I grinned at the ground and shook my head. A comfortable silence settled over us. The light was nearly gone from the sky now as the sun descended behind the trees. Things were, for once, peaceful.

My instincts suddenly prickled. It was quiet, but it seemed too quiet. There was no happy chatter coming from behind us as there should have been, no muted huffing as Jett struggled to pull the targets from the ground. I jumped to my feet suddenly, spinning wildly as my heart jumped into my throat.

My arms rose with the gun automatically, forgetting

momentarily that it was empty. My body reacted before I fully had time to process what I was seeing, aiming it at the man who stood behind Jett, his arms locked around his shoulders while he held the sharp, glinting edge of a knife to his throat. Jett's eyes were wide in panic while he tried not to cry, his face contorted with the effort.

Everyone was frozen in place: Jett, paralysed with fear, his captor, Grace next to me, hands completely empty of any potential weapon, and me, raising a uselessly empty gun at the enemy who had intruded upon our camp. An enemy with a large red 'W' painted on the sleeve of his jacket.

I knew the raid today had gone too well. The large 'W' on the jacket told me so, which could only stand for one thing: Whetland.

Chapter 21 – Retaliation
GRACE

My breath caught as my eyes landed on the red 'W' painted onto the man's jacket. Realisation quickly settled over me as I recognised the symbol; he must have followed us back from Whetland after we had been convinced it had gone well. Oh, how wrong we had been. My muscles were tense as the knife pressed harder against Jett's throat, straining the thin skin over his neck but not yet breaking through. Hayden was frozen beside me, aiming the uselessly empty gun at the man's head, which was dangerously close to Jett's.

'Let him go,' Hayden growled, his jaw clenched tightly as he spoke. The muscles in his arms were flexed tightly as they remained straightened out unwaveringly in front of him.

'You and I both know that's not how this works, boy,' the man spat, leering at Hayden. He looked to be around forty, with grey specked into his hair and ragged beard. It was common for people to always be in a state of mild distress, but this man looked as though he'd been living in a pile of dirt for years. I noticed several dark spots where teeth should have been as he bared them at Hayden.

'What do you want?' Hayden demanded harshly, still aiming the gun at him.

'For starters, you're going to put your gun down,' the

man said. His grip on Jett was so tight that I feared he was having difficulty breathing, a feat made no less difficult by the sharp blade at his throat. His brown eyes were so wide it looked as though his eyeballs were trying to escape their sockets, and he was visibly shaking with fear. My heart beat a little faster for him, upset that he was so terrified.

'Put your knife down,' Hayden countered, not moving.

'Ahh,' the man said, pressing harder on his blade. A thin red line appeared at the edge of it, minuscule droplets of blood leaking from the skin. Jett let out a tiny squeak of pain, pressing back into the man as if trying to escape the knife. 'You're going to put your gun down.'

Hayden huffed angrily, his entire body so tense he looked like he might crack if touched. Slowly, he took one of his hands off the gun, raising it by his side as he bent down cautiously to set it on the dirt. It wasn't going to do much good anyway, but at least it gave the illusion of defence. The man shifted his gaze to me, taking in my empty hands and defensive stance.

'You armed, Blondie?' he snorted, his tone mocking and condescending as if he didn't think for a second that I was dangerous. My blood boiled through my veins at his assumption and I was suddenly even more determined to save Jett.

It wasn't the first time someone had underestimated me, though it was usually the last thing they ever did.

'No,' I growled. I was suddenly extremely aware of the metal, warmed now after hours against my skin, that was pressing into my lower back secured by the waistband of my shorts – the gun I'd used on the raid and hadn't had time to put back yet. That gun could be our saving grace if I could only get to it before the man slit Jett's throat.

'What do you want?' Hayden spat, drawing the man's

attention back to him. Jett whimpered as the man shifted his body slightly, digging the knife a little deeper into his skin.

'It's very simple,' he started slowly, tightening his grip around Jett's shoulders. 'You stole from Whetland, and I can't allow that without retaliation. You must pay for what you've done.'

'Are you alone?' Hayden demanded, glaring daggers at him. He didn't answer as he continued to leer unnervingly at Hayden. 'Are you alone?!'

Hayden's voice echoed around the trees, the sound of it roaring toward the man and rebounding around for a few seconds.

'He's alone,' I said, carefully observing his face as I spoke. A flash of irritation crossed his features, confirming my suspicions. If he had backup, they'd have shown up before now to make sure I wasn't armed or to take us out. Hayden's head ticked toward me for a fraction of a second before he took a slow step forward.

'Ah, ah, ahhhh,' the man scolded Hayden, shaking his head at him. 'You don't move another inch or I'll spill this boy's blood into the dirt.'

'Why would they send one person after us? What kind of plan is that?' Hayden questioned harshly, trying to make sense of things. Again, the man didn't answer. His eyes were oddly yellow as they focused on Hayden. Something seemed to click in Hayden's mind just as it occurred to me.

'They didn't send you,' Hayden mused aloud. His brows knit tightly together and his hands clenched by his sides as if restraining himself from launching his body into the man's.

Hayden's guess was confirmed once again by a sneer so deep I felt my stomach twist over. There was something very off about the man and I wondered if he was slightly crazy.

He was wearing a jacket with a 'W' on it, after all, which clearly gave away his home while most of us did everything we could to keep that information secret.

'What do you want?' Hayden growled, his frustration growing considerably at the man's reluctance to speak and lack of information. My eyes darted to Jett's, which locked with mine. He looked absolutely petrified, his face frozen in terror while tears leaked from his eyes. My heart pounded behind my ribs, afraid for him.

He watched me closely, silently begging to be saved. My eyes darted up to the man's face to see him focusing on Hayden. I reconnected my gaze with Jett and ticked my head to the left almost imperceptibly. Confusion crossed his features, sending a wave of frustration through me. I repeated the motion, exaggerating the movement a little more. My hand formed the shape of a gun by my side, slowly ticking my thumb down as if taking an imaginary shot. Realisation seemed to click finally in Jett's mind, because his eyes widened, if possible, even more for a moment. I gave a tiny nod, silently telling him to wait.

'What do I want?' the man said, repeating Hayden's question. 'I want you to take me to where you put our medicines and give them back.'

'Never,' Hayden said instantly, shaking his head.

'Then I'm afraid your little friend here . . .' the man trailed off, digging the knife even deeper into Jett's skin and causing a thicker line of blood to seep out over the blade. Jett whined uncomfortably, the pain written clearly across his tear-soaked face. '. . . is going to have to pay for it.'

'No!' Hayden shouted, taking another step forward. Tension sizzled around the clearing so thick I could practically feel it weighing down on my skin. The man's eyes nearly bulged from his head at Hayden's movement and I knew

I had to act now before it was too late. Jett's watery eyes locked on mine once more as I tilted my head to the side, signalling to him silently.

All at once, several things happened. Jett leaned far to his right, digging the knife along a new part of skin deep enough to draw blood. The man appeared surprised, glancing down at Jett to try and subdue his movement. Hayden froze, halting his progression so as not to cause further damage to Jett. And finally, my hand whipped behind my back, grasping the handle of the gun and jerking it forward.

In less than a second, I aligned the three guides mounted on the top of the gun with the man's forehead. Without hesitating, I squeezed the trigger, sending a loud bang echoing around us as the barrel released the bullet. A sickeningly wet *thunk* sounded as the bullet struck, sending a spray of red shooting out behind it.

The man fell to the ground with a tiny, almost non-lethal looking hole through the very middle of his forehead leaking only a small trickle of blood. Jett was released from his grip as he fell, and the knife landed on the dirt with a soft thud, the edge of it smeared with blood from Jett's neck. Hayden whipped towards me, taking in the gun in my hands and the offensive stance I was in before he jerked his attention back to Jett.

Hayden had barely managed to open his arms before Jett crashed into them, his body colliding solidly with Hayden's torso as he hugged him tightly. Sobs echoed out around us as he cried, clinging to Hayden's body as if terrified the man would get up and take him again. Hayden's arms wound around his shoulders, hugging him back before recovering enough to speak low to him.

'Hey, it's all right . . .' he said quietly, running his hand over his back. Jett sobbed into his stomach for a few seconds

251

before Hayden grabbed him lightly and pulled him back to inspect his throat. 'Are you okay?'

A thin line stretched across his skin, bleeding but not too deep. The pressure of the blade had split his skin, but hadn't managed to open any arteries. After a quick visit to Docc, Jett would be just fine.

'I-I think so,' Jett stammered, reaching up to attempt to wipe away his tears. He sniffled loudly before detaching himself from Hayden suddenly and running toward me, just as he had done with Hayden.

I felt his thin arms rope around my waist, hugging me tightly before I managed to recover and loop an arm somewhat awkwardly around his shoulders.

'Thank you, Grace,' he said, pulling back to glance up at me.

'You're welcome,' I answered, surprised by his sudden show of gratitude. He looked younger than his ten years, tears soaking his face. He shot me a shaky smile before glancing back at the man crumpled on the ground.

'He must have followed us from the trees outside Whetland,' Hayden mused aloud, frowning at the body in the dirt. 'I bet Renley didn't even know he was here.'

'Who's Renley?' Jett asked, frowning in confusion. He sniffled again and gingerly touched his neck, paling when he saw blood stain his fingertips. He brushed them against the legs of his shorts while he waited for Hayden to answer.

'Leader of Whetland, remember? I've told you,' Hayden said patiently.

'I thought that was Celt?' Jett asked.

I nearly choked on my air at the mention of my father's name, which luckily went unnoticed by the two of them. They did not know who my father was and I had no intention of telling either of them as I was certain it would benefit me in absolutely no way.

'No, that's Greystone,' Hayden said, glancing at me. It was as if he just remembered that that was where I was from. He blinked and a sudden relief washed over his face.

'You're from Greystone,' Jett pointed out, looking at me.

'Yes,' I said simply.

'Are you going to go back?' he continued, watching me with wide eyes.

'No, I can't,' I said slowly, unable to look at Hayden and meet his gaze. I didn't want to see whatever was on his face at that moment.

'Well, I'm glad you're staying,' Jett said, like it was my own decision. 'I'd be dead without you!'

'No, you wouldn't,' I said, shaking my head. 'Hayden would have saved you somehow.'

'But you're the one who did,' Hayden interjected, breaking into Jett and I's conversation. 'You're making this a habit of yours.'

'What?' I asked, frowning in confusion.

'Saving the people I'm supposed to,' Hayden said slowly, his eyes burning into mine. 'First Kit, now Jett . . . We owe you.'

'It's fine, really . . .' I said, feeling, of all things, oddly embarrassed. I wasn't used to getting praise, much less from someone I had finally admitted to having feelings for. What a strange sensation it was, indeed. I needed to change the subject.

'Should we, um, you know?' I said, pointing at the body. I didn't want to speak of it in front of Jett, but we had to do something about it. Hayden shook his head as Jett took a few apprehensive steps away from where the man had landed.

'No, I'll send someone. Let's get back,' Hayden said,

253

putting a hand on Jett's back to guide him away. He scooped down to grab the remaining items that Jett hadn't managed to gather and stuffed them into the bag before slinging the strap over his broad shoulder. Jett took a deep, shuddering breath that sounded very loud in the quiet of the trees, clearly still very shaken up by what had just happened.

'We'll stop by Docc to get your neck looked at, buddy,' Hayden said gently to Jett, who nodded.

'I'm not going to have to get stitches, am I?' he asked, cringing.

'I don't think so,' I answered, squinting at it in the darkness. All things considered, it really wasn't too bad. A good cleaning and a few bandages should do the trick, but I'd leave it up to Docc to handle.

'Okay, good,' Jett said, clearly relieved.

Hayden remained fairly quiet as we moved through the camp toward the infirmary, thinking about something that kept him trapped in his head. Jett chattered away, claiming he hadn't really been that scared all along. I appeased him, agreeing that he looked like he had things under control as we walked through the doors to the infirmary. Jett darted away in search of Docc, leaving Hayden and I to move through the small building alone.

'You don't have to lie to him, you know,' Hayden said with a hint of amusement.

'What do you mean?'

'You told him he looked like he could handle it when he was nearly pissing his pants. You can tell him that, you know? He needs to hear it, sometimes,' Hayden said quietly.

'He's going to have a hard time being brave if people are always telling him he's not,' I pointed out.

'Hmmph,' Hayden muttered, not responding any further as we entered the main part of the building. I was surprised

254

to see Kit sitting up in one of the beds, looking much better than the last time we'd seen him. His bandages were clean, his face had a healthy flush of colour, and he showed no signs of fever or infection from what I could tell. It appeared as though the antibiotics we'd got him were already working wonders.

'Hayden, Grace,' he greeted in surprise. 'What the hell just happened to Jett? He ran through here with his neck bleeding all over and looked as happy as a clam.'

'Someone from Whetland followed us and had a knife to his throat before Grace shot him,' Hayden explained, giving him the abridged version. Kit nodded, as if this news wasn't something that shocked him.

'You guys are all right?' he asked, glancing at both of us. I nodded while Hayden muttered a quiet confirmation.

'Good,' Kit said, nodding slowly.

He stood from the bed, a tiny twinge of his jaw the only thing giving away the fact that he was still in significant pain. He was healing, but he clearly still had a long way to go before being fully functional again. I was shocked when he moved forward and roped an arm around me, giving me my second surprise hug in less than thirty minutes. I froze for a second before managing to respond, hugging him lightly in return. When he pulled away, my eyes darted immediately to Hayden to see him glaring at Kit, his eyes narrowed along with his jaw sharply set. I couldn't ignore a small twinge of happiness as I let myself think for a moment that he was jealous.

'I've been such a dick to you and I'm sorry,' Kit said, surprising me even more than his hug had. 'You've done nothing but help everyone here and I've only doubted you. I couldn't really help it since that's how we're raised, you know?'

He grinned apologetically at me, sitting back down on the bed as a little bit of colour drained from his face at the small exertion.

'I completely understand,' I said. And I did. I was raised similarly – you only trust your own. I was not part of their own, so naturally they did not trust me. I couldn't hold that against Kit for going by what he'd known his entire life. 'Don't even worry about it.'

'Brilliant,' Kit said with a wide smile. Hayden cleared his throat loudly next to me, jerking my attention toward him. He looked tenser than the situation warranted as he took a step forward.

'Right, well, good to see you're feeling better, Kit,' Hayden said tightly. I bit back a smile that tried to force its way through at Hayden's obvious jealousy. It was like I'd won a small victory, and I suddenly felt like shouting in joy. As if on cue, Jett reappeared from wherever he'd been with Docc, a fresh bandage wrapped around his throat just as I had predicted.

'Guys! No stitches!' he cheered, pointing at his throat with a wide grin on his face.

'Yeah, lucky you . . .' Kit muttered before chuckling at him. 'We'll both have neck scars now, little man.'

'Wow! We will!' he said in excitement. 'Awesome!'

Kit grinned at him before reaching forward to ruffle his hair lightly.

'We should get going,' Hayden said, shuffling backward slowly as he stuffed his hands into his front pockets.

'Okay,' Jett said, ducking away from Kit's hand and bounding toward the door.

'See you, Kit,' Hayden said before following Jett. I raised my hand to wave goodbye, still feeling awkward about the hug but pleased it had got such a reaction out of Hayden.

A cool breeze whipped through the camp, which was now completely dark.

'Hayden, can we get hot chocolate?' Jett asked suddenly, wrapping his little arms around his body. 'It's cold!'

'Jett . . .' Hayden trailed off, clearly exhausted.

'Please? I just about got killed!' he said, pointing to his neck once more.

'Isn't it too soon to be using that as leverage?' Hayden asked, chuckling quietly. Jett beamed up at him, baring his teeth in a silent plea. 'Fine. One quick cup but then you have to go home and tell Maisie what happened.'

'Yes!' Jett said, jumping excitedly and starting off across the short path to the kitchen.

'You interested in hot chocolate?' Hayden said, glancing at me while we walked.

'What is it?' I asked uncertainly. Hayden's jaw dropped as he gaped at me.

'You don't know what hot chocolate is?'

'No . . .' I said, suddenly feeling stupid. Hayden stifled a laugh as we followed Jett through the door to the dark building that was the kitchen and mess hall.

'I guess that makes sense,' he said mysteriously. 'You'll see.'

'It's sooo good,' Jett said. 'Hayden makes it the best!'

'Yeah, Hayden makes it the best!' Hayden repeated, referring to himself in the third person and mimicking Jett's seemingly constant excited tone. I laughed as they led me back into the kitchen where usually only Maisie and her helpers were allowed. A small table stood in there, surrounded by four stools. Light flickered suddenly as Jett lit a candle on the table, casting us all in a soft glow.

'This had better be good,' I joked, settling onto one of the stools.

257

'Oh, it is,' Hayden said. He moved through the kitchen, pulling open cupboards and retrieving a few supplies. I couldn't see exactly what he was gathering but I heard the soft sizzle of a hot plate turning on. He filled a large bowl with water from the vat that stood in the corner and set it on the hot plate. His hands moved surely as he added mystery ingredients to three mugs he had gathered.

'It's better with milk but we don't exactly have a ton of that sitting around . . .' Hayden said softly.

Jett sat on the stool next to me, watching Hayden eagerly. Before long, the water had started to steam. Hayden removed the bowl and poured the hot water into the mugs, mixing each of them with a spoon before carrying two over to Jett and me at the table.

'Let it cool, Jett,' Hayden instructed. It sounded as if this was something he said often but was probably frequently ignored. He returned to the table with his own mug and set it down in front of him. I looked down at the mug he'd handed me, which was filled with a brown, steaming liquid.

'Try it, Grace!' Jett said excitedly, grinning at me with anticipation.

I picked up the mug, raising it gingerly to my nose. The chocolatey scent was delicious and the smell sparked a memory from years ago when Celt had found a few candy bars for Jonah and I to split. Of course Jonah, being Jonah, had taken them all for himself the moment Celt was gone, forcing me to watch him eat them without tasting a single one. The scent had been all that had lingered in the air, but it had been enough to make my mouth water.

I took a small sip, the liquid so hot it burned the tip of my tongue but undeniably delicious.

'Oh my god,' I muttered. We didn't get a lot of sweet

258

things to eat so it was like liquid magic. Hayden, who had been watching my reaction closely, grinned at me.

'You like it?'

'It's delicious,' I told him.

'My mum used to make it all the time before . . . everything,' he said, a flash of sadness crossing his face before he wiped it away. 'Glad you like it.'

I felt a pang of sadness for him. Again I was struck by how tragic it was for him to remember such things only to have lost them for ever. He had suffered so much at such a young age that it broke my heart.

'It's really good,' I reassured him. Jett appeared unable to hold out any longer, because he started taking swigs of his own, not pausing long enough to let it cool down. He muttered a quiet 'ow' when he burned his tongue, earning an unsurprised shake of Hayden's head.

'I told you to wait,' Hayden said smugly.

'I know, I know,' Jett muttered, waving him off. He quickly became engrossed in his hot chocolate, ignoring Hayden and me as he devoted his concentration to the sweet liquid.

'I've been meaning to ask you . . .' Hayden began. He leaned on his elbows, hunching over his shoulders slightly across the table from me.

'Ask me what?' I said, heart thumping nervously.

'That guy we saw in Whetland, how did you know he had cancer?' he asked slowly, as if afraid I would be upset by his question. His careful gaze stayed fixed on mine, waiting patiently for my response. I drew a shaky breath, ignoring the pang in my chest as her face flashed across my mind again. He'd revealed more than I ever imagined he would to me, so I could share at least a bit of myself with him.

'My mum died of cancer,' I replied quietly. I found

259

myself unable to tear my gaze away from his. 'Of all things to die of in this world . . . She looked the same way before she passed.'

'I'm sorry,' Hayden said sincerely. His hand inched forward across the table as if he meant to grab mine before he retracted it, his eyes darting to Jett at the other side, oblivious to us.

'It was a while ago,' I shrugged, responding the same way I always did.

'But it still hurts, right?' he asked, as if seeking confirmation that it was normal to continue to grieve the death of a loved one years after they were gone. I knew, in that moment, he was thinking of his own parents. We'd both lost people we loved very much.

'It still hurts,' I agreed softly. This time his thumb brushed lightly over my knuckles. He only did it once before retracting his hand once more, but it sent a jolt of fire up my arm and straight into my heart.

'So your mum's gone . . .' he said slowly, flinching slightly at his words. 'You still have your brother. Anyone else?'

'My dad,' I replied, tension twisting at my stomach. It felt weird to tell him these things, as if the more I revealed about myself, the harder it would be to stay protected.

'Wow,' Hayden said, as if surprised so much of my family remained alive. It was a true tragedy that things like this were considered rare these days. 'What's your dad like?'

He leaned towards me as if he found this all fascinating. Having no family remaining of his own, I supposed he was very interested in what it was like to actually have one alive.

'He's . . .' I trailed off, unsure of what to say. 'He's amazing. Kind, sweet, funny, selfless. I couldn't ask for a better father.'

A soft smile tugged at Hayden's lips before he leaned back, sagging into his chair. 'Sounds like it.'

The smile quickly slid off his face, something more difficult to read taking its place. He didn't speak again as he became lost in his thoughts. My opportunity to observe him in calm silence was interrupted, however, by a quiet snore sounding from beside me, I jumped before letting out a low chuckle at the sight of Jett sound asleep, his face resting on his arms on the table.

'Kid can sleep anywhere,' Hayden muttered, as if this wasn't the first time this had happened. He drained his cup and pushed his hand through his hair once before heaving himself to stand. I copied him, drinking the rest of my delicious hot chocolate and rising from my chair. Hayden moved around the table, scooping Jett up easily to lift him without waking him. Jett's head lolled around until it settled onto Hayden's shoulder where he continued to snore lightly.

'Come on,' he said quietly. 'Let's call it a night.'

Chapter 22 – Struggle

HAYDEN

Jett's head rested on my shoulder as we walked down the dark path, his body warming mine in the chilly night air. He continued to snore lightly, the sound of it accompanying the quiet crunch of our boots in the dirt. My arms were taut around his body as we neared the hut he lived in with Maisie. I could feel Grace's gaze linger on me for a few seconds, but she didn't say anything.

'Nearly there,' I said quietly, my voice dropping deeper than usual. We passed countless huts that all looked very similar, little touches like tattered flower pots and handmade signs the only things setting them apart.

Finally, Maisie's hut came into view, distinguished by a wooden flower Jett had tried to carve. I nodded at it, silently telling Grace which it was. She turned off the path and raised her hand to knock gently. A quiet shuffling came from inside before the door opened, revealing a very tired-looking Maisie. It suddenly occurred to me that she probably didn't know what had happened tonight or she would have come and found Jett much sooner.

She smiled sleepily at us, taking in Jett snoring on my shoulder before her eyes landed on the bandage around his neck. Her eyes widened, concern flooding over her features.

'Maisie—' I started, only to be cut off immediately.

'What happened to him?!' she demanded instantly, stepping forward to brush her fingers along his neck. Her eyes flashed back and forth between Jett and my face.

'He's all right,' I assured her, shifting his weight as he slipped down my torso slightly.

'How did this happen?' she pressed urgently.

'Someone followed us from Whetland and threatened him while we were practising shooting,' I explained. 'He had a knife to his throat before Grace shot the guy.'

Her eyes flashed to Grace beside me, who had remained silent.

'You saved him?' she asked. Grace's mouth opened before closing once more. Her lips pulled together in an awkward smile before nodding slowly.

'I guess so,' she said modestly. I could tell she was somewhat uncomfortable with the amount of recognition she was receiving today. Maisie didn't hug her, but the gratitude was evident in her expression.

'It was a lucky day for us when you came to Blackwing,' she said slowly, her voice dripping with sincerity. I couldn't help but silently agree. Grace appeared stunned by her words and mumbled something quietly in reply, a blush creeping into her cheeks.

'It's nothing . . .' she said, glancing to me to save her from the conversation. For all the shit she gave me for being bad at talking, she wasn't much better.

'Want him in bed?' I asked, diverting Maisie's attention from Grace.

'Yes, please,' Maisie said, stepping back to let me into her softly lit home. The hut was even smaller than mine, the single room taken up mostly by two twin beds, two chairs, and a dresser. A few of Jett's things were aligned neatly on top of the dresser, treasures he'd collected over his years growing up here. Smiling, I noticed a small toy helicopter sitting in the centre. I carried him to the bed against the wall, which I knew to be his. This wasn't the first time I'd brought him home in a dead sleep.

He didn't wake as I lay him gently onto the bed, his head tilting to the side on the pillow. Grace surprised me by arriving by my side and throwing a blanket over his thin body. I shot her the smallest of smiles before we rejoined Maisie at the door.

'Thanks for looking out for him,' she said to the both of us. 'As always.'

'No problem,' I said casually. 'We should go, though. It's late.'

'Of course. See you around,' Maisie said as we stepped out the door. She gave a small wave before closing it, leaving us alone in the night air once more. My feet automatically started to carry me back to my hut while Grace moved next to me.

'You know, for all that shit you gave me earlier, you really aren't much better at talking to people than I am,' I said with amusement. She shot me a quick glare before a soft smile split across her face.

'I can talk to people,' she defended. We weren't far from my hut and it was already coming into sight.

'Right,' I scoffed. 'You're shit at taking compliments or thanks, then.'

She let out a soft laugh. 'You've got me there.'

'Why is that?' I asked casually.

'I don't know, why are you bad at saying what you really mean?' she fired back, arching an eyebrow at me. She spared me from answering by continuing. 'We all have our flaws, Hayden.'

'Hmm,' I hummed softly in agreement. However, this

264

flaw she had, if you could even call it that, was really the only one I'd seen so far. In my opinion, her humility was just another strength.

We reached my hut, where she waited for me to open the door. Her gaze suddenly snapped to the line of trees behind the row of tiny houses, focusing into the darkness.

'What?' I asked. She squinted into the darkness and was quiet for a few seconds, her muscles tense.

'Nothing,' she said slowly. 'I thought I heard something but it was probably just a rabbit.'

'I'd rather not take the chance,' I said, adrenaline peaking in my system. 'Give me your gun.'

She pulled it from her waistband and handed it to me silently. My eyes focused on the space where she'd been looking, seeing nothing but darkness. I crept around the edge of my hut to draw closer.

'Stay here,' I commanded, not even looking at her as I inched forward with my gun raised.

'Hayden—'

'Stay here!'

Thankfully, she listened to me and stayed where she was. I moved forward through the night, finally drawing even with the line of trees. My eyes squinted to try and see something but all I could see were the dark outlines of trees. My gun aimed around me as I shifted deeper into the trees, searching for the source of the sound and fully expecting to find an enemy of some sort, but there was no sign of anyone. I waited for flashes of movement, but none came.

There was no one there.

I retreated from the trees after one more careful glance around to find Grace exactly where I'd left her, hands twisting anxiously in front of her. She let out a sigh of relief when she saw me approaching once more.

'Anyone there?' she asked, her eyes darting to the trees once before refocusing on my face.

'Nothing,' I said, shrugging. She heaved out a sigh and nodded.

'Okay, good.'

I nodded as I opened the door, shifting easily through the darkness until I found the box of matches to light a few candles. Grace shut the door behind her as she followed me. For the first time, I noticed dirt streaked across her cheek, spatters of blood flecked onto her skin, and other smatterings of the day marking her. I was certain I didn't look much better.

'Do you, um, do you need to shower?' I offered, uncertain. I set the gun down on my desk.

'Could I?' she asked hopefully.

'Of course,' I said, feeling overly polite. My mind drifted to the first shower she'd taken here, when she'd boldly removed her clothes and joined me beneath the spray of the water. That had been the first time I'd kissed her, despite my reluctance and denial. 'Um, you go first then I will if there's water left.'

She blinked, frowning slightly before nodding. 'Okay.'

She moved to the dresser, pulling out some of the clothes I'd got her, before heading to the small bathroom. She shot me a small smile as she passed, closing the door behind her. An odd sense of déjà vu settled over me, my mind drifting just as it always seemed to do.

It seemed like no matter what we talked about or what we did, she was continuously surprising me. I was constantly discovering more and more about her and had yet to find a flaw in her. She was strong, brave, selfless, and good. More than once, now, she'd given much of herself to save the life of another who in reality, shouldn't have meant anything to her. Both Kit and Jett were, essentially, enemies, yet she'd saved them without a second thought. I found it impossible to believe that anyone else in Greystone would have done the same.

What struck me more, however, was her ability to see through me. She'd thrown my act in my face earlier as no one had ever done before, seeing through the image I worked so hard to portray. Yes, I knew I was tough, dangerous, and brave, but she easily saw through my insistence that I didn't care. It was something I'd grown up thinking would make me tougher, stronger, but something I'd never really been able to shut down. No matter how hard I tried, there was no denying that I cared for the people around me. She saw that easily, which made me feel vulnerable.

Everything about this situation was so strange, so foreign, so uncertain. I had no idea what I was doing, what I wanted, or what she wanted. No, I knew what I wanted, but I didn't know how to go about it. I wanted Grace and I wanted to be able to fully admit it to myself and to her, but I couldn't seem to stop the inner battle that had waged inside me from day one.

It was in moments of chaotic vulnerability that I revealed the most to her, my true feelings and emotions leaking out in the cracks that formed in my façade. In those moments, she either returned or accepted my sentiments, which was a good sign. I still, however, had absolutely no idea where we stood, a fact made more difficult yet by the world we lived in. Could people really even hope to have something semi-normal in a decidedly abnormal world?

My thoughts were cut off by Grace emerging from the bathroom, her hair dripping wet around her face, and skin still damp beneath the white tank top and black shorts she wore. She ruffled her hair quickly with a towel before flashing me another smile, which I focused determinedly on as I forced my gaze to stay put.

Her being so damn beautiful really wasn't helping my inner struggle.

'There should be about half left,' she told me, raking her fingers through her hair.

'Thanks,' I mumbled. My feet carried me toward the bathroom and I realised I'd been pacing the entire time she'd been in there. I really needed to sort my head out soon or I was going to go insane. Even after telling her how I cared for her and how I wanted to protect her, I still had absolutely no idea where we stood, a fact that both concerned and comforted me.

'I'll be right out,' I told her before closing the door. I stripped down quickly, shoving the waistband of my jeans past my hips before ripping my shirt over my head, the collar of it clenched in my fist tightly. The water was cold as I stepped beneath it, the cool streams trailing over my scarred back to soothe my skin. I forced all thoughts of Grace from my mind as I cleaned my body, determined to shower quickly and attempt a few moments of quiet peace before being confronted with Grace again.

All too quickly, the water ran out, leaving my wet hair clinging to my skin in thick clumps before I managed to push it back off my face, like when a dog shook off the water from its fur. As I dragged a towel over my skin, I realised I had forgotten to take another set of clothes with me. When I re-entered the main room, Grace averted her gaze quickly. A small smirk pulled at my features, pleased she'd got caught looking.

She gazed determinedly away from me as I crossed to my dresser and pulled on a pair of boxer briefs and shorts, not bothering with a shirt. The towel dropped to the ground before I bent to hang it on a hook next to where Grace had hung hers. She was already snuggled beneath her blanket but still very much awake. I felt a pang of guilt for making her sleep on it for so long and was struck with a sudden idea that sent a wave of nerves through me.

I sat on the edge of my bed after blowing out all but one of the candles in the hut, plunging us into relative darkness.

'Hey, Grace?' I said slowly.

'Yeah?' she answered, finally looking at me once more.

'Do you, um, want to share the bed? It's a lot more comfortable than the couch . . .' I trailed off, feeling annoyed at myself for being so nervous about asking. She was quiet as she considered my offer.

'You don't mind?' she asked cautiously.

'No,' I answered honestly. After the night we'd spent in the city, I was eager for another chance to feel her chest pressed into mine and the steady way she breathed when she slept.

'Um, all right,' she said, slowly pushing her blankets down.

She got up and avoided looking at me as she moved across the room. She tentatively pulled down the blankets on the other side before crawling in. I leaned forward to blow out the last candle, leaving us surrounded by complete darkness. It was impossible to ignore the pounding of my heart as I lay down, the distance between us too great to feel her warmth.

'This is way better than the couch,' she said with a soft laugh, breaking the tension that seemed to have settled over us once more. I chuckled and shifted my broad shoulders, attempting to relax into the mattress but instead feeling even more tense as I felt the urge to move closer to her.

'Told you,' I replied. I felt like my body was vibrating and I couldn't get comfortable, as if every cell in my body could sense how close she was even though we weren't touching. I couldn't even see her thanks to the darkness, but I could feel her there and hear the soft whispers of her breath as it escaped her lips.

'You're really good with Jett, has anyone told you that?' she said suddenly.

'What brought that to mind?' I said with a low laugh. It seemed like such a strange thing to bring up . . . now.

'I dunno, I was just thinking it earlier and thought you should know. Not everyone is good with kids like that.'

'Hmm,' I said, unsure of how to respond. In truth, Jett was the only kid I'd ever really interacted with. Most of the others seemed to be too afraid of me to approach, but not Jett. Ever since he could walk, he'd been trying to keep up with Kit, Dax, and I. He'd given us no choice, really, not that we minded now.

I jumped when I felt her hand brush down my forearm lightly, her touch surprising me. My head turned on my pillow towards her, the only thing I could see was a very dark blur where I knew she was. Her hand didn't leave my arm as it continued to rake up and down my skin slowly, raising goose bumps on the surface. My heart pounded a little harder.

'I'm glad you're here, Grace,' I admitted quietly. Her touch paused for a fraction of a second as she absorbed my words before restarting. 'I know you'd probably rather be home with your family, and I don't blame you. If I had a family, that's where I'd want to be. But for what it's worth . . . I'm glad you're here.'

'I do miss my family,' she said quietly. 'But . . . I'm glad I'm here too. With you.'

I sucked in a quiet breath at her confession, my shoulders lifting from the bed so I could roll onto my side to face her.

I could feel the heat of her body now, inches away from my own as she lay on her side to face me. My hand shifted, covering her own as it glided lightly up and down my arm. I moved my hand up her arm, over her shoulder, and up along her jaw, the feel of her skin guiding my touch in the darkness. I could feel her jaw shudder gently as she drew a shaky breath at my touch.

I wanted to take in every detail of her face despite the dark; I wanted to memorise the curve of her lip and every inch of her skin covering her soft cheeks. I wanted to sink into the moment of dark vulnerability and just settle with her. I wanted to forget everything except for her and let her in, really let her in, but the walls around my heart were high and strong, making the task difficult.

She didn't say anything as my thumb ran over her lip once more, but I could feel her breath, ragged and warm. I knew her heart had to be pounding just as mine was, revelling in the way I touched her just as I was enjoying it. Without even realising, my body had shifted much closer to hers, mere inches separating us now.

'Hayden,' she breathed softly, stilling my touch. My fingertips had woven into her hair as my hand cupped the side of her jaw.

'Yes?' I replied. My voice was deep and low.

'My heart is beating really fast,' she whispered, the air between us so thick with tension that it almost seemed to dull the words. I shifted forward, closing the remaining distance between us and sending a jolt through my body.

'So is mine,' I admitted, relishing in the harsh thumping of my chest against my ribs. It was a rush unlike anything else. It took every bit of self-control I had to restrain myself, though I could feel my resolve slipping through my fingers with every beat of my heart.

'Kiss me, Hayden,' she breathed, her words so soft and quiet I was certain I had made them up in my head. The tiniest movement of her body forward amplified her whispered statement, however, as she pressed into me. Without further hesitation, I drew a deep, shaky breath and leaned forward in the darkness, my lips easily finding hers.

It was as if the world fell away. Sparks fired from all my nerves, shooting through my body and waking up every single cell. Every inch of me that was pressed into her seemed to be buzzing excitedly, making it impossible to draw back from her now that I had given in. My skin craved hers, the only relief to the burning desperation to be near her only soothed by actual contact.

All of my efforts to subdue these feelings crumbled at my feet the moment I let myself kiss her. Despite my inner struggle and my determination to remain strong, she was breaking me down bit by bit, and there was absolutely nothing I could do about it.

Chapter 23 – Fervour
GRACE

Heavy thudding resounded in my chest, so hard that I could feel the shudder through my body. The heat of Hayden's lips on mine seemed to be melting away the stress of the day. There was something so undeniable flowing between us, sparking through my veins when he so much as shifted next to me. I couldn't seem to escape the pull I felt to him, every moment I spent with him only dragging me closer and closer.

I'd never felt anything quite like I did now as he kissed me. The vulnerable, dangerously unguarded words we'd exchanged had built up the beautiful tension I felt in the pit of my stomach, the feeling overflowing through my limbs when he'd kissed me. It was so rare that he showed his true emotions or verbalised what was actually on his mind, so to hear his admission and to see the unguarded side of him had been incredible.

Even though we were both reluctant to admit so, we both felt a strange, unimaginable pull toward each other.

My pulse pounded through my veins now as his lips melded into mine, moving slowly, carefully. His hand cupped my cheek lightly and his thumb brushed along my cheekbone as he kissed me, setting my skin and blood on fire alike. My body shifted forward against my will, pushing into his without my permission.

Everything about him was so familiar yet unfamiliar; I felt like I'd spent years watching him and the way he moved but so little time actually touching him. His chest was firm and warm as I pressed into him, the pressure returned ever so slightly as his hips met mine.

I sucked in a breath when the kiss intensified as he swiped his tongue smoothly along my lower lip. I found it difficult to maintain my composure when he let his tongue push against my own lightly. My hands wove around his neck, clutching him to me in a desperation I could not control. His insistence on keeping the pace slow and steady only served to build up the tension I could feel in every cell in my body.

My teeth tugged lightly on his lower lip, pulling it back and earning a quiet groan from him as I released it. Encouraged, he dove back in feverishly, letting his lips melt into my own and his tongue push into my mouth once more. I was surprised when my leg wound around his hip, both of us still lying on our sides, and drew him even closer.

A quiet gasp left my throat when he let out another groan, the pressure between us getting to him as he tore his lips from mine and pushed me onto my back before pulling his body over mine. Immediately, my hands tangled in his hair, tugging his lips back down to mine while his body fell between my thighs. His body weight alone was enough to put pressure on my core.

He hadn't even touched me and I was already coming undone.

Perceptively, his hips shifted to allow him to rock his body slowly over mine, grinding himself into me in the most teasing way possible. A whine left my lips as he kissed me, before disconnecting the kiss to drag a hot trail down my neck. My eyes closed as I relished the feel of his lips on my throat; they parted slightly to wet the skin before moving down the line.

It was like every muscle in my body was rebelling against me, tightening and relaxing in time with the kisses he placed on my skin. My fingers were absolutely enmeshed in his hair, tangling through the strands and tugging gently, while my thighs tightened involuntarily around his hips. The amount of self-control it took for me not to rip his clothes off at that moment was astronomical.

When he placed a heated kiss over my collarbone, my back arched off the mattress, shifting my hips along with his and earning another groan from Hayden. I somehow managed to untangle my hands from his hair to let them rake down his back. I felt a pang as the pads of my fingers ran over the rough texture, the countless scars and flaws connecting with my touch. I felt him exhale softly as he noticed me touching his back, pausing as if unsure I really wanted him even though he was damaged.

God, how I wanted him.

My hands travelled slowly down their path, feeling the scars gently without hesitation as the strong muscles passed beneath my touch. It wasn't until my hands reached his lower back that he resumed his actions, deciding I wasn't scared off by his scars. His lips pressed once at the hollow of my throat before finding my own again, parting them gently to kiss me once more.

My blood felt like it was actually boiling in my body as he rocked his hips slowly once more, driving me absolutely insane. There was so much to consider, so much confusion, but in that moment, all I cared about was Hayden.

My thumbs hooked the band of his shorts before sliding around the sides, reaching as far as I could before I was stopped where our bodies were pressed together. I sucked in a deep breath before I slowly inched the band over his hips. My heart thudded more rapidly than it had in my entire time at Blackwing, terrified and exhilarated all at once.

I had managed to shift his shorts down only a few inches when he stopped kissing me, dropping his forehead to mine and letting out a heavy sigh.

'Grace . . .' he said, his tone sending a wave of embarrassment and disappointment through me. His eyes flicked open after closing momentarily and I tried to suppress the sting of rejection. My hands shifted upward once more, resting on his hips.

'I'm sorry,' I mumbled, sure my cheeks were burning red.

'Don't be sorry,' he said quietly, sitting up enough so he could see me better. His face hovered inches over mine and I flinched slightly when I felt his hand brush back a few strands of my hair. I couldn't find it in me to look him in the eye as I let my mortification wash over me. I had pushed him too far.

'Hey, seriously,' he said, ducking his head down to force me to look at him. 'You have no idea how much I want that, okay? I just . . . I don't want to rush into anything.'

'Sure,' I murmured, still too embarrassed to believe him. I'd tried to take things further and he'd stopped me, sending me into a quick downward spiral of self-doubt.

'I mean it, all right? I . . . god, Grace, I want to so bad. But I care about you too much to rush into something and ruin it,' he said softly. He sounded completely sincere, making the sting of rejection hurt a little bit less. I wondered if that was something that had happened to him before.

'It's not . . . because of me?' I asked, feeling more self-conscious than I ever had.

'*No*, not at all. You're so beautiful, Grace.'

I sucked in a short breath at his words, the sincerity

behind it striking my heart like a lightning bolt. I felt the ache of embarrassment and rejection start to slip away as I met his unwavering gaze, slowly starting to believe him. As if he could see me struggling internally, he dropped his head cautiously to press his lips ever so lightly against mine, in a feather-light kiss, but it was enough to send a shockwave down my spine and ignite my blood once more.

'Sorry, again,' I whispered. I had no idea what to say to his compliment, something I was terrible at accepting.

'Stop apologising,' he said, a hint of a laugh crossing his features.

'Okay, okay, sorry,' I said before I even realised what I said. A light giggle came from my throat, lifting what remained of my embarrassment. Hayden grinned down at me, his stunning features lighting up as he did so.

'Get some sleep, Grace,' he said quietly, running his thumb across my lower lip once before sliding off me. He landed next to me, rolling onto his back and letting his arms fall on either side of him. I remained where I was, staring at the ceiling as I tried to decide if I could cuddle into him or not. He let out a quiet sigh and lifted an arm to rope around my neck, hauling me into his side.

I let him, resting my head on his shoulder and tentatively looping my arm across his stomach. His arm drifted across my back, holding me gently to him as he tugged the blankets that had got pushed out of the way back over us.

'Goodnight, Hayden,' I whispered, settling into him completely.

'Goodnight, Grace,' he returned softly. I felt his fingers tickle slowly across my back, the gesture comforting and sending a wave of butterflies through my stomach.

My heart was finally beginning to return to its normal pace, though I still felt the heat searing through my veins as

I pressed into him. While the embarrassment and rejection in my system had been eradicated, the disappointment lingered. There was no denying the fact that my body was pent up, frustrated from the way he made me feel with no way to ease the tension.

He was the biggest tease I'd ever encountered and I didn't even think he was aware of it.

Despite the tension lingering in my body, the quiet lull of Hayden's breathing and beating heart soon melded into the perfect lullaby to soothe me to sleep. I slept hard, once again exhausted by the day and deeply comforted by the heat of Hayden's body so close to mine.

My sleep was interrupted hours later by a round of knocking at Hayden's door. I groaned as my face pressed into whatever it was resting on, which turned out to be Hayden's arm. At some point during the night, we'd shifted so Hayden was now behind me, his arm looped around my waist to hold me against him. His breath was soft as it whooshed past my ear, blowing the stray hairs across my cheek.

I squeezed my eyes shut, hoping that whoever insisted on knocking would go away and leave us be for a while, but the mystery person did not hear my silent plea as they knocked again. A sharp inhale from behind me told me that Hayden had awoken. This seemed to be a common thing for him, to be awoken in the morning by a knock at the door, because it had already happened several times since I'd arrived here. There were times when I forgot he was the leader of an entire camp.

'Hang on,' Hayden called, his voice raspy and impossibly deep in the morning. His nose nudged the back of my neck gently before I heard him whisper quietly, 'Morning.'

'Morning,' I responded easily, a gentle smile pulling at my

lips once more. Our greeting was cut short, as he untangled himself from me and crawled out of bed. He pulled his arms out in front of him, stretching and flexing the muscles in his back tightly before letting his arms fall back to his sides, his shoulders shifting in the process. I couldn't tear my eyes away from him as he pulled a shirt from his dresser – maroon and red plaid with the sleeves torn off. He buttoned it only a few times before moving to the door. When he reached the handle, he paused and turned back to me.

'Um,' he said somewhat awkwardly, glancing at me in his bed before his eyes darted to the couch apologetically.

'Oh, right,' I said, realising that it probably wouldn't look good for me to be caught sharing his bed. I ignored the gentle wave of sadness that rolled through me. I understood why even though I didn't want to leave the blankets that still held his warmth. As quickly as I could, I moved to the couch, pulling the blanket over me to make it look like I'd just woken up. He nodded once and shot me another apologetic grimace before opening the door.

Bright light streamed into the room, causing both of us to squint as the visitor greeted Hayden cheerily. Once my eyes adjusted to the new brightness, I realised it was Maisie.

'Sorry to wake you,' she said as she took in Hayden's bleary appearance.

''S'all right,' Hayden murmured, running his fingers over his eyes to try and wake himself up. 'What is it?'

'We used up the rest of the venison this morning,' she said, frowning. 'We're going to need more soon or I'll have difficulty feeding everyone.'

'We're out already?' Hayden asked, frowning down at her. It was so interesting to see this side of how a camp really worked. In Greystone, Celt was in Hayden's position, but I rarely got to see the things he dealt with on a daily basis.

279

Seeing Hayden's continuous role as protector, provider, and overall leader of Blackwing really made me realise just how much weight rested on his shoulders. For every single issue that Blackwing had, he was looked at to help solve it.

'I'm afraid so,' Maisie said apologetically.

Hayden sighed and ran his hand down his face, pausing at his jaw to run his thumb and forefinger along his lower lip.

'All right. We'll get a hunt going, I guess.'

'Thank you. Want me to tell Dax?' she offered. It was then that she finally glanced at me on the couch, shooting me a soft smile before refocusing on Hayden.

'No, Grace and I can handle it,' he said, copying her to glance at me as well. I shifted under my blankets, trying to appear casual.

'Okay,' Maisie said, nodding. 'Stop by the mess hall before you leave and I'll give you some food. The usual amount?'

'Yeah,' Hayden replied. 'Thanks.'

'No problem,' Maisie answered with a soft smile before walking out of the frame and out of my sight. Hayden closed the door and pushed his hand through his hair absent-mindedly before turning to me.

'Ever been hunting before?' he asked, looking to me as I pulled myself from the couch.

'No, actually,' I replied. I'd never gone but I imagined it wouldn't be much different than going on a raid. Only this time, the targets wouldn't shoot back.

Hayden nodded. 'Well, get some stuff together. Pack a day or two of clothes and whatever else you might need. We'll get the other stuff from storage before we go.'

'A day or two? How long does this take?' I asked, surprised. When people went on hunting trips in Greystone, they were usually back in the same day.

'Usually two days. The animals don't come close enough to camp so we have to go pretty far away then settle down before they come out again. Takes a while.'

'Oh,' was all I said. 'Makes sense.'

Hayden didn't respond as he started pulling various items out of his dresser and stuffing them into a duffle bag he retrieved from beneath his bed. I copied him, pulling the few articles of clothing I had from the drawer he'd given me before I realised I had no bag to put them in. The backpack that contained my stash of feminine products was still full, and had been ripped the night I got it.

'Here,' Hayden said, seeing my dilemma and tossing me a medium-sized backpack that must have been stored next to his duffle bag.

'Thanks,' I said gratefully, stuffing my items into it.

Moments later, we had our supplies from his hut packed and strapped onto our backs as Hayden led us towards one of the storage buildings. Once inside, Hayden started pulling supplies from shelves. I watched as a tent, two sleeping bags, a lantern, a first aid kit, fire-starting supplies, a kettle, a knife kit, and several other items were piled onto the floor.

'Are we driving?' I asked, beginning to worry about the amount of things Hayden was piling up.

'Yeah, we'll take a truck,' he said, selecting a flashlight off the shelf and shoving it into his bag. 'I'll go get it if you'll start moving this stuff outside?'

'Sure,' I answered without thought. It suddenly occurred to me that it meant he would leave me completely alone for the first time since I'd arrived at Blackwing, if only for a few moments. My first thought wasn't of escape, however, but of pleasant surprise that he trusted me enough to do so.

He nodded and went out, setting off at a jog for the garage while I started to move the supplies outside. It was still early and the sun was just starting to rise, setting a warm glow around the camp. No other humans could be seen in the street, and things were quiet. In the distance, I heard the gentle roar of the truck's engine, the sound growing louder as Hayden drove it back to me.

When he pulled to a stop in front of me and parked, I was surprised to see several bags already loaded into the vehicle. As I added some of the supplies, I saw that it was the food Maisie had promised, already loaded and ready to go for us. Hayden helped me get the rest of the supplies into the vehicle before we jumped in and drove the short distance to the raid building to collect our weapons.

I was pleased when Hayden handed me a gun again – the same one I'd used yesterday that he must have taken from his hut. He then grabbed a rifle and, to my surprise, a crossbow.

'Why the crossbow?' I asked. He gathered up a bag of ammunition and slung it over his wide shoulders, the strap of the heavy bag cutting into his muscles.

'It wastes less ammo,' he explained, shrugging. 'I don't want to waste bullets on something we're going to eat.'

He handed me the crossbow to carry back to the truck. Finally, we were loaded up and ready to go. Hayden climbed into the driver's seat while I sat in the passenger's, pleased to be out of the back for once. Blackwing was quickly left behind as Hayden drove, bringing us deeper and deeper into the woods that surrounded the camp. More than once, I was certain we would get stuck between tree trunks as Hayden manoeuvred the vehicle through impossibly small spaces.

'So what do you hunt for?' I asked. I was curious about this, and it occurred to me I'd been eating meat here for a while now without always knowing what it was.

'Deer, hopefully. But they're hard to find so we'll take anything really. Turkey, duck, beaver—'

'Beaver?!' I said suddenly. My nose wrinkled in distaste.

'Yeah,' Hayden said with a laugh. He glanced at me quickly before refocusing on the road. 'It's better than it sounds, I promise.'

'I'm not sure if I believe you,' I laughed.

'Food is food,' he said, shrugging. 'Just hope we don't have to go for squirrel or anything.'

'Ugh, please no. Celt used to make us eat squirrel when we were little,' I said before I realised my mistake. I cut myself off and glanced nervously at Hayden to see if he noticed.

'Celt?' he said slowly, a frown settling over his features. 'You actually know Celt?'

'Um, yeah,' I said, unsure of how to proceed. 'He's . . . he was around a lot. Everyone knows Celt.'

Technically, it wasn't a lie. Celt *was* around a lot, always interacting with the kids and other members of Greystone. I'd just left out the fact that he was my father.

'Oh,' Hayden said simply. 'Okay.'

I suddenly felt very desperate to steer clear of any conversation that could potentially lead to the disclosure of information, nervous I'd got so close just now.

'So, um, we what? Camp in the tent and wait for animals to wander by?' I asked, hoping to divert his thoughts away from Celt.

'Yeah, basically,' he said. I let out a silent sigh of relief. 'That's why it takes so long – they hear us coming in but after a day or so they settle down and go back about their business. That's when we get them.'

'Strategic,' I joked, shooting him a smile. 'What about bears? Don't bears like to attack people camping?'

'Bears?' Hayden repeated. He belted out a laugh and

glanced at me, his brows raised high. 'There are no bears in these woods.'

'How do you know?' I shot back, giggling at his certainty.

'Because. I've lived here almost my entire life and I've never seen one,' he explained, his mood restored.

'Maybe the bears are smarter than you.'

'I don't think so.'

'You're not afraid of big, scary bears coming to get you in your sleep? I am,' I teased.

'I'm not afraid of anything,' he said, straightening up and puffing out his chest before chuckling.

'Ah, right. Okay, Hercules,' I chuckled.

'Hmm. Fitting,' he said, nodding thoughtfully.

'Yeah? All right then, Herc. Better live up to the name now. I'm talking completely fearless and cutting the heads off monsters and saving damsels in distress,' I said, grinning widely at his profile while he drove.

'Damsels in distress, right. So I'm Herc?' he asked. A dimple dotted into his cheek as he shot me a sideways grin.

'If you can live up to it, you're Herc,' I said with a giggle.

'Deal,' he said, shaking his head in amusement. 'So you think bears are scary, huh? Seems kind of irrational.'

'Bears are ferocious, all right? It's perfectly fine to be afraid of them,' I said, only half joking. I didn't really think we'd get attacked by a bear, but I didn't like the idea much anyway.

'You're kind of like a bear,' he mused aloud.

'Me? How?'

'Yeah, ferocious, lethal, kinda scary but also . . . strong and tough,' he said, surprising me with the depth of his compliment. He nodded as if reaching a decision. 'If I'm Herc, you're Bear.'

I felt my lips pull into an even wider smile, as butterflies fluttered in my stomach.

'I like it,' I admitted, watching him closely as he focused on driving. His eyes crinkled slightly in the corner thanks to his grin and the dimple in his cheek was deeper than ever, framed by the sharp angle of his jaw.

'I like it too, Bear. I like it, too.'

Chapter 24 – Hunt

HAYDEN

'Grace, hand me that stake,' I said, crouching in the dirt as I aligned the clips of the tent to the long, wobbly pole. I held out my hand in time for Grace to place the small metal stake into it, which I shoved into the pole before hammering it quickly into the dirt to secure it. It was the last piece of the frame to set up, leaving only the canvas left to secure over the poles.

'Want help?' she offered, crossing to stand on the other side of it.

'Yeah, thanks.'

I bent to pick up two corners of the tent, which was about ten feet by ten feet. A small burst of wind blew through the clearing, sending the fabric billowing up in my hands before Grace caught the other side and helped me string it along the poles. Soon, the tent was fully set up and ready for usage.

'Looks pretty good, huh, Bear?' I asked. My mood had been light all afternoon, the playful banter Grace and I continuously exchanged making for a pleasant time. She let out a wispy laugh at the nickname, her wide grin telling me she liked it despite its abnormal nature.

'Sure thing, Herc,' she shot back cheerfully. We'd spent the last hour setting up our camp, gathering firewood, and getting situated. What had been an empty clearing only an hour ago now housed our truck, a small tent, a makeshift fire pit, and a log we'd rolled over to sit on. Our supplies were strewn about on the ground, waiting to be put away into the tent now that it was finally constructed.

I watched quietly as Grace bent to pick up the supplies from the grass and haul them into the tent. Her shirt lifted slightly as she carried them to reveal a small strip of stomach. It took my eyes a second or two longer than it should have to divert their attention.

Ever since stopping what could have quickly escalated into something very serious, I had been having trouble controlling my thoughts. It was as if my body and mind were at war with one another; my thoughts continuously worked to think of anything other than Grace and the way her body had felt pressed to mine, while my body seemed to be working towards anything to achieve that feeling again. It was like torture now to be alone as before and try and hold back.

As Grace rustled around in the tent to set things up inside, my mind continued to think about earlier that morning. She had been clearly embarrassed and disappointed when I'd stopped things, but my words had been true. The last thing I wanted to do was rush into something physical when I was just starting to admit my emotional attachment to her. I didn't want to ruin whatever the hell was going on between us before it even started. Things in our world had a way of becoming more complicated than expected, so it was necessary to take things slowly to avoid disaster later on.

It was similar to what had happened with Malin. We'd started off as friends, which was more than one could say for Grace and me, before shifting to a physical relationship. We had both been lonely, desperate to be needed by someone or to feel something, but it hadn't worked. Despite sleeping together, the feelings had never come. We'd never been able to fall for each other or develop any emotion, crippling our chances from the start. Our time together had been strictly physical, leaving me feeling even emptier than I had before.

This was what haunted me – the fear that moving too quickly would stifle any chance for feeling, for emotion. Grace made me feel warm, needed, alive. It was something I'd never felt from another person and I was too greedy to let it go. I didn't want to lose what I was starting to feel for her by repeating my mistakes from before.

'Hayden?' Grace called from inside the tent, ripping me from my reverie.

'Yeah?' I responded, moving from where I'd been standing for the last few minutes. I lifted the flap and stuck my head inside to see what she'd been doing. Two sleeping bags had been unrolled, with our bags of clothes placed at the foot of each. The lantern was between the sleeping bags, the rest of our supplies lining the edges. Our weapons, including my crossbow, were sitting in the middle, ready for use.

'Does this look okay? I'm not sure if there's a specific way you like it or . . .' she trailed off, arching an eyebrow at me as she looked for approval.

'Yeah, looks fine,' I said, my eyes lingering on the separate sleeping bags. I'd packed them both with high hopes that I'd be able to resist her, but I couldn't deny the lingering hope that we'd end up together as we had last night. Now that I knew what it was like to hold her through the night, I didn't want to go back to sleeping alone.

I shook my head suddenly as I realised how pathetic I sounded.

Get your shit together, Hayden.

She smiled at me, pleased at my approval. My breath was momentarily caught in my throat as I took in the way she seemed to glow in the soft lighting from the tent. A thin sheen of sweat had settled over her shoulders and chest, making her complexion dewy and tantalisingly beautiful. The green of her eyes, offset by so many different shades of the colour provided by the forest, appeared even brighter than usual. I blinked and drew a breath to try and gather my thoughts, something that was becoming increasingly difficult around her.

'Ready to learn how to hunt?' I asked, stepping fully into the tent to help gather the weapons.

'Yeah, definitely,' she replied, shifting to gather up the pistol she'd used earlier. She hesitated before grabbing the rifle but scooped it up anyway, slinging the strap attached to it over her shoulder before standing up and leaving the crossbow for me. I strung the sheath of arrows over my shoulders and picked it up. It felt heavy in my hands as I turned to leave the tent while she followed.

'So,' I started, raising the crossbow to show her how it worked. 'You pull on this cord here to cock it back.'

I demonstrated, pulling on the string to set the bow. She nodded as she watched closely. I reached behind my shoulder to pull out several different arrows to show her the difference.

'See the different sized darts? The smaller ones are more accurate. We have more of them. You load it by setting it here, but make sure it's aligned with the string or it won't work. I'll show you how to aim more once we get out there, but do you get how it works?'

'Yeah, it's not too bad,' she said, focusing on the crossbow a bit longer before nodding once and looking at me.

'All right, if you say so,' I said, smiling challengingly at her. 'Ready to go, then?'

'I am if you are,' she replied, adjusting the strap of the rifle over her shoulder.

'Let's go, then. Try to be as quiet as possible so we don't scare anything away,' I instructed, dropping my voice. She nodded and followed me as I set off into the trees.

The sun that managed to sneak through the cover from the trees was hot as it hit the back of my neck, easily drawing sweat as we moved. I was thankful I'd worn a shirt with the sleeves cut off that allowed the light breeze to billow though armholes, but it wasn't enough to stop me from getting warm. Grace, too, seemed to notice the heat as she wiped sweat from her brow without complaint. I could feel the strands at the back of my neck sticking to my skin, the sweat weighing them down, and I regretted not grabbing a hat or bandana to keep the strands off my face.

Our feet were nearly silent as we moved, our years of training for raids naturally aiding us for hunting. The only sounds to be heard were the calls of birds singing in the trees, the gentle rustling of creatures unknown moving through the brush, and the quiet whisper of wind that shuffled the leaves. Despite the slightly overbearing heat, it was a beautiful day outside.

We'd moved about a mile before I held my hand out to slow Grace, my forearm colliding lightly with her shoulder as she walked into it. She stopped moving and glanced at me before looking around, trying to figure out why I'd stopped. I raised my finger to my lips, ensuring her continued silence before pointing ahead to the left, where a small pool of water sat in the middle of a clearing. It was where we often came to hunt, as the animals were drawn to the water on hot days like today.

Grace nodded silently in understanding and watched as I crouched behind a bush. I flattened myself out to my stomach, settling into the dirt to hide myself as much as possible. She copied me, lowering her body next to mine with an excited expression on her face. Her eyes widened as I set the crossbow in front of her, and I couldn't help but smile at her uncertainty with it.

'You ready to learn?' I whispered, keeping my voice low.

'I guess,' she replied quietly, resting her elbow in the dirt to pick up the crossbow as I showed her earlier. I reached behind me again to grab an arrow and hand it to her. Her fingers closed around it as she accepted it and loaded it into the bow. She smiled triumphantly as it clicked quietly when she did it correctly, green eyes flashing to me only a few inches away. 'Now what?'

'Now . . .' I started, glancing at her hands and their position. I shifted my body and slung my arm across her shoulder, my chest pressing into her back as I nudged her hand slightly with my own to readjust her grip. 'Keep your hands there to aim.'

I tried to ignore the way my heart sped up when I pressed into her, but it was difficult. I could hear her breath catch slightly as I ducked my head next to hers, looking down the shaft of the arrow to show her how to aim. My lips were only inches from her ear as I muttered the instructions quietly.

'If it's close, aim one or two inches above where you want to hit. The farther away, the higher you have to aim.'

She nodded slowly, raising the crossbow an inch as she aimed at a tree stump about fifteen feet away. As she moved, her ear brushed lightly against my lips, sending a jolt through my body. She inhaled sharply at the feeling and I caught the way her eyes flicked towards me for a second before refocusing on the stump.

'Don't flinch when you pull the trigger,' I whispered, closing my finger over hers as it rested on the trigger. My chest, arms, and hands were all touching her. My breath washed over her neck as I resisted the urge to let my lips land on her soft skin.

'Ready?' My voice was so quiet it was almost silent. She held her breath as she prepared to shoot, steadying her hands. It was then that my eyes dropped from her target to scan her face. Her eyelashes cast a shadow across her skin, but the flush to her cheeks from the heat made her face look healthy and alive. Her lips were parted slightly as she blew out the breath she was holding.

As if she could feel me studying her, her eyes flicked towards me once more, this time landing on my lips that were only inches from her own. She drew a ragged breath as her eyes lingered on my mouth, and I felt the shudder that ran through her drag down my spine as well. I wanted nothing more than to close the space between us, our lesson all but forgotten thanks to the electricity that seemed to run through our every point of contact.

Without any degree of control or resistance, I inched forward, her lips inches from my own. My blood pounded through my veins, making my skin tingle all over. Her lips were impossibly close to my own when a sudden rustling sounded ahead of us, snapping both of our heads away from each other and toward the sound. The moment washed away, leaving me feeling slightly disappointed, as we focused on the source of the disturbance.

Grace kept the crossbow raised, shifting it ever so slightly to aim it at the wild turkey that wandered into our view. Its round eyes didn't see us observing from across the clearing, and it didn't seem to sense our presence as it wandered into the open.

'Slow and steady, Grace,' I whispered, hunkering down as far as I could to see what she saw. I could feel her finger start to tighten over the trigger as she aimed, preparing her first ever shot with a crossbow. She drew a silent breath and held it as she had before, steadying her hands before her finger pulled the trigger all the way, releasing the arrow with a soft whisper. It flew through the air for a fraction of a second before landing with a soft thud in the chest of the turkey, sending it to the ground almost instantly.

'Yes,' she cheered quietly, a grin breaking across her face. She shifted in the dirt, preparing to push herself up before I stopped her.

'Wait, sometimes there's more than one,' I whispered. She settled back down to her position quietly with my arms still wound around her shoulders. Sure enough, only seconds later, a second turkey appeared from the brush, apparently taking no notice of the one Grace had just killed.

I felt her shoulders shift against my chest as she readjusted the crossbow, loading another arrow silently in place. I watched her face as she took aim, her lips parting again and eyes focusing on the turkey. Her finger squeezed the trigger slowly, and she sent the arrow flying into the neck of the turkey.

Her grin widened again, pleased with her triumph and natural talent at shooting the crossbow. It didn't really surprise me with the amount of weapon training she'd had, but it was nice to see how excited it made her to succeed at something. Without even thinking, I went to press my lips lightly against her jaw. Her breath caught slightly as I did so, just as surprised by my action as I was.

'You did it, Bear,' I said quietly, unable to suppress the grin.

'I had a good teacher,' she whispered, glancing at me with an excited look on her face. To see her so happy sent a wave of warmth through my body. It took everything in me to retract my arm from around her, shifting to settle back into my previous position next to her.

'Clearly,' I said lightly. 'Now keep watch, you don't want to miss anything.'

She nodded silently and bit back her smile as she faced forward once more, searching for more prey to hunt down. I watched her happily, completely captivated and enthralled.

The afternoon passed quickly, and before long, we had almost more game collected than we could carry back to the campsite. Grace had managed to shoot down seven turkeys before we'd had to go retrieve the arrows, piling the catch next to us to wait for more. I'd managed to bring down a possum that had wandered by as well as two ducks. The sun was starting to set when we called it a day, more than pleased with our haul.

After tying a few strings around the necks of the game, we were on our way. Grace carried one bundle while I carried two others, the crossbow slung back over my shoulders while Grace carried the guns in case we ran into something we didn't want to.

'Pretty successful day, I'd say,' she said happily. Her walk seemed to have a little bounce to it and her tone seemed lighter than I'd heard it in days. The dead birds swung freely by her side as she walked through the brush and I couldn't help but chuckle.

'You're a natural,' I agreed. She beamed up at me, pleased.

'Thank you, thank you,' she said, tipping her head playfully.

'Not that I'm surprised with the amount of training you've had but still, a crossbow is different to a gun.'

'I like it,' she mused. 'It's so . . . mechanical. With a gun you just aim and shoot, but there's more to a crossbow. It's fun.'

'Fun,' I repeated, laughing again. Before it had always seemed like something that had to be done – a necessity to keep my people alive – but now that she said it, I could see how hunting and shooting a crossbow could be fun. 'I guess you're right.'

Our camp was thankfully undisturbed. The temperature had dropped noticeably as the sun dipped behind the horizon, but the lingering heat of the day still radiated up from the dirt as we tied our prizes to a branch in the tree to keep them out of reach from any scavengers.

'I'll make a fire if you get out the food?' I suggested, glancing at Grace.

'Sure,' she replied before heading into the tent.

I moved over to the stack of wood we'd built up earlier, pulling a match from the box we'd set next to it. Matches were something, luckily, Blackwing had in abundance. A few years ago, Barrow and Kit had hit the jackpot on a raid, finding enough cartons of matches to last Blackwing for years. I dragged the match over the side of the box, igniting a flame, before lowering it into the pit to light the kindling beneath the logs. I bent down and blew lightly, curling my lips into an 'O' as I did so.

Fire had just sparked through the kindling as Grace reappeared outside, laden with food Maisie had packed: two packs of jerky, two bottles of water, and two apples. Fruit was difficult to come by, so seeing that Maisie had packed some for us both made me happy.

Once I had the fire going to my satisfaction, I shifted back to sit on the log we'd rolled over a few feet away. Grace joined me, handing me my half of the food. It was almost completely dark now, so the soft glow of the fire provided our only source of light. The flickering flames illuminated her skin and reflected in her eyes.

'So I've been wondering,' she asked, before taking a bite of her jerky.

'What's that?' I asked. Questions always made me feel a bit uneasy.

'How did you come to be the leader of Blackwing?' she asked. My eyes focused on the fire in front of us, unsure if I wanted to answer or not.

'You don't have to tell me,' she added softly, noting my reaction.

'No, it's all right,' I said. Fire bit into the log in front of us, consuming the energy from the wood to fuel its life. My head ticked to the side as a flash of fires a thousand times larger consuming things like homes, businesses, and worst of all, people, flitted through my mind. I shook away the grisly images.

'From day one, Kit, Dax and I were trained by those who formed Blackwing. They knew they'd need knew leaders someday so they started with us since we had no families left. We all trained and learned what we know now but to this day I don't know why they chose me over either of them. A woman named Melinda was in charge before, but she got killed when we were raided . . . I was barely eighteen when they picked me,' I explained, my eyes never leaving the fire even though I could feel Grace studying me closely as she absorbed my words. I was twenty-one now, but it felt like so much more time had passed since I'd become leader.

'Who is "they"?' she asked gently. I took a deep breath as I fought to suppress the memories.

'People in charge of things, mostly. Like Barrow, Maisie. Other people you haven't met. Some people were upset that they chose someone so young but I dunno . . . it wasn't really my decision. One day I was just this kid running around looking out for only myself then the next I was in charge of all these people . . . That was when I decided to grow up,' I said.

My mind flitted automatically to Malin. Our time together had ended months before I was put in charge, but my ascent to leadership cemented my belief that I couldn't mess around with situations like that again. If I was going to be a leader, I needed to earn the respect of the people I was in charge of.

I shook my head, letting out a heavy sigh before continuing.

'I really don't get why they chose me. Why not choose someone else? Barrow, Kit, Dax? Barrow was older, more experienced . . . Kit would have done whatever needed to be done without a second thought. And Dax . . . well he might have been a disaster, actually, but everyone loves him.'

'I know why they chose you,' she said softly.

It was only then that I was able to rip my gaze from the flames to refocus on her. I stayed silent as I waited for her to continue.

'The fact that you don't see it only proves it even more . . . You're just . . . better, Hayden. You genuinely care about every single person you're in charge of and you'd do anything for them. You care more about doing what's right for everyone than for doing things for yourself, which is rare in the world today. You're honest, selfless, loyal . . . They didn't choose Kit or Dax or even Barrow because they don't have the qualities you do. You're everything a leader should be and you're just . . . a good person.'

She thought far too highly of me, seeing qualities I knew I didn't have. I had no idea how to respond because she was so completely wrong. I had far too many flaws and wasn't nearly as great as she gave me credit for. She held my gaze in the flickering light and seemed to be fighting in her head before she decided something. She sucked in a breath before opening her mouth, saving me from responding to her inaccurate yet flattering speech.

'Hayden . . . I have to tell you something,' she said quietly. If I wasn't mistaken, I thought I saw a flash of guilt cross her features. My stomach twisted nervously.

'What is it?'

Her gaze dropped from mine momentarily as she glanced guiltily down at her knees. My heart thumped heavily as I waited patiently.

'I should have told you sooner but . . . Celt is my father.'

Chapter 25 – Trust

HAYDEN

'I should have told you sooner but . . . Celt is my father.'

Grace watched me carefully as she stopped speaking, her jaw tense after the bomb she'd just dropped. I felt the muscles in my chest tighten as I absorbed her words. I was too stunned to reply and my jaw seemed to be clenched shut, making speaking impossible. She sat stiffly next to me, the firelight flickering over her soft skin to illuminate the tension on her face that was growing by the second.

'What?' I finally managed to say, my voice deep and sharp. Her eyes flickered back and forth between mine, trying to gauge my reaction.

'Celt is—'

'Your father is the fucking leader of Greystone?' I spat, reality starting to sink in. She opened her mouth to reply before she bit it back, cutting herself off. She blew out a short huff of air.

'Yes.'

My brain seemed to race in a thousand different directions at once as it tried to process this new information. Every emotion I felt flashed by in a fraction of a second only to be replaced by a new one. Anger seemed to be the most prevalent, and I felt myself latch onto it as a scowl scored across my features.

'Why the hell didn't you tell me?' I demanded. I tried to ignore the sting of betrayal I felt as I realised she'd lied to me on several occasions. I couldn't stop myself from standing up, needing to put some space between us for the moment. She remained seated on the log by the fire as I stood and moved a few feet away, my shadow casting a darkness across her face as I towered over her.

'I didn't know how to,' she said slowly, her voice serious yet strong, not giving in to my anger. She continued to watch me carefully as I glowered down at her.

'No? What about the time I flat out asked you how you know Celt? Only a few hours ago?' I spat, letting my anger get the best of me.

'I don't know, Hayden—'

'You lied to me,' I accused, cutting her off again. My hand shoved through my hair in frustration. I felt strangely vulnerable and it made me wonder what else she'd lied about. I suddenly felt like the trust she'd started to build up was caving away, breaking into crumbs at my feet.

'I know,' she admitted, exhaling slowly as if trying to keep herself calm. I, on the other hand, wasn't managing so well. It seemed that every emotion I was feeling had intensified tenfold as they coursed through my veins. Anger, betrayal, hurt, confusion, and embarrassment all seemed to be fighting for attention as I continued to glower down at her.

'More than once,' I added, stoking the fire.

'I know.'

'Why?' I demanded, furious she wasn't arguing with me. I wanted to scream at her. I wanted her to fight back. I wanted her to defend herself but all she did was sit there. She was quiet for a few seconds, and her gaze finally dropped from me to land in the fire while she collected her thoughts. I felt jittery with impatience as she stalled.

'*Why*?' I repeated, frustrated beyond belief. Her eyes flashed up to mine in a split second as she caught my tone. She launched herself to her feet but didn't come near me as she finally seemed to get mad as well.

'Don't you yell at me,' she hissed, her brows knitting together angrily.

Good. It looked like I was going to get the fight I wanted, and the masochist in me dug in for the exchange. I felt the muscle tic in my jaw as I clenched it tightly, waiting for her to answer my question before I shouted it yet again.

'What would you have done if you'd known I was the leader's daughter that first night you found me, huh?' she pressed, glaring at me across the fire.

'Nothing,' I said honestly. Even if I'd known then, I wouldn't have been able to kill her. Her being Celt's daughter didn't change the fact that I owed her.

'Yeah, you maybe, but can you say the same for everyone else? Dax? Kit?' she continued, raising an eyebrow at me.

'No,' I admitted, seething. But her point still stood. She might not be in danger from myself, Kit, or Dax anymore, but there were others in Blackwing that I couldn't vouch for.

'Exactly,' she spat, crossing her arms over her chest. 'If I would have told you then, I'd probably be dead. Or tortured or something. Either way, it would be the stupidest thing in the world for me to tell you that.'

'Maybe then,' I said, fighting back the sting of betrayal I felt starting to creep up. 'But what about now? Why lie about it until now?'

'I just told you about it,' she argued. Her voice was tight as if trying to remain calm.

'After lying about it only hours ago!' I growled, throwing my hands up by my sides as my restraint broke. I wasn't sure what I was most upset about: the new information or the fact that she'd lied to me on several occasions.

'Jesus, Hayden, I just told you! What do you want me to say?' she asked in exasperation. My chest heaved as I blew out a huff of angry breath, trying to sort my thoughts out. What did I want her to say? I didn't even know. I was too livid to think straight.

'Do you know what this means, Grace? Do you realise what could happen now?' I questioned harshly. My tone was dark and deep as I stared her down.

'Nothing has changed, Hayden. I've been Celt's daughter the entire time I've been here,' she dared to point out.

'*Everything* has changed! Do you know how dangerous it is for you to be here? Do you think your precious father is just going to let you hang out over here if he finds out where you've been?' I spat, glowering at her as I waited for her to answer. She glared back at me, her jaw clenched tightly and nostrils flaring as she failed to hide her anger.

'No,' she said reluctantly through gritted teeth.

'No,' I repeated angrily. 'He's going to send an entire freaking army over if he finds out where you are. You being here makes it ten times more dangerous for all the people I'm trying to keep alive.'

She didn't say anything as my words hit her like a brick wall, her chest heaving as she struggled to maintain even breathing. My anger only seemed to grow as I saw more and more potential dilemmas that could arise thanks to this new information.

'And you,' I spat, blowing out a derisive breath and shaking my head slowly. 'Do you know what they'll do to you if they figure out who you are? Forget about ever blending in, they'll make your life *hell*. That is if they don't kill you first. I might not do it, Kit and Dax might not, but

302

there are people here who won't give a shit what you've done. They'll see you as the public enemy number one and a source of information, nothing more. People might seem nice now but if they find out who you are, they won't hesitate to do whatever it takes to get information out of you. Do you understand what I'm saying?'

Throughout my rant, I'd unknowingly started pacing, my tone growing angrier and more frantic by the second. It was like the more I talked, the more I realised how devastating this information could be. Not only was her identity a risk to my camp in the form of Greystone attacking, but Grace herself was at risk from my own camp.

'Yes,' she said bitterly, angry with me for being right.

'And, if somehow you ever did end up back in Greystone, you'd be a huge liability. You've seen everything here . . . You can bet your father will more than thrilled to get some new information.'

I was ranting now, getting carried away with hypothetical situations, but my mind couldn't stop. This could potentially ruin everything.

'I wouldn't do that,' she said, her voice finally losing some of the anger it had held. Instead, hurt lanced through her tone. I scoffed.

'I wouldn't,' she repeated when it was clear I didn't believe her. A few hours ago, I wouldn't have doubted her at all but now . . . 'I wouldn't put you in danger like that. Or Jett. Or Dax or Kit or Docc . . . I couldn't do that.'

Her words did little to soothe the ache I felt at her lies, but thankfully my anger was still masking most of my emotion.

'I can't trust anything you say now,' I grumbled.

'Hayden, you're overreacting,' she said, shaking her head at me incredulously.

'Overreacting?' I repeated angrily. 'Grace, I just found

303

out how dangerous it is for you to be here, don't tell me I'm overreacting.'

'It doesn't change anything! I'm still the same person I was, you just know who my father is now,' she countered sharply.

'What happens when other people find out, huh? What happens when others find out who your father is and what they have sitting in front of them?'

My hands continually clenched and unclenched by my sides and my feet never ceased their pacing. A small path had started to wear into the dirt next to the fire where I moved back and forth.

'No one will find out if you don't tell them!' she argued back, her voice laden with frustration.

'They will,' I said, shaking my head slowly. 'People always find out sooner or later. Secrets don't stay secrets for long.'

She blew out a sharp exhale and I thought I heard her actually stamp her foot into the dirt in frustration, but I couldn't look at her. I couldn't see the way her green eyes burned into mine, trying to bring me back from the anger that had taken over while trying to rein in her own. Clearly I had reacted just as she feared I would, which was probably why she avoided telling me for so long.

'I won't tell anyone,' she said slowly, her voice forced into an even tone. 'I'll . . . stay hidden if Greystone raids, I'll be extra careful when we go on our own . . . no one will find out, Hayden.'

I shook my head and bit my lip into my mouth. I clenched my jaw too tightly, drawing blood from my own lip. The bitter, metallic taste drifted over my tongue as I silently cursed myself.

'You can try but honestly . . . it's only a matter of time

before someone else finds out,' I muttered. My hand shoved through my hair again before raking down my face in frustration. Stress seared through my body, tensing my muscles and twisting my stomach into knots.

'I knew you would be angry,' she said cautiously, crossing her arms over her chest again.

'No shit,' I growled, casting a glare at her from across the fire. She shot me a disapproving look.

'I know you're mad now but . . . I think you'll realise it's not that bad in a while.'

'No, I won't. I'm putting my people in danger for you, Grace. For you.'

'Why don't you just kill me then and save yourself all the stress?' she suggested, her tone flat and sarcastic. I could feel her gaze burning into me as I turned my back to her and pressed my hands into my temples.

'You know I can't,' I answered.

I felt weak, vulnerable. I hated that the safety of my people hinged on this one person that I wasn't strong enough to get rid of, my feelings for her making it impossible to do what I should have done the moment I laid eyes on her. This was exactly what I'd been afraid of from the start – that my selfish desires of keeping her around would end up causing trouble for my people. My fears were coming to life right before my eyes, the potential for something to go wrong vastly increased now that I knew exactly who she was.

If I had known from the beginning . . .

I shook my head, clearing away the thought. I never would have been able to kill her, even from day one. This was what I got for giving in to what I wanted for once rather than doing what I knew was right and staying away from her. It was a sick poetic justice that I should have expected.

'This is . . . everything . . . it's all ruined now,' I said, feeling dramatic but not caring. In that moment, I couldn't see how this could ever work out positively. She'd betrayed my trust and would have to do a lot of work to get it back. Trust was a dangerous thing in this world, potentially the most dangerous of all. Slowly, without even realising, I'd come to trust her.

Not anymore.

'Hayden, come on,' she pleaded. For the first time she didn't sound angry, just sad. I turned around and faced her, taking in the tiny step she'd taken towards me and the way her lips parted as she watched me.

'You lied to me,' I said, repeating my words from before but without the same conviction. Before when there'd been anger and disbelief, now there was only hurt. Regret flashed across her face momentarily and she took another step toward me before pausing uncertainly. My face remained stonily blank, hopefully making it difficult to see what I was thinking.

'I know,' she repeated calmly. Her breathing had calmed and her arms were no longer folded over her chest or clamped into fists by her sides.

'I trusted you,' I said slowly, giving in to the hurt I'd managed to hold off until now.

'You can still trust me.'

'I don't know what to do,' I admitted flatly.

'I don't know what to say,' she returned. She was closer than she had been during the entire fight but still too far away to touch me.

'You could say sorry,' I shot reproachfully, upset she hadn't even bothered trying to apologise for lying. I was surprised when I heard her scoff, causing my eyes to flick back up to where she stood. Her eyes were once again narrowed at me.

306

'I didn't ask for this, Hayden,' she shot back, her voice cracking with anger once more. 'Do you think I wanted this? You think I want to be here?'

It was like she'd dug a knife straight into my heart. My shoulders hunched forward momentarily as I sucked in a disbelieving scoff. I pinched my lips together and nodded as I let out a self-deprecating, humourless chuckle.

'Right, got it,' I snapped. Of course she didn't want to be here. Hadn't she said that from day one? I'd tricked myself into thinking that she really did like it here, that it could be home. I made myself believe that she liked it here with me. Obviously I was wrong. Her eyes widened slightly as she realised what she said.

'Wait, Hayden—'

'Nope, it's fine. I understand now.'

I bent to scoop up what few supplies remained outside, actively avoiding looking at her as I moved around in the darkness.

'Hayden,' she said, merely stating my name in an attempt to get me to stop and look at her. I ignored her.

'You coming inside or what?' I asked gruffly as I unzipped the flap of the tent. She frowned at me. Even now, in my cold, angry, hurt state, I couldn't deny that it hurt me to see her upset, but I was too preoccupied with my own issues to do anything about it. She sighed heavily as she took in the tight expression on my face.

'Yeah.'

I nodded sharply before turning and heading inside. I heard her boots scuff in the dirt as she kicked some into the fire, quickly extinguishing the light and plunging us into complete darkness. I didn't even bother to turn on the lantern as I threw myself down on my sleeping bag, facing the wall so my back was to her. A few seconds later, I heard her

307

enter the tent and zip it shut. She didn't say anything as she copied me, settling herself onto her own sleeping bag on the other side of the tent.

Sleep felt impossible as I lay in the dark, my mind swarming over everything that had been said. There was nothing I could do about the fact that she was Grace Cook, daughter of Celt Cook, the leader of Greystone. There never had been anything I could do, no matter how early I'd known. This information wasn't what I was so upset about.

I was upset about the potential for danger now that I knew. Her being Celt's daughter put everyone I was in charge of, everyone I cared for, at extreme risk. If someone from her own camp found out she was here, we potentially faced massive attacks to try and get her back. If someone from Blackwing found out who she was, Grace was in danger of being tortured for information or killed. If she somehow ended up back at Greystone, all of Blackwing would be in danger thanks to the massive amount of knowledge she had about us. Even if she didn't willingly give it up, I had no doubt in my mind that those in Greystone would have ways of getting it out of her.

The only way of preventing any danger to anyone was if no one else ever found out who she was or that she was here, a feat I was convinced was nearly impossible. How close already had we got to someone from Greystone seeing her? They'd raided Blackwing only weeks ago, missing her by a second. It was more than possible that the same situation would happen again, only with a completely different outcome.

It also wouldn't be hard for someone from Blackwing to discover that the leader of Greystone was missing his daughter. It wouldn't take a genius or even that much information to connect the dots and figure out it was Grace.

Everything came back to me – bringing Grace back to

Blackwing had sealed this. If anything bad happened to anyone, it would be my fault.

All these thoughts were enough to cause the stress and tension I was feeling, but the thing that struck me the deepest, the thing that hurt the most, was the fact that Grace had lied to me. It cut me deeper than it should have and I knew I was being dramatic, but the ability to trust someone in this world was so rare that I hadn't even realised I'd trusted her so much until it was gone. I resented her for destroying that, and I hated myself for resenting her.

I was stuck in my head, chasing myself in circles as I tried to calm down when I heard her shift in her sleeping bag. For a moment I thought she was getting up to join me, but soon the rustling stopped. I felt a weird mixture of relief and disappointment when she didn't appear beside me.

'I'm sorry,' she whispered, her voice laden with regret and sadness. Her words lingered in the air between us, waiting for me to either accept them or swat them down into the canvas floor of the tent. I drew in a deep breath as I tried to accept them, begged myself to accept them, but I just couldn't.

Not tonight, not yet.

The silence stretched on between us, too long now to accept the words sinking to the floor. A quiet sigh from across the tent told me Grace knew I wouldn't reply. I felt the words on my lips, my tongue fighting to hold them in while I debated internally.

It's all right, Bear.

I wanted to say it.

I wanted to feel it.

I wanted to let the words loose and forget the fight had ever happened, but I couldn't. The silence stretched on, smothering her apology and suffocating any potential for relief from the crushing weight that had fallen over us.

Chapter 26 – Fair

HAYDEN

I awoke before I was ready, the light of the sun and the song of the birds pulling me slowly from the comforting depths of sleep. It seemed to be the only place I could find solace and reprieve from the stress and pressures of discovering exactly who Grace was and realising the repercussions that went along with it.

It appeared that I hadn't moved in the slightest while I slept, my body still resting on its side so I faced the canvas wall of the tent. My arms were crossed over my chest tightly, my shoulders hunched. I found it difficult to imagine how I had possibly slept like that the entire night, because my entire body felt stiff.

My eyes remained closed, shutting out the intruding light that insisted on shining, and I listened to the soft sounds of the birds in the trees. I heard the gentle rustling of leaves that always seemed present around here, and the soft tickle of the wind on the tent.

My eyes sprang open suddenly as I realised a very specific sound I'd come to recognise easily was missing. There was only one person breathing in this tent, the sound echoing from my own chest.

I sat up in an instant, my body screaming in protest with the quick movement. My torso twisted anyway as I whipped my gaze across the tent, causing my heart to drop into my stomach when sure enough my eyes landed on an empty sleeping bag, the middle of it slightly crinkled and clearly empty.

Of course.

She was gone.

GRACE

My palms pressed into my eye sockets as I took a deep breath, bringing little white bursts of light into the darkness of my vision as I pressed down. A knot the size of a dinner plate seemed to have settled in my stomach, every thought I had twisting and turning it until I found it difficult to even move. My elbows dug into my knees as I leaned forward to rest my head in my palms, a weak attempt to block out the world.

A cool breeze whispered over my skin, the temperature of the morning considerably cooler than the sweltering heat of yesterday. It only seemed appropriate considering how I felt inside.

Never in my life had a fight with someone affected me so much. Usually, I felt only anger, which passed quickly after a few rounds of shooting or a bout of training. This fight had been different. I'd felt, and continued to feel, like a piece of shit. My emotions had ranged full circle. Anger, sadness, regret, hurt, compassion, everything. They'd ripped through me like a tornado through a field, until everything was raw and exposed.

I couldn't stay in that tent with him. The ignored words I'd uttered seemed to haunt me along with the rest of our exchange. I'd felt like I was slowly being smothered by

311

the whirlwind of emotion I felt, my capacity for it tested beyond belief. I had to leave, put some space between us, and try and clear my thoughts. It was impossible there with Hayden and his stony silence.

Hayden was, in every way, justified in how upset he'd got. While my actions had been motivated purely by self-preservation, Hayden's were not. Hayden's main priority, whether he wanted to admit it or not, was and has always been keeping those he cares about safe. I understood why he was angry and I couldn't blame him at all.

There was nothing I could do about it, but being who I was put Hayden and his entire camp, every single person he cared about, into danger. Already, I had got dangerously close to being discovered at Blackwing. My own brother, who would recognise me in a second even if he believed I was dead, had been mere feet away from me. It was more than rational to assume this could, and most likely would, happen again, making it far too easy to spot me.

I knew without a shadow of a doubt that if my father found out where I was, he would raise absolute hell against Blackwing to get me back, putting everyone Hayden cared for in danger just as he feared.

Not only were Hayden's people in danger, but I was as well. It wouldn't be hard for someone to go on a raid to Greystone and overhear that the leader, Celt, had lost his daughter a few weeks ago. Everyone knew I was from Greystone. It would take about three seconds to put two and two together and realise I was Celt's daughter. I knew Hayden wasn't lying when he said there were people in his camp who would take advantage of this information, hurting me or using me malevolently to get a step up on their enemy.

In all honesty, I wasn't concerned about the second option. I'd been selfish enough already. I probably deserved to be found out by Blackwing. Better I get hurt than any of them.

The only point of Hayden's I didn't agree with was the fear that I would be a liability to them. Not that I ever would get back home anyway, but if I did, the last thing I would do would be to volunteer information about Blackwing. Despite my resistance and reluctance, I'd come to care about these people. I couldn't set them up for slaughter simply to please my violence-happy home. I wouldn't.

Everything had spiralled too far out of control, ruining everything in its path. Everything, including how Hayden had potentially felt about me. That, I could admit, was what hurt the most. I was just starting to get to see what it was like to be with him and I'd lost him before we'd even really started.

I should have told him sooner.

Maybe at first I was right to not tell him, but the moment I realised I had feelings for him, I should have told him. Already I trusted him enough to know he wouldn't kill or hurt me. I could have trusted him with this. Maybe if I'd told him sooner I'd still be in the tent with him, curled into his side rather than out in the woods on my own.

The palms of my hands pressed even harder into my eyes in an attempt to wipe away the memory of how Hayden had looked at me. Nothing seemed to work, and I appeared to be doomed to see Hayden's hurt and disappointed face no matter what I did. Guilt surged through me when I thought of how his face had fallen when I'd said I didn't want to be here. His entire demeanour had changed, dropping the anger to form a flat, hollow state I did not like in the slightest. I hated myself for saying it, because I knew I didn't mean it.

An unidentified rustling from behind me jolted me from my self-loathing. I jerked toward the source, not sure what to expect as my heart slammed into the back of my ribs. My breath seemed to catch in my throat when I saw him, his face masking the momentary relieved surprise with a scowl quickly. He frowned deeply at me as he emerged from the tent.

Hayden.

'You're still here,' he muttered deeply, his face blank.

'Where else would I be?' I asked softly, my voice laced with resignation.

I didn't care if it hurt my pride, I wanted this fight to be over. Something told me it wouldn't be that easy, however, and that I'd spend a lot of time trying to make up for it. Trust was life or death in this world, guiding every action and every decision. It was easily broken and not easily gained. Trust was hugely important to Hayden and I'd broken it, simple as that.

He didn't reply and merely shrugged as he moved to stand on the other side of the makeshift fire pit. He crouched down and began to coax a fire to life. I watched as his hands moved expertly, stacking the kindling and arranging the logs so his match caught the rest on fire almost immediately. He blew on it softly, eyes focused on where the flames sparked to life.

I wanted to talk to him, fix what I'd broken, but I didn't know how. Instead of sitting next to me on the log, he remained crouched by the fire, staring into its depths and getting lost in his own thoughts. I bit my lip, trying to hold back the words fighting to be said. My control was weak, however, after a night of virtually no sleep and continuous regret.

'I should have told you,' I said quietly. 'As soon as I started to . . . trust you, I should have told you.'

He didn't say anything or even look at me, but I caught the little tick of his eyebrow that told me he'd heard my words. I sighed heavily and shoved my hand through my hair before getting slightly tangled in the unruly strands. I appeared to have picked up the gesture from Hayden.

'I know you don't want to talk, and that's fine . . .' I started, hating how vulnerable the words made me feel. 'But I just need you to know that you're right. I should have told you and you have every right to be upset.'

'Do I?' he asked suddenly, his gaze flicking up to meet mine. He appeared frustrated as he looked up at me from beneath his brow. 'Do you understand why I'm upset?'

'Of course, Hayden,' I said, shaking my head slowly. 'I'm putting everyone you care about at risk. It's not my fault I am who I am and there's nothing to be done about it, you and I know that, but I could have told you so at least you knew.'

'Everyone I care about,' he repeated thoughtfully, dropping his gaze from me once more.

'Yes,' I said simply. 'And I'm sorry.'

I held my breath as I waited for him to reply, praying he'd accept. It wouldn't fix much, but it would be a step.

'I get why you didn't tell me at first,' he said, ignoring my apology once again.

'And?' I prodded gently.

'And I don't blame you, I just wish you'd told me sooner. There's nothing we can do about who you are, but I would have been much more careful if I'd known from the start.'

'We've been lucky,' I thought aloud. It was so strange that the word 'we' kept getting thrown around, but I couldn't deny it made my heart soar. Maybe there was a glimmer of hope after all.

'There is no "lucky" in this world, Grace. People live and they die. That's it.'

He readjusted his position so he was settled on the ground

now rather than crouching, choosing to sit in the dirt rather than sit next to me. His words were so heavy, and there was a darkness creeping into his tone that chilled me to the bone. I didn't like the weight that had landed on him, dragging him down even further than his position in Blackwing already did.

'There's more to life than just living and dying,' I said slowly. I hated that whatever mood he was in now, whatever thoughts were going through his head, was pretty clearly a direct effect from what had happened last night.

'Like what?' he asked bitterly. His mood seemed to grow worse by the second and I couldn't help but frown at him.

'Like . . . friends. Family, blood relatives or not. Honouring those we've lost. Laughter, hope for the future . . . love,' I paused, suddenly needing to take a deep breath. I felt a blush creep up on my cheeks. I wasn't sure how this conversation had started but it suddenly felt extremely serious. 'There are still beautiful things in the world, Hayden, you just have to let yourself see them.'

'That's the problem, Grace.'

I frowned in confusion as my heart thumped in my chest, my body reacting to his words even though I didn't fully understand them. 'What do you mean?'

He sighed heavily and ran his thumb along his lower lip before shaking his head slowly.

'Never mind.'

I pinched my lips together, not wanting to push him, while I tried to ignore my disappointment.

Neither of us spoke for what felt like hours even though it was only a few minutes. Then, without a word, Hayden rose suddenly from his position on the ground to start preparing a quick breakfast over the fire. We ate in silence, before beginning to pack up our supplies into the truck. The lighthearted banter from yesterday seemed like decades ago as the last piece of equipment was loaded into the backseat. The game, which thankfully hadn't started to rot yet, was loaded into the trunk.

As we drove away from our temporary campsite, I hoped desperately that Hayden would leave his bad mood behind as well. I wanted him to go back to the Hayden I had been coming to know – the kind, selfless, good person he was despite his attempts to appear unattached and hard. The Hayden I had started to fall for. He was still there now, lurking beneath the weight of the stress that had newly settled on him, and I desperately wanted to free him.

We arrived back at camp much quicker than I would have thought, my distraction making the trip fly by. When Hayden pulled the truck up in front of the kitchen to deposit the game with Maisie, I was surprised by who greeted us.

'Kit,' I said in slight shock. I hadn't been expecting him to be out of the infirmary.

'Welcome back,' he said with a wide grin. He moved to open the trunk, where I joined him. 'See you guys had a good hunt.'

'Yeah, I guess,' I said distractedly. 'Are you sure you should be up and walking around?'

'I'm fine,' he said. He sounded mildly offended but chuckled nonetheless. 'Docc said the sooner I'm up and moving the faster I'll heal. You want to challenge Docc?'

'No,' I admitted with a small grin. It felt like the first time I'd smiled in ages. He helped me carry the game into the kitchen while Hayden ignored us completely and unloaded the rest of the supplies, hauling them over to the storage building across the path.

'What's with him?' Kit asked quietly, immediately noticing Hayden's mood. We moved to the back of the building where the freezers were. The kitchen was one of three buildings in Blackwing with a generator, making it possible to keep small amounts of food cold in the freezer.

'Nothing,' I said, attempting to sound casual. We threw the birds into the freezer and slammed it shut quickly so as not to let the cool air out. 'I think he's just tired from the hunt.'

'Hmm,' Kit said, frowning. He seemed unconvinced but didn't press things as we reappeared outside. I was surprised to see the truck gone, though I could hear it rumbling in the distance before the engine was shut off as Hayden put it away. Kit didn't say anything else as he scratched lightly at the bandage still around his throat. I didn't know what to say to him so I chose to just stay silent as I watched Hayden's figure stalk back towards us.

'Relax, mate,' Kit said calmly when Hayden drew nearer, sounding the calmest I'd ever heard him. 'You look like you've been through hell.'

I resisted the urge to laugh bitterly in Kit's face.

'Yeah,' Hayden said flatly. 'Long trip, sorry. I'm just tired.'

Kit nodded as Hayden's made up story miraculously coincided with my own.

'Go and relax a bit. If anything comes up, I'll handle it,' Kit offered. 'Dax is running around somewhere, too. You've earned it.'

Hayden didn't argue but sighed heavily before nodding. 'All right. But come and get me if anything happens.'

'You too, Grace. No offence but you look like you haven't slept in days.'

'Ha, ha,' I said flatly. I wasn't offended because I knew he was right. He shot me a small grin before saying goodbye and heading off away from Hayden's hut. Hayden didn't speak to me as we walked quietly down the path. I noted the way he held his shoulders, unnaturally high for him as if his muscles were rebelling against the rest of his body.

The door to his hut was shoved open before we moved inside. Hayden immediately moved to his bed and sat down on the edge, leaving me to stand somewhat awkwardly while I tried to decide what to do. Hayden tilted his head to the side, flinching slightly as if his neck was sore. His eyes closed as he reached behind him, gripping his shirt behind his neck to haul it over his head. His lean torso was revealed, the skin littered with tattoos.

With his eyes still closed, he rolled his head from side to side, trying to relax the muscles. I took a tentative step forward, pausing momentarily before continuing on my way.

'Here, let me . . .' I offered, gingerly climbing onto his bed to crawl up behind him. He didn't answer but I caught the reproachful look he cast me as I scooted closer to him. My hands reached up slowly to land on his damaged skin. He flinched away from me momentarily before he caught himself, and I tried not to be offended. It was the first time I'd touched him since our fight.

His skin was warm as I moved my hands up his back, sliding over every curve of muscle and jagged scar before reaching his shoulders. I let my fingers knead over them. He hissed quietly when I dug my thumbs into a particularly large knot just above his shoulder blade but didn't stop me as I tried to work it out.

'Remember what you said earlier?' he said suddenly, surprising me. My hands continued to knead at his muscles, loosening the tight fibres slowly.

'About what?' I asked gently. My thumb ran over a particularly long scar that trailed down from his shoulder and I resisted the urge to press my lips into it.

'About everyone I care about being in danger,' he said, his voice slow and deep.

'Yes, I remember.'

He paused, flinching suddenly away from me as I found a new enormous knot at the base of his neck. He was quiet for so long that I thought he was finished talking again.

'You know that includes you, right?' he finally said slowly. My hands stilled for a fraction of a second on his shoulders as my heart flew up into my throat. I paused for a moment to collect myself before I answered.

'I hoped so,' I admitted. It wasn't that I wanted him to worry about me, I just wanted him to care.

'I don't want them to find out who you are. I don't want them to hurt you.'

I desperately wished I could see his face but didn't want to risk interrupting and losing the moment. My fingers worked the last knot out of his shoulders, earning a sigh of relief from him. I let my touch trail lightly down his back, tracing the scars there and taking in the ragged beauty of his sacrifices he'd made over the years.

'We'll be careful. No one will find out,' I promised. My voice was a mere whisper. My hands settled low on his torso, and my thumbs dragged slowly over his skin.

'I want to trust you, Grace,' he said slowly.

'You can, Hayden. I'd never do anything to hurt you or anyone else here,' I said honestly. I was in too deep to do anything do these people. Despite my better judgement, I couldn't stop myself from leaning forward to press a light kiss into his shoulder blade. My lips lingered on his skin as I waited for him to tell me to stop.

He didn't.

'It'll come back . . . just not right away. I can't trust you so quickly after this, but some day . . .' he trailed off. His head dropped down as his gaze fixed on the floor near his feet that hung off his bed. His hands remained by his sides, one of his fingers tapping irregularly as if he wasn't aware of it.

'That's fair,' I agreed quietly. I rested my lips against his shoulder again, pressing them to his skin lightly while I waited for him to continue. He didn't speak again, however, as his hand that held the tapping finger rose from his side. Slowly, he put it over mine on his side, covering the back easily and picking it up to drag to his lips. I sucked in a breath when he pressed his lips into my palm before lacing his fingers in the gaps between my own. I was certain he'd be able to feel my heart pounding as it pressed lightly against his back.

'Be patient with me, Bear.'

I could see his profile as he turned slightly, the way his brows were set low and I saw the vulnerable expression on his face. It was obvious there was still so much going on inside his head, his words revealing only a small fraction of the storm brewing inside.

'Of course, Herc.'

Chapter 27 – Free

GRACE

Hayden's back was still pressed to my chest, and my lips remained on his shoulder blade while he held my hand in his own in front of him. A combination of relief and joy seemed to be flooding through me as I rejoiced internally at his quiet words. He hadn't fully let his guard down yet, but I could feel him slowly letting me in, bit by bit. The cracks in his harsh exterior were widening, revealing the vulnerability he tried so hard to hide.

I let my other hand wind around his waist to hug him fully from behind, the skin of his bare back warm and rough against my cheek. I felt a spark of heat shoot up my arm when his fingers raked lightly over the backs of mine.

'Hayden,' I said quietly, my words softened by his shoulder. I felt the tight muscles in his stomach expand beneath my palms as he drew in a breath.

'Hmm?'

'When I said I didn't want to be here . . . I didn't mean that,' I said quietly, desperately wishing I had a clear view of his face. Suddenly he moved, squeezing my hands lightly before unwrapping my arms from around his waist. His long legs swung up from the side of the bed as he turned, so he was facing me. He straightened out his legs, one either side of my hips so I sat between his knees. My knees, bent to sit criss-cross, landed on his thighs as he leaned back onto his hands.

'No?' It was difficult to read his expression. His eyes were narrowed slightly as he studied me, and his face held a soft frown.

'No. I . . . of course I miss home and my . . . father,' I said, wincing slightly now that he knew the truth. 'Even my brother.'

He frowned deeper, as if discouraged by my words but didn't say anything.

'But being here, with you . . . it's different. I feel . . . free.'

My words were true; here I felt free to be who I was without the pressure of living up to the expectations of being Celt's daughter. I felt free to make decisions based on what I really wanted for once rather than what my father or brother did, even though I was technically still a prisoner. I was in no way actually free, but I felt it all the same.

'Free,' he repeated thoughtfully, his frown softening. His gaze flicked down to where my hands rested on his thighs but he didn't move to accept or reject the touch in any way.

'Yeah, which is ironic considering the circumstances,' I said, letting out a half laugh, half sigh. Again, he didn't reply right away. He claimed he wasn't good at the whole talking thing but in reality, I wasn't much better. His intense scrutiny made me feel exposed and vulnerable.

'It is ironic,' he finally said with a tiny hint of a smile. My pulse jumped at the small change in expression.

'I shouldn't have said it. I was angry and it just came out . . . I didn't mean it, I want you to know that,' I said. I felt like I was rambling even though I was hardly saying anything. My thoughts seemed to bounce around so quickly in my head that it made it difficult to form a coherent train of thought. I took a deep breath before continuing. 'And I'm sorry.'

His gaze held mine, no less intense that it had been. 'I thought you were gone this morning.'

'I was right outside,' I pointed out gently. Without my permission, I felt my thumbs slide slowly over his thigh, searing through the fabric.

'I know, but when I woke up and you weren't in the tent I thought you'd run for it,' he explained, a flicker of sadness crossing his features. 'Even though I was mad at you, I still didn't want you to leave. It made me . . . sad.'

I sucked in a short breath at his confession, the selfish side of me extremely pleased he hadn't liked the idea of me leaving and the side that cared for him upset that he'd been sad.

'I'm not going to leave, Hayden,' I said softly. I felt the word I hadn't said stuck behind my teeth: you. I'm not going to leave *you*, Hayden.

'I don't want you to.'

He surprised me by leaning forward, taking the weight off his hands to bring one up to my face. His fingers snaked into my hair as his palm rested where my jaw met my neck. I couldn't even find enough breath to reply as my heart pounded, the constant thudding of my pulse drowning out any sound besides Hayden's voice. He was too near now, too close to even think straight as I held his gaze from mere inches away.

'I don't know what this is, Grace but . . . I feel it. I've never felt something like this before,' he said quietly, his voice low and deep and dangerous to my already fragile condition.

'I feel it too, Hayden,' I replied, my voice no more than a whisper. 'You're . . . something to me.'

A tiny flicker of a smile pulled at his lips at my words, as if they amused him.

324

'Something,' he repeated. I noticed he did that a lot.

'You know what I mean . . .' I said, blushing. 'You're just . . . something.'

I couldn't miss the hint of amusement written across his features. I really was bad at this.

'You're something to me, too, Grace,' he said quietly before dragging his thumb over my cheek once more. His other hand rose to mirror it, encasing my face gently in his palms. I managed to suck in a short breath before his lips seared into mine.

Everything seemed to be piling up in an attempt to destroy me. I found it so hard to believe that he felt the same things I did. I couldn't ignore the inexplicable pull to him despite all the reasons I shouldn't, the belief that he was far too good for this world, and the intense desire to be the one for him to share the burden of all the responsibility he carried. I wanted to be the one he could lean on when he felt like he couldn't, and I wanted to help him realise what an incredible man he really was. He was so completely oblivious to how he actually was that it killed me.

My heart pounded out of control as he let his lips fold over mine, fitting perfectly in the gaps created by my own. His hands remained on my face as he kissed me, and my hands rose from where they rested on his thighs to land on his bare chest.

Hayden's grip on my face pulled me forward, bringing my body closer to his. Without even thinking, my legs unfolded to either side of his waist, my thighs resting over the tops of his so my knees could tuck in around him. The kiss was sensual, tender, and slow, so vastly different from the last kiss we'd shared when things had escalated almost to the point of no return.

I could feel the words we had struggled to say now as

they passed unspoken through our kiss. Neither of us were particularly good at expressing ourselves, but the way he kissed me now made it very clear how he felt. Just as I wanted to be that special person for him, I could feel he wanted it for me, too.

I was surprised when I felt Hayden's hands leave my face, his palms trailing lightly down my sides before he replaced them on the bed to shift us backwards. He leaned back against the wall, I bent my knees on either side of his hips to straddle him. He continued the slow motion kissing of his lips over mine. Once settled, he returned his hands to my hips where they proceeded to practically sear a hole in my clothes.

I'd been with others before, but never someone I actually cared much about. Never someone who claimed to care about me. I knew what to expect physically from being with someone, but had no idea what emotional attachments were possible. I knew with Hayden, it was guaranteed to be different. The emotional connection between us was too much to ignore, and I knew it would change things.

My thoughts were interrupted, however, by Hayden's hands snaking under my shirt to land on my lower back. His palms heated my skin, and I felt the way his fingertips dug into my flesh as he pulled me against him. My arms rose to link around his neck, bending at the elbows to allow my hands to tangle in his hair as he deepened the kiss. His tongue pushed deeper into my mouth and I felt the way his body pressed forward to increase the contact between us.

Without my permission, my hips ground down against him, earning a soft groan from his throat that was stifled by our kiss. His hands shifted lower to rest on my bum, guiding my hips downward once more against him. I felt a jolt of electricity run through me at the contact, and I was suddenly reminded of the first and only time he'd really touched me, easily undoing me with his fingers alone.

'Grace . . .' he murmured, his voice laden with need. I didn't know if he had anything else to say, however, because he didn't continue. I loved the way my name sounded rolling off his lips in the heat of the moment.

When my hips ground down against him again, I could feel the bulge that had formed. The last thing I wanted to do was rush things, especially after how embarrassingly it had ended last time, but I ached to feel him.

I gasped quietly when he tore his lips from mine to trail them down my neck, his kisses growing feverish and more urgent now that our bodies had started to wake up. What had started out so slow and emotional had suddenly shifted to an atmosphere of desperate want. My head rolled to the side as he nipped at my throat, his breath hot over my skin as he sucked lightly. A light sigh fell from my lips as his tongue lapped over my skin to soothe the dull ache that had settled in from his teeth.

The bulge beneath me was even more obvious now as I shifted my hips downward, earning another soft groan from Hayden. My hands fell from where they'd tangled in his hair to trail down his chest, the skin there hot beneath my palms.

When my fingers reached the waistband of his jeans, his lips pulled from my neck. I hadn't noticed, both of our breathing had grown slightly ragged as the heat of our kissing had increased. He hovered inches away from me, his lips parted while shallow breath blew out. His eyes were dark and his hair was messed up from my hands, making him look slightly wild. I could see the inner battle he was fighting past his eyes while my fingers worked slowly to undo his jeans. I bit my lower lip, holding his gaze as I waited for him to tell me to stop.

No such message came, however, as I managed to fully undo his jeans. I reached down to run my hand over him, the bulge hard beneath my palm through the layers between us. It was as if my touch snapped him out of the internal battle, whatever side had been arguing for him to stop losing. His eyelids fluttered lightly as he ducked forward again to press his lips into mine, silently giving me permission.

It was difficult to breathe as he kissed me harder than he ever had, his tongue pushing into my mouth while his hands rose to cradle my face tightly. I returned the kiss and tried to ignore the tension in the pit of my stomach as my hands tugged down on the waistband as best I could, my body shifting back to rest on his thighs as I worked the layers down enough to free him. My gasp was stifled by his lips as I took in the size of him, the impressive length shocking me slightly.

Without further hesitation, my fingers closed around his shaft to feel the warm, silky skin there. A deep moan rumbled from Hayden's throat as I touched him. He was hot and thick in my palm as I slid my hand slowly down his length, noting the way the skin seemed to move with my hand and the subtle shift in Hayden's lips against my own.

It was so strange yet incredible to see him like this, so open and unguarded as I touched him. His actions were rough and urgent, matching the pace of my hand as it slid up and down his length. I let my thumb roll over the head a few times, collecting the tiny drop of fluid that had leaked out. Another quiet groan escaped his lips as I gripped him firmly, and I could feel the way his hips shifted without his control when I moved my hand.

'Ahh, *shit*,' he muttered, the heavy tone in his voice sending a jolt straight through my body.

When my hand stroked up and down the shaft a few

more times, I pulled my lips from his to trail them down his neck. His head rolled backward, eyes closed and lips parted, as I let my teeth sink lightly into his throat before running the flat of my tongue over his skin. I could hear the way his breathing had grown uneven and shallow as well as the way his heart thumped heavily. The skin that covered his chest was a light, flushed pink colour, telling me he was nearing his end.

His hands gripped my hair, tugging on the strands lightly as my hand moved from the base of his shaft to the head and back down, the action repeated over and over. That seemed to do it, because his groan was louder than ever as I continued my actions.

'Let go, Hayden,' I breathed into his skin, my voice no more than a whisper. I could feel him resisting letting his body release and I wanted him to let himself enjoy it.

I felt his lips crash back into my own, kissing me firmly despite the heavy way we were both breathing. He gave one final groan before I felt his body tense, the warm liquid suddenly coating my hands telling me I'd succeeded in unravelling him. The fluid made it even easier to slide my hands as I coaxed him through his release, giving him one final stroke before pulling my hands away from what was now surely sensitive.

Hayden's lips were pressed to mine but he'd stopped kissing me. His eyes were clamped shut and his hands were still holding my face firmly on either side as he started to come down. His breathing was still heavy as he leaned back against the wall again. I hadn't even realised he'd sat forward, but in our desperation for each other he must have closed the distance even more.

'Holy shit,' he breathed, his eyes still closed. I giggled quietly, taking in the flush to his face and the glow that seemed to set on his features. His lips were a dark pink, parted as he breathed more evenly now.

I jumped slightly when I felt his palms push up my thighs, not expecting him to move just yet. My breath hitched in my throat when his fingers reached my centre and grazed over it lightly. He appeared to have recovered enough to lean forward and press a kiss at the base of my throat. My body squirmed uncontrollably over him as his hand slipped between my legs, putting pressure there and setting my nerves on fire.

'Go and clean up and get back here,' he murmured quietly, pressing another soft kiss on the other side of my neck. My eyes fluttered closed at the feeling before I managed to reply weakly.

'Okay.'

I nudged the door open with my shoulder before disappearing inside, cutting off his intense gaze. Once inside, I reached for a few tissues that had been placed inside, wiping off my hands before throwing the soiled tissue into the makeshift latrine. I splashed a little water from the basin in there onto my hands, cleaning myself off.

I was about to head back into the room when I felt a sudden dull ache in my abdomen. Immediately, I knew what it meant. My hands clenched into fists in frustration, my body far too pent up to deal with this right now. Of all times for my period to come, now was the absolute worst. A string of silent curses flowed through my mind as I prayed I was wrong.

Unfortunately, upon further inspection, I discovered that I was right. I'd just started to bleed, luckily sparing my undergarments in time to locate the supplies I'd stashed in the bathroom. It was with a deep sigh that I finished my business in the bathroom and re-entered the hut. I quickly saw that Hayden had discarded what he'd been wearing, his jeans replaced now by a pair of black athletic shorts. He still looked like he was glowing from his high, which only dug into me even more now that I knew I couldn't let him touch me.

'Hey,' he said, crossing the room from where he'd stood by his dresser. Immediately, his hands landed on either side of my face, then his lips on mine, kissing me softly now in comparison to how he'd kissed me so hungrily before. I felt the shock shoot through my body, teasing me with what I couldn't have. It was with all the self-control I had that I managed to put my hands lightly on his chest and push him back.

'Um, it's not . . . a good time,' I said, embarrassment tinting my cheeks pink. He looked down at me, briefly confused before my words made sense.

'Oh,' he said simply, blinking once as he understood. 'All right.'

His hands remained on my face, and his thumbs brushed along my cheeks once more. I sighed in disappointment as his lips pressed into mine again, cursing my body for its bad timing.

'God, you're so tempting, Grace,' he whispered. I felt beyond thrilled he felt the same desperation for me that I felt for him.

'I know the feeling,' I replied with a soft smile. His lips quirked up to one side before I continued. 'Hey, there's um, something I need to do.'

His brows furrowed downward in confusion and he hesitated to answer. I realised why he did so.

'I'm not going anywhere, I told you that,' I reassured him. He blew out a soft sigh before nodding slowly. 'You can trust me.'

'You're still earning that but . . . All right. Do what you need to do. I have to go see Kit and Dax anyway,' he responded, dropping his hands from my face. 'Just . . . don't talk to anyone you don't know. Do what you have to and come right back here, okay?'

'I will,' I responded, nodding quickly. I was surprised he was choosing to trust me with going off on my own after how much I'd betrayed that trust already. I could tell he was very reluctant to do so, but I suspected my promise to stay here was helping things. 'I'll be back soon.'

'I know,' he responded lightly, holding my gaze until I broke it, shooting him a soft smile before I turned to head to the door. I pulled it open and slipped outside with a final goodbye.

My stomach twisted nervously as I moved down the path, my mind whirling to try and think of what to say. If what had just happened was any indication of what could potentially happen between Hayden and me, I wanted to be prepared. Malin's words flashed through my head as I walked, and I found myself hoping Docc would be able to read my mind so I wouldn't have to repeat them.

Far too soon, I arrived at the infirmary. It was still daylight out, so I hoped he would be inside. Alone. I pushed through the door and was relieved when the building appeared to be completely empty as I moved towards Docc's makeshift office. Sure enough, he was sitting there reading a book. He didn't look up as I approached nor as I came to a halt in front of his desk. I stood somewhat awkwardly in front of him while I waited for him to acknowledge me.

'Hey, Docc—'

'Wait,' he said, holding up a finger without looking at me. His eyes scanned across the page he was reading. I clamped my mouth shut and folded my hands together in front of me, forcing myself to stand still while I waited. Seconds seemed to drag on and on as he continued to read. Finally, he closed his book and looked up at me.

'Grace,' he greeted pleasantly. 'You're alone, I see.'

'Um, yes,' I answered awkwardly. 'Hayden had to meet with Kit and Dax.'

'Ahh,' Docc said calmly, nodding once. 'What can I do for you?'

'Well, it's kind of . . . awkward, but . . . I need you to promise not to say anything,' I started, certain my face was beet red. The last thing Docc probably wanted to hear about was this.

'A doctor never tells, girl,' he said patiently. He peered at me over his desk. Apparently he didn't feel the need to stand, leaving me on my feet awkwardly in front of him as if I were giving a presentation.

'Right, good. Well, um, I spoke to Malin a while ago and she told me about this shot you have . . . for birth control,' I muttered, unable to hold his steady gaze. I focused on the wood of his desk, too uncomfortable to look him in the eye.

'Yes, I have such a thing,' he said evenly.

'Um, I was wondering if I could get that. Just so I have my period less frequently,' I lied, hoping he would believe me even though I knew he knew better.

'Of course,' he replied. 'When was your last menstrual cycle? You need to start it within five days of it.'

'Erm, now,' I said, relieved at my luck in timing.

'Wonderful,' Docc said. My eyes flitted back up to his face to see him smiling gently. He rose from his seat and moved to a cabinet behind the desk, opening it and pulling out a syringe and a small vial. He flicked his head, drawing me towards him.

'Now you'll need this every three months,' he explained

as he inserted the needle into the vial to draw up the solution. 'After a few months, you might stop getting your period altogether, but that's normal. It takes about five days to be completely effective the first time, but subsequent shots will be effective immediately.'

'It's just for my period,' I blurted quickly, too quickly.

'Yes, of course, but just so you know,' he said with a small smile. I was beyond relieved that even though he seemed to sense the truth behind my motivation, he wasn't judgemental or disapproving. He was simply fair and impartial, as all doctors should be.

I felt a cool wetness over my upper arm as he ran an alcohol swab over my skin, cleansing the area. He let it dry for a few moments before he positioned the needle.

'One, two, three,' he said evenly before jabbing the needle forward. The medicine stung slightly as it was plunged through the syringe but the needle was pulled from my arm before I was even fully aware it was over. Docc replaced the cap on the needle and threw it away before pressing a tiny bandage over the site.

'There you go,' he said with a gentle smile. 'Come see me if you have any problems, but I don't anticipate any.'

'Thank you, Docc. I appreciate your . . . discretion,' I said, feeling extremely lame.

'Anytime, girl. You've helped me enough to deserve this.'

'Thank you again,' I said, starting to move back toward the front door. 'I'll see you around.'

He nodded peacefully, his eyes closing once as he did so. I retreated from the infirmary quickly, still slightly embarrassed even though Docc had been so understanding. I had barely made it three feet out the door when I accidentally bumped into someone walking down the path. Their chest collided with my shoulder and I hissed slightly when a dull ache shot through my arm. I glanced up and was surprised to see a very familiar pair of green eyes looking down at me.

'Hayden,' I greeted, surprised.

'Hey,' he said, equally as surprised. I noticed he held a sheet of paper in his hands that appeared to be a list, which explained why he'd run into me without seeing me. Lists never seemed to be a good thing.

'What's that?' I asked, hoping it was simply a list of dinner options for the evening but very much doubting it.

'We're running low on some supplies,' he told me, frowning gently. 'We're going back into the city tomorrow.'

Chapter 28 – Arbitrary

GRACE

I didn't remember falling asleep. One second I had been talking with Hayden about all that needed to be accomplished on the raid, and the next second I was waking up in his bed. I was pleasantly surprised to find his arm linked over my waist and feel his breath tickling the back of my neck.

I allowed myself a few seconds to drink in the quiet peace that had settled over us, revelling in the warmth of his chest at my back and the dim glow that seemed to linger in the pit of my stomach. The glow, however, was slightly dimmed by the dull ache in my lower abdomen, the harsh reminder of nature's extremely unfortunate timing. Either it was my body's way of telling me to get myself under control, or Mother Nature had a sick, twisted sense of humour.

It was with a deep sigh and slow, gentle manoeuvres that I managed to shift myself out of Hayden's grasp and slip out of bed. I cringed when the frame of the bed squeaked under my shifting weight, as I had been hoping not to wake him. He looked much younger now in the depth of sleep, the harshness of the world leaving him for a few blissful hours before it came crashing back down around him.

I stepped as lightly as I could while I made my way to the bathroom, grinning as I managed to close the door without waking him. Once inside, I retrieved my supplies and took care of the necessities: brushing my teeth, combing the tangles from my hair, and most importantly, taking care of the great annoyance that had interrupted yesterday.

Yesterday, which had been one of the most surreal yet exhilarating moments of my life, only to end so abruptly. It seemed impossible that the man sleeping in that bed out there, who was so hardened to the world and so closed off when it came to his feelings, had allowed me to see him at his most vulnerable. My stomach flipped at the thought of touching him and seeing the way he reacted, setting my skin abuzz with goosebumps just at the thought.

A soft knock on the door succeeded in making me jump. My hand accidentally knocked my toothbrush off the rim of the basin, sending it clattering against the floor before I managed to collect myself.

'Grace?' he called softly. His voice was laden with sleep.

'Yeah?' I responded.

'Are you, um, going to be ready in ten minutes? We have to meet everyone and get ready,' he said. His voice was muffled by the door and his rough early morning tone.

I shoved my things into the small bag I kept in the bathroom and took a deep breath before opening the door to reveal a ruffled looking Hayden. His dark hair stood up on one side where it must have kinked when he slept, and his skin appeared a bit pinker than usual as if he were warm. His eyes blinked blearily at me as he tried to wake himself up.

'Yeah, just need to change,' I said, sending him a gentle smile that he tried to return but ended up mostly squinting at me because of the light streaming into the hut.

'Great,' he said, standing aside for me to leave the bathroom so he could take his turn. I went out and moved to the dresser as he closed the door to change.

Not even ten minutes later, Hayden and I were walking

down the now familiar path toward the raid building. I immediately noticed the truck sitting outside with a noticeably larger group of people than usual. I had been expecting Dax to be there, but was surprised to see Kit, Malin, Docc, and Jett also standing around the truck as well.

'Are they all coming with us?' I asked Hayden, my brows knitting together in concern. In my past experiences, raids with more than four people never went well. A large jolt of concern shot through me at the thought of Jett going on a raid, but it was quickly neutralised as I realised Hayden would never allow that.

'No, not Docc and Jett,' he said quietly, keeping his voice low. 'Docc doesn't do raids really. He's more valuable to us here and safe than out there.'

I couldn't help but agree with him, thinking the lives Docc saved with his medical knowledge had to be more significant than the number he'd potentially save by going on raids.

'Malin's coming?' I asked, surprised. Hayden had mentioned once that she'd kill me without a second thought. Despite his warning, she'd been nothing but nice to me so far.

'Guess so,' Hayden said, shrugging. Our hushed conversation was cut off as we arrived at the circle. Now that we were nearer, it was easy to see those who planned to come along all had weapons strapped in various places. Knives in sheaths hung off Kit, Dax, and Malin's belts, the strap of a gun cut across Kit's chest, and each of them held pistols in their hands.

More weapons waited on the ground, presumably for Hayden and me. Without hesitation, Hayden stooped to collect his 9mm handgun and slid a switchblade into his back pocket. Next he slung a backpack that clinked with ammunition over his shoulders before giving me a meaningful glance. I blinked once before copying him, loading myself

338

with similar weapons.

'Hayden, I helped get the guns ready,' Jett said proudly, breaking up the quiet conversations between Kit, Dax, Malin, and Docc. He bounced on the balls of his feet as he waited for praise.

'Did you make sure everything is loaded correctly?' Hayden quizzed, shooting him a look with his eyebrow raised.

'Sure did!' he said happily.

'I double checked,' Kit said quietly, shooting the tiniest of smiles at Jett. 'Kid did well.'

'Does that mean I get to come with you?!' he asked excitedly.

'No,' Hayden said firmly, dropping the ghost of a smile that had formed on his face.

'But Hayden—'

'Listen boy, how about you help me with some stuff in the infirmary today, how's that sound?' Docc said calmly, drawing Jett's attention. The look of disappointment at Hayden's denial was quickly replaced by one of excitement.

'Really?!' Jett asked excitedly.

'Really,' Docc repeated, smiling gently at him before shooting a slow wink at Hayden. Hayden nodded in silent thanks as Docc steered Jett away from the circle.

'See you when you get back, guys!' he called excitedly, waving enthusiastically over his shoulder before allowing Docc to take him away. Everyone returned their goodbyes before turning to Hayden for further instruction.

'Well, fearless leader, what's the plan?' Dax asked as he leaned casually against the hood of the truck. Kit and Malin stood across the circle, waiting quietly.

'Kit, you sure you're up to this? No shame in waiting until you're fully healed,' Hayden said, postponing Dax's question.

'Jesus, I'm fine! You guys act like I'm made of glass,' he

said exasperatedly. I got the feeling it wasn't the first time someone asked him about this, which was confirmed when I caught the pointed look he threw at Malin. She rolled her eyes as if they'd had this argument several times now.

'All right, whatever. You're the one who got shot in the neck, not me,' Hayden said, raising his hands in surrender.

'So, plan?' I prompted, getting us back on track.

'We've got this whole list of stuff – batteries, anything usable for buildings, some other small stuff – but mostly we need fuel,' Hayden said, frowning. The others frowned as well and I knew why: petrol was one of the most difficult things to find. Not only did the vehicles of Blackwing run on petrol, so did the three generators that powered a few of their buildings, including the kitchen, which made it essential for survival.

'Where are we going to go for that? Every place we've tried in the last few months has been dry,' Kit pointed out with a frown.

'I know,' Hayden said. 'I was thinking the suburbs? We could siphon it out of the cars there since most people go into the city to raid.'

Everyone nodded, agreeing with the plan. It was as good as we could hope for, plus not going into the actual depths of the city would hopefully mean fewer run-ins with enemies.

'Right, well, let's get on with it then,' Dax said heartily, rubbing his hands together before jumping into the passenger seat. Kit and Malin climbed in the backseat, leaving a small space for me between the middle where Malin sat and the edge of the car behind where Hayden sat. It was quite a tight squeeze with the five of us, something I was not used to. The loaded trunk, full of empty gallons and duffle bags, combined with the extra amount of people, made me feel like a rat stuck in a cage.

Hayden began to drive, and we quickly left Blackwing behind. I felt uncomfortable as Malin's thigh pressed into mine, her shoulder shoving me into the wall of the vehicle with every bump we hit. She seemed relatively uninterested in me, after saying a brief hello, a confusing surprise, as she focused mostly on talking with Kit. Dax chattered happily to Hayden in the front seat, laughing at something I hadn't heard over the roar of the engine.

For a moment, I was really reminded that I was the odd one out here. I didn't belong with them, hadn't grown up with them. These people, who had known each other nearly their entire lives, had deep bonds that went back years and years, built stronger every day by trust that could only grow by earning it over and over again. A sting of jealousy shot through me as I realised they all had something here I didn't: friendship.

I really only had one good friend back in Greystone, a twinge of guilt prickling in my stomach for just now having thought of her when I was surrounded by obvious friend-ships. Leutie had been my best friend when I was little and remained so as we grew up, although I suspected she thought me dead now. She was so very the opposite of me – sweet, warm, selfless, beautiful. Everyone loved her, and she had a lot of friends, but she'd been my only one. Unless you counted my brother, which I didn't. I felt a trickle of sadness run through me now as I thought of her as I realised, once again, that I would never see her again.

I was snapped from my thoughts when I saw a flash of green in the rearview mirror as Hayden's eyes locked on my own. He sent me a soft smile through the reflection, erasing the sense of exclusion I'd felt moments before and replacing it with a warm glow in my heart.

Maybe I wasn't completely alone.

I hadn't even been aware of it, but we'd long since entered the ruins of the city and were now slowing to a stop among several broken-down vehicles in the streets of a neighbourhood. My eyes immediately scanned the area, but it was relatively unfamiliar to me. I hadn't spent much time out here among the houses and was much more used to the feel of the city that once housed millions of people.

Finally, the engine was shut off and the doors were opened, letting me out of the tight confines and allowing me to take a full breath. Everyone's weapons rose automatically as we scanned around us, but no movement was visible.

'All right,' Hayden said, drawing our attention while he continued to scan the areas behind us. 'Kit, Malin, you guys take the list.'

He pulled the sheet from his pocket and handed it to Kit.

'Dax, you're on electrical. Get whatever you think we'll need – you know best,' he said. 'Grace and I will work on siphoning the petrol. If you see anyone, you know the signal.'

Everyone nodded, accepting their assigned duties before splitting into opposing directions. 'The signal', I had learned, was simply two low whistles meant to alert others of impending danger. After gathering a few empty jugs from the car, I followed Hayden down the street, watching as he manoeuvred quietly through the streets and avoided the debris scattered about. I imagined it looked much like the day the bombs fell, as no one was around to clean up after.

As we walked, it occurred to me that Hayden was being quiet. Or rather, quieter than usual. He was never particularly talkative, but he hadn't said two words other than to give instructions. I could practically see the memories flashing through his mind as we walked and I desperately wanted to draw him out. I wanted to make him think of anything other than the ruins of a neighbourhood, the ruins of people's lives. I was positive he was thinking about that day that ended life as he knew it, and the thought sent a jolt of pain straight through my heart.

HAYDEN

It was difficult to focus on the task at hand as we moved through the shattered remains of my local area. Every few steps, I'd see something that looked vaguely familiar yet different, the damage incurred having marred it almost beyond recognition. Almost. I saw bits of the playground my neighbours had had in their backyard strewn across the street. A grill I'd smelled so many hamburgers cooking on lay in a mangled, melted heap in what was now a weed-overgrown lawn. A bike I remembered the neighbour's kid riding around on lay twisted and charred in the gutter – a kid who was no longer living.

'Hayden,' Grace said gently. I jumped when I felt her hand touch mine gingerly, my arm yanking away instinctively before I realised it was just her. A flicker of concern crossed her features when I looked down at her, taking in the way she watched me.

'Sorry,' she muttered quietly as she took in my instinctive reaction.

'No, it's fine,' I mumbled, too preoccupied with memories to focus on much. This happened every time I came to any residential area, never mind the place I'd grown up. Or started to grow up, at least.

I shook my head in an attempt to clear the thoughts as my eyes settled on a car. My stomach clenched painfully as I realised it was in front of the remains of a house that once had been my home. My eyes closed and I blew out a deep breath as I tried to block out the memories stampeding through my mind.

'Hey,' she said gently, touching my forearm this time and letting her hand linger there. I opened my eyes and looked down her. 'Teach me how to do this?'

'You don't know how to siphon petrol?' I asked sceptically. She shook her head slowly, her eyes strangely intent.

'No.'

'Here, let's try this one,' I said, stopping at the car right in front of my old house. I tried my best to look anywhere but at it so I focused solely on Grace. She waited as I tugged off my backpack and unzipped it before pulling out a bit of plastic tubing and a rag. 'Okay, so, open the petrol tank.'

She did as I instructed. 'Okay, now what?'

'Put the tube into the tank and stuff the edges with the rag,' I said, watching closely as she did as I said. I ducked down to put one of the empty gallons I held on the ground below the tube.

'Like that?' she asked, squinting back and forth between her handy work and me. She'd tied a tidy knot in the rag, sealing the petrol tank off perfectly. I nodded.

'Mmhmm. Now blow into this end of the tube. It'll offset the pressure and force the fuel out of the tube,' I said, pointing at the bit she held in her hand. 'And put it in the gallon immediately after or you'll get a mouthful of petrol.'

'Okay,' she said, nodding before doing as I said. Her lips wrapped around the tube as she blew one lungful into it and dropped it into the gallon, into which almost immediately a trickle of petrol started to flow. She grinned down at the petrol proudly but not at all surprised. It had been a little bit too easy.

'Something tells me you already knew how to do that,' I suggested evenly. She shot me a guilty grin and shrugged.

'Maybe. I'm just trying to get you out of your head,' she said honestly, watching me closely. I frowned gently, a wave of warmth passing through me that she'd not only noticed my mood but had wanted to do something about it. She had, in fact, distracted me enough from the memories that haunted me, if only for a few moments. She surprised me again by taking a small step forward so she was close enough to press her lips gently to my jaw, heating the skin where she'd kissed me.

Once she pulled back, she gave me a soft smile before bending to kink the tube and switch over the gallons, having filled one successfully.

'Of course I know how to siphon petrol,' she said with a slight chuckle, a hint of mock insult to her light tone. I let out a half sigh, half laugh as I watched her drain the rest of the petrol from the car after nearly filling the second gallon.

'I'd be embarrassed for you if you didn't,' I teased. My mood lightened a bit thanks to her efforts but I still felt heavy. My eyes landed on another car on the other side of the street and I nodded at it before crossing over to it, Grace trailing behind me after retrieving our supplies from the now empty petrol tank.

'Want to know something?' I asked her, my gaze focused on the new vehicle.

'I do,' she replied.

I automatically started setting up the second one, trading places with her. She stood next to me with two empty gallons of her own. I didn't look at her as I spoke, determined to remain calm and even.

'That was my house,' I said casually, ticking my head across the street but not looking at it or her. I heard the quiet gasp as she sucked in a breath and saw the flash of movement in my peripheral vision as her gaze turned automatically toward what remained of the house. I knew exactly what it looked like. I didn't need to see it again. All that really remained was the brick fireplace surrounded by a sea of rubble, my belongings indistinguishable from shattered bits of the structure.

'Oh, Hayden,' she said quietly, the surprise stealing the volume from her voice. I knew she was trying to see past all that remained to the life I had before. 'Does it . . . is it difficult to be here?'

'Yes,' I admitted. I turned my gaze determinedly back to the car and away from her. Petrol had started to trickle slowly down the tube and into the jug. She was quiet for a while, as if choosing her words carefully.

'Why here, Hayden? Of all places to do this raid, why come here?' Her words were not accusatory or sceptical, merely cautiously curious. I could feel the shift in her gaze as it settled on me now, but still I didn't look at her.

'I don't know,' I admitted. In all honesty, I hadn't even known I was heading here until we were driving down my street. There was no real reason to be here. There were broken-down cars all over the city, it didn't have to be here.

'Have you ever gone in it?'

'You mean what's left of it?' I joked lamely. My voice sounded the exact opposite of joking. She gave me a soft frown that finally drew my gaze to hers. I let out a deep sigh at my pathetic attempt to act like being here didn't affect me.

'No, I haven't,' I finally answered. The closest I'd ever got was the pavement before I turned and ran away like a coward. I'd tried several times, and that had always been the outcome. I wasn't strong enough to face that. 'I can't.'

I felt weak admitting these things, but for the first time I didn't mind. I knew, for some reason, that Grace would understand. She would see why it was so difficult for me because she held a certain compassion that others around me lacked. Kit and Dax didn't understand why I never made it past the pavement, and I hadn't bothered telling anyone else. Why admit yet another weakness I struggled to hide every day if no one would get it anyway?

No one, that is, except Grace.

'I imagine so,' she said gently. Her gaze never left mine as I finally gave up trying to preoccupy myself with the petrol. There was no judgement to her voice, no arbitration or forced sorrow, only understanding. I felt a surge of appreciation for her and was relieved that I'd told her. It was such a strange feeling to share these types of things with someone – difficult, exhausting, and foreign – but I had to admit I liked it.

'Come on,' I said, changing the subject. 'Let's move on.'

I screwed the lid onto the single gallon I'd filled, leaving us with one more before we'd filled four. She nodded silently, accepting my ending of the conversation. We moved past what remained of my house and I noticed it draw her gaze once more. I didn't look and kept my eyes focused on the car we were approaching. Her gaze stayed fixed on the wreckage of my house the whole way, craning her neck backward until she was forced to look forward again. A thoughtful, determined look had settled on her face and I thought I saw a hint of something in her eyes, but she didn't say anything as we prepared to fill the final gallon.

I'd just reached the car when a flash of movement from the other side of the vehicle drew my attention. I jumped back in surprise as three men appeared with heavy weapons – knives, makeshift clubs, and what appeared to be a lead pipe – in their hands as they sneered at us over the hood. My heart jumped in my throat, their sudden appearance taking me by surprise as my hand flew out to grab Grace's wrist instinctively.

'Grace, run!' I shouted, taking a step backward and dragging her with me as one of the men let out a snarl of a laugh before easily sliding over the hood of the car in pursuit. Grace appeared stunned for a second before her training kicked in, her feet turning to run with me away from the men. Cackles of dark laughter and curse words were hurled at us as they chased us through the debris-ridden street. Heavy feet pounded on the cracked pavement behind us as we ran, my body suddenly buzzing with adrenaline. Air ripped through my lungs and my muscles stretched and flexed while I ran. My hand remained locked around Grace's wrist, my pace no faster than allowed her to keep up.

'Wait,' Grace yelled suddenly, ripping her hand from my grip before I was even aware enough to stop her. In a flash, she turned on her heel and sprinted back in the direction we had just come.

'Grace!' I shouted. My muscles seemed frozen in place, every instinct I had screaming for me to keep running while my heart held me there, watching desperately as she ran farther and farther away from me.

'Grace!'

I watched in horror as she ran back toward the men, each step bringing her closer and closer to them. Derisive grins stretched across their faces like hyenas whose prey was coming running for dinner. No matter how many times her name flew from my lips, she never stopped.

'Grace, stop!' I called, unable to move as my heart pounded painfully.

But she didn't hear me. Her feet carried her farther and farther from me, my plea for her to stop dropping dead and ignored on the cracked pavement between us, left behind like dust in her tracks.

Chapter 29 – Trepidation

HAYDEN

My feet seemed cemented to the ground, legs unable to react to the sudden turn of events despite my years of training. I watched in horror as she drew even nearer to the three men, who were charging toward her quickly. I didn't recognise any of them, but I wondered if Grace did. She didn't slow down as the distance between them practically disappeared.

It wasn't until she reached them and ducked under the heavy lead pipe swinging in her direction that I was finally able to break out of my trance; the defensive manoeuvre telling me she did not, in fact, know these men. My feet broke into a sprint, charging after her as a guttural half groan, half yell ripped from my throat. I was closing the distance quickly, but not quickly enough. With how fast they were all moving, I didn't dare use my gun for fear of hitting Grace.

She seemed to move at twice the speed of the men, but she was outnumbered. Each time she ducked a blow from one, another would swing, their barbaric weapons more than effective as they tried to attack her. While she managed to dodge a lot of the attacks, the lead pipe connected with her body more than once, as did the makeshift club. The knife tore at her skin, missing her mostly but reaching her enough to bleed.

My legs carried me ever closer and I saw her lean back out of the way of a jab with a knife from one before throwing her knee into the ribcage of another, sending him sprawling to the ground. She ducked to the side quickly, side-stepping a second man as he charged at her. Again, her foot connected with the man on the ground, a sickening crack sounding through the air as she connected with his nose. He stopped moving on the ground, clearly unconscious while blood poured from his nose.

The third man, wielding a knife, leered at her as he taunted her by twirling it around in his fingers. The second man, taking advantage of her distraction, lunged at her and knocked her to the ground before raising his makeshift club, aiming directly for her face. He lifted his arms to swing downward just as I reached them, my entire body slamming into his and knocking him from where he stood over her into the pavement.

I landed on top of him with a heavy thud and was immediately hit with the rotten scent of unwashed human. He wasted no time in trying to throw me off, but I managed to keep him pinned down as I pulled my fist back and let it fly into his jaw. My muscles felt tight as I swung again and again, the harsh sting from the connection radiating up my arm. I was surprised when I felt a heavy punch meet my jaw, splitting my lip and sending a thin trickle of blood down my chin.

'Pretty little girlfriend you have there,' he jeered, his eyes bulging out from his skull. I landed yet another blow to his face. His head snapped to the side and he spat a mouthful of blood before letting out a derisive laugh. I saw his eyes flicker to the side, where I could see Grace fighting the remaining man. She ducked under the reach of his knife as he jabbed it at her again before slamming her elbow down over his arm, sending another sickening crack through the air as his arm broke.

A guttural scream ripped from his throat as he felt the pain, his weapon falling to the ground from his now useless arm.

'You stupid bitch!' he swore at her. Grace didn't reply but swung her leg to kick the man's arm again, earning another scream of agony from him before he collapsed to the ground, clutching at his arm that was bent at an unnatural angle.

'Feisty thing. Can't wait to see what a good fuck she is,' the man pinned beneath me dared to say. Something inside me seemed to snap as his words crashed into my brain. I had no control as my fists flew through the air, landing with loud thuds and hollow smacks against whatever part of him I could reach.

'Don't.'

Smack.

'Even.'

Thud.

'Look at her!'

Crack.

My chest was heaving as I realised the man was no longer moving, out cold on the pavement beneath me as blood poured from unidentified places on his face. My hands were covered in blood that was not my own, and I could feel the dull ache in my knuckles from the repeated abuse. My body was shaking as I stared down at what I'd done, somewhat ashamed that I'd lost control so badly.

I pushed myself off the ground and whipped around, noticing that I was alone besides the three unconscious men. Grace was, once again, gone.

Or so I thought, as a flash of movement to my right quickly corrected me. She appeared seemingly out of nowhere, jogging towards me with something clutched in her hands. She was also covered in blood, though it was difficult to tell if it was her own or not. I'd seen her take far too many blows to be completely uninjured, and the thought of her getting hurt terrified me. My heart was thudding so hard I thought it might burst out of my chest, and my breath was coming in short pants from the exertion of the fighting.

'What the hell was that?!' I demanded, furious at her for running back blindly into obvious danger for no apparent reason. I stormed forward, meeting her halfway now that she'd jogged back over to me. Now that she was closer, I could see an obvious bruise forming over her cheekbone and several cuts to her face that were bleeding rather profusely.

'They're just some random Brutes, Hayden,' she said as calmly as she could while she tried to catch her breath. Sweat trickled down her face, joining the blood as it trailed down her body. My jaw clenched tightly as I glared down at her.

'*Just Brutes*. They had weapons and there were three of them! Why the hell would you go running back like that?' I all but shouted. I was livid with her for being so reckless.

'I had it under control,' she said. She narrowed her eyes at me as she saw just how upset I was.

'You can't just do shit like that! It's dangerous,' I said, hating the way I sounded like I was scolding her. Technically I was.

'Really, I had no idea,' she said sarcastically. She rolled her eyes at me. A flash of fury rose in me at how casual she was acting. She had nearly just got herself killed and didn't even seem to care. The thought alone sent a jolt of pain through my body.

'Do you not understand? People *die* out there, Grace,'

I said, a hint of hurt leaking into my voice and weighing down the anger. 'They die and they don't come back.'

'I know,' she said softly. Her face dropped the hints of anger that had started to build up at my attack. 'I just . . . I didn't think.'

'Well, you have to think. You had a gun and you didn't even use it. You can't just do whatever you want and run around like you're invincible because you're not, Grace. You're good, yeah, but you're not invincible.'

She studied me for a few seconds. Not once had my gaze broken from hers; it was as if I was physically unable to break the deep connection.

'You're bleeding,' she said, changing the subject abruptly. Her eyes darted to my lip where it had been split and I felt a sudden sting of pain as if her noticing it had reminded me to feel.

'So are you,' I countered. My stomach clenched as I took in the damage done to her, the unsettling feeling spreading through my body as I realised there was probably much more that I couldn't even see yet.

'You weren't supposed to follow me,' she stated slowly. 'You weren't supposed to get hurt.'

'Did you really think I wasn't going to follow you? That I'd just let you get your arse kicked by those three?' I asked, raising an eyebrow sceptically.

'I don't know what I thought,' she admitted. She shrugged and winced quickly but tried to hide it.

'Where are you hurt?' I questioned, not buying her act.

'I'm fine,' she said, shaking her head and dropping my gaze as she lied.

'No, you're not,' I argued, frustrated. She was clearly not fine, but I knew she would never admit it.

'Look, you might not give a shit if you get hurt but I do,

353

okay? Now what's hurt?' I said in exasperation. I almost didn't even notice the confession that slipped past my lips, but I saw it register on her face as she blinked slowly before recovering.

'Hayden, I'm fine!' she said, raising her voice in protest. She took a deep breath and frowned at me. 'Really.'

I looked down at her disbelievingly but decided to drop it for now.

'Now will you tell me what the hell you were doing?' I said, changing the subject once again. I crossed my arms over my chest and stared down at her expectantly, ignoring the throbbing in my knuckles as they pressed into my arms.

Grace opened her mouth to speak and closed it again, deciding against her words. Her eyes darted down to her hands, and for the first time I realised she was still holding something. My eyes dropped down to it as I heard her let out a low sigh. She held it out to me, her hands slightly unsteady and stained with blood.

I felt my heart hammer my stomach twist as I realised what it was. The edges were burned black, and water seemed to have leaked into most of the inside, but it was in one piece. It felt far too heavy in my hands as she handed it to me, as if the emotional weight had manifested itself physically. Both of us were silent as I took in the object.

I ran my hand gently over the charred cover, feeling the subtle grooves that had been all but erased by the fire. My fingers trailed down the spine before reaching to open it, my hand shaking slightly. I'd grown up with it always sitting in the same place – on the coffee table in the living room. I would recognise it anywhere: the family photo album.

The pain that always seemed to linger in my heart seeped into my veins, enveloping me in a mess of emotions I'd struggled to keep locked away. Tentatively, my finger hitched under the cover, frozen in place as I tried to force my hand upward. I could feel Grace watching my every move but couldn't bring myself to meet her gaze. My attention was fully captivated by what I held in my hands.

Slowly, as if it might bite me, I picked up the cover and started to open it. My breathing seemed impossibly fast for simply standing in place, but my heart was pounding so quickly I almost didn't even notice. The cover was nearly open now and my eyes landed on the first page, the tiny, tiny glimpse of the first photo more than enough for me to slam it shut quickly. My hand pressed on the cover again, holding it closed as if it would spontaneously fly open.

'You shouldn't have done that, Grace,' I said quietly, still unable to tear my gaze from the photo album. It felt rough against my palm as I took in the details of what I thought was surely lost to the fall of the world.

'Probably not, but I did and I'm not sorry,' she said quietly. My eyes darted up to meet hers. The pulse in my ears seemed to drown out the world around us.

'You can't do that, Grace. You can't put yourself in danger for me.'

'I wanted to get it for you,' she said matter-of-factly. My heart jumped, but I refused to feel happy that she wanted to help me while endangering herself.

'It was dangerous,' I repeated. 'And pointless. I can't look at it.'

'Sure you can—'

'No, I can't. There's a reason I don't want to remember everything. There's a reason I can't go into my house. It's just . . . it's easier if I don't.'

'Things aren't always easy but that doesn't mean they're not worthwhile,' she said quietly. Her green eyes peered into my own, as if she were trying to see into my mind. She took a small step forward and placed her hand, just as battered as my own, over the back of mine that rested on top of the photo album between us. 'You don't have to look at it now, just . . . keep it, okay? Maybe you'll change your mind.'

'If I keep it, will you promise not to go running straight into a death trap again?' I pressed, arching an eyebrow at her. A ghost of a smile pulled at her lips.

'I promise.'

'You'd better remember that. I told you I don't want you to get hurt and I mean it,' I said, my voice dropping in volume now that I seemed to have calmed down. I hadn't really been aware of it, but my anger at her had melded into a tense concern, the fear that she was badly injured subsiding a bit now that she stood there in front of me.

'I'll remember, I promise,' she said earnestly, holding my gaze. I nodded slowly and let out a sigh as I folded the photo album into my chest, cradling it there with one hand. My other hand rose automatically to run lightly along her lower lip, which was swollen thanks to one of the men now unconscious on the ground.

She seemed to be holding her breath as she watched me watching her, my frown deep as I took in her face. The moment seemed to linger between us, growing more palpable by the second as our breath caught in our throats. Time seemed to disappear around us as I let my thumb run over her lip again, my fingers snaking into her hair at the base of her neck.

'Jesus, what have you done to me, Bear?'

My voice was a mere whisper, as if I was afraid of the answer. She had such a grip on me and I wasn't even aware of it until moments like this – moments when I feared for her own safety above my own. Moments where I was struck by just how much I cared for her, something that surprised me every single time I realised it.

'Whatever you've done to me,' she replied, her voice shaky for the first time. My eyes flitted back and forth to hers, noting the hint of vulnerability there as she spoke her true feelings. I couldn't resist the lure of her, like a drug. I was drawn to her against any will I might have had, and I gave up resisting as I let my lips brush lightly against hers with my hand lingering on her cheek.

The warmth of the gentle kiss seemed to soothe the various aches that had settled into my body, and my heart hammered on for what seemed like an unhealthy amount of time. The warmth enveloped me, spreading through my veins and taking me over completely. With a quiet sigh, I pulled back and dropped my forehead against hers. Her eyes were closed as she settled into me, the photo album she'd retrieved still cradled in my free hand.

'I'm going to protect you, Grace. You just have to let me.'

Her eyes flitted open at my words, meeting my gaze that was so close to her own. Her lips parted as she drew a short breath and absorbed my words.

'You deserve someone to protect you, too,' she whispered in return. A ghost of a smile pulled at one corner of my lips as I leaned back a few inches to gather more of her reaction.

'I protect you, you protect me, is that it?' I asked, trying to mask the quiet amusement that had started to creep up.

'Yes,' she said seriously. 'That's exactly it.'

'As long as you keep your promise not to do anything stupid or reckless, you have a deal,' I offered slowly. It was progress from her whole 'I don't need anyone to protect me' thing. She truly didn't, but there was no way she could ever stop me from it.

'Good,' she said, a small smile pulling at her lips. 'Deal.'

It suddenly occurred to me how strange the setting of our conversation was. There we stood, in the rubble of where I grew up, surrounded by broken homes and memories alike. We were on the street in front of my old house, halfway between where we'd fought the Brutes and where she'd retrieved the photo album. What had once been a normal, quiet neighbourhood was now a graveyard for the world that was; the shattered remains that were scattered on the street the only evidence that life had once been simple.

Two low whistles pulled me from my thoughts, the sound drifting from down the street. Grace's eyes widened as she recognised the signal. Both of us turned to head toward the sound before I remembered something.

'Wait,' I said, throwing out my arm. 'The petrol.'

'Oh yeah,' she said, blinking in surprise as if she'd forgotten all about it. She glanced around quickly before spotting it only a few yards away. We jogged over and collected our items before hurrying back to where the signal had come from.

As we approached where the men lay unconscious, it quickly became clear that the one with the obviously broken arm was starting to wake up. He let out a low moan and rocked to the side, his face screwed up in pain as if he wasn't fully aware of what was going on. Grace and I jogged by, and I was very surprised when Grace's foot darted out to connect with the man's face. I'd lost count now of how many times today I'd heard the snap of bone, but it was clear she'd just broken his nose again as he plummeted back into unconsciousness. She continued to jog next to me without the slightest pause, her action so casual it was as if she'd waved goodbye to someone.

'Pig,' she muttered, a scowl settling on her face for a

moment. I couldn't help but feel swelling admiration for her tenacity.

'Remind me never to piss you off,' I said lightly. We jogged a little faster as a second signal sounded out, concern flashing through me. My muscles stretched as I pushed forward, the exertion actually easing some of the ache out of my body.

'You have and you will again,' she said, shaking her head. I caught the sly grin on her face before letting out a low chuckle. We continued to run forward, the truck now in view as we approached.

Relief washed over me as I counted the three of them waiting there, all standing casually around the truck. I could see no obvious injuries, though we were still too far away to tell for sure. Sweat started to trickle down the back of my neck again as we finally met up with everyone, stopping a few feet away.

'What the hell happened to you two?!' Dax demanded, his eyes widening at the sight of us. For a moment, I had forgot we were both bruised and bloodied. Everyone was, thankfully, unharmed. Except for Grace and me, that is.

'Brutes,' I explained shortly. 'Three of them.'

'Are you guys okay?' Kit asked, frowning deeply as he took in the state of my knuckles and the various other injuries between the two of us.

'Just fine,' Grace reassured him. Flashes of the way she'd moved when she fought replayed in my mind and I was impressed all over again. She fought just as well, if not better, than a lot of men I'd seen.

'What was the signal for?' I asked after seeing they were clearly all right.

'I saw some Brutes a few blocks down and figured it was time to clear out,' Kit explained.

'And by the looks of you two, there are probably more around here,' Malin said, eyeing us apprehensively. She wasn't as used to raids as everyone else, so she was a bit more unsettled by the danger.

'All right, let's get out of here then,' I said, nodding. Everyone agreed and helped Grace and I load our stuff back into the truck along with their own prizes they'd already loaded. With a wary glance around, I waited for everyone to pile into the vehicle. The same positions were resumed, and Grace crammed herself into the seat behind me without complaint.

Only minutes later, we were zooming out of the city and back toward Blackwing. Once we'd cleared the limits of the city, everyone seemed to let out a sigh of relief. Kit, Malin, and Dax chattered to each other about the success of the raid while I settled into content silence. My eyes flitted to the backseat in an attempt to meet Grace's gaze, but it wasn't there.

She was leaning forward against the back of my seat, her head resting lightly on her forearms while her back rose and fell slowly as she breathed. A jolt of concern flashed through me as I realised her insistence that she was fine really was just to shut me up. She clearly wasn't fine, and it frightened me to see.

'Grace, are you okay?' I asked suddenly, interrupting whatever was being talked about around me. Her head snapped up as she blinked and met my gaze in the rearview mirror. She attempted to smile at me but it came out as more of a grimace.

'Mmhmm, I'm fine,' she said unconvincingly. We hit a bump in the dirt and a tight grimace flashed across her face. 'Just . . . try to avoid any big bumps.'

I nodded, my brows knit tightly together. My jaw

clenched sharply and I felt the muscle jump in my cheek. I had to get her back to Docc before her pain got any worse. She must have easily seen the concern on my face because she shot me another attempt at a smile, this one working better than the first and actually looking genuine.

Anxiety twisted at my stomach and a surge of unexplainable guilt flooded through me. The sooner we got back, the better.

'Hang in there, Grace. Almost there.'

Bonus Chapter
DOCC

Chaos whirled around us as bomb after bomb decimated London. Planes whizzed overhead, spraying bullets at whatever and whoever they passed. Each time the ground shook, the group of people I stood amongst let out screams of terror, grasping each other close in an effort to remain strong. The bridge we'd gathered beneath gave us a little cover, but it wouldn't last for long.

This was supposed to be the meeting place should anything like this happen.

So far, roughly only thirty had made it here.

There were supposed to be over a thousand.

My eyes narrowed as I searched the quickly deteriorating street, desperate to see more of our group arriving. A flash of movement caught my attention; I jerked my gaze to them as two figures appeared from around a corner. They moved quickly, one adult and one child. A bomb went off behind them, causing them to duck while their feet carried them onward. It wasn't until she hastily pushed her hair back from her face that I recognised her.

It was Sophie Abraham, and the small figure could only be her son, Hayden.

My heart panged painfully as I noticed the significant absence of one other who should have been there. Sophie's husband and Hayden's father – Noah – was gone. I knew what that must have meant, and I felt a disappointed breath escape my lungs. Noah had been one of my most trusted confidants, one who I relied on heavily in the escalating turmoil, and his death would be a major loss not only to his family, but to everyone in our group.

Others around me noticed Sophie and Hayden now as they ran towards us, so close to the safety of the bridge. I waved my arm, encouraging them forward, when suddenly Sophie was jerked backward, stopping in her tracks as she fell to the ground and yanked Hayden down with her. Horrified gasps sounded from the group, including my own, as we witnessed her death in a split second.

'The boy's alive,' said a voice next to me. I glanced over to see Barrow, a young man of around Noah and Sophie's age.

'We have to get him,' I replied quickly. My eyes found Hayden again to see him crouching over his mother, an easy target for the desolation raining down around him.

Without another word, Barrow darted forward from beneath the safety of the bridge, sprinting the short distance to Hayden.

It only took him seconds to get there. They had been so close.

I watched as Barrow pulled Hayden from the ground, wasting no time in standing and rushing back toward us. Hayden writhed in his arms, clearly reluctant to leave his mother as he reached behind Barrow. He was too young to know the finality of what had just happened.

A breath of relief pushed past my lips as Barrow returned. Hayden was now screaming for his mother, desperate to get back to her. Barrow patted his back and tried to calm him, keeping his protective grip firm. My eyes looked past them both, scanning for any other survivors making their way to us, but I saw no movement other than the continuous explosions and chaos overtaking the city.

'We can't wait any longer,' I said, raising my voice to address the group. Fear-stricken eyes focused on me. 'If we stay here, none of us will make it out.'

'You're right,' Barrow nodded. 'Everyone, get on the bus!'

Immediately, people turned and hurried to board the bus that we'd parked beneath the bridge a few weeks ago. It looked broken down, which is why no one had bothered to touch it since we'd placed it here.

People continued to pile on while I ducked down, searching a small ledge on the bottom of the vehicle until I found the key I knew was there. Relief soared through my body as I straightened up and boarded, successfully starting the engine. My eyes caught Barrow's, who was still holding a very upset Hayden. He gave me an affirming nod.

So far, our plans were working, if only for a fraction of the people we'd hoped for.

The engine rumbled as I drove forward, swerving to avoid blasts in the road and scattered debris. Screams sounded as another bomb shook the earth, rattling the windows of the bus.

'Keep your heads down!' I called just before a round of bullets ripped through the roof. I heard a scream of agony but didn't dare tear my eyes from the road.

Bombs continued to fall, and the road didn't clear, but the longer we drove, the farther we seemed to leave the chaos behind. Finally, mercifully, we reached the edge of the city and burst onto a dirt path towards a small wooded area outside of London. The bus rumbled on the rough terrain, but people had finally seemed to calm down enough to stop screaming. Only a few muted moans could be heard as whoever had been hit by the bullets earlier felt the pain of the wounds.

When we reached the trees, we only made it a few feet into the shelter of their branches before we had to stop the bus. It was far too large to manoeuvre through the woods; we would have to carry on by foot.

'That's as far as we'll get,' I said, turning to face those aboard. 'Those of you who have been out here already know the way. If not, stay close. It's not too far.'

People hung on my every word and followed my actions as I left the bus, stepping aside until everyone had piled out. I saw faces I recognised – those I'd met with countless times before today to plan out what we'd do when the inevitable war finally came to London. Other faces I didn't know – those trusted enough by those who had worked to prepare for this situation. I hoped there would be time for introductions later.

'Let's go,' I instructed as I started to walk down a lightly treaded path.

Barrow appeared beside me. I noticed he'd finally put Hayden down, though he still held his hand to lead him along as he walked next to him. Hayden had stopped crying and obeyed in silence. Sadness rolled through me again as I felt the loss of Noah and Sophie.

'Do you think anyone else made it?' Barrow asked, keeping his voice low.

'I hope so.'

Barrow was silent for a few minutes as we continued. Quiet murmurs could be heard as people behind us talked in shaky voices.

'Do you think . . . Noah?' Barrow murmured, eyes darting to Hayden as if hoping he wouldn't hear.

'I didn't see him,' I admitted, sadly. 'He'd have been there if he could.'

Barrow sighed and nodded. He'd been close friends with both Noah and Sophie.

We carried on the rest of the way in silence. About an hour passed before we came upon a familiar clearing and the looming watch tower, left over from when families seeking a bit of nature come here to visit. The tower had been used to see the view of the city and the surrounding area. Now we would use it for protection.

A few other small buildings were scattered around the area, obviously neglected but still standing. Only one had electricity, and it had once been a small café. I was pleased to see that the place looked undisturbed, and even more pleased when I spotted a woman named Melinda. She was another who I'd met with countless times before. She caught my eye and gave me a sad, determined nod.

I watched as she moved toward the nearest building and pushed the door open, inspecting the contents before coming back to the group.

'Some luck. Our supplies are still there,' she announced. A wave of relief washed over the crowd as she approached me.

'This is what we planned for, right?' she said. Barrow joined us, Hayden still trailing along.

'On a smaller scale, yes. We should proceed as we intended.'

Barrow nodded in agreement.

'Okay, everyone,' Melinda called. Everyone turned to listen. 'If you're here, then you either helped plan this or know someone who did. I'll admit, we hoped more would make it, but some may come later. Those who couldn't meet at the bridge know where we are, and they'll make it here if they can.'

My eyes landed on a young woman, Maisie, who was wiping away tears and an older woman who had her arm wrapped around her shoulder. I recognised them and knew there were at least three more that should have been with them. Perhaps they had gotten separated and they'd show up later.

Perhaps they would never make it.

'In the meantime, it's up to us to get things moving here. There are supplies and food in each of these buildings, but they are limited, so use caution. Hopefully once things settle down we can go back into the city to get more, but for now, let's behave as though this is all we'll ever have. We need to be rational.'

People nodded in agreement. She continued.

'I know many of you know this, but for now, it's not safe to go anywhere. The city will be unpredictable, and there will be others like us, but not on our side. We've heard of other groups of people, and I'm sure some of them will have survived today as well. We don't know where they plan to settle, or how many there will be, so everyone be alert. We can only trust those we know.'

Melinda looked around at the crowd, her face set in strong determination. She caught my eye and nodded. I cleared my throat and stepped forward.

'For those of you who lost ones you love today, I am sorry. I know it's not easy right now, but we need to focus on survival. We've planned ahead for a day we hoped would never come, but it's here. We just need to stick to our plan, and we will carry on.'

The crowd was silent, and a few people nodded resolutely.

'Go on, everyone. Start setting up.'

With that, people began splitting up and taking action. Supplies that had been crammed into the buildings were brought out and organised so everything would be as practical as possible. I watched as those I'd met with before delegated tasks to others so that the camp could start to take shape.

We worked for hours, setting up tents, starting fires, organising supplies. All the while, the faint booming continued to sound as the carnage carried on in the city. I tried to tune it out as I set up the few medical supplies I'd managed to stash out here.

As evening approached, the air quieted. A soft rustling of leaves was all that remained as the chaos finally subsided. I breathed a sigh of relief, hopeful it was finally over.

It was nearly dark by the time the first survivors showed up. I couldn't help but smile as I saw the group of around twenty break through the clearing to join us. They were familiar faces, bloodied and battered, but they were alive.

Over the next few hours, more and more people would show up. Still fewer than we'd planned for, but by the time morning came, our number had grown to nearly five hundred. Children were put to rest in some of the larger tents we'd set up, some of them orphans now, like Hayden. The adults remained awake, working relentlessly to get things moving in our new home.

Eventually, days passed and no more survivors came to join us. It seemed we'd finally reached the limit of those who had survived. In that time, our camp had transformed. People relied on the skills they'd learned in their normal lives to improve our conditions. Those with knowledge of construction had been busy building more solid structures. Those with electrical experience attempted to give power to as many buildings as they could with their limited materials.

A few stepped up as the designated food coordinators, taking inventory and rationing out meals as best as they could.

Very quickly, everyone found their place, the desperation to survive forcing people to what they knew best. Everyone had a role, and it was defined very quickly in order for us to carry on.

The most difficult part was the children. They did not understand what was happening, especially those who had lost their parents. The adults took turns staying with them, attempting to distract them from what was happening around them, but it didn't always work, and the questions poured in. I answered them honestly, certain no good would come from lying to them.

It was a warm day about two months after we'd settled in the woods that I came across three young boys all around the age of five or six. They were slightly secluded from the rest of the group, and I noticed one of them drawing in the dirt with a stick. Hayden. A sad smile pulled at my lips as I recognised the other two boys, both of whom were now orphans as well. Their names were Kit and Dax.

'What are you boys up to?' I asked, startling them all. They glanced up at me guiltily.

'Nothing,' Hayden said quickly, leaning forward in an attempt to conceal whatever it was he'd drawn in the dirt.

'Let's see,' I said gently, resting a hand on his shoulder so I could see.

I couldn't help but notice what could only be a rough map of our camp. He'd drawn little squares where the buildings were, and a large triangle that must have represented the tower dominating the centre. Things had changed drastically from the first day we'd settled here, and his drawing reflected that. We'd managed a few trips back into the city, greatly increasing our supplies and ability to expand and improve our camp.

'Blackwing?' I was still getting used to the name we'd chosen for ourselves.

Hayden nodded, and Dax picked sheepishly at a blade of grass that had sprouted through the dirt.

'Why do you need a map?' I asked softly, studying him.

'I just like to know where stuff is,' he replied. Kit gave a shy nod of agreement.

'You don't need to worry about that just yet,' I told him.

He frowned. 'Why not?'

I sighed. This was not the first time I'd caught them doing something like this. Only a few days ago, I'd broken up what I thought was a fight when, actually, they had just been practising their combat. It was clear they'd observed what the adults in camp were doing and had tried to copy them even if they weren't sure why.

'Just not yet. Run along with the other kids, now,' I instructed calmly.

They were just boys. They were too young to be concerned with training and maps.

'Yes, Docc,' they all mumbled before standing and hurrying away. My eyes followed them and caught Hayden's green gaze as he turned to look at me over his shoulder. A frown remained on his face as he turned back around, settling in with the other kids who were gathered around Maisie, who was reading a book aloud to them. The loved ones she'd cried fearful tears for the first day here had never made it.

My eyes settled on Hayden, Kit, and Dax once more. Guilt weighed heavily on me, and I made a mental note to be more careful about what the children observed. Most took no notice, but it was clear that Hayden, Kit, and Dax were different. There would come a time for them to step up, but it wasn't now.

Now, they had to be children, even if the world had fallen apart.

First, there was *Anarchy*.

NOW COMES

Read on for an extract from the next epic story in the series.

CHAPTER ONE – RELIANCE

GRACE

I blew out a deep breath as I squeezed my eyes shut in an attempt to block out the pain radiating from my ribcage. Every tiny bump we hit was like a sledgehammer to my side, no matter how carefully Hayden drove. I kept my face buried in my arms to hide my grimace; there was nothing Hayden could do about it and I didn't want him to feel bad for something he had no control over.

The truck hit a divot in the road and I felt the sharp pang vibrate through my ribs again, forcing air through my clenched teeth. My hand on Hayden's shoulder gripped the fabric of his shirt tightly in my fist as I tried to ward off the pain, and I felt the truck slow a little as he tried to be more careful.

I hadn't noticed the pain until after I'd climbed into the truck, the adrenaline from the fight and Hayden's words masking the injury. Now, however, it was impossible to ignore as red-hot pain seared through my ribs. I felt the sticky, warm wetness of blood plastering my shirt to my stomach, but the ache from my ribs seemed to be causing the most discomfort.

A shaky breath ripped from my lungs as I felt the truck manoeuvring through the trees, telling me we were finally nearly back to Blackwing. I jumped when a hand landed on my back, the movement causing pain to shoot through my nerves once again.

'Are you all right?' Malin asked from beside me, her voice equal parts concerned and confused. No one seemed to have realised I was injured at first, just as I hadn't. No, that was wrong – Hayden had noticed.

'Mmhmm,' was all I managed to reply, nodding slowly while I kept my face pressed into my arm that leaned against the back of Hayden's seat. Hayden seemed jittery beneath my touch; my hand on his shoulder was the only thing keeping me grounded as I tried not to let the pain take over.

'She's not all right,' Hayden snapped, his voice laced with anger. He mumbled something else I couldn't quite hear over the roar of the engine. My heart thumped once at his concern for me, even if it was hidden beneath his angry tone. I couldn't find the strength to reply, though, as yet another bump in the road sent a jolt through my body.

After a few more agonising minutes, Hayden finally pulled the truck to a stop. I hardly managed to lift my head from my arms when I heard my door fly open. Blood rushed to my head and I felt woozy as I turned to where he stood in the doorway. He took one look at me, his eyes darting to the red stain in my side, before stepping forward and looping his arms beneath my knees and back. He pulled me from the back of the truck easily.

'Hayden, I'm fine,' I lied, blinking once to try and clear my head. His arms held me securely to his chest as he started walking, and my arms looped automatically around his neck despite my protests.

'No, you're not,' he argued gently. The truck still hummed in the background with the engine running and presumably filled with the rest of our raid crew. Hayden hadn't said a word to any of them before pulling me from the back and carrying me away.

'No—'

'Grace, dammit, you're not fine,' he said firmly. I could practically see the frown on his face even though my head had fallen to his shoulder. The pain was making me dizzy. I felt pathetically weak that I had to be carried off like this; I'd endured worse pain and had made it through alone. I could take care of myself.

Or so I tried to believe as I let Hayden carry me further. I could feel the warmth of his body through his clothes and the way his heart hammered as I rested my head on his shoulder. I was relatively useless as I felt Hayden push a door open, cutting off the sunlight beating down on us.

'Docc!' he called sharply, making me jump slightly and sending another shot of pain through my body. Hayden noticed the wince I failed to suppress. 'Shit, sorry.'

''S fine,' I mumbled in reply, squeezing my eyes tightly closed once again. I felt his thumb stroke lightly over my shoulder as he walked, the gentle touch soothing a little bit of the ache I was feeling.

'What happened?' Docc soothed as he appeared beside us.

'She tried to fight three Brutes at once,' Hayden explained quickly.

'Oh Grace,' Docc said quietly, partly disapproving and partly impressed. 'Set her on the bed, Hayden.'

'I'm going to put you down, all right?' Hayden said quietly. He sounded very close, which I found to be true when I opened my eyes. His face was only inches from my own, and concern was etched clearly across his features. His bright green eyes were locked on mine, and his brows were pulled low over them as he watched me.

'All right,' I responded weakly. I hated how shaky my voice was and I hated him seeing me like this – weak, vulnerable, everything I hated and tried so much not to be. As a girl it was already difficult enough to be taken seriously, worse was being an injured girl who had to be carried into the infirmary. There was no hint of pity in Hayden's gaze, however, as he gently set me down on the bed. His arms stayed around me until he was sure I was settled, and he only withdrew after I gave him a small nod.

'Where are you hurt?' Docc asked calmly as his deep brown eyes settled on me. I found it difficult to look at him, however, as Hayden's gaze burned intensely into my own. The moment seemed to linger on for far too long, and Docc had to repeat his question before I was finally able to look at him.

'Where are you hurt, girl?' he repeated patiently. My eyes flicked to meet his.

'My ribs, left side,' I said, grimacing as I tried to point at the area. The area was soaked through with blood by now, something he surely noticed as he leaned closer to inspect.

'I'll have to cut away your shirt to get you cleaned up. Hayden, if you'd kindly step out—'

'No!' I blurted quickly. Too quickly. I swallowed harshly before continuing. 'Hayden can stay.'

Docc studied me for a moment with a hint of a knowing glint in his eye before he nodded slowly. 'All right, girl.'

He turned and walked away for a few moments to retrieve whatever he needed, and my gaze quickly returned to Hayden. He leaned forward onto the bed, his hands splayed wide over the thin mattress only a few inches away from my own hand. It occurred to me that he might not want to stay even though I had just told Docc he could.

'You, um, you don't have to—'

'Shut up, Grace. I'm staying,' he said quietly, shaking his head slowly. My breath caught as his hand shifted to cover mine, his fingers winding between the spaces created by my own as he picked it up gently. My heart fluttered at his insistence, and the pain suddenly didn't seem quite so bad. Our moment was interrupted as Docc reappeared. His eyes flitted to our joined hands; he said nothing.

'Here, take this,' Docc instructed, holding out a pill and a bottle of water. 'For the pain.'

I did as he said and swallowed the pill. I felt the cool metal of scissors Docc had procured as he cut along the hem of my shirt, causing the fabric to quickly fall away. I was left in just my bra and shorts. Docc was very professional, and Hayden had already seen me like this, or even more intimately, countless times.

I winced as Docc probed gently around my ribs and resisted the urge to look. Past experience with wounds told me that looking only served to make the pain worse; it was better not to see the damage and let it impair your judgement. My gaze stayed fixed on Hayden's, whose eyes didn't waver from my own. His thumb trailed lightly across the back of mine, and he squeezed my hand encouragingly.

'Is it the cut that hurts?' Docc asked. I could feel him wiping away some of the blood with some kind of gauze, and the sharp sting of alcohol used to cleanse the cut.

'No,' I said honestly. The cut hurt, but it was just a flesh wound similar to the many I'd endured before. This pain I was feeling now was deep and achy, much different from the pain of a cut.

'Hmm,' Docc hummed quietly. He continued to study my ribs and I couldn't stop myself from looking down. I sucked in a gasp when my eyes landed on the damaged area, which only served to send another rocket of pain shooting through my ribs. A long, jagged gash ripped diagonally down my side, starting on the front of my ribcage just below my chest and trailing four or five inches, and producing more blood than I had been expecting. It wasn't particularly deep, but the length of it made it look scarier than it was.

Much more serious, though, was the dark purple bruise that had already formed over my ribcage. Such instant bruising couldn't be a good thing, and I already knew what I feared before.

'Broken rib,' I muttered quietly, assessing along with Docc. The pain seemed to increase just as I knew it would now that I'd seen it.

'I'm afraid so,' Docc said calmly. His fingers put a light pressure on both sides of my ribcage that caused me to wince again and suck in a harsh breath.

'Don't!' Hayden said quickly. Docc's eyes left my injury to study Hayden curiously.

'You're hurting her,' Hayden added quietly, holding Docc's gaze.

I squeezed his hand lightly as I returned my gaze to him. He was looking at Docc with a deep frown before he felt me watching him and turned to look at me.

'It's all right,' I said. Concern flickered across his features again as he blew out a deep breath.

'Maybe you should step outside, son,' Docc suggested gently. I knew he would have to do more that would cause me pain, just as he knew Hayden wouldn't want to see it.

'No,' Hayden said firmly. 'I'm staying.'

'All right,' Docc sighed. 'Just know, she'll have to endure a bit more pain, so you be there for her instead of telling me to stop.

'Good. Now Grace, I'm going to have to feel around a bit, so you tell me where it hurts the most.'

'Okay,' I said before taking a deep breath to ready myself. Hayden's hand was gripped tightly in mine as I nodded that I was ready.

Docc's hand slid gently over my ribcage, feeling cautiously for any protruding fragments of bone. The pressure hurt, but not unbearably as he tried each bone. He made it three or four times around before his fingers ran over one site that caused me to gasp in pain.

'There,' I wheezed breathlessly. My body shook as pain radiated through me.

Hayden let out a heavy huff next to me, and I felt his other hand land lightly on my shoulder. His thumb ran over my skin slowly, his touch distracting me just the slightest from the pain.

'All right,' Docc said evenly, noting the area before moving on. 'Tell me if it happens again.'

I nodded but didn't respond as I tried to block out the discomfort. I felt his fingers tickle along my ribs, but the sharp, stabbing pain I'd just felt didn't reappear. He finished assessing my bones and removed his hands, allowing me to open my eyes once more. They flitted to Hayden's, still watching me, before looking to Docc.

'Well?' I asked, afraid to hear him confirm what I had guessed.

'I think you're lucky,' he said slowly, gathering up supplies to stitch up my cut. 'It's hard to say without X-raying, but I suspect you've just broken the one. It seems to be a clean break and should heal well, but you'll have some pretty bad pain for a few days before it starts to get better.'

I blew out a deep breath of relief. One broken rib wasn't too bad, especially if it was broken cleanly. Shattered or fragmented ribs became much more dangerous as they tended to damage internal organs, so I was lucky to have avoided that.

'Unfortunately you can't splint a rib, so you'll just have to take it easy for a few weeks until it starts to heal,' Docc continued. He poured what I identified as disinfectant over my cut without warning, causing me to hiss in pain. Hayden's hand tightened around my own, as if it had hurt him, too.

'I guess that's good news,' I said through gritted teeth. He had started to poke around the cut, preparing to suture it. I already knew there wasn't anything to do for broken ribs, so this wasn't really news to me.

'So she'll be all right?' Hayden asked, speaking for the first time since Docc told him off.

'Oh yes,' Docc said, nodding slowly as he focused on my ribs once more. 'Ready for the stitches?'

I nodded and clamped my jaw shut, preparing for the familiar sting of the needle. I knew how rare anaesthetic was, so I didn't even consider asking for any. I wasn't from Blackwing and I didn't want to take away what was theirs.

I turned to look at Hayden. He shot me a tight grimace and leaned closer, his hand sliding up the side of my neck before landing on the side of my face. I could feel his fingers tangle into the back of my hair while his thumb lightly stroked my cheek.

'Just look at me,' he said quietly. 'It'll be over before you know it.'

I nodded and tried to keep my breathing even. I focused on how it made me feel to have Hayden there with me, by my side, when he didn't have to be. As much as I wanted to be strong and independent, I had to admit it felt good to know someone else cared for me enough to help. It was such a strange thing – to have someone clearly care for you – because I was used to handling things on my own.

Even back in Greystone, the only person I'd ever really leaned on was my father. Celt was always there for me when he could be, but his position made his time limited and thus made it difficult to really use him as a support system.

My brother had always been too brutal, too brash to really be of much support outside of physical backup, and I couldn't remember ever having a conversation with him that didn't revolve around some type of violence.

Leutie had been my best friend, but she'd been too fragile to count on. I had always been the one to support her, for her to lean on, not the other way around. She probably would have been there for me if I'd ever needed her to be, but the fact was that I never had.

But now, as the needle ripped through my flesh to stitch me back together, I needed Hayden. I needed his hand on my face, his other hand in mine, and his steady gaze to hold me together. I needed the reassurance and the strong support, even though I was scared to accept it. As much as I didn't want to admit it, as much as I knew I shouldn't, I needed him.

My gaze never wavered from his as I tried to block out the pain, and his gentle touch never stopped as it brushed along my cheek. I found myself transfixed by his gaze, the intensity taking over my thought process so much that I could hardly feel the pain anymore. The blood that had dried on his face remained ignored, and I felt the urge to clean him up despite the fact that I was in the process of getting stitches. He was potentially hurt as well, but his every action so far had been to fix me.

'Almost done,' Docc said, breaking into the spell I'd fallen under. Hayden's brows jumped up once as he shot me a reassuring look.

'You're doing so well, Grace,' Hayden murmured, his voice low and soft. My lower lip bit into my mouth as a particularly sharp jab of the needle shot up my nerves. I blew out yet another shaky breath as I refocused on Hayden and his gentle touches. My heart hammered, although I suspected it didn't have anything to do with my injury.

With one final stitch through my skin, Docc cut the suture and placed a thin bandage over the area. My shoulders drooped with relief, the tension I hadn't been aware I was holding releasing now that he was finished.

'All done,' Docc announced. He gathered up his materials and straightened back up. Hayden surprised me by leaning forward and pressing his lips into my forehead lightly before pulling back again.

'Good job,' he whispered. His thumb ran across my cheek one last time before his hand fell away and he straightened up.

I could feel Docc's eyes on us, but again he remained silent, choosing not to comment on the obvious affection between Hayden and me.

'I'll get you something for the pain and then you're free to go,' Docc said as he moved toward his storage cabinet.

'Oh, no, that's fine,' I said quickly. I didn't want to take more of their supplies.

'Hush, child. You got half of this stuff for me so it's the least I can do.'

I sighed and accepted this, feeling selfish for not arguing further because it really did hurt. The sting of the cut would subside in a few hours, but the severe ache of the broken rib would linger for days, if not weeks.

'Here, take one of these every six hours, two if the pain is really severe,' Docc said, handing me a bottle.

'What is it?' I asked, squinting at the label that had worn off slightly.

'Hydrocodone,' he said evenly. I nodded as the familiar name registered and he pressed two different pill bottles into my hands. 'After roughly a week, switch to the Aceta-minophen. You can take that every four hours as you need it.'

'Thank you, Docc.'

It seemed like lame appreciation for all he'd done for me since I'd arrived here, but I didn't know how else to say it.

'Of course. Now get some rest, the both of you. Hayden, get yourself cleaned up as well. I don't want to see you in here with an infection,' he said sternly, his gaze flitting back and forth between us both.

'Will do,' Hayden said before refocusing on me. His eyes glanced down my body quickly before he seemed to realise I was still in just my bra. His hand reached automatically behind his head to grip his T-shirt. He pulled roughly, whipping the fabric over his head before sliding it off his arms and handing it to me.

'Here,' he said quietly. I accepted the shirt with a soft smile.

'Thank you.'

I managed to lift the shirt over my head with my arm that wasn't on my injured side, but ran into a few problems as I found it difficult to lift my other arm. Without a word, Hayden's hands landed on my wrists to help guide me into the shirt before he released me to pull it down fully. I tried not to blush, feeling ridiculously helpless already.

'Thanks,' I mumbled again. He nodded gently before speaking once more.

'Want me to carry you?'

'No, I'll be fine,' I said, waving away his offer. I leaned forward slowly and focused on keeping my face blank as I swung my legs to the side of the bed. Hayden hovered close by, clearly not believing me.

'No, here, let me—'

'Hayden, seriously,' I insisted. 'Just . . . give me your arm. You don't have to carry me.'

He sighed in frustration before extending his elbow to me so I could loop my arm through it and hoist myself up. A jolt of pain shot through my ribs again but I ignored it as I took a shaky step forward, leaning on Hayden for support.

'You two take care of each other, you hear me?' Docc called from behind us. I couldn't help the tiniest hint of a smile that pulled at my lips, liking the way that sounded.

'Of course,' I replied when Hayden didn't. He appeared too focused on getting me safely out the door. A low chuckle was all I heard from Docc as we finally made it to the door, which Hayden held open for both of us. The sun had started to go down now, setting Blackwing in a soft, golden glow.

I was surprised to see Dax waiting outside the infirmary as he leaned against the wall. The truck was gone, assumedly returned to its place and the supplies we'd gathered put away as well. As soon as he saw us, Dax pushed himself off the wall and came to join us. It was only when he was a few feet in front of us did I notice he had the photo album I'd retrieved for Hayden in his hands. He took in Hayden's lack of shirt before he realised I was wearing it.

'Hey,' he said, his voice sounding the most serious I'd ever heard. 'Are you all right?'

I couldn't tell whom his question was directed at, but Hayden remained silent so I answered.

'Yeah, I'm fine.'

'She's got a broken rib,' Hayden said after a heavy sigh. Clearly our definitions of 'fine' were somewhat different.

'Ooh, ouch,' Dax hissed, grimacing sympathetically as he glanced at me. 'Those Brutes will getcha.'

'I'll heal just fine,' I said stubbornly. Dax let out a low chuckle while he shook his head slowly.

'I'm sure you will. But hey, I, um, I found this in the front seat and . . .' he trailed off and glanced down at the photo album in his hand. Hayden's gaze landed on it before he reached forward to take it.

'It's mine,' he said flatly. Dax watched him curiously.

'Where'd it come from?'

'My house.' Hayden's voice was stony and firm, as if he didn't want to discuss this right now.

'Did you finally go in?' Dax asked in awe, his eyes widening slightly. It was clear he knew, to some degree, that Hayden had difficulty going to that place. Hayden sighed heavily and shook his head.

'How do you think she got hurt?' he said, flicking his head towards me.

Dax's gaze flitted to me, a mixture of awe and surprise written across his features. 'You got this for him?'

I could feel my brows pulled low over my eyes as I returned his loaded gaze. 'Yes.'

He looked impressed. 'Wow.'

Everyone was quiet as Dax seemed to figure it out: not only did it mean Hayden had told me that was his house, but he knew that I'd risked my own safety to get something for him. The weight of this was not lost on Dax as he took in our linked arms and the heavy expression on Hayden's face.

'You two . . . you're like . . . *together*, aren't you?' he said. It was a statement more than a question. In all honesty, what we were remained indefinable. I wasn't sure of much besides the fact that I had feelings for Hayden. Strong, strong feelings.

'We have to go, Dax,' I said finally when Hayden declined to speak once more. He seemed too focused on getting me back to his hut to be bothered with talking to Dax right now.

387

He frowned at me as we took a step forward and ignored Dax's statement. I didn't mind that Hayden didn't answer. We made it a few yards away before Dax spoke again.

'I'm still okay with it,' he called, his voice loud enough for us to hear but not for anyone else who might have been around.

'Bye, Dax,' Hayden called deeply, disregarding his declaration once again as we moved down the path. I couldn't help but chuckle, liking the united front against Dax's attempts to clarify things.

Our steps were slow and steady to cause the least amount of pain possible, so it took a while to finally reach Hayden's hut. I felt myself falling into a weirdly pensive mood as Hayden led me to sit on the edge of the bed. The pain didn't seem so bad anymore, and I suspected the pill Docc had given me was finally starting to kick in.

'Are you really okay?' Hayden asked quietly. I resisted the urge to roll my eyes, finding his concern sweet, but embarrassing.

'Yes, Hayden. I swear.'

He knelt down in front of me so his face was level with mine now. His hands landed on my knees, and I felt his thumbs trail lightly over my skin, making sure I was telling the truth. Without really thinking, my hand reached forward to land lightly on his jaw. He sucked in a breath when my thumb traced along his lower lip, feeling the cut there that had dried with blood.

'Let's get you cleaned up, yeah?' I said quietly, my urge to take care of him kicking in once again now that I was, for the most part, taken care of. He sighed heavily, fighting his instincts to make me rest.

'Please, Herc?' I asked quietly. I wanted to wash the damage away, clean him, fix him. I wanted to be there for him like he'd been there for me. Slowly, gently, he leaned his cheek into my palm as he blew out a sigh of defeat.

'All right, Bear.'